MATTHEW ZORICH

Bastards of Liberty

The Conspiracy of Crows Book One

First published by Raccoon County Press 2023

First edition

ISBN: 979-8-9876861-0-2

Editing by Katrina Robinson
Cover art by Dawid Gardias Bestselling-covers.com
Editing by Kavin Space Mage Press

This book was professionally typeset on Reedsy.
Find out more at reedsy.com

For my father

Preface

~Bastards of Liberty~
The Conspiracy of Crows Trilogy
Book One

I love history, and this passion brought me not only to reading piles of books on history, politics, and journalism but also to the realms of fantasy, which remained on the outer edges of formal education. After I graduated college, inspiration from my favorite authors like Jack Kerouac, Hunter S. Thompson, and F. Scott Fitzgerald melded together with my love of comics and the lore found in books by the great Tolkien, Joe Abercrombie, and George R. R. Martin. I came up with Runt and his two siblings, Alysha and Ben, as they follow their hero paths in this novel.

Bastards of Liberty evolved into an alternative history of America called Vineland, but I twisted the story too much and landed on more feudal mythology instead. I liked creating a version of a mythos stretching Vineland into a fantastical place filled with powerful weapons, old and new religions, nation-states, and a bunch of sorry bastards trying to do something right for a change. I hope you find the story of the Ashburn family and their bastard friends as engrossing and harrowing as I did while writing it.

Thanks,
Matthew~

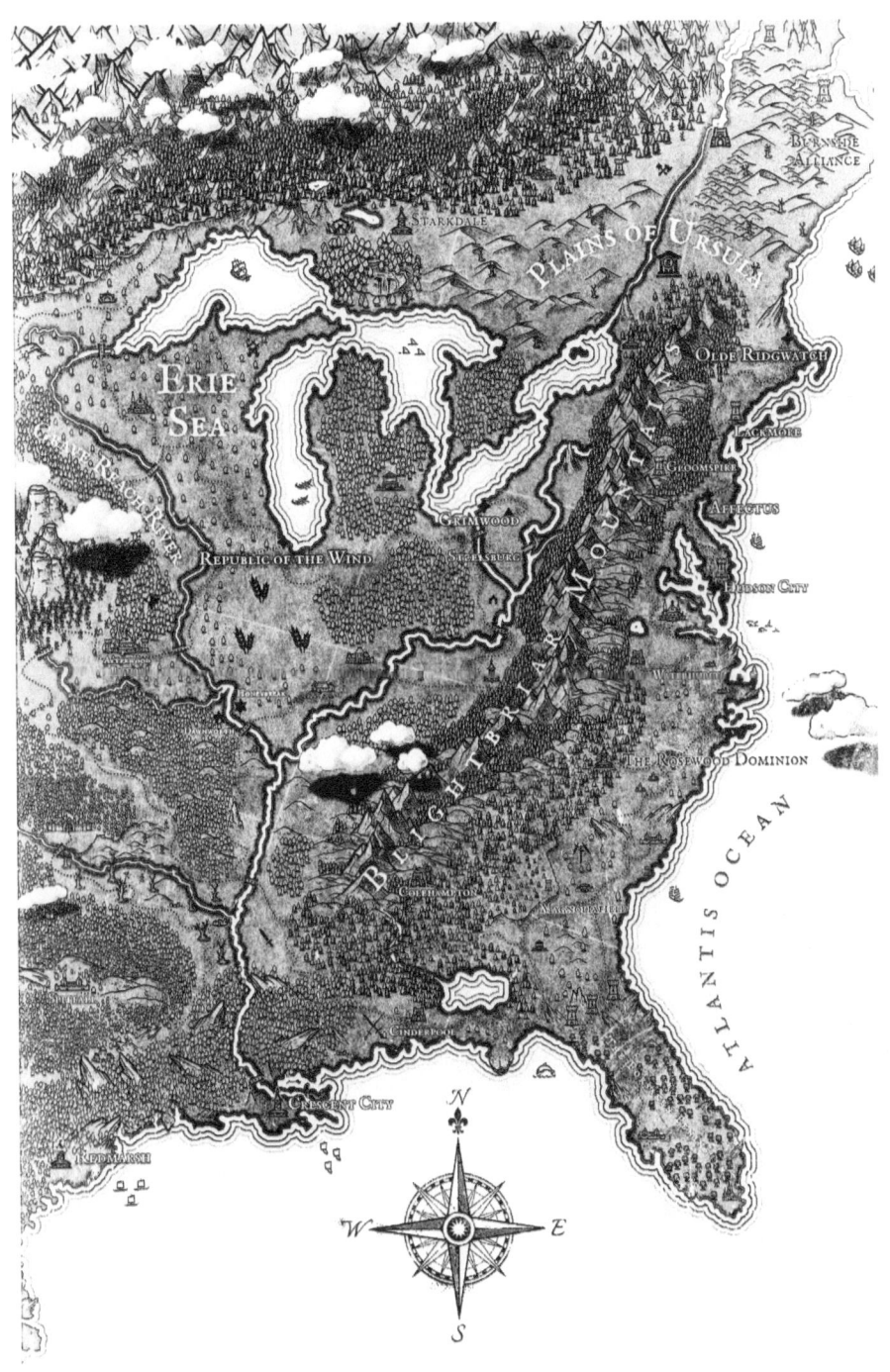

Eastern Vineland

iii

Northern Vineland & the Capital

Prologue

The pine tree's sap stuck to Runt's hands as he climbed higher. His older brother Ben moved him towards the top of the four-hundred-year-old pine tree. The boys had hollowed out the interior of the branches, so it felt like a ladder as they climbed higher. It was just enough so their young bodies fit, and they could climb and look out across the valley of their homestead, watching the sunset, birds take flight, and their neighbors below them, unseen and unheard like two crows taking in their territory.

"You okay, Runt?" asked Ben, a slight worry for his younger brother.

"Of course, just my hands sticking to the branches," said Runt as his breath shuddered along with his nerves. The summer season, known as the time of the god Jupitor, left the days long and gave the two boys the ability to play after getting their chores finished before dinner. Ben stopped climbing, which forced Runt to pause as well.

"Think this is far as we go, I don't want to snap the top of the tree off."

Ben switched his handholds and moved his feet, so he faced out now, looking past the valley. Runt looked at his brother's feet and along the valley at their neighbor's homes.

"Okay, going to move over to the other side," said Runt. He shuffled around the grand old pine tree and looked out past the river used by everyone in the area to bathe and fish in.

"Be careful, Runt, don't want some warhawk to pluck you from the tree and tear you up, becoming food for its little ones," his older brother said with a giggle.

"I will, I will," Runt whined, annoyed, his face red. His feet trembled from the height, and the thought of a giant bird of prey tearing him to pieces mid-flight.

Runt, the younger of the two, adjusted around the branches, just a bit below Ben, his head high as Ben's stomach but on the other side of the tree. He sat on a branch, keeping balance by using one of his arms to hold onto another branch above him as the tree swayed along with the life of Wolf Hills below.

"Did you see that the old lady across the river, Miss Rowan, has a black willow tree and two oakthorn trees? I wonder if we could find some cast off wood from the oakthorn trees and see if Angus might be able to make something out of it, like the handle to a sword or axe." Runt smiled. "I bet Alysha would help too, and maybe Helena."

Ben sighed deeply as if being older and smarter were a chore he dealt with when speaking to his younger brother. "Best not, the black willow trees are dangerous, that fog around the trees can burn you pretty badly. Besides Alysha and Helena don't care for that stuff anymore, or at least not as much." Ben took a deep breath and changed the subject. "When I go off to squire for dad, are you going to work with Angus at the tavern? He said he'd love to have you around if I can't help anymore."

"Yeah, Ma said I could but only when we are caught up around the house, so maybe during big celebrations or when there is a market day. Ben, do you really want to be a soldier when you grow up?"

Ben shifted and sat on a branch, peeking over at his brother. Ben was eleven summers old and angling upwards in height. He saw two crows circling off in the distance, cackling and spinning around in a deep orbit.

"I want to be like father. I want to be a soldier, a knight, killing savages in the mountains, battling orcs in the wilderness, and maybe marry a grand duchess somewhere off the coast of the great Atlantis Ocean," said Ben. The wind picked up, and they grabbed onto the branches tighter with both hands.

"Dad's never home. I miss him. Alysha said he's at court trying to end the war and keep the Nation of Stouya and Legion of Carigreed from taking over Vineland," said Runt. "I dunno what she means, he's a soldier, he commands other soldiers. The court of the capital, it's confusing. So many titles, names, and bowing. That's not fighting battles, glad we don't have to be there."

Ben sighed deeply, thinking about the Brotherhood of the Rose and the Order of the Crimson Cloaks. They were two ancient orders steeped in history and chivalry. His heart ached to achieve membership in one or the other.

"What about you Runt? What do you wanna be when you grow up? Do you want to battle a hoard of goblins deep in dwarven caves, explore the grand labyrinth of a library at a university, or meet a powerful wizard who'll whisk you off on an adventure?"

Runt made a face and smiled. "You mean not like some made-up things like the spooky old bog witch in the woods, the orc king of the Gloomspire, or an elven knight of the Hazefire Federation out west?"

"Where did you hear about all that stuff?"

"I read about them in the books dad left us, and the ones borrowed from Angus."

The branches shifted again and the slight taste of Sif, the bringer of harvest, drifted through the valley, but the late summer heat kept the season of autumn away.

"Well, I don't know, Ben," said Runt. "You're going to be a soldier. I guess I just want to be like you. Strong, tall, and smart, be a soldier like you want to be, like Dad."

Ben looked at Runt for a moment but didn't delight in the reverence his brother had for him, so he turned away and looked out at Wolf Hills. "We better get down. I think the weather is changing. Head down slowly and be careful. Okay, buddy?"

"Okay Ben, okay."

BASTARDS OF LIBERTY

Doc - Wrong Kind of Smoke

"You can't smoke reefer in here. It's illegal from the Stagger Wall to the Atlantis Ocean," whispered a teenager wearing rounded spectacles.

"What? For Maker's sake, why not, Maynard? It's my fundamental right to smoke whatever I want. I saved thousands of lives at the Battle of the Reaping. I took thousands of lives, but that's beside the point," the drunken man mumbled to himself. "All of Vineland should know—this entire world of Midgard should know of me, dammit. I'll smoke whatever I want!" yelled the crazed man sitting across from Maynard.

"Excuse me, sir, do you need another?" asked the kitchen helper.

"What? Yes, of course, and please, call me Doc. This is my assistant, Maynard. Been here a few days—should have introduced ourselves. Yes, another round. We celebrate tonight, young man. We celebrate those lost on the battlefield and from the Smoldering Plague. It's the anniversary of the Battle of the Reaping. The veil between here and the other side weakens, and we toast to our departed friends and family members." Doc gestured toward everyone in the bar as he spoke to Runt and Maynard. Several soldiers in the corner took notice of his loud, blasphemous tone. "We also drink to those lives we took, now haunting our thoughts and dreams," Doc muttered. "What a wonderful autumn evening to be alive and with the spirits of the dead."

Maynard wrote down the last bit Doc had whispered to himself. He had no idea where the reefer his mentor smoked came from—or the white powder known as wizard salt that Doc was now sniffing up his nose. They were too broke to afford either. The reefer and wizard salt were illegal throughout the Holy Imperium and independent city-states, including Grimwood's

1

surrounding territories. He knew Doc didn't care, and his mentor often indulged to forget or to awaken the muse so he could expand on numerous topics for later publication at one the universities or in the local paper.

Maynard pushed up his spectacles and moved his hair away from his eyes. His mentor was drunk. Both were hedge mages. The older man was in a deliriously thoughtful state, ranting to anyone who would listen. In past times, Doc had created remarkable experiments and taught Maynard mysteries others couldn't imagine, but those had been private moments after long days of study. Tonight, it looked as if he were far wasted, and they were far from Grimwood University. Doc continued drinking, smoking, and gathering rumors, hoarding them as if they would disappear if not written down. To those encountering him tonight, he appeared as a manic drunk, but Maynard knew his mentor was the most dangerous man in Vineland.

"Ahh, the Wayward Tavern, home for travel-weary journeymen. This place is full of tired eyes, hard feet, calloused hands, and pure hearts." Doc sniffed another line of wizard salt quickly. "Well, some of them. Most men my age couldn't go on like this, but here I sit, taking in these fine people and this fine stinky weed, so beautiful." The drunk mage pulled in a large inhalation of smoke from his pipe and pushed it out his nostrils. "All of the candles are lit, and the beer and wine flows! This'll be a night, my young apprentice, a historic and memorable night.

"Did you know, my young apprentice," Doc took a deep toke and puffed it out, "past generations leveled the top portion of this hill, taking the stones to make the walls for the large tavern. The second floor is of stout wood, mostly pine and oak, from the valleys and hills where the forests run deep and spirits seep from the land. Grimwood's city-state and its knights, the Grim Vultures, protected the Wayward Inn and the surrounding town, although I have not seen any in some time."

"I love this town and its freedom and righteous justice." Doc stood now, coming into a fever as he spoke. "It's justice is only superseded by Grimwood for higher crimes. Wolf Hills is known for its local population of wolves and its maple syrup. This town and the more prominent city-state of Grimwood attempted to stay neutral during the Crimson Struggle, but one cannot remain uninvolved throughout years of war! Now Grimwood is surrounded by cemeteries for its mistakes, and ghosts and ghouls haunt its shores. Many volunteered to join the Holy Imperium ranks. Others joined the Nation of Stouya, better known as the Nation. Others joined the Legion of Carigreed, known as the Legion. They fought over the continent of Vineland for years after two families' bloodlines, the Ruinthorns and Hawthorns, died out. It's over now, thanks to me." He smiled with pride.

"I know, I know—I was already taught this. Why are you lecturing me?" Maynard mumbled as he quickly wrote down what Doc stated, nearly breaking his quill.

Doc's back faced Maynard. A single troubadour in the corner played music poorly. His lute sounded like he should have practiced more at his home's hearth before attempting to keep soldiers and patrons cheerful in the town's only drinking establishment.

Above the troubadour, the second floor lay open to an expansive balcony with room for tables of four or two seats, a long table at one end, and a bar at the other. Those above could look over the railing to the lower floor, at the patrons eating and drinking below. The Wayward Tavern held weddings, dances, and town meetings due to the place's two floors and overall size.

"This beer is exceptional," Doc said to himself, Maynard, and anyone else within earshot. He stood, spinning a hand in the air, trying to conjure more thoughts. "The lute player sounds like he's dragging a cat across a washing board. I can't believe he's wearing a white wig. What a fop."

The kitchen helper moved on and started picking up empty dishes and wiping tables. He kept track of the drunks and those in need of another drink. He also updated the cook on how the guests had received the food.

Maynard and Doc held down a table on the first floor of the tavern. Doc emptied a long clay pipe and packed it as a thought bubbled up into his blurred brain. With the pipe in his mouth, he lit it. The smoke lingered in the air, creating a purple haze. Several soldiers near the door took notice of the off-putting smoke coating the ceiling in colors. Two of the soldiers spoke to each other over their mugs of ale.

Maynard watched his mentor with concern. "Don't you think you've had enough, mentor?"

"Never enough for the likes of me, boy. If I don't drink, smoke, or indulge—" Doc paused for a moment and looked away. He glanced back at Maynard with a sad smile. "If I don't, the screams, the voices, they come back. Remember, what we do has a toll. It always has a toll. Now let us celebrate!" And he raised his cup to drink.

Mentor was a term used for a teacher at Grimwood University, part of the Silver Ivy League. Places of wealth, knowledge, nobles, and snobbery. Maynard felt a slight sense of pride and yet disdain in using the term towards his teacher.

* * *

Runt, the kitchen helper, had watched the two of them and their antics since they'd shown up a few days back. Tonight, his double shift wore on. He hadn't seen his mother or older sister since a little before lunch and wouldn't see them until he hiked home after the witching hour. Runt hoped there wouldn't be trouble with a crowd like tonight, as real coin could be made.

The Holy Imperium soldiers inside the tavern meant profitable business, bringing more money into everyone's pockets. Sure, there was a lot of talk— odd talk, too, from the soldiers and townsfolk—but stories kept everyone up to date on the news around Grimwood. Runt heard complaints of new taxes to the east of Grimwood city-state and other areas. He also heard mutterings of the Holy Imperium attempting to unify the city-states across all of Vineland. His father had shown him a map of the territory of Vineland once; it was unbelievably vast and barely connected by a few sets of poorly guarded old roads created when King Christopher and his savage wife, Erica the Red, had forged the country whole.

Now their bloodlines dead and the Crimson Struggle finally over, everyone felt a sense of ease, and even a little hope for better days. After so many years of strife, folks just wanted to be left alone to make it through the winter, which lingered in everyone's thoughts around this time of year. But unfortunately, all three nations still fought across the Atlantis Ocean.

"Unify" the lands by Prince Damon and the Holy Imperium, Runt thought. It was unthinkable. Orc warbands ran through the dark forests of Vineland, and tribes of goblins crawled out of caves and fought dwarven clans in the mountain ranges to the east. There could be no unity, especially with the savage native elves raiding homesteads and fortifications near crossroads.

Runt walked to a table of soldiers who were seated, talking, and barely playing a game of bones. "Do you need anything further? Would you like to see what the kitchen has available?" asked Runt.

The Holy Imperium soldiers looked at Runt. He was all blue eyes and light-brown hair cut near ear level. He could stare a man in the eye without flinching, even if he was a little short for his age. He thought of his brother—how he longed to travel and become a soldier like him, like these men in the Holy Imperium Army, but he was stuck in Wolf Hills to farm and take over the household.

He looked at the men, the dice on the table, the coins, the empty cups and blades at their sides, stained silver armor. He stepped back and bowed quickly. "Let me see if I can grab you a round on the house." He turned and walked away, hoping not to cause any trouble. He was tired and had worked hard this holiday night, hoping for extra money from the serving girls so he could buy another book before winter settled in. Runt looked at the troubadour and hoped he'd start to play a catchy tune soon.

* * *

"What are we even going to call this country, Maynard? Vineland is a fine name. The Holy Imperium sounds stupid. Maker's milk-filled tits, so unoriginal! Only Prince Damon could have come up with that name. What shit. Trying to spit the Holy Imperium out every time he acknowledges a country even as it's divided. It's not the best-selling point to the common folk."

The drunken mage spoke to Maynard but primarily to himself. Unfortunately, he was plastered and continued to talk more loudly as surrounding patrons heard him whether they wanted to or not. The young boy sat at the table nervously, writing down as much as he could while the older man spoke.

Over the past few days, he and his apprentice had written down as many stories as they could hear from the townsfolk. They heard about James Wolfe, the scout and messenger, the town's pride, fighting for the Holy Imperium against the Legion and the Nation. Currently, a few sang of James Wolfe and his wondrous deeds. When the song ended, it drew a look from Doc.

"I guess it's fortunate he was there to save the day from the Legion of Carigreed and the Nation of Stouya." He took a deep pull from his cup with no smile on his lips.

Other townsfolk told tales of three witches telling fortunes, stealing away children in the night, or of goblins and orcs in an ancient keep in the mountains, waiting to take over the world.

"The Castle of the Mists, or was it the Gloomspire? I always forget," he muttered and asked the locals to carry on with their tales.

Lately, travelers thought they heard goblin laughter from caves and recalled worse crawling about at night. Yet others spoke of giants and dragons from antiquity, yet they remained vividly in everyone's imaginations through stories, songs, poetry, and the deadliest form of communication: gossip.

Doc heard all the stories, drank more than his share, and became depressed and angry because nobody ever mentioned his talents and power. He was technically a member of the Order of Redcloak, a knight and ranking noble, the only surviving battlemage this side of the ocean, but nobody believed him. The man was broken like a fallen egg.

"He's cracked, a grade-A lunatic," Maynard had told one of his schoolmates one day at the University of Grimwood. Maynard hadn't had many friends, but he'd been drunk and had needed to unpack his problems. He didn't even know Felix's name, but he listened because Maynard had offered to split a half bottle of whiskey with him.

The jacket Doc wore tonight looked dark, faded crimson near the top. It used to symbolize those higher in ranking than a belted knight. It didn't matter to the men sitting near the door with their swords on their hips, spears standing against the wall behind them. They were the law with only a few areas or city-states where the Holy Imperium and prince did not rule. After the Battle of the Reaping, the Crimson Struggle ended. The Holy Imperium reigned victoriously. Now birds pecked at the dead after the battle in the north. Nothing grew anymore due to the blood spilled, magic thrown, and souls crushed for the sake of pride, patriotism, and the Holy Church. The prince decreed the continent of Vineland now be called the Holy Imperium, a monument to his majesty and governance.

The populace had had enough war for a lifetime. The natives, known as elves, kept to themselves on the other side of the Grave Reach River or stayed away from any civilization by living in the deep woods, swamps, and mountains where no sophisticated folk wandered. Along with goblins and orcs, the elves were sold as slaves on this side of the river, with the elves favored among the races, as most humans felt they were easier to subdue and restrain.

"Sir, please sit," said Maynard. Nevertheless, Doc did not. Instead, he stood, arms waving about, a pint of brown ale sloshing in his pewter cup. Under his darkened jacket, he wore a leather-layered shirt with metal laced with silk. It was unlike anything ordinary folk wore. Doc had said a mystic from an island in the south had made it for him for trade. He never said what he traded it for.

"Listen here, you fat little weasel, and listen close." Doc's pipe stuck out through his teeth as he spoke out of the side of his mouth. His eyes glowed through his dark-tinted glasses. He looked at his apprentice; fear crawled through other patrons' bones, and the music and talking dulled.

Maynard pushed his spectacles onto his nose and swept back his hair, as it continued to fall into his eyes. He wasn't fat, but he was neither an athlete nor built for military service and he'd spent more time with a book than splitting wood. The apprentice believed in sunny- and rainy-day reading, and his body showed it. It was pale and rounded, but his mind was sharp, and he knew when his mentor's eyes glowed, he and others were in for an awful time.

"Forget it, forget it. I—I lost myself for a moment. Forgive me, Maynard. They're always there inside my head, whispering."

* * *

Runt walked over near the bar's edge, trying to get the owner's attention as he poured drinks. At fifteen winters, the kitchen helper knew trouble was coming and did his best to stop it from escalating into a bar fight—or worse.

"Quiet over there, or I'll sick the constable on you," the owner, Pete, screamed back at Doc. Pete was not as sharp as Runt but had the right of it as the owner and elderly member of the establishment. Runt looked for a serving girl and found none. Tonight, there were three upstairs on the balcony or talking to the cook, a dwarve named Angus, about a dish.

Smoke loomed above the heads of the people around the bar from pipes packed with tobacco. Laughter filtered above a heavy game of cards in the corner over a dirty joke. Those in the Wayward Tavern ranged from trappers to farmers and neighbors, yet the Holy Imperium soldiers outnumbered everyone tonight. Oddly, Runt didn't see any Grimwood soldiers in attendance either. The tavern allowed for all kinds. It was not unheard of to see a native or even a dwarve come through; several years back, there had been an orc trader with three human companions looking for antique weapons. Of course, they hadn't been able to find any info on what they sought, but they were kind to everyone, and the orc even gave one of the local girls a piggyback ride around the tavern.

* * *

"Music, minstrel, I need music! Please play the song about the—" Doc looked around and forgot what he wanted. He looked on, a bit bewildered and disheveled.

The barkeep looked at him with sad eyes, glanced at the troubadour near the end of the bar, and nodded his head. The man with the lute started playing again.

"Kind sir, please, a round of drinks for all in attendance. I am paying for it. For the prince and the free city-states! For Sir Thomas Casting and the Holy Imperium!" He raised his mug, and the people sitting at the bar cheered and drank. Doc sat with a frump, his worn-out patchwork coat falling around him, denim breeches sticking out underneath. His glasses changed colors from red to pink, then blue, his eyes no longer glowing. The glasses constantly altered themselves, having been bewitched years ago. He pushed the hood off his shaven head. He was older than his apprentice by two scores, but the age barely showed. His face was the same as his head—well shaven—and his lip garnered a clay pipe which stuck out the side of his mouth, constantly moving about.

Runt set drinks on the table where four soldiers of the Red Army played bones. They didn't say thanks, grumbling about the bald lunatic who bought a round for the bar.

"You know why we are here tonight, correct, young apprentice? Tell me and make it snappy before I lose my temper." Doc leered. Most folk couldn't figure out his mad gibberish, which worsened as he drank.

"We are here for a boy, sir," Maynard said.

"Damn right. He is more of a young man now, and he's essential for the cause. He's about your age, with book learning, and knows how to fight. He will attend my old friend the squire until he is ready for more responsibility. *Do you get me?*" Doc took a long pull from his cup, finished off the beer, took a massive hit off his pipe, and blew the smoke into the air.

"A squire to your squire? That doesn't make any sense," said Maynard.

Runt showed up, arms muscled from carrying mugs of beer night after night. "Your bill, sir."

"What? This is outrageous. Wait, what is your name, boy?" asked Doc.

"They call me Runt, sir."

"Runt, hmm. Interesting." He scratched his chin and took his glasses off. He looked at his pipe and put his thumb into it, snuffing it out. "I believe it is time to pay up, my young apprentice. And you, boy, what is your given name?"

"Ahh, it's Rhett. Rhett Ashburn of the Wolf Hills," said Runt. "Most folks call me Runt."

"Ashburn of the Wolf Hills, of course. This forsaken tavern is at the peak of the Wolf Hills, yes, yes. Let me ask you, boy, have you seen your father lately? Never mind, don't answer. This is a fine place, a fine town. Everyone here keeps worshiping their gods privately. Yes?" asked Doc but did not wait for an answer. "Worships whatever gods you want around here, pays no taxes, and makes no trouble. Dammit. This place is the very heart of freedom!" he yelled.

"Sir, please keep quiet. You are upsetting a lot of folks, good paying customers from out of town. And no. No, I haven't seen my father. I'm sorry, sir, I need to get back to work," said Runt.

"Yes, of course. Apprentice, have you paid our tab?" asked Doc.

"No, I haven't. We have no money. You spent it on other matters last night while I slept with the donkey in the barn."

"What? Yes, yes, of course. A man has to attend to his needs. No matter, I am sure those Red Army chaps will take care of it." Doc paused. "Those Holy Imperium soldiers are here to collect taxes!"

The music stopped again. In a moment, every conversation stopped, and every drunk, mercenary, farmer, young rogue, and old man eyed Doc. He smiled and pointed to the soldiers in the corner, wagging his finger like a schoolchild pointing out a misbehaved friend. "Taxes and green leaf. They have come for taxes and to stop us from ingesting our sweet green leaf, and they want you to lie in bed with Prince Damon of the Holy Imperium and the prince's Holy Church!" yelled Doc. He didn't need to shout. Everyone was quiet and staring at him, his apprentice, and Runt.

"Ahh, crap," said Maynard. He started gathering books, papers, bottles, and implements spread across the table as chairs moved, and bottles and mugs fell.

"Don't stare, boy. Assist my apprentice before he breaks something exotic. I must have my potions and my medicines!"

Alysha - Harvest Fires

The smoke from the Harvest Festival bonfires filled the peaks and valleys of Wolf Hills in the northern portion of Grimwood. Alysha finished her work around her home, which was nestled in a deep valley. A winding river flowed past a clearing and down a footpath from her front steps. The sun lingered above the tree line as the smell of bonfires, leaves, and apples drifted on the breeze. The valley held several homesteads that tended to fend for themselves, only going into town for needs they couldn't produce. The area's thick trees, along with the local wolf population and a little lore, kept the valleys of Wolf Hills safe from highwaymen and bandits. The town belonged under the protection of the city-state of Grimwood yet remained independent enough not to be hit with taxes as much as other towns. The hills and valleys grew hearty folk with too much wildness in their veins. They were a kind people to look at, who could withstand the cold and snowy winters near the Erie Sea.

"Mother, they are lighting our bonfire soon down by the river, and if you look up, you can see smoke from a few valleys over!" yelled Alysha into the door of her house. Her dark copper eyes matched the dress she wore.

Alysha's mother remained inside, performing last-minute adjustments to the jack-o'-lanterns, one for each family member.

"Come in here and help me carry them out," said Maria Ashburn.

Cinnamon and cider drifted around the air in the house. It was Alysha's favorite holiday.

"It's too bad Runt can't be with us tonight," said Maria, her voice strong and confident. "Or even Ben—I'm sure he's missing the festivities."

The local cook and a family friend, a dwarve named Angus, had asked for help at the tavern, stating an uptick in patrons the last few days, so Runt spent time cleaning and serving at the bar. The Ashburn family needed the money, Alysha knew, but she stayed home with other plans tonight. Her older brother was away playing army man with her father. Correspondence from her brother and father, who were stationed together, withered as of late. It had been a year, and no letters from either.

Alysha grabbed two of the pumpkins and placed them near the front door. At five feet seven inches and seventeen summers, she was every bit a woman as her mother. Her hips swayed, she could run in the fields and hop boulders across the stream by the house as much as the boys around the valley. She was strong and split wood better than her fifteen-year-old brother.

Women in Wolf Hills did just as much as the men to keep a family together, fed, and alive—better than those living in big cities like Grimwood or Olde Ridgewatch, where orc, native, and even goblin slaves did the work. In Wolf Hills, the wildlife was abundant and dangerous. The winters dumped snow for days, and folk would go out and remove it from their roof, or it would suffocate them and their livestock.

"Alysha, take those two jack-o'-lanterns and place them near the front door as well," said Maria, her dark-blond hair streaked with the polish of age. Her mother never called Alysha by her first name, Bella. That was the name her father had given her before he left to serve in Prince Damon's endless wars. Nobody in Wolf Hills called her Bella either.

"Yes, Mother!" Alysha said with a bit of attitude. She wanted to be finished with her chores. Alysha pulled her hair into a ponytail and tied it up with a bit of leather. Her hair grew in long curls, and she forced it straight when she could, which was not often. It was wild and the same color as her mother's hair. She had her father's sharp nose, but the rest of her was Maria.

Her mother stood next to Alysha as she carried the two pumpkins, carved out in smiles and frowns, and placed them in front of the door. She took a wick from the hearth and lit the tallow candles inside the jack-o-lanterns, giving even more aromas to the cooling autumn twilight. Maria hugged her daughter, breathing in her scent, thinking of her daughter's childhood and how much she had grown. Alysha pulled away, aching to finish her chores.

The wind picked up for a moment. The last breaths of summer came through, and Alysha felt warmth, or maybe it was from the bonfires lit all over.

Small towns all over the country of Vineland performed harvest celebrations, whether they worshiped the Maker of the Holy Church or prayed to the dwarven gods of the Sword and Stone or to the Profane gods based on the four seasons.

She loved her mother, but they constantly fought over Alysha's responsibilities at home while she took on side work at the town's blacksmith shop, always flirting with the boy who worked there.

In most towns outside cities, the children worked the land and carried on after their parents passed. Maria wasn't sure what she wanted for her children. Benjamin was off in the army already, but her youngest, Runt, and Alysha, a mirror to herself, remained in Wolf Hills. She taught all three to read in hopes they would become more than farmers, but she was frightened of what the future would bring them, like any parent.

Before he left for a position in the Holy Imperium Army, Benjamin had been an adequate reader but hadn't loved books as Alysha and Runt did. They both read and reread the few books in town and nearly memorized the books the Ashburn family owned. Stories of witches speaking to ravens and cats, stories of pirates without ships, and those stories of ancient dwarven castles nestled in the hills fending off hordes of evil creatures. Those household books were from their father, who had brought them home primarily as war souvenirs years back, now cherished by his family in his absence.

The fall winds kissed the leaves off the trees, and the sunlight danced them to the ground. The valley held several cottages and a few barns. All dressed up to enjoy the last feast before winter pushed everyone inside for several months. There was no proper road to get down to where Alysha lived, only a footpath wide enough for a cart and horse. Other smaller paths led into the valley. Each path was used by the valley folk and by the wolves, the deer, and the few elves trading on the fringes of Wolf Hills. The main trail had no name, but everyone in town knew everyone, so a local traveler could easily ask where they lived and receive an answer. They would point in a direction and say, "Two hills and a valley over yonder," or, "Travel that way along the trail as the crow flies until you hit the river and follow it down. You'll see it."

Everyone worshiped their deities however they wished. The town of Wolf Hills held no official church. However, the Holy Church held a mass in the local courthouse basement every Sunday, and the People's Church had its services in the same place on Saturdays. Others worshiped deities quietly, keeping to themselves.

"Mother, the pumpkins are lit. May I go?"

"No, dear, just a moment." She looked to the sky, and a stray lightning bolt streaked across the tree line. "Our gods bless us with sky kisses," she said to Alysha, pointing to the sky. "Did anyone stop by today with word or mail?"

"No, I'm sorry. No mail today, no word from father," said Alysha, who blew her mother off. She knew her mother was disappointed. Maria asked about it daily, hoping her husband would send a letter from the capital, Hudson City, where he was stationed. Her Benedict may have shipped elsewhere; Maria didn't know. So, she'd ask Pete, the local tavern owner, of any news or rumors, hoping for some information from her husband.

"I guess we shall carry on." Her smile fell, and then she perked up. "I married into this; he is a noble, and I am a commoner. This was to be expected." She smiled again and pressed down her dress. Alysha waited, nearly bouncing in place, and Maria smiled. "Sorry, love. Go gussy yourself up so you can see that boy you like." Alysha was off without another word. "I hope Mr. Purenut's son is only teaching you smith work and nothing else," Maria said, primarily to the leaves twisting in the wind.

Alysha went inside, grabbed her mask, and snagged a bottle of wine from her father's reading den.

"I'll be down by the river in a few moments. If that blacksmith boy, Ryan Purenut, calls on you, behave! We do not want to add another pumpkin to this bunch yet," said her mother.

Alysha blushed and put on the mask her brother had made earlier in the month, knowing that would not be a problem. Her mother had nothing to worry about. She ran out of the house, down past the front field, and toward the riverbank, where six homes decided to burn a large bonfire to celebrate their dead ancestors and a good harvest late into the night.

The sun sank below the trees as each maple, oak, and ash whispered to one another when the wind picked up. Golden and rust-colored leaves crunched as she padded her way down the path. Folk recently called for early snow, while others argued it would be warm for another few weeks. The conversations were long and lively at the Wayward Tavern, where her brother Runt worked this time of the year.

Alysha ran past the remaining trees by the river, and the bonfire stood as high as one of the pine trees surrounding the clearing. The smell of pine and oak drifted through the air as the light reflected off parts of the river nearby. Earlier, the neighbors cleared the area, laid the wood for the bonfire, and set up makeshift tables on large stones.

There were a few barrels of ale, cups, and tankards near every hand. Cider and wine flowed, and younger children stole sweets or were provided treats like pie balls or apples by the adults. The river flowed north toward the sea, but it was slow and easily crossable as long as no heavy rain fell. The valley and hill people would pull fish from it until midwinter. It provided for them and the local animal population.

The woods surrounding the valley held maple, red oaks, and white and blue pine trees and across the river stood a small solitary home accessible through a ford in the river when it ran low.

The Catseye family, Alysha's direct neighbors, were at the edge of the clearing, enjoying the festivity's start.

"Oh, Alysha, will Runt be home before the fire burns down tonight?" Helena Catseye said as she met up with Alysha to walk down to the creek. The two were close friends, mirrored both in age and a lust to escape their small homestead. Alysha held her breath for a moment unsure of what to say. She almost felt jealous of Helena asking about her brother. She wanted to see Ryan but also wanted to spend time with Helena tonight as well.

"I dunno. He's working with Angus at the tavern, and I heard they're pretty busy," she said.

"Drat. I was hoping to share a dance with him," said Helena.

"Really? I'm sure he wouldn't know what to do if he were around to offer. Boy can barely walk at times before he trips over his feet." She smiled at Helena and thought about what she had said. "Oh, I'm sure he would be smitten to even be in your presence. Still," she paused, slightly jealous for some reason, "it would be nice to have at least half my family around tonight. It feels like we're off in so many directions all the time." She pushed her mask, so it sat at the top of her head.

"It's a dance, Alysha. I wasn't going to marry him. There aren't a lot of decent boys around," Helena said and then looked at her friend. They smiled at each other and turned away. She was shorter than Alysha by two inches, and where Alysha's hair was a dark blond, Helena's was a darker brunette. They both held the curves that girls in northern Grimwood were known for, and boys noticed when the two girls were together.

"I know—sorry I was being rude. Runt is a well-behaved young man who has grown a lot since Ben left to make his fortune in the Red Army. Anywho, Helena, do you think Ryan will make it to our bonfire?"

"You didn't hear? It's the talk of the hills and valleys," said Helena.

"Hear what? I've been helping my mother as we prep for winter these last few days. What? Tell me, Helena, tell me!"

"Soldiers in the area are pressing men and boys into the Holy Imperium Army. We don't know what for or why, but Ryan was taken a few nights back. His parents were furious, but Mr. Purenut couldn't do anything about it, and Ryan is the older of the two boys. It was expected that one of them would serve. We didn't think they would come here; the big war is all over."

Alysha's shoulders slumped, and her smile faded for a moment, but then anger took over. She stood tall, her expression now more severe than easygoing. "How dare they! We're not part of the Holy Imperium. Wolf Hills tried to stay impartial during the bloody war; the town provided comfort and care to all if they passed through. Besides, we're under the protection of Grimwood."

The music picked up.

"Hello, Mr. and Mrs. Catseye!" Alysha said to show proper manners as they walked by Helena's parents.

16

"Hello, deary!" Mrs. Catseye called.

Boys and girls and the older folk danced around the fire. Mr. Rankle drank from a jug of ale, fiddled a tune as folk danced, and whooped it up. Helena grabbed Alysha's hand as they walked by a table. They grabbed a cup of they weren't sure what and downed it. Tears welled up in both girls' eyes, and they nearly coughed the liquid back up. Alysha pushed her mask down. The drink warmed her face; she looked at the fire through the eye holes.

"Alysha, you look absolutely wicked," Helena said.

"Thanks, Helena. Let's dance this news away. I don't want to think for a moment," and they joined in and spun around the fire, trying to forget their thoughts.

The night's darkness drifted in with smoke from the bonfire as neighbors wore masks of all kinds, drank, and spoke of their past relatives and the coming winter. Usually, people didn't stay out too late because of the valley's darkness, but tonight was special.

At night, the town of Wolf Hills kept a brazier lit outside the city's edges, where the main road crossed in both directions, welcoming travelers. There were rumors that the town constable kept a dwarven light for emergencies. Inside a homestead or within town borders, the people felt safe at night, but on nights like tonight, all of the families would get together outside and celebrate, dance, and sing to keep up their spirits as winter neared along with a sense of dread and death.

Alysha took off her brother's mask, which had been made from a wolf skull and padded with soft felt her father had given her a few years back. Her brother had taken his time as he made it, painted it sable, and adhered wolf fur around the skull to give it a mane. She looked scary in it, and a few younger children ran from her when she drew near them earlier. She was frustrated and wanted to hit something. When she danced, she spun around the circle, whooping, hollering, and looking for Ryan Purenut with slight hope in her heart. The laughter, yelling, and fiddling was intoxicating, and she stopped thinking for a few moments.

Helena and Alysha left the dance after several songs and grabbed a cup of spiced wine warmed by the fire. They walked hand in hand closer to the stream to cool off and feel the air on their faces.

Helena took off a shaggy fox head mask. "Special night tonight, you know. They say you can see ghosts gliding off the Erie Sea and onto the shores of Grimwood if the moon is right. We should play ghouls in the graveyard like the ones in Grimwood forest or tell tales of the bogey of the headstones of Black Willow Falls."

Alysha smiled, grasped Helena's hand, feeling its warmth, and shivered a bit, unsure if she was happy or scared. "Some say the old witch of the Litchbury Mire to the west leaves her tower tonight to trick children with sweets so she can feast on their carcasses throughout the winter."

"Okay, you win, Alysha. Wow! So gross. Where did you get that story from?" asked Helena.

"Bits here and there—a little from my mom or Runt and what he picks up while working late at night," Alysha said.

They walked toward the stream and saw a person by the water, sitting on a large rock.

"Now, who would want to be alone on a night like tonight?"

"I dunno; let's find out," answered Helena.

Doc - Slight Disagreement

"Hey, you over there! What did you say?"

Four Holy Imperium soldiers stood and looked at the drunken mage, Maynard, and Runt nearby.

"You two! Pay up and get out. You've been running this tab up for days. And you four—take it outside if you need to, but you pay up first!" yelled Pete as he walked from behind the bar to get in between the two groups.

He'd forgotten about the soldiers upstairs. Pete's girth showed on his belly, and his attitude displayed through his frown. At fifty winters old, he took no shit and tried to show authority at his place of business. Pete's common sense and ability to read a situation and break it up before it became an issue kept the Wayward Tavern running, but he was off tonight.

Maynard gathered his mentor's tools and trinkets, pushed them into an old leather satchel, and slung them over one shoulder.

Doc stood as well and reached into a coin purse to pay. "Runt, would you be a good boy and saddle up our donkey for us, please? Apprentice, follow the young lad out with the bag," he said. He put his hand on Maynard's shoulder and whispered, "Follow Runt; stay true to your education. I'll meet you at Runt's home." Then he started pushing both boys toward the tavern's back exit, where everyone pissed, shat, and threw up throughout the night. "Go now, go now! Off with you," Doc said.

"But you have no money to pay," said Maynard.

"There is always a way to pay, Maynard. Have I not taught you? Go now and be gone; I'll meet you soon." He pushed them out the door and slammed it shut.

Both fell into sawdust and mud on the ground. It smelled of urine and shit.

"Now, where were we? Ahh, yes, payment. How much was it?" asked Doc as he looked toward Pete, who stood behind the first-floor bar.

He stumbled over to the bar and half hung, half stood against it, using the edge for guidance. He appeared drunk yet determined to pay off a several-day-old bar tab.

"Two full crowns now, and be off with you," said Pete.

"The prince's balls two full crowns!" yelled the drunken man.

"And he also pays for our tab, the loudmouth prick."

Doc looked around through his tinted glasses as smoke drifted from his pipe. The four soldiers near the door now appeared at both of his sides and behind him. The biggest one stood like an ox, stout and strong, his face wearing a scraggly beard. The rest of the men looked to be tired and drunk.

"You'll pay for our drinks and dinner tonight. Your insolence to the prince and the Holy Imperium will not be tolerated," said the scraggly-bearded man.

"What? For the prince and country, I thought. I'll have you know; I've personally met the prince. Well, I forgot who I am. My apologies." He was visibly dizzy, spinning one hand around in the air for balance. "I am the last damn battlemage of Vineland, and I will not be bullied by the likes of you!"

"Gentlemen, please, no trouble. We are under the sovereign state of Grimwood here at Wolf Hills. No need to throw around your authority; we can call the local constable," said Pete.

"Horseshit on you, magic man! Grimwood is now under the control of Prince Damon and the Holy Imperium. And we'll not hear another word of it!" said the scraggly-bearded soldier, his anger rising.

Three of the four soldiers put hands on their sword hilts, and the patrons, quiet before, started to grumble.

"What do you mean? Grimwood is a free city-state, and Wolf Hills is a patron of it," Pete said. He was a bit beside himself. He didn't want trouble, yet the soldiers proclaimed the Holy Imperium was in control of Grimwood. The two were separated by nearly a month of hiking, shorter if traveled by horse.

The closest law outside the town constable, Junior, was the court of

Grimwood and knights order the Grim Vultures based in the city. They checked in on the town twice a year to collect small taxes, usually maple syrup, pelts, or fish.

All attention turned to look at the drunken mage as he stood wobbling, holding on to the bar with one hand and his staff in the other. His body slowly shifted back and forth. The drunk consistently fell but caught himself as if he were a puppet. His frayed dark cloak moved as if it were windy inside the tavern.

Pete stood, arms folded across his fatness, a head taller than Doc, and looked at the drunk in front of him, the four soldiers, prince's men, all standing straight and aching for a fight around him. There was a definite feeling of wrongness about the situation, yet he wasn't sure what to do. Typically, there was merriment, laughter, and a sense of hope on holidays like tonight. Pete blinked and looked around at a den of wolves.

"Not anymore, you pig-serving bar leech," said the scraggly-bearded man.

"You four, may I suggest a compromise?" Pete stood straighter. "How about you take your short, pointy swords, shine them up real nice, and shove them up your ass. This is Grimwood, and your kind is not wanted here!"

The rest of the bar patrons cheered and stood. Three soldiers turned their backs to Doc as they assessed the situation.

The scraggly-bearded soldier stared at the drunken fool. "Is that how it's going to be?" he asked.

"Yes, and you will be paying my tab with your cock-sucking prince's money," said Doc, half insane and half drunk.

"Prince Damon will soon be king, and you are under the law of the Holy Imperium," said the soldier as he drew his sword.

Pete backed away from the scene, moving behind the bar, noticing the soldiers wore a mixture of chain mail and leather. The rest of the guests wore their everyday work clothes: shirts, pants, and coats for the walk home. None wore armor to deflect a sword cut or spear attack.

The larger soldier started laughing loudly. So loudly that the patrons relaxed and giggled. He brought his fingers to his mouth and whistled. Chairs pushed aside, tables moved, and other noises echoed above.

The drunken mage looked at the balcony surrounding the first floor above him and saw twelve soldiers leaning over the rail. "Oh shit." Doc squirmed, grabbed the top of his staff, and started coughing loudly, leaning onto it.

"What's wrong, you stupid fool? Think your independence still matters? Think you and this shithole of a town will get away for not paying taxes? It's about time you and the rest of you lot start paying for the war we fought. Our commander says this place is to burn. There are no churches here. You people worship the woods, the wolves, and whatever else you Profane believe," said the scraggly-bearded man to the entire tavern.

"We worship freedom, you bearded asshole! And I've already paid, you stupid pig-fucker!" Doc screamed as he guided the bottom of his staff into the larger soldier's crotch, cutting deep through his leather and chainmail. The staff's concealed blade sliced up the man's groin through his body, splitting him to his breastplate.

There was a moment of calm, then a bolt from a crossbow upstairs released, missing Doc and hitting Pete directly in his bulging stomach. The mage pulled out his staff's blade and pivoted the top toward the closest of the three remaining soldiers' faces. The other end mashed into a soldier's face, breaking his nose, eye socket, and skin. The top of his staff carried a large white stone set into it, kept in place by what appeared to be a murky wooden grip, like a tree's roots. Blood and gore from the soldier's ruined head stained it now, bits of brain matter dripping off its sides.

"Talleyho, shit bags!" Doc loped for the back door.

The patrons rushed the other soldiers, who stood in shock, having watched two of their comrades murdered before them. One cut in two, the other's head mashed in, slumped on the floor, lifeless. Angry yells came from the second floor, along with further crossbow bolts. A slight mist appeared from the floorboards.

"Fire!" someone yelled near the back as a door slammed shut.

Bar stools tipped over as patrons and soldiers wrestled and punched one another. They fought, consumed by drink, excitement, pent-up anxiety, and rage.

The tavern's floorboards warmed as thick black smoke curled around everyone's feet. A wall caught fire. Violence and panic remained inside as the back door opened, and casually, Doc trotted out, closing the door as if nothing had happened. The smell of beer and blood drifted into the air as glasses broke and wooden chairs crashed over people's heads.

"That was close." He brushed off his coat and walked away. Screams came from inside the tavern. "Now, what did I do with my pipe?"

Ben - Another Parade

"Olde Ridgewatch, this worthless city or whatever the locals call it, smells like fish all the time," said Stu. "Seriously, the place is filthy. The streets curve like a broken pecker, and everyone speaks a bastardized version of the Holy Imperium's tongue." Stewart Slickback complained, the natural right of any soldier.

Stu and Benjamin Ashburn were archers in the prince's Second Army, stationed by the Atlantis Ocean in one of Vineland's oldest cities—thus its name, Olde Ridgewatch. It was early morning, near the end of autumn, and they had drawn patrol duty again.

"I've never even seen a city like this, much less attempt to guard it against looters and rioters. How am I supposed to know if folk are up to trouble when it feels like everyone hates us?" Ben said.

The two young men were well equipped compared to a mercenary or highwayman found in the city's hovels or shadows on the roads outside of town. Their archer kits consisted of half chain mail shirts, dyed red leather, and half helms. Ben carried a short sword and crossbow, illegal unless in the prince's army. Stu carried a spear and short sword.

Ben kept the crossbow at hand but not spanned to shoot. It was more of a tool to threaten from a distance than anything else. The armor kits were expensive for soldiers, and the Holy Imperium forced those who joined the army to pay a share for their kits. Ben's father had paid for his gear with little to no effort, while Stu had worked to pay his off through his first year of service to Prince Damon. Once paid down, Stu would move forward into the ranks, higher if a noble chose to make him a man at arms. Ben expected to be knighted eventually but worked at it as if it were not a foregone conclusion. With luck and years of service, he would be a Redcloak like his father—one of the highest honors a soldier could receive.

Stu had received an education in Hudson City and, thus, compared everything to it. Most sailors considered Olde Ridgewatch the most valuable port in all of Vineland, more essential than Hudson City, the capital of the Holy Imperium, yet Olde Ridgewatch still didn't measure up to his expectations.

General Ashburn traveled to Olde Ridgewatch from the capital and stayed at the Red Maple Keep. The governing commander, Lucas Slickback, asked Sir Ashburn if he would take his son Stu on as a squire. Ben's father declined but hired him as a new archer after receiving a generous contribution from the same lord. This was the highlight of the trip up to Olde Ridgewatch. Ben's father remained morose during the rest of the journey, keeping to himself, and barely speaking to Ben. Rumors spread of Sir Benedict Ashburn's argument in court with another noble over a woman. This embarrassing event earned him both exile from the court and Prince Damon's anger. Ben heard the rumors and did his best to think of his father as a quality man who wouldn't dishonor his mother. She was at home in Grimwood, celebrating the fall harvest.

General Benedict Ashburn had moved after orders came via raven, making his way quickly to Olde Ridgewatch. Already a distant and professional man to the point of annoyance, Ben's father turned even further inward during the march, collaborating with his staff as needed and sitting alone most evenings.

When Ben had initially joined Prince Damon's Second Army, he wished to squire for his father. However, after traversing the wilderness over the king's and queen's roads, he found the task taken by another lord's son. Ben had remained quiet while his father spoke; his hopes and dreams slowly left him as his father explained his decision to choose another over his birthright.

Alfie Von Dyke, Benedict's new squire, was one year older than Ben but looked five years younger. Alfie's blood ties to Prince Damon were the essential factor. Ben's father treated Alfie more like a son than Ben. Inwardly, Ben was distraught at the news but remained stoic, as his father had taught him. Enough anger and spirit remained inside him to show his worth to his family, so he stayed on and joined the Second Army of the Holy Imperium ranks.

After joining the army, Ben found his father would not let him join his lance. A lance was a knight's household and command, featuring a squire or multiple squires, various archers, pages, and servants. Ben was assigned to the lance of Sir Donald Williamson, a semi-retired knight. His father had showed an act of kindness and bought Ben's armor, which allowed Ben more financial freedom than his peers as he worked to become a man at arms.

Stu had happened along and managed to join Sir Williamson's lance as well. They both tried to serve with respect and loyalty, but they often found themselves put on guard duty because of Sir Williamson's nature. They felt shunned and never really part of the lance. Stu and Ben did their best to stay out of Sir Williamson's way. At sixty summers with a thick frame, the man had a voice that boomed when he gave orders; he was not a man to anger. Ben had heard stories of his dad's war buddy Sir Williamson when he was younger. His face held creases from time and stress as his dark, sunken eyes showed the wear of multiple engagements. Nevertheless, he led his men with dedication, and they followed, doing their best not to let the old man down.

"Ben, what are we supposed to be doing again?" asked Stu.

"Sir Williamson's squire advised us to guard the streets by the river for the next several hours and win hearts and minds. Whatever the Hades that means. So, I guess we patrol, show the locals we are here to protect them and we're in charge," Ben said.

"You trying to convince them or yourself?" Stu looked at him.

Ben was about to retort but decided to be a good soldier for the prince and Holy Imperium. But what were they doing in Olde Ridgewatch? Who was the enemy—the woman throwing refuse out her window, the boy running across the street delivering a message to the butcher, or the fishmonger yelling about his newest catch?

"I mean, these people have been here for years. Doing what they do, scraping by, growing, and making this city what it is, as shitty as it is. But it's theirs, not ours. None of the army in the barracks is from this area. We're from Hudson City, the Commonwealth of Erieland, or the south, not to mention mercenaries from the old world, the Brotherhood of Bitterleak. Shit, they're something terrible," Ben said. "I swear, all they talk of is drinking and making locals squeal like pigs when they die. Glad I don't have to face them in battle. Can't be good for the city's morale and overall disposition."

"Just because they're an ancient military order from across the Atlantis Ocean doesn't mean their shit doesn't stink when they eat spicy food." Stu looked at the brick buildings along the pier and took a deep breath of ocean air. "I hate this place because it's not Hudson City. It's not my home. It's theirs. Let the rats have their nest. I want out of here," he said. "Sorry, just talking. I thought when I joined that it would be more than guarding a street or alley in a port city. Where's my mythical battle with mages throwing fireballs, lightning, and flowers and shit, and the prince calling down a dragon on the Legion's army?"

"I know, but wait, flowers?" Ben asked. "Mages don't throw flowers." Ben looked at Stu. They were quiet for a moment and then laughed. "It's okay. I understand you can't complain up. It's the army—either complain to someone of equal standing or get shit on even worse. But try not to say it too loudly, or we'll get lashed again."

"Yeah, I know. Still itches," said Stu, scratching at his back.

Both had received lashings as punishment for infringement of the dress code, profanity, and laughing while at attention.

The streets previously well worn paths from antiquity were now covered by a mixture of dried mud and broken stone or cobbled red brick. They stood for a moment and looked at the buildings on the other side of the street. Each was one to three floors high, with basic stone foundations and wood the rest of the way up, with roofs overhanging one another. The town also had watchtowers and a keep on the other side of the bay overlooking the town.

"Did you know the towers in Hudson City are poured stone, iron, and steel? Mostly dwarven made or at least engineered by dwarves. Olde Ridgewatch, the Child's dirty diaper of a city, was built by humans using a poor version of dwarven red brick. No wonder they want us to stop rioters. One torch to a roof, and half the city would burn—look how close these buildings are to one another," said Stu. "It's older than Hudson City. Nothing compares to the city of towers. Olde Ridgewatch—how pretentious! Doesn't even have a proper name. What a mess of a port surrounded by farms and a half-assed university."

Crimson Yard University was not half assed. Even Ben knew it rivaled those universities in prestige and age across the ocean. Crimson Yard University had helped make Olde Ridgewatch one of Vineland's most critical Holy Imperium cities. The rich sent their children to be educated before becoming members of higher society.

Ben walked on, doing his best to look authoritative and menacing. The last punishment had opened his eyes, and he resolved to become a better man. He wanted to be a knight of the first order, a Redcloak, but his eighteen summers made his mind wonder if he'd be happier at home with his brother and sister. It was fall, and the leaves had changed. He thought about his hometown in Wolf Hills, of his house in the valley where his mother, kid sister, and little brother still lived.

"It's near time for the harvest festival in my hometown. There'll be warm apple cider, dancing, a bonfire, and fresh brown ale. I wonder what Olde Ridgewatch does for harvest time," said Ben. He thought of pine branches waving above the river and watching fallen maple leaves drift along the water.

They neared a market. Merchant stalls stood on the left, selling wares and the daily catches while yesterday's rotting meats mingled with the bay. The city breathed in as if it were building up to let out a scream.

"I'd love to see a parade. I haven't seen one in ages. A little celebration at the end of the season," said Ben.

Stu listened and shifted the conversation. It was unwise to linger thinking of home as a soldier. They both learned about this early in their careers, getting drunk one night and moping about their pasts.

"Did you hear the guards working last night caught a couple of locals up to mischief?" Stu asked. "They found a few folk drunk and pissing on a fire built over an effigy of the prince. Guess the rumors were true. The new tax levies incense the locals, including the merchant class." He looked at one of the stalls selling stringy smoked sausages not fit for a dog. They walked on, growing hungry. "Anyway, our guards found this lot by the fire, middle of the street, way past curfew, and beat the piss out of them. Killed two of 'em and left the bodies in the street as a warning. Heard it from an old foot soldier named Drew as I was taking a piss early this morning."

Ben and Stu were in their late teens, men by most standards, but neither had killed a man outright. They shot their crossbows in minor skirmishes and didn't know if they'd hit or killed anyone before the cavalry ran down the group of townsfolk they were supposed to disperse. The action occurred outside of the city, and they both felt detached from it. They were *green*, as the veterans would say: *Stupid fresh fish, greenhorns*. They were trained and knew how to react if it came to it and could manage themselves in a fistfight, but for guard duty, it was not wise to be out without a veteran to show them the way.

Stu scratched at his crotch and continued, "So a few of ours beat up a few locals nice and proper—pirates and sneak thieves, the lot of them. They need to pay their taxes and get on with their life. That's what I say." He tried to sound reassuring, but it was a fake boast.

"Not so loud, Stu," said Ben. Stu looked at him and nodded. "It's all a bit jacked up though, ain't it?"

Stu wasn't finished, though. "The prince needs money to build bridges, maintain towers and other public works. The Holy Imperium is growing. It needs roads, more castles. Prince Damon, by rights, has to pay for those, right? Our own army pays down the war debt because these men fought on our shores, in our fields, and on our homesteads to protect us. We gotta pay for our swords, pikes, and whatnot. The war is over now; the Crimson Struggle, it's over. And the Battle of the Reaping solved it, right? Great battle with magic, fireballs, dwarves, orcs, and all the races fighting on three different sides. And we won. The Holy Imperium and Prince Damon beat the Nation of Stouya and the Legion of Carigreed, sending their asses back across the ocean. The prince was, well, he was in Hudson City and nowhere near the Battle of the Reaping with the wizards and orcs, dwarves, and all the fighting and killing, but you know what I mean. It's over now. Time for peace, songs to be sung. Time to rebuild Vineland into a greater country. It takes taxes from merchants and common folk to do it."

"But he didn't raise taxes on the nobles. I heard he cut taxes for them because they helped him win the war. He cut their taxes but implemented this new tax," said Ben. The sun warmed the boys as the breeze whipped around red dust from a stone archway. "So, the prince cut taxes for the nobles, who have most of the money, and raised taxes on who? The merchants and the well-educated. I mean, he raised taxes on those people and anyone drinking tea. Those people stuck in the middle."

"You got that right," said Stu.

"So, the sons and daughters of nobles are still noble, but not as well off. I dunno all this shit—politics, it's complicated. The nobles get taxed, but it seems like he cut taxes for those who could afford it and raised taxes on the lower classes," said Ben.

"Aren't we nobles too?" asked Stu.

"I guess. Don't feel it, though."

They heard drums before they saw them. A young girl carried a drum strapped onto her stomach, hitting it to a rhythm. They saw a line of the townsfolk, including elvish slaves mixed in with dwarves, down the street and past the market. The people in their stalls stopped talking and looked on. Those wearing hats took them off. Others placed their hands on their hearts. Those still shopping moved away from the street center out of respect.

"I think we may get our parade," said Stu.

"Maybe . . . what the Hades is going on? It's early morning. We get this shift because ain't shit going to happen except for the drunks walking off the night's drink and the opening of stalls and shops and whatever," whispered Ben.

"They're everywhere," said Stu.

The buildings to the left of Stu and Ben stood tightly together with only a few darker alleyways.

"Parade's taken up the whole street, ain't it?" said Stu, stating the obvious. He looked around, realizing they stood in the middle of the street like two idiots, the only uniformed soldiers of the Red Army around.

The drummer walked through the morning mist, followed by a woman wearing a black dress and veil. Others wore black, carrying large staves,

30

shovels, or axes. The woman in front walked stoically with tears in her eyes. Behind the first line of people, they carried a box above their heads.

"Shit, it's not a parade, and we're right in the middle of their path," said Ben.

"What is it? It's not a parade?" asked Stu with mild stupidity.

"Funeral," said Ben quietly.

"Funeral—it's for the two that the guards killed. Can't be, though. The prince outlawed burial in a public cemetery for those turning against the crown. They can't bury the dead on sacred grounds in the city. We have to stop them," said Stu.

Ben wanted to be a good soldier, wanted to be better, and wanted to prove himself. "No way we're stopping them. Look how many there are," he said.

They were frightened deer in shock, too stupid to run as the hunter aimed their bow for the kill.

The drumming continued, a flute played, and singing softly yet rising with emotion flowed from the crowd. The mob sang of loss, home, and an unfulfilled future with sadness dipped in anger.

"The hymn sounds familiar, but it's not from the Holy Church," Stu said. "They're flaunting their noses at us."

"Let's move off the road and let them pass. Say nothing; bow your head when they come by," Ben said. He could hear the pain in the song and see the anger in their eyes now.

"Bit wrong, though. I mean, it's not illegal to worship another god other than the Holy Church. That's a lot of them . . . okay, agree. I ain't going to start shit," said Stu.

They moved off the road to the stoop of the cobbler's shop as the funeral procession came closer. Ben could see two caskets at the front, one smaller in shape, he thought, and one larger being carried on shoulders.

"Are those children's caskets? Thought maybe it would have been about the fight last night, but—"

"Shut it, Stu!" hissed Ben.

As the procession moved toward them, the woman in front stopped. She wasn't old, only in her mid-thirties. The men in the funeral procession wore black armbands over their shirts. Stu and Ben stood quietly in their uniforms of the Holy Imperium. The woman looked at the two of them, a steady fury in her eyes, bracketed by tears. She spat and continued walking past them.

Stu and Ben stood at attention, heads down to show respect. After the procession passed, they followed safely as the two coffins moved along. According to one of the prince's new laws which forbade burial in the King's Church for any disloyalty to the crown, the procession passed a cemetery. The two soldiers watched as the coffins were placed in a boat along with several large stones. The boat was rowed out, and the bodies were weighed down and dropped into the Atlantis Ocean. The coffins were brought back to the shore for reuse.

Ben and Stu observed as the procession dispersed to two local taverns to toast the dead. They turned away and finished their rounds on guard duty, staying clear of the pubs. Later, two other soldiers relieved the boys, and they headed back to the barracks.

"Odd shit we saw today. Should we report it?" asked Stu.

"We should write it up and report it to Sir Williamson," said Ben.

"You think he'll get pissed?"

"I dunno," Ben said. He thought nobody should have to bury their children, no matter what.

So, they walked back in silence.

Alysha - Cleansed Earth

Alysha and Helena walked beyond the dancing and drinking, toward the shoulder of the river where the cottages and homesteads like Alysha's stood. The stones of the riverbed were flat before the river started mixing with sand. The opening slope had been created from years of cattle and sheep crossing from the other side into the shallows. A man sat on a large boulder overlooking the small drop as the water ran below. Alysha recognized him immediately from her treks into town to the tavern, where her brother Runt worked, or to the blacksmith shop, where Ryan Purenut apprenticed.

"Hi, Mr. Wolfe. Are you having a good evening?"

"Ladies, ladies, you startled me." The man, Junior Wolfe, smoked a pipe, resting a large mug on his leg. The man was a bit taller than Alysha, his hair matted and long, looking like the mask she wore. His face showed his age with lines and creases along his eyes and mouth.

He was the son of the late James Wolfe, a legend in the area. James had served as a foot soldier for the Holy Imperium's Second Army under Sir Donald Williamson. The songs told the story of James Wolfe, who had been wounded in battle while returning a message to Sir Williamson that had helped him devise a plan to win the next day and the battle. But, after delivering the message, James Wolfe succumbed to his wound. The songs said that as he died, he howled like his namesake, in pain.

Junior had done his best to live up to his father's great name but had failed in most cases. He drank more than most and served as the town's constable. He was named after his father, but most folks called him Junior. The Wolfe family lived in the area for generations and had nearly died out. Junior, one of two living relatives left, lived in Wolf Hills, and his younger brother worked at Grimwood University. Junior never married and, as a trained warrior, was a constable who protected the town. He sat on a rock, bare feet in the stream, staring out toward the north.

"Well, isn't that a scary mask? Did you make this?" he asked, pointing with his pipe.

"No, my brother Runt did. I just borrowed it. He's up at the tavern helping out tonight," Alysha said.

Junior nodded. "Hello, Helena, how is your beautiful mother this evening?" He paused, then continued, "The tavern, you say, Alysha? The place will be a madhouse tonight. With all the Holy Imperium soldiers in town, I decided it best to leave for a bit." He scratched at his patchy beard with worn and calloused hands.

"My mother is fine as ever, sir, and still married if you do forget," said Helena.

"Oh, oh, you're as perky as your mother, Helena. I meant no harm. Sorry. I get a bit off on this night, thinking about a few friends I've lost in my days here and away." He drank from his mug, took up his pipe, and drew in for a smoke.

"Come, come, sit for a moment. It's okay. I won't bite." He moved over, making room.

The girls looked at each other, back at the festivities, and at the gruff older man, his black-and-peppered beard and mangy hair. They took sips from their wine cups and sat on the large rock with him.

"Do you know anything about the Holy Imperium and them pressing boys and men into service around here? We heard they took Ryan Purenut and others from a few valleys away a few days ago," said Alysha.

"Yeah, we heard whispers about it up at the tavern. Unfortunately, it's nothing I can do. Even if we were to get half the town into a mob or a brute squad, we couldn't stop as many armed men as they have. There are several knights in the tavern right now—and talk of an actual Redcloak about. You know—real, old-blooded nobles like your father, Alysha. At least that's what

Donald, the pig farmer with the awful hair, told me," said Junior.

"Donald? My mom says he's more pig than a farmer—and a drunkard." Alysha took a sip of her drink. "And she doesn't gossip much."

"Either way, there are too many Red Army types around. Could be trouble. I sent a messenger to Grimwood as a complaint and tried to speak to the captain of the soldiers after the fact, but they did not take too kindly to me and my family name," Junior said. He took a deep pull from his cup.

"But how can they do this? Don't we fall under the laws of Grimwood? Don't they protect us?" said Helena.

"We are indeed a free town, just as Grimwood is an independent city, and they do protect us. I can't figure out why so many of the soldiers are in the area and why no word from Grimwood has returned. An emissary or even a few guards could clear this up. They took Ryan and a few other younger men from around Wolf Hills, and nobody has heard of anything from any other town since those men showed up." He took a deep pull from his pipe, smoke drifting over its ornately carved markings. Junior smiled, the night's amusements having a positive effect on his sour mood. "I wouldn't worry too much, though. We should hear from Grimwood no later than tomorrow night, I think," he said.

Helena and Alysha looked at Junior, realizing he was smoking illegal reefer, which they had never seen. They both coughed, and Junior smiled.

"Sorry, lasses, been a stressful night up by the tavern. Just unwinding. Alysha, you are looking at my pipe. It was my father's. One of the few keepsakes I have of his. The pipe came with the sword I wear—and with a bloody reputation. My younger brother, Felix, got lucky; he got neither the pipe nor the bloody sword and all its problems. It's okay, though, we are both Wolfe, I say, but he's been more like a cat," finished Junior.

The fiddle started up, but it was a slower, sadder tune. The girls looked back for a moment. Alysha stood, grabbed a few rocks, and started throwing them over the river. She tossed each stone back into oblivion after they'd spent years working on getting to the shore.

"Miss Alysha, if you don't mind an old man saying, you got strength in those arms."

She tossed the last stone away. "Ryan Purenut let me work the bellows and even started showing me how to smith a little the last few summers—and even a few times during the winter. He was nice to me, didn't treat me like a girl who washes clothes by the stream or a bloody cook . . . no offense, Helena. Junior, will Ryan come back soon or ever?"

"I'm a great cook, Alysha, and someone has to wash. No man has the guts to be responsible for daily living," Helena said.

"You're right, Helena, sorry. You've always been more right than wrong," said Alysha, looking at Helena.

"Well, ladies, sometimes the soldiers return if they keep their heads down and listen to the commanding officer. Most sign a paper to soldier for a year and return with a few coins in their pockets, a few scars, and bad dreams in their heads," he sighed, tapped out his pipe, and stood, "Sometimes not." He looked back. "Let's get, let's get back to the party now. Drink a glass for our loved ones, the dead, and the missing. It's what this night is for. So put your masks on, girls. Let's go dance."

They walked back from the river. The party continued, and time moved as the water flowed over the stones in the river.

Alysha spun and danced hand in hand with her friends and neighbors. The music played on, and she pushed up her mask, taking a moment to breathe in deeply. She grabbed an apple and bit into it, and the juice ran down the sides of her mouth. Everyone danced, laughed, and drank, and Alysha relished the warm energy of her family and friends. She took in all of them enjoying a blessed night to the Profane, celebrating the lives of those who had passed beyond the veil. A loud, shrill horse neighed at its bridle, bringing Alysha to her senses. A horse rode down the path toward the river, and she saw movement in the woods by the shore where the bonfire lit up the night sky.

It was dark, and the glow from the fire and torches didn't provide enough light when Alysha and Helena peered into the pine and oak trees. The fiddle and drumming stopped playing behind her.

Junior Wolfe walked toward the path, looking beyond the bonfire into the night. "Who goes there? Show yourself!" He put his hand on his sword hilt.

A dark horse walked out of the shadows, as somber as the sky above.

"Townsfolk, children, and fools, I am Jared of the Blackheart family, and you are now under the protection of Prince Damon's Holy Imperium. Path of the Blessed is with you all. Those between the ages of fourteen and forty summers are pressed into the service of General Flint's First Army. You will assist in our endeavors as we quell the criminal elements residing in the city of Grimwood."

Jared Blackheart wore plate armor and clasped to his shoulders, a tarnished white cloak bearing the marking of the Holy Church: a sword facing up with a candle as its blade. He was not a simple bandit. Strapped to the horse was a large sable shield, shining unnaturally.

A party of ragged-looking monks and soldiers moved from the woods onto the riverbank from both sides. Each wore a black heart sigil on their monks' robes or surcoats and bore the marks of the Holy Church, a sword with a flame for a blade. Holy ravagers on a quest to purge sin from the heathens. The lead soldier coming out of the woods was shorter than the rest, wearing boiled leather and holding a compound bow. "Fall to your knees and accept the Holy Church and the faith of the Path of the Blessed," he sneered.

Alysha saw hunters use the bow for big game like hogs and bears. The man's teeth, visible in the firelight, were yellow against his pale-white skin. Alysha thought she could see a green tint in the man's eyes.

Another stood near the edge, a woman older than the rest of the soldiers; she was dressed like the monks, wearing armor and robes as if she used to be a nun. She carried a short sword and had a book open, reading loudly to those around her.

"What is the meaning of this fire and these lanterns with faces?" demanded Blackheart, pointing at several jack-o'-lanterns. He was a strong, imposing ox of a man.

"Sir, we're celebrating the harvest and remembering family fallen during the long winters. It's tradition hundreds of years old," said Mr. Catseye.

"It's blasphemy to the King's Church to the Path of the Blessed. Men, sanitize this place. Keep only the worthy, bleed the rest, and burn the houses," ordered Jared. "I will erase the blight of unholy blood from this land."

"What, no!" Helena cried.

"You can't!" one of her neighbors said.

The monk-like soldiers moved quickly as Alysha's friends and neighbors screamed and yelled. Jared moved forward on his horse, pulling a large, bladed mace from his shoulder, and swung it quickly, shattering Junior in one sweep. His body bounced, landing several feet from Alysha.

Chaos consumed the valley.

"Cleanse the Profane from this earth!" yelled Jared Blackheart.

Alysha ran and fell over Junior, trying to stop the bleeding, but he was more gore than human. Blood quickly covered the front of her dress. Helena ran from the men, toward the river. Jared Blackheart passed by Alysha on horseback as if he were making his way to mass. Alysha grabbed Junior's body as if to put it back together, trying to ignore the screams and sounds of death around her.

She looked around, saw houses on fire, and turned toward her home, the biggest in the area. Alysha watched as Jared rode toward her mother, swung his mace from below, and thrashed her to the ground. She looked on and down again at Junior and her hands. She heard screams. Or maybe she screamed. The smoke from the fire and her tears blurred the violence, and soon she felt no pain.

A few valley folk ran, and crossbow bolts feathered their backs. Any man or woman showing resistance grew swords from their bellies, joining their ancestors as the magic of the night slipped into the river and blood fed the ground.

"Drown any child that can't stop crying and take the rest to camp. We need slaves and servants to work for the army near the sea. Those left will be part of our camp work detail. We don't want our drinks poisoned or throats slit while we sleep. Line them up, and we'll get the rules straight," said Jared.

Junior's sword rested at his side; he gasped, trying to speak to Alysha. A blood bubble popped, splashing her face. His arm twitched, and he reached for his family pipe. He moved his hand ever slowly to hers, whispered "Brother", and was gone. Tears fell, but no sound came from her mouth. She hadn't known him well, but he'd been part of the town and well known to all. Technically, she was of noble blood, and they should respect her, but these soldiers did not seem to care. They only cared about violence and the power of control through its use.

Jared stepped down from his horse. "Line them up. I said do it!" he screamed as spit came from his mouth. His sunken-in eyes held a yellow tint to them.

Alysha got up and walked toward where the others made a line. Everyone stood, lost in grief beyond remembering. Alysha slipped the pipe into her skirt pocket. She thought about grabbing the sword but knew better.

"I am Sir Jared of the Blackhearts, and you are blessed. Blessed to breathe, lucky to be of service, and if you work hard, you will be free when the campaign is over and paid for any grievance you feel Prince Damon may owe you. I am harsh and strict, but I do reward diligent workers. Welcome to the Holy Imperium. The Maker's blessing be upon you, sorry sinners. I'll shackle you until we believe you can be trusted. If you work hard and don't complain, you'll be fed and treated better. Some could win a better station in life rather than toiling away on a piece of ground. If you revolt, if you argue, I will decimate those left from your town, lining you all up and randomly picking people to face the blade. The ones not chosen will perform the killing. Is that fucking clear?"

Neither the dead nor the living answered.

General Flint -No Further Troubles

The tip of the spear of his majesty's First Army, known as the Prince's Army, halted. Robert Flint, Redcloak of the First Order, sat on his horse, speaking to his squire, who stood near his side. Flint's cloak symbolized pride and power, showing more than noble blood, his status above all other knights. He looked ahead, as they were on top of a hill, waiting for the scouts to report and the rest of the army to catch up. Flint's riding party consisted of four knights: two in riding kits and two fully armored, ready for confrontation with any destitute highwaymen or giant wolves, which had been reported in the area. The wildlife became aggressive the farther they moved from the Atlantis Ocean, and there was gossip of monsters and beasts from childhood lore making the rounds the more his army marched into northeast Grimwood. The rumors had started in the Commonwealth of Erieland as they traveled the Queens Roads through the Blightbriar Wilds and persisted the more they traveled west.

The trip proved shorter than expected, only three weeks from Hudson City by the Atlantis Ocean to where they stood on the edge of northeastern Grimwood territory. So far, the worst bit had been a harassing group of goblins and orcs, which his second in command, Jared Blackheart, had taken care of a week back.

Jared Blackheart was both a gift and a curse provided to General Flint. He commanded a crazy band of religious zealots called the Genteel Monks which gave any respectable noble pause. They were violent criminals picked from the stocks and jails of cities off the coast. Jared advised each to repent and cast their lot with him and the Holy Church. He offered them absolution through blessings. His men sinned daily and purified themselves each night through Jared's prayers. Although not proper knights, they worked well in small sets, causing chaos on the outer flanks of a battle, and if the Genteel Monks could get into house-to-house fighting, they were nearly unmatched. Their methods caused terror everywhere they met resistance. Unchivalrous, yes, but battles needed to be won and songs needed to be written. The group numbered fifty men, all specializing in death and destruction.

They came across six adolescent orcs whose skin still held the youthful green hue all young orcs had before turning to mature colors like gray, dark blue, brown, black, or white or yellow in exceptional cases. The smallest orc was under six feet tall with his horns just budding from his head. They all carried brutal-looking axes, swords, and maces. They had been hunting homesteads near a mountain pass in the Commonwealth of Erieland between Mount Nittany University and the city of Affectus.

Flint had attempted to get into better graces with a local lord who held a mountain pass; he had sent Jared Blackheart to deal with the troublemakers. He'd found them as they dined on a family of peasants inside a two-story cabin. Jared and his men slaughtered five of the orcs and took the sixth captive. Flint knew Jared had plans for the orc but kept those thoughts to himself. His band of monks spent a week hunting goblins and any remaining orcs, trying to extinguish the threat to the supply line of the army and local villages. The goblins' diminutive stature and brackish, blotchy skin kept them camouflaged and harder to find. After a week, Jared and his men considered the deed complete and joined General Flint and the rest of the First Army. Jared, like some humans, believed both the orcs and goblins were the races best fit to be slaves. General Flint concealed his personal feelings, instead focusing on using his resources to complete his orders.

"I belong back at court," Flint declared, sitting straighter on his horse. He'd been exiled from court by Prince Damon after he and General Benedict Ashburn argued over a woman while in Prince Damon's presence. The worst part was that General Ashburn was already married to a commoner living on the outskirts of Grimwood, hundreds of miles from the prince's court. After the fight, General Flint was exiled from Prince Damon's court, an embarrassment to his family. His rival, Benedict Ashburn, lost the leadership of his army and was exiled from the court. Now Flint hoped to earn Prince Damon's favor by taking the city-state of Grimwood by siege and putting it under the yoke of the Holy Imperium. Neither Flint nor Ashburn knew Prince Damon lusted after the same woman.

Flint was a calculated and stern man, open to using any resources to win a battle or get his way politically. He worshiped the Profane gods but, in public, functioned as a member of the Holy Church. Constantly conflicted by his beliefs, he strove to remain a committed soldier for the honor of the Flint family.

Jared Blackheart never doubted the Maker and was devoted to the Holy Church's rule and the Path of the Blessed without question. The Holy Church taught that God was the Maker, the Child created an example of right and wrong, and the Servant provided a path toward righteousness. The Holy Church believed King Geordie of Great Brightland and his offspring, including Prince Damon, came from a long bloodline of the Maker's Child. They worshiped the trinity of the Maker, Child, and Servant as one or separate, pending their wishes and needs to force their point.

* * *

The Holy Church believed the world had been created by the Maker, who had made five races, four of which had lost favor with the Maker, falling from grace. Some races were worse than others: humans were above dwarves, elves, orcs, and goblins. The Holy Church believed humans were closest to the Maker, chosen to rule over all other races.

Historically, the Holy Church's power ebbed and flowed with the king and queen at the time, but it began to grow into an independent authority. The Order of the Blue Rose, known as the Blue Templar, was the Holy Church's military order. They reported to the Council of Inquisitors, the judicial branch of the Holy Church.

After the Golden Age of King Christopher and Erica the Red, the Council of Inquisitors tried to weed magic and heresy from the land. This eventually pitted the two most influential families on this side of the Atlantis Ocean against each other: the Ruinthorn and the Hawthorn families. Both bloodlines claimed sovereignty over Vineland. The Council of Inquisitors used this newly granted power to destroy books, art, and other forms of entertainment they found lacking in holiness; they then started the judicial use of executions of those found lacking in the eyes of the Maker. In addition, they used the Holy Church's religious readings to justify further violence, slavery, and prejudice against anyone who did not see the world as they did. The Order of the Blue Rose had been the heavy fist of the Holy Imperium in Vineland and Great Brightland for decades.

Other parts of the Holy Church participated as well. Still, the Order of the Inquisitors and, thus, the Blue Templar took these notions beyond everyday prejudices, attempting to kill off all elves, orcs, goblins, and dwarves ill-favored by the Maker, Child, and Servant.

The Purge of Thorns, started by the Council of Inquisitors, had spread like a plague from Great Brightland across the Atlantis Ocean to Hudson City's peninsula in Vineland. The flames of the Purge of Thorns had ended in the year of the Maker in 1693.

When the purge ended, the Holy Church was scarred, and the Council of Inquisitors weakened. The king of Great Brightland had broken up the Order of the Blue Rose by placing them under regional bishops who reported to their respective cardinal. This reigned in the Council of Inquisitors, who had no strength to fight slights against the Holy Church. The Council of Inquisitors was not permitted to add members to their council, and after years, they gradually died down. The Council of the Inquisitors, now appointed by the king, numbered less than a handful.

The end of the Purge of Thorns led to the Thornbriar War between the Ruinthorn and Hawthorn families. After both families' demises, the war continued for fifty years in what was now known as the Crimson Struggle. Thus, Vineland was a vast and fertile country bathed in a history of war and strife.

* * *

General Flint tweaked the edges of his mustache and smoothed out his short hair. He wore short hair on the sides and a bit longer on top, parted and greased, to stay down, which was not of the style of Hudson City's capital. Many barbarians, highwaymen, and other fools' long hair blinded them for a moment in battle, long enough for them to lose their heads, and Flint did not take chances. He chose to ride in a heavy riding kit as a precaution, and he rested on the fact it would keep him in shape throughout the ride to Grimwood. The ride itself was near its end as he saw his favorite scout gallop up to him.

The First Army moved from the coast westward on the Queens Roads, burning any town that did not align with the Holy Imperium's new authority. They were on a mission to keep peace and create order across Prince Damon's lands. Several forts and towns supplied the army with crops and men to join the First Army's ranks, while others attempted to remain nonaligned or thought themselves under the care of their local liege lord or mistress. Those fools fell to sword, stone, and fire.

Although the public mission was to keep peace on the Queens Roads and, thus, in the Holy Imperium, General Flint was to take Grimwood, an independent city-state, by the end of spring. Winters were notorious in the north; General Flint knew this well. In the past, he had dealt with them himself above the Erie Sea. To keep an entire army warm, fed, and alive through a harsh winter near Grimwood would take a tremendous force of will and a little luck.

"What do you think, my lord? Shall we ride straight to Grimwood and bring this madness to an end? We picked off a squad of Grim Vultures surveying the outer edges of their boundaries. They will not be making any reports back," said Ian Shortstride. The Grim Vultures were the pride of Grimwood, their elite military order and defenders of the city-state.

Ian was General Flint's most trusted scout, the two having bonded through several military campaigns. Ian Shortstride was also a native elve and was hated by everyone. The term "native" would prick his staff's ears because most humans called the scout a savage or even slave. Dwarves, orcs, and even goblins speaking in a common tongue would call him savage in human company. Ian Shortstride's skin was not a prominent elvish color of red, brown, or even gray, but paler in comparison. For the cultures of elves, dwarves, orcs, and goblins, the red, brown, and dark skin was honorable, as lighter hues were considered deplorable. To some, the paler the color, the more likely the bloodline was impure and tainted by humans mingling into their family trees.

Ian Shortstride's ears came to a sharp point, causing easy ridicule in military encampments. He kept them hidden most times, but it did not help. He dressed more like a savage who had stolen a soldier's clothes, with a mixture of the army uniform and light leathers and furs with two short swords at his hips and a compound bow and quiver on his back. He carried General Flint's family emblem on his cloak, a black bear on a green background, so he could make it through any lines and sentries without being killed for looking like "the enemy."

"There appears to be no resistance as of yet. Only a few keeps, mostly tall log houses with stone bases on the road, and they are sparsely guarded," said Shortstride.

"We should be at Counselor City shortly. You can nearly smell the Erie Sea. What an asset of Vineland, the largest freshwater source possibly in the entire world," said Flint. "Shortstride, please come have a glass of wine."

The few men around Robert Flint remained on their horses and made room for Ian. Flint's squire presented a skin of wine. Ian bowed thanks and felt the soldiers' eyes on him, their distaste for his kind shown on their faces.

"I thank you for the opportunity, sir," said Ian. "Where is your mad dog Jared Blackheart."

Flint nodded at the men around him, and they moved on. The rest of the army continued passing Ian and General Flint. The two watched the soldiers as they marched.

"I've sent Jared Blackheart and his Genteel Monks to sow chaos around the area, and if he comes across the Ashburn family, he is to bring me their heads."

Ian raised an eyebrow but didn't say anything. This could bring General Flint's rivalry with Benedict Ashburn to further hostilities. Two soldiers in

45

places of power who hated each other.

"I've also engaged an agent, a witch hunter, to get me back in favor with Prince Damon. Jared and his men follow orders to an extent, and the witch hunter, Samuel, owes me a life debt, so he's searching for a family heirloom that Benedict Ashburn's family may have in their possession or, if that is not the case, anything resembling a Gift of the Maker."

While they were equal in size, strength, and battle prowess, General Flint was Jared's superior. Still, neither he nor anyone else wished to meet with Jared; his war mace; and the legendary shield, Midnight's Veil. Flint believed he could take Jared in a fight, as his skill was unmatched. However, the lingering knowledge that Jared's shield held no dents, looking like a polished shadow, gave even Flint pause.

"You speak of the Maker's Gifts your religion believes exist?" asked Ian. "We call them Paragons."

"Yes. While Samuel searches, Blackheart's men will harass local villages, gather a labor force, and send them to Counselor City, which will be under our control by morning. We'll use the villagers to start working to fortify Counselor City for the winter, and those surviving winter get to dig trenches if there is to be a siege of Grimwood. The people in this area worship a medley of idols, gods, and such. Blackheart will be happy to purify them all. If he converts a few, so be it," said Flint. He took a deep drink from his cup.

"There are also creatures in the state of Grimwood who may offer Blackheart and his Genteel Monks resistance, or if the Grim Vultures turn wise to the harassment from Blackheart, they could present problems," said Ian. He sipped from his cup and looked around. "Not to mention Black Willow Falls and the surrounding Grimwood forest."

"If any of Grimwood's soldiers vex Blackheart, he will sink back into the woods and make way to Counselor City. The main part of the First Army will have Counselor City in a suitable defensible position. If the Grim Vultures question any of us, we will act as if the prince sent an army to assist Grimwood in protecting their lands from rogue highwaymen and marauders bent on the city's destruction. Send reports via horse, not bird. I don't trust birds this far into the season," Flint said. "As you say, I don't trust the deep woods here. There is old magic here, whether our men believe in it or not. Old wives' tales always hold a grain of truth. Wolves, witches, and such—best to take precautions. We'll stay away from the eastern gate of Grimwood just as others have done in the past. I do have a plan, you know, to take this city."

"Understood, sir," said Ian. "Several stories of Grimwood are true. Although the local elven tribes are weak and keep to themselves, the rumor of the witch of the Litchbury Mire is not to be taken lightly. The same is said of the wildlife. The Grimwood area is known for its wolves and brown bears, not to mention nobody enters Grimwood from the eastern gate or even ventures into the actual wood. The fog is too dangerous because of the black willow and oakthorn trees. I'll do my best not to overextend my scouts."

"Grimwood will quickly find out what is happening, but it will be too late. Winter is near, and nobody moves once the snow falls. We shall put this entire country to the flame before the end of spring." General Flint smiled. "I hope Blackheart finds Lord Ashburn's family and pays them a visit," he said, looking down at Ian. He took a sip of his wine. "A noble lord living like a pauper in a backwoods town. What a joke."

"Blackheart's ways are vulgar. He thinks of me as less than an equal. The Holy Church, this way of believing the Path of the Blessed, is justified by his Maker's teaching. It will be his downfall," said Ian. "Jared's second in command, Bernard Caldwell the half goblin, and Mother Softfellow lead prayers over those monks like they are holy angels." Ian scoffed. "As if their Maker promotes rape, theft, and terror."

"Jared Blackheart is a tool, and I need to wield him to make Prince Damon's nation grow from this ground. As I use you as my eyes and ears, I use Jared Blackheart as a hammer and anvil. I do my best to respect you and him as much as I can," said Flint.

"His noble blood is filled with decay and bitterness," said Ian. "Nobles, what rot. To them, being in the presence of an elve is an insult to the Maker himself. They don't understand the history and the land they walk on."

"We're friends, Ian. I share wine, blood, and family with you, and many of the nobles at Prince Damon's court hate me for it. I'm a leader to all these men. Specifically, to Jared, yourself, and other tools at my disposal." Flint held his hand out as soldiers marched by. "I must allow Blackheart to be himself because he is needed. Soldiers use both arrows and lances in war, Ian. Let it pass. I will make sure he doesn't harm you. Now," he said, "let's get to Counselor City. The mayor sympathizes with our cause and wants to be in Prince Damon's good graces. She thinks if Grimwood falls, her city will build up and take its place. If we take Grimwood whole, we have a new base of operations. If not, we'll build up Counselor City as Grimwood burns to ash before us."

Alysha - Putting in the Work

Following the initial carnage, the soldiers placed shackles on everyone as they stood in a line.

"I am looking for members of the Ashburn family. They live in the area, specifically this valley," said the leader of the monks, Jared Blackheart.

Everyone was in some form of despair and shock. Helena looked at Alysha but didn't say anything. Neither had any family left in the valley.

"Shut your fucking holes. You can cry in your sleep," said a man to Jared's left. His name was Caldwell. Alysha remembered hearing it a few minutes ago.

These soldiers, these so-called Genteel Monks, were looking for her family, Runt, who was hopefully safe, and her mother, who was now dead.

Alysha took the chance. "Sirs, I know where the family is." She stepped forward the best she could.

"Speak up, wench!"

"Maria is dead over there by the burning two-story house. Their daughter Bella was sick with a fever tonight; she was in the home when it burned," she said weakly. Of course, it was a lie, and she hoped they wouldn't know any of their names. Her hands shook; she was sure this wouldn't work.

"Is that so?" Jared looked down at her.

Alysha stared at his eyes with fury, then changed and glanced down, attempting to be humbled, as if she had nothing to live for. She would remember that face for the rest of her brief time on Vineland.

"And you, who are you?"

"Alysha Wolfthorn. This is my cousin," she lied, nodding to Helena.

"Good, our camp has use for the likes of both of you." He smiled through his beard and moved on.

The Genteel Monks marched the remaining villagers past burning cottages and over their dead relatives' bodies. When Alysha looked at her house and saw her mother's headless body, she forced back tears and swallowed back vomit.

The old woman behind her waited until the rope pulled tight, picked her up by the arms, and pushed her on. The old woman whispered, "Live for her memories, girl. Live to show her you will grow stronger and better than she ever thought you could. Go on, girl, go on. Be quiet, obey, and listen to what they say. Survive this and grow strong."

Alysha looked through the snot and tears crawling down her face, ignoring the burning acidic taste of the vomit, and saw defiance in the woman's eyes, as if this weren't the first misfortune to befall her.

She drew closer. "You'll know when to take revenge. It may take years, but you'll know," the old woman whispered. "You kept to the old ways, yes, you and your family. You did. I know who you prayed to: Jupitor, who gives us light and day; Sif, bringer of the harvest, change, and death; yes, and Stribog. During the winters here in our hills, he smiled at us. But you know who I see in you? Judith. You are a child of Judith, bringer of rain, growth, lightning, and storms. Let her guide you through this terrible time."

Alysha didn't say anything, she just nodded in a flash of clarity. She didn't see Runt or Angus, but she saw others from town in the line of prisoners. They cried the courage out of themselves as they walked in two lines away from the fires of their homes and the deaths of their fallen loved ones.

"Shut up, shove on, or die," a soldier ordered.

Alysha looked back and burned the image of her house and her mother into her mind.

Shackles chafed Alysha's skin and weighed on her physically and mentally as she shuffled along. A rope tied around her neck kept her and her remaining neighbors together. Helena walked in front, sobbing quietly, as the older woman walked behind her. She remembered her mother calling the woman Miss Rowan Wightland when she'd fished near her house across the river, as if she were some form of a noble. Today, Miss Wightland looked wild and thin. Alysha tried to console Helena, who had seen her little sister drowned by soldiers. She ignored the memory of her mother's death even as it lingered like burned bread. Everyone struggled to process the events that had just occurred. Oddly, a smoldering fury blossomed inside her instead of sorrow. Alysha tried to remember faces in case she survived, a thirst for revenge seeding. In the furthest parts of her mind, she tucked those thoughts away.

They moved north, away from the flames and bodies toward the Erie Sea. Alysha was lucky enough to wear her warmer cloak, wool dress, and boots. They drank water downstream from the river near noon, weary and unsure if they would be fed. The water tasted like the blood of the dead. They pushed through late afternoon, and the wind's chill twisted down the line of captives. The chain of prisoners crested a hill as a deep, bright gray and blue line from the sea peeked over the horizon.

"See, girl? See it? We're near Counselor City as it lay on the edge of the Erie Sea—the poor stepbrother to Grimwood," the old woman crooned behind her. Miss Rowan Wightland pointed. "We go there now. It'll be your home. Or prison. Don't make waves on the Erie Sea this winter. Grow there like Judith grows flowers. Learn and grow," she whispered.

Helena tugged Alysha forward, and Miss Wightland continued behind, mumbling to herself.

Grimwood was a large walled fortress backed by powerful merchants and guilds, while Counselor City was free of union guilds, allowing for cheaper and poorer-quality goods than those produced in Grimwood. While Counselor City grew from the hands of local humans and nobles, Grimwood's lineage twisted from elvish to dwarven settlers, on to a city council of human and dwarven people reigning over the city-state matters, guarded by the knighthood known as the Grim Vultures. Grimwood's port had been carved deep by dwarven hands with cut stone and etched runes, allowing larger ships to access city stores. Counselor City's port and buildings used brick and grout in stark contrast.

Counselor City had lost a sizable militia for the Holy Imperium in the hills of the Commonwealth of Erieland during the Crimson Struggle, with sons and daughters lost to a never-ending war. Yet, Grimwood had proudly remained an independent city-state during the Crimson Struggle, accepting all sides in trade and industry after the Thornbriar War. Grimwood had its own wicked past filled with betrayals, slavery, and political maneuvering.

The caravan of human flesh slinked its way through a field, a column of trees and woods to their right, and a hill with no vegetation except ankle-high grass to their left. On top of the hill, Alysha could make out a large stone pile.

"You see the altar to our friend and our sister," said Miss Wightland, her hair streaked in silver and gray, a natural wave to it. Her face was timeworn, and her hands were thin and knotted.

"Are we related? I'm sorry. You must have me confused," said Alysha quietly. She sniffed and wiped her nose to clean herself up a bit.

"Oh, we're friends now, Alysha, and to the left upon the hill is not a bench but an altar to Judith. The storm comes, and it seeks an offering. Do you not feel it?" asked Miss Wightland.

"I never told you my name."

"There is no need, as we are friends, you and I," said Miss Wightland. "Now is the time. Judith requests a gift, a sacrifice. Feel the wind; see the power in the sky."

The gusts picked up and blew Alysha's cloak. She looked to the heavens and watched lightning flicker between two clouds. The remaining prisoners slumped closer to the ground.

"You're one of three. Two brothers and you, soon to be two, and there are three sisters and a lover's triangle all winding in the storm, making history."

After the lightning and thunder rolled, two children slipped off their ropes and ran, shackled yet quick as rabbits, attempting to escape toward the forest.

"Release dogs on them!" yelled a fierce-looking man.

Alysha had heard his men calling him Blackheart, while his second in command, Bernard Caldwell, had called him Jared during the march. Bernard Caldwell sat on his horse next to Jared Blackheart, looking peculiar. His pale skin carried a brackish tint as if he were part orc or goblin. He smiled with a nasty mouth full of decay. She remembered Jared Blackheart running down Junior Wolfe two hours ago. She now carried Junior's pipe, stashed away in her dress, and promised to present it to Junior's brother, Felix, in Grimwood—if she could ever reach him.

"Those attempting to escape will meet the Maker!" yelled Blackheart, his shield like a shadow hooked up to his saddle. The large, short-haired, and visceral dogs ran toward the children. Everyone watched as the two children, younger than Alysha's brother, sprinted off through the field, toward the woods on Alysha's right. The dogs raced toward them, mean and hungry. The soldiers cheered, watching the dogs leap on the children's backs, ripping their flesh as they screamed.

"Now's the time I pay my respects to Judith for us," said Miss Wightland from behind Alysha.

She didn't understand what the old lady was referencing. Alysha's eyes widened as she looked on. As if no one were watching, Miss Wightland casually tugged the rope from around her neck, slipped it off, and started jogging toward the hill and the altar; her shackles made no noise. She moved up the hill, past a set of stones and briars, toward the summit. None of the guards noticed as the old woman hiked up the hill at a speed that would have made Alysha breathless. Everyone heard animals eating and growling. Thunder rolled against the sky, and there was a scream. Alysha's attention turned to the hill. She saw Miss Wightland standing on top of the altar, shouting and naked, her shackled hands in the air, trembling toward the sky.

"How did the old witch get up there?" asked Jared Blackheart. "Caldwell, take care of that madness on the hill."

He aimed his compound bow at an angle. The shot looked unbelievable to place as the storm rose. Alysha looked on and breathed in deeply as he released the arrow toward Miss Wightland at the top of the hill. The arrow peaked and fell toward the woman. A flicker of lightning reached from the sky and grasped the old woman on the altar. It was a quick moment, and Miss Wightland and the arrow disappeared in a flash of power and fire. The altar was lit aflame along with the vegetation around the stone.

Caldwell whistled and stuck his tongue out of his yellow teeth. "Was that good, sir?" he asked.

Jared grabbed his long dark beard. "I guess so, I guess so. She is right and dead now. Move the rest of these pigs on. Let's get done with this march before the rains take us all," he said. He waved his hand, and Alysha and Helena pushed on.

The rain fell hard, and Helena complained, muttering to herself. Alysha didn't say anything as she tried to understand what had occurred. After the storm, she felt different, as if the water had cleansed her of fear and pain. They marched on toward the Erie Sea.

* * *

After a long march, they could see Counselor City and stopped so Jared Blackheart could assign new lives to those captured. Alysha's feet were bloody and blistered, and her mouth was dry as her body ached for water and food.

"Everyone here will be supplied with a purpose or job. We'll walk down the line, and if you have any skills, speak before you're assigned a job or station. You'll be provided shelter and food if you are part of the encampment, and if not, you'll make do with the provisions provided by your new masters," he said.

The old, young, and broken lined up and waited their turn. The sounds of "labor, cook, servant, and slave" rang through the line along with "washerwoman, whore, and tailor."

Finally, Jared stood before Helena and Alysha. He grinned at Helena and glanced at Alysha. Two other men stood off to Blackheart's side. One of the men wore spectacles and carried a flat board and parchment, writing down names and positions. The other, Bernard Caldwell, leered at Alysha and Helena with his filthy grin, smelling of sweat and sour food.

"Lord Jared, these pretty ones, might I sample them here before they start their new lives?" said Bernard Caldwell.

Helena looked down and grasped her fingers. "I can wash and farm and split wood, sir. I can cook."

"We have plenty of those people, plenty. It's all your entire town is good for, chopping wood, farming, and anyone can wash," said Jared. "Whore!" And he moved on to Alysha.

"No!" she screamed.

Bernard Caldwell grabbed Helena and pushed her off to a new life, and Alysha looked at Helena's back, tears in her eyes. She balled up her fists.

"You there, you're a wh—"

"Sir, I can smith, sir," said Alysha.

"Smith, you say." Jared paused. He grabbed his black beard, which showed spots of red in it. His hair was black, and his eyes held large, dark circles under them. He was a mammoth man, one of the biggest Alysha had ever seen. He stood nearly six feet seven inches. "Show me your hands."

She put them out. They were coarse and rough; her arms flexed, showing her muscles.

"Never heard of a whore smith. You sharpen knives, swords?" asked Jared.

"My boyfriend showed me. He was an apprentice. It seemed like a lark at first, but I enjoyed it. I can shoe a horse, sharpen knives, make nails, fix harnesses," Alysha said.

Her voice didn't quiver as she stared right at him. Jared Blackheart, the man who had slain her mother.

"Fine, head over to the Hob and Bob smithy. If you don't work out, my boys will take you out back and break you in like the horse you said you could shoe. Now get out of here," he said. "Mark it down, Professor Nester. The Maker's will be done."

The man with spectacles and a mousy look bowed at Alysha. "Name, lass?"

"Alysha, Alysha Wolfthorn," she said. She didn't know why she changed her name but considered her mother's death, the incident at Judith's altar. She wasn't sure, but it felt prudent to say.

"All right, Alysha, work hard for Hob and Bob, or you will be Alysha Whoresmith in a few days," said the spectacled man, and he spat at her feet. "Claudette will walk you down to your new home."

Alysha walked away, head up, yet unsure what would come next.

The town was busy as laborers dug around the city, creating trenches, and putting in stakes. Alysha and her family hadn't traded or gone to Counselor City often. Her mother had preferred to go to Grimwood. The surrounding area's pine trees were logged out, creating a new palisade wall.

The townspeople from Wolf Hills with no fundamental skills dug trenches to prepare the town for an attack and carried stones from the Erie Sea to help reinforce the new walls.

Alysha walked to a building near a freshly built wall where sap dripped from one of the sides of the barricade. The stone building was not even a month old. It stood three sides squared out, and one side next to the door had a rounded kiln fire on the outside, set up so the same fire pit was inside, like a fireplace for a window. The roof held two chimneys, one for the kiln and another on the building's other side. It was one generous affair with a loft for sleeping and an open outside room with an overhang and fire pit, which allowed work to be done outside during the summer. She walked in, not knowing what to say or think.

Two men worked, one pumping the billows, another hammering. Sparks flew, hitting the large leather aprons hanging on their muscled bodies. The men were dirty and older. She felt the heat and percussion of the hammering, but there was limited smoke. They both looked up but continued to work, so she stood and waited as the hammering continued. Alysha could have left, but she remained shackled by the wrists and legs. She wouldn't make it far. Then, finally, a man with a short, grayed goatee and a lined face acknowledged her. He looked in his fifties but had youthful eyes. He nodded to the other man to get his attention. They pulled cotton from each of their ears.

"You there, what do you want?" said the man with the goatee.

"Sir, the man up there sent me to help," said Alysha.

"What? Wait, what?" asked the one with the mustache and long white beard. He was bald, while the other man had a full head of hair.

There was confusion between the two men. The one with the silver-and-white goatee muttered to the other, who wore a curled-up mustache.

"The last smith, if you can call him one, was sent to join the labor camp. Didn't like the work, didn't like us, and couldn't sharpen his dick. You don't have a dick, do you?" the one with the mustache asked.

"No, sir." She stood taller. "But I can swing a hammer like I got one," she said.

"What do you know," said the other smith with a smile.

The two men walked over. Both were thickly cut, broad around the shoulders and waist. The one with the goatee had darker hair, cut short and grayed at the ends. The other with the mustache was bald on top as if he had taken a razor to it, but his mustache and beard made his face look full.

"So, you were sent here to serve for the prince and country," commented the one with the goatee.

"A female smith and human. Only female smiths I ever heard of were dwarven, but they wore bigger beards than most," the other said, chuckling with slight mockery.

They stood above her with their arms crossed.

The one with the mustache twitched his nose and curled its ends. "Gonna need to get those manacles off, I suppose," he said.

The other gripped his goatee, pulling at it. They looked at each other again and nodded as a decision was made.

"Fine. We'll feed you and work with you. Listen to us, learn, and if it gets too much, you head out and start digging ditches until you die. You work hard, and you'll find life no trouble here. I'm Hob. Notice the goatee." He pointed at his face. "Bob has a mustache and hates everyone except me. Got it?"

Alysha nodded. "They took us from our village and burned it down, so all I have is what you see. But I can work. I've done smithy work in my town. Nothing with weapons or armor. Really, I sharpened knives and shoe horses," she said. She was taking a chance here. Her lie had held up to the soldiers, but these two men seemed as if they could chew through bullshit like a freshly sharpened wood saw.

"Let's keep it simple. Now you say your name," said Hob.

Alysha was confused. She thought she'd be a slave, but not now. She stared for a second. "Alysha Wolfthorn. I'm from a little south of here, about half a day's walk."

"Well, lass, there's bread, a few pieces of cheese, and a wineskin by the workbench near the window. Sit and eat. We'll sort out your shackles and where you'll sleep shortly," said Hob.

They turned, moved back to the fire, and started hammering again. Alysha walked over to the table, grateful for the room's warmth, and devoured the food. The wine calmed her, and soon, she slept at the table. When she awoke, she found a piece of fish in front of her and a blanket over her shoulders. After eating, she walked out to find them finishing shoeing a large horse.

"You're awake. Come over and take the reins here. I gotta piss."

She ran over and took the horse. Hob left, and Bob finished up.

"Thanks, lass. It's late tonight. We're going to finish up and knock those manacles off. Tomorrow, you're in charge of getting us water, cleaning up the shop, fetching tools, and doing as we say. Easy as that. You sleep inside the shop. Once we leave, we lock you in. It's more for your safety and our tools than anything else. You'll be one of the few warm people this winter. Any disagreement?"

"No, sir," said Alysha.

"Sir? Ha! I'm no knight, lass. Just trying to make my way through this bloody life. Work hard, and we'll do our best to take care of you." Bob smiled and finished the work on the horse.

"I thought you were the grumpy one," said Alysha.

"Don't let Hob know." He smiled again.

She breathed in deeply and went back inside the shop.

Runt - Heartwarming

Maynard pulled the donkey loaded with saddlebags, out of the barn near the Wayward Tavern.

"Follow me down this path, and I will get you on your way," said Runt. "We'll move off the main road until I can get you to the crossroads." Runt heard a scream from the darkness behind him as Maynard followed.

"What was that?" Runt asked.

"Can't be good; my mentor gets into trouble or ends up in the middle of some calamity through no fault of his own. He just finds bad situations. Best we keep moving. He'll find us eventually."

They walked a short path away from the tavern, not saying much, just breathing and pulling the donkey along. Shortly, they made it to the town's outskirts. They stood in the shadow of one of the lit braziers on the northern edge of town. The firewood snapped and popped, lighting up the crossroads as shadows danced around them. There were lights off in the distance, along with yelling and screaming past tall pine and maple trees that lined the edges of the village like a fence.

Runt began to worry as the seconds passed.

"We should stay off the road," Maynard said. "Those soldiers were looking for a fight, and my mentor isn't afraid of starting one."

"What do you mean? I need to get back to work. My boss, Pete, or Angus will whip me if I don't get back," said Runt. "I'll lead you down the way a bit. Walk until you see the sea, turn left and walk until you see the spires of Grimwood, and you'll be on your way back to the university."

The donkey, oblivious to the world, looked at the two teenage boys as it veered toward the side of the road.

"Who's Angus? Come on, donkey, walk straight," said Maynard as the donkey fought against the apprentice's pull.

"Angus is the cook. He's a bit gruff, but you get used to it," said Runt.

Suddenly there were footsteps, and both boys looked back as fear ghosted through them. The donkey looked as well.

"Hey! You boys, okay? Anyone see you at all?" asked Angus, bent over, heaving breath in a hushed tone.

"Angus, that you?" said Runt. "What happened? You aren't mad, are yah?" Runt left the donkey's side and looked at Angus. "I was just heading back. Did you butcher another pig tonight because it was so busy? You have grease and gore all over you." Runt saw fog rolling in behind Angus as he walked toward the pair of boys.

"Don't, boy. It's madness, worse than the bar riots I've been in Steelsburg. Soldiers and the crazy old drunk set fire to the tavern." He looked at Maynard. "He's started a shitstorm and pissed off Imperium soldiers. They've taken to killing anyone that doesn't bow to them in honor of Prince Damon. Vulcan's beard, I thought it was a few drunk mercenaries, which is concern enough, but it's worse. We need to leave, now!"

He caught his breath after a moment. Angus stood in front of the two boys, about the same size, only older, arms knotted with muscle and age. Lines circled his eyes, and his mustache braided into a long red-and-grayed beard.

Most dwarves stayed near the Blightbriar Mountains and the carved-out cities below the earth, but a few dwarves like Angus found solace above ground in Wolf Hills with its trees, valleys, and open sky. He brushed off his trousers, his face a smear of snot, blood, and sweat, just like his hands. Angus wore a simple tunic, a light leather apron with studs, a belt with a sheathed kitchen knife and cleaver, and a pair of trousers. He had a large pan slung over his back like a shield a warrior would wear.

"Angus, you have mud or some of the butchered pig on your face there. Wait, that's not pig. What the Hades is happening?" asked Runt.

"I dunno, boy, the Wayward Tavern is gone. Or will be soon. The courthouse and the mayor's house are now under guard. The Holy Imperium has taken over. Other buildings have been set to torch. They gathered anyone loyal to Grimwood, anyone who looked like trouble, and the town's leaders and led them to the courthouse when I snuck away. They're looking for you, asking for *you by name*—your sister and mother, too. Maybe they know about your dad and brother in the army. My hovel's burned up, gone now, the bastards. All I managed to get were my cooking utensils and my favorite pan." He slapped his back where the pan sat. "Ahh, come here, fella." He nodded over to Maynard, the apprentice. "What's your name?"

"My mentor calls me apprentice, but you can call me Maynard."

"Maynard? Where you from?" asked Angus.

"Best for me if we get going. I'm sure my mentor can clear everything up," said Maynard. His tone was both defensive and nervous.

"Come closer here, Maynard." He moved closer to Angus. The dwarf grabbed Maynard's dark-gray robes with one hand, took the torch Maynard was holding, and threw it on the road. Angus wiped his hands all over Maynard's robe and cleaned his large cleaver and butcher knife on the fabric, daring Maynard to complain while he sneered at him.

"Now, like your mentor, the dim-witted idiot, you have blood on you. He owes me for the dinner I cooked, if not my home and job. Most likely, the soldiers would have burned the town whether your mentor got involved or not. Still, dwarven principle—he owes me for the dinner I cooked, and he failed to pay. You going to see him soon? I saw him get out of the tavern after he killed a few of the soldiers, starting all of this mess," said Angus.

"I suppose . . . he said to meet him at home, which is the University of Grimwood. He does this often—makes an odd remark—and I have to figure it out. It's part of my teaching. Maybe he meant Runt's home?"

"Well, shit, that is confusing as all get out. Let's get Runt home, and we'll try to find out if his ma knows anything." Angus placed the cleaver inside his belt and the knife at the other side. "Runt, put out the torch. It's not safe in Wolf Hills any longer. Let's get going," he said. "Try to keep quiet. If we come across soldiers from the Holy Imperium, run, split up, and hope they can't catch us all."

"Where's your house, Runt?" asked Maynard.

"Follow me. It's a way into the wood," he answered. Runt led Maynard the apprentice, Angus the dwarven cook, and a skittish donkey into the darkness, leaving behind the fog, smoke, and blood.

The thick darkness of night surrounded Angus, Maynard, and Runt as they moved away from the top of Wolf Hills; the burning tavern and surrounding buildings behind them no longer back lit their escape. Runt could walk the path quicker alone, having done so on a nightly basis, but tonight, with a donkey, a dwarve, and another human tagging along, he slowed to make sure nobody stumbled or fell into a ravine or stream.

* * *

Wolf Hills was built on the highest slope around the Erie Sea and was one of the first settlements in Grimwood before the Golden Age of Erica the Red and her beloved King Christopher. It remained as other cities grew in prominence, yet it didn't outgrow itself and crumble like other cities had after the Golden Age. It plodded along, staying out of trouble like the donkey Maynard led down the dark path. Wolf Hills held a courthouse, tavern, and close access to a crossroad, which gave the town the status to keep it alive but not enough to grow. Grimwood became a sprawling metropolis due to the nearby sea and trade from other local municipalities and sea bordering city-states.

Grimwood's access to the Erie Sea helped it outgrow Wolf Hills, becoming a walled fortress with towering spires. Its influence in trade and arms helped keep the peace and brought justice to the surrounding area, including Wolf Hills.

King Geordie of Great Brightland lived a lifetime across the ocean, but his bastard son reigned in Hudson City. As far as everyone knew, Prince Damon's political ambitions had previously been his father's. Although technically in charge of territories, fortresses, and castles near the sea, Prince Damon had no sway in this part of Grimwood or other parts of Vineland like the Commonwealth of Erieland. Political power had shifted to Prince Damon after the Battle of the Reaping and the belligerents stopped killing one another.

In the chaos following the bar fight, the Holy Imperium soldiers had burned the Wayward Tavern, the mayor's house, residents' homes, and businesses on top of the hill. The area where the mayor's residence and tavern smoldered was the tallest peak in the region. It was dependable ground to hold. Unfortunately for the Holy Imperium soldiers, Wolf Hills was surrounded by a thick forest with hills and ravines. Holy Imperium soldiers couldn't hold it unless the capturing force knew the paths, caves, and other isolated regions. Groups of soldiers, including the Carigreed's Legions, and the Nation of Stouya had tried to take the town by force or guile early during the Crimson Struggle and ended up losing entire platoons of soldiers to the deep woods surrounding the village of Wolf Hills. Rumors suggested wolves, witches, or demons, but the town knew local farmers were using hit-and-run tactics in the dark, feeding the bodies to the local wolf pack.

* * *

There was a scream behind Runt, Angus, and Maynard, coming from the direction of the town, making all three and the donkey stop and look back.

"More looting, maybe worse. Soldiers aren't kind to anyone. Let's keep moving," Angus said.

Runt picked up the pace, giving way to quickness instead of safety in the dark. He was worried for his mother and sister.

Around the town, there were small valleys and hills featuring groups of homesteads. Runt's small valley typically took over two hours to walk to, but it would take over three in the dark.

"Angus, you said 'Reds'—you mean all those soldiers serving the Holy Imperium?" Maynard asked as he tried to keep up with Runt.

"Reds, yeah, the shortened term for soldiers in the service of the Holy Imperium," said Angus.

"I still don't understand. Do they not know the area or who we are?" Runt said. "Our townsfolk don't put up with highwaymen or other criminals. The people from those houses will gather and pick off the lawbreakers from trees and bushes using a blade, bow, and steel-made claws passed down from generation to generation. We know the land and have the advantage. I've heard drunks brag about it into their cups late at night—how they took their first life in the dark, sneaking out from an apple tree. Those soldiers back there can't expect to hold the town, right?" Runt questioned himself out loud.

"Don't think they want the town, Runt. I think they want to sow fear and may have a bigger game in their sights," said Angus. "Plus, much of the town was up there tonight, except a few homesteads like yours."

"What they did was dishonorable," said Runt.

"You spoke of stabbing people in the back at night hiding behind a tree, you shithead," Angus said. "There's no law or honor in war, no matter how many stories you read about knights, dragons, and beautiful ladies in distress. Tall tales are for milk-drinkers and putting kids to sleep. Now let's get you home, grab your mom and sister, and head into a cave where we can be safe for a few days. I know a few in the area."

Runt said nothing more. The night's shock wore him as they walked and worry slowly seeped into his thoughts. Maynard tried not to stumble and fall as he led the donkey on the path.

The going for Runt, Angus, and Maynard wasn't easy, but the path started to lessen up, and morning colored the sky.

"Come on, you two, we'll be just in time for breakfast. My mom makes the best eggs. Maybe we'll have a slab of bacon since Maynard is a guest and all. Heck, having you over is news for our neighbors—a scholar from Grimwood!"

"Runt let's hope we can get her, your sister, and anything we can grab and head up into a safer place by the river caves until we figure out what's going on. It was nasty back there. Father Winter is going to punish all of Vineland," said Angus.

"I didn't think. Yeah, you're right, Angus," the boy said. His face turned from excited to worried.

Runt walked to the top of another hill and started down a well-worn curved deer path as the sun peeked above the horizon. Red maple, pine, oak, and black walnut trees mingled around the path as leaves crunched under his leather boots. Runt jogged ahead of the group. The colors of the fall started to show in the early morning. An odd smell came to Runt's nose. *Bonfire*, he thought, but after a moment, he realized it was too late to smell the bonfire. Runt broke through a turn in the trees, and anxiety rose into his chest. The wind warmed as he moved closer to his two-level home at the valley's base. Runt moved faster now, and he sensed it through the trees as the smell of burning leaves and wood grew stronger. Smoke came from the houses he could see. One more turn, and the ruin fell before his eyes.

Angus looked farther and saw Runt's neighbor's house, black and burning. Runt ran down the trail. Leaves hit his face, and branches snagged at his jacket. A large black walnut tree passed to his right as he pumped his arms, breaking out of the woods and the well-used path. He ran through the tall grass. His legs churned toward his house. He made it past his neighbors' homes, and smoke drifted past him, blocking his view. He paused at a house, a chimney half fallen, wood and timber smoldering. Janice, a girl he'd played with since they could crawl, and her parents lay near the front of their house, heads removed, bodies shattered.

"No!" He ran again toward his home, where smoke billowed from the windows and door, nothing but ash and burned wood, and the smell of roasted meat lingered. He knelt when he found her and grabbed at his mother's body, tears traveling down his face, but she was gone like the neighbors. Runt's chest became wet and slick, but he didn't notice through his echoing despair. Maynard and Angus appeared, both out of breath, eyes wide. Angus carried his cleaver and butcher knife in his hands and slowly turned his eyes, looking for trouble. Maynard stepped closer to Runt, and the grief spread to everyone still living like a disease.

Runt leaned over his mother's body. His shirt was dark crimson from her blood. He looked up at Maynard, his eyes nothing but tears. Maynard saw the body, its chest a gaping hole, like a cruel surgery gone wrong and the head missing. This was the last time Runt would hold her. There would be no more breakfasts, smiles, or hugs from her. She'd never remind him to wear his cloak because the weather was sure to turn cold. Runt moaned a muffled scream as he breathed in, an inhuman rattling growl like the broken purr of a mangy cat, and Maynard looked, taking in the loss.

"Oh, shit, your mom." Maynard paused. He had witnessed death before and worked with cadavers under the tutelage of his mentor. He understood basic anatomy and the process of life and death but had never witnessed the sorrow it brought when one so close passed. Maynard understood the process but not the emotional damage that occurred. He'd seen dead homeless in Grimwood, watched people die in bar fights, and even saw the horrors of a small battle as a water boy and surgical assistant, but he looked at it as a form of education. Seeing death up close like this, as more personal, even for a person he barely knew, made it complicated.

"Look, look, look, look, we need to step away from this, get near the wood, and take stock of the area. The people who did this may still be here. These fires, this all just happened," Maynard said in a worried tone, out of breath, leaning on a dark wooden staff.

Angus walked over, his hand up to his face, blocking the heat from the houses. The donkey lingered on the trail farther behind them.

"Maria, no," Angus whispered, then composed himself. "Aye, Runt, we'll bury them, but we need to look at this from a distance for the moment," he finished through wet eyes.

Angus grabbed Runt and pulled him up, the body falling back into the grass. Runt's eyes went wide, but he was out of it, his body and mind no longer registering the reality around him.

"Look at me! Look, you need to live. If you want to find out who did this, why they did this, you need to live now. Listen to me. Now! Understand? Let's move," commanded Angus.

Over the fires near the main entrance to the valley, the noise of a horse echoed around the trees. The two boys and dwarve ducked and half ran into the tall grass and into the brush, the sound of leaves cracking and sticks breaking as they moved.

"Did the soldier see us?" asked Maynard in a hushed tone.

Runt lay curled up in a ball, eyes closed, hands covering his face. Angus placed his hand over his mouth. The valley's main entrance broke directly out of the woods into a short grass area only as wide as a hay cart. They looked hidden by the tall grass, brush, and prickers as they watched from the valley's edge.

Out of the entrance trotted a man on top of a giant horse, baring a shimmering black shield. He looked like the soldiers from the Wayward Tavern. He looked again at the fires and laughed, his black-and-red beard shaking as he spat at the burning houses, kicked his horse, and guided it back up the trail, away from the wrecked valley.

"Son of a bitch," said Angus. "I didn't think they would venture out at night or, if so, on a horse in this area. Takes real stones."

"Who was that? Did the Holy Imperium do this? Did the Holy Imperium kill my mom? *Why?* My dad's a Redcloak! My brother is part of the Red Army now. I was going to join soon. Why, why, why, why!" He couldn't see anymore. Tears blocked his vision, so he pointed to where the man on the horse had been, crying silently like an infant who was mad for the first time.

"Look, Runt, you saw what they did in town and here. I don't know what to think, but Redcloaks, soldiers of the Holy Imperium . . . I wouldn't trust either," said Angus.

Runt wiped his eyes with the backs of his hands, sniffed, and took a deep breath. The air shook his chest when it came out. "Okay, Angus, what do I do?" Runt pleaded. His thoughts were muzzy as he searched for a reality he couldn't grasp. It only spun out of control as the world finished burning to the ground in front of him.

"I dunno, I dunno." The dwarve shook his head. "We should try to bury your mom, grab what we can from around here, and see if Maynard knows where his mentor was going. The man may be crazy as Vulcan's brother, but it sounds like he has an idea as to what the Hades is happening."

Maynard took a walk around the perimeter of the valley and came back. "It looks like the people who did this are gone. Probably the soldiers of the Holy Imperium, similar to those who burned the tavern. I need to find my mentor; I think he'll help us. Let's do what we can here, bury those who can be buried and say some words," said Maynard. "Runt, we need a safe place to hold up. Where can we go?"

Runt thought for a moment. "I know a place." Runt walked toward his burned-down house and started dragging his mother's mutilated body toward the others. They both looked on, and Angus shrugged his shoulders, moving toward Runt to help. He grabbed the body's legs, and helped Runt bring the corpse into the woods.

"Okay, now we start digging. The ground will be softer here."

They dug into the soft forest floor using sticks and hard bark. Movement passed between the trees behind Runt, twenty feet away. It was the quiet yet defiant movement of a large predator. Maynard stopped digging, along with Angus, who put his hands on his cleaver and knife.

"It's fine. The wolves won't hurt us," Runt said.

"What do you mean?" asked Maynard.

Runt's voice faltered, "I just know they won't bother us, and with any luck, they may pick off a few of those soldiers, wherever they are now."

Maynard looked at Runt. "It's been like that for a bit, right? You know they won't hurt us?"

"Yeah, I've been able to be around the wolves like this for a while. I can't talk to them or anything, but they are friendly to me, and I to them," said Runt.

Maynard nodded and didn't say more. They started to dig again. By midday, the lack of sleep started to take its toll on all of them. They made their way toward a small grove on the other side of the valley across the river, away from the skeletons of burned-out homes. They saw more corpses whom Runt knew. His friends and neighbors lay broken on the ground. He looked with tears dried up, but the emotions of anger and bitterness stayed. Runt, Angus, and Maynard quietly walked onto a deer trail as if at a wake.

"I used to play up here with my friends, now dead behind us. Pricker bushes and briars surround it, so most people stay away, but I know how to get in. Crawl for a bit."

They crawled under the brush and ended up at a small clearing about halfway up one of the hills in the woods across from the creek. Their feet were wet and muddy, but it felt safe. Maynard and Runt fell to the ground. They had left the donkey on the other side of the creek, stripped of its gear and bags.

"You boys stay here. Rest. I'll go scrounge up food and wood. We should be okay to cook for now, with the fires burning on the hills and valley here."

The afternoon melted into the evening, and they fed on fish over a small fire, a deep melancholy looming over them along with the lingering smoke of the houses in the valley.

Hudson City - Maker Save the Prince

Geneneral Casting stood on a balcony in the highest tower of Hudson City, one of the grandest cities in Vineland. In a city full of towers, he looked down on all of them from Trinity Cloudreach Spire. The air was crisp as he breathed in the essence of the Holy Imperium, which one day could rival Thamesbridge in Great Brightland. Trinity Cloudreach Spire stood taller than the cherished clock tower in Thamesbridge. The architect of Trinity Cloudreach, Perri Stonegazer, was a meticulous and crazy dwarven mage. Her family said she loved the sky more than she loved the mountains while she lived. During the Golden Age, she was a fixture at Erica the Red and King Christopher's court and had built the tower as a gift for their wedding, years before Casting was born.

All of the towers in Hudson City were dwarven-made, no human builders rivaled the imagination and ingenuity of their dwarven counterparts. Casting thought the two beautiful human-made cathedrals lying in the shadows of the city's towers were an apt metaphor for what the dwarves created compared to the works of human hands.

Prince Damon, court members, and several noble families lived in the capital. Still, the power of the merchants and underclass tugged below the city's surface, creating a bloodless battle of ideas moving the city forward each new day. General Casting looked out on the balcony and saw the business, wealth, and strategic importance of Hudson City as it moved in a constant state of flux.

His morning reports sat on his desk, offering news from across Vineland. A small riot in Olde Ridgewatch, food shortages in the south near Cinderpool, outlaws on the Kings and Queens Roads, and religious disputes by the Stagger Wall rolled in after the cease of hostilities between the Holy Imperium, the Legion of Carigreed, and the Nation of Stouya. Now that he thought about it, nothing had changed after the Crimson Struggle had ended. The actors moved or positioned themselves anew in this grand play full of bastards, royals, and bandits, but nothing felt entirely different. Every day was a struggle; some days, more blood was on his hands. He ran his fingers through his hair, not wanting to even think about the politics and policies concerning the Stagger Wall. A great river and massive wall divided Vineland in two, keeping the wild and free tribes of elves, goblins, and orcs generally on one side of the great continent of Vineland and the civilized on the other side. The Holy Imperium needed to solidify their holdings in the near east before they considered providing further soldiers and supplies to General Jacob Blackheart and his Fourth Army in the west.

"Families, clans, dukes, and barons all gnawing on the bones of the Holy Imperium. It appears there will be losers even on the winning side," Casting said, looking at a map with his reports in his hand, his assistant listening.

The Crimson Struggle had ended on this side of the Atlantis Ocean. The plotting, murdering, and fighting continued between the regimes of Great Brightland, the Legion, and the Nation across the ocean's dark, bottomless waters. The Holy Imperium owed allegiance to Great Brightland, as Prince Damon owed his power to his father, King Geordie. Casting continued to deal with the fallout from the Holy Imperium's triumphant win at the Battle of the Reaping. Thousands lost their lives in an unimaginable feat of magic between three mages. Only one mage remained after the battle; he'd been a man of the Holy Imperium, but the mage had been incoherent after and broken in his mind. After joining Prince Damon's court, Casting forced the mage into an asylum under sedation, placing rings of binding onto him. A hero gone mad.

After the battle, peace delegations from the Legion of Carigreed and the Nation of Stouya met with the Holy Imperium in Hudson City. A sense of joy and happiness reached hamlets, towns, and cities across Vineland, but General Casting didn't reflect too much on the peasants' emotions. To

71

General Casting, ceasing hostilities on one side of the world and fighting on another didn't feel like peace. It felt more like biding time until another disaster occurred.

Now the weight of command from a giant military organization and the control of a new nation overwhelmed him. He wore no crown, but the burden was genuine. He was second only to the king's bastard son Prince Damon. General Casting rose high.

Matters remained in disarray. The coinage continued to be an issue, with insufficient unity and no consistency. There were prisoner-of-war trades to complete, bounties to be paid off, and the remaining independent city-states to be brought under control. Prince Damon wished those issues to be dealt with before the end of next fall. Casting wanted all city-states united under the Holy Imperium flag even while dealing with a poor growing season, which could lead to food shortages. There were also rumors of plague sprouting up in local papers from soldiers coming home. "Maker save the prince," and all of that.

These problems matriculated, creating protests and riots in principal cities like Olde Ridgewatch, a large harbor above Hudson City. Other city mayors or important dignitaries constantly begged and petitioned to see him or Prince Damon. They wanted reassurance, land, money, power, and leniency on taxes, all grabbing, gaping, and fawning for attention.

"Victor! Please bring me any further reports and summon the council for a meeting. We need to get our affairs in order. Oh, and Victor, make sure Prince Damon is aware. He needs to learn how to lead, not control a country," Casting said.

Victor Parish, Thomas Casting's assistant, nodded. Victor was dressed impeccably with round spectacles and short-cropped and combed dark hair. He was well-built, wearing his customary suit jacket. Even though Victor was not a military man, he snapped tartly and moved to meet General Casting's request. He was undoubtedly the most important man in the court of Prince Damon, Casting thought. Victor assisted and moved about Thomas Casting's advisors and the council smoothly. The council ran Hudson City and, thus, the entire Holy Imperium through much effort. Victor worked with the old and new bloodlines, bending their will to General Casting's commands and assertions. He worked best in the mid-afternoon and evenings. Victor could force treaties and alliances big and small with a nod and a few whispers during a gala event or impromptu party.

Casting was more of a battle strategist than a politician. He used those organizational tactics and understanding to deal with the political landscape and unite a loose bundle of cities under one flag, religion, and man. Yet, every day, he felt as if he were failing.

Noble bloodlines could trace their ancestors back to Great Brightland in the old world. In contrast, royal bloodlines cited connections to King Christopher and Erica the Red here in Vineland. King Christopher and Erica the Red Goldthorn were now deceased, and other family members from the Ruinthorn and Hawthorn lines were all but dead thanks to the Thornbriar War, which had led to the Crimson Struggle and now Thomas Casting's current position.

He poured himself a small brandy, lifted the glass to his lips, said a prayer to the Maker, the Child, and the Servant, and drank deeply. General Casting was thankful to be a human and chose to lead them all. He sniffed deeply and threw back another brandy. He tasted the heritage of Great Brightland, and it burned lightly. He was curious to know if his prayer was to be a cruel or fair leader. Of course, it could have been to brandy distillers for all he cared, as his thoughts on organized religion were not as strong as Prince Damon's aggressive stance. Either way, his devotions were done for the day. The papers appeared on the table as requested. Victor stood five feet away from the desk. It always felt as if Victor had emerged from the shadows. The window let in the sunshine, and dusk particles floated in the air on the light.

"Excellent. Please carry on and let me know once all the council have been notified of our gathering this evening."

Casting looked up after speaking. Victor was gone already. *Yes, indeed, he is an asset*, Casting thought. He picked up his new reports and read, fingers running through his mustache. The report was from General Flint about his march into the city-state of Grimwood. Flint's troops would soon begin the harassment of Grimwood and outlying villages supporting the city and castle.

This action included burning villages and controlling essential crossroads. It wasn't a siege yet—only a show of muscle, standard shit. General Flint knew not to engage the cities' forces until spring. Under General Robert Flint's command was Jared of the Blackheart family. Flint assured Casting that Jared Blackheart would behave himself after the siege ended so there would be something left of Grimwood to rule. Casting requested no more than one day of looting and burning once the city was taken. He had faith in Flint. Blackheart and his monks were known more for their sins than their saintliness for their bloody work. They could manage the winter conditions; they knew which towns to destroy and the ones to control as strongholds throughout the winter. Soon Flint would be back in the good graces of Prince Damon.

After Flint's dust-up with Benedict Ashburn while at court, both were exiled. A slight incident had turned into a major scandal when Prince Damon overheard the scuffle between Flint and Ashburn. It shamed the Flint family and brought down Sir Benedict Ashburn's rising star. Unfortunately, they hadn't realized the woman they lusted for was the same woman Prince Damon had pined for as well. After the skirmish, Casting conferred with Prince Damon and talked the prince out of a worse punishment for Ashburn and Flint. Casting managed to separate the two by several thousand miles in doing so. It was a military-ordered exile, but they would be allowed back at court if either could partake in their orders professionally and with poise.

General Casting knew it was right to get Flint and Jared Blackheart away from court as a safeguard. The Flints and Blackhearts grasped for power, thinking their families could govern the Holy Imperium better than those in charge. Jared lived in the shadow of his twin brother, Joseph, one of the heroes at the Battle of the Reaping, and Flint ate up an opportunity wherever it existed. Casting sighed and moved his thoughts to other, more complex issues, like Prince Damon's grand designs for all free city-states.

"Sir, an emissary from Steelsburg is here to speak to you. Should I send him in?" asked Victor.

"Yes, of course, please do so, and bring some of our best ale as well. It's time to move another piece on the game board."

Casting looked at the map of the vast area of Vineland and smiled, knowing he was progressing toward the unification and control of all of it.

Runt - Hello Again

"Wake up, you nitwits!"

Maynard, Runt, and Angus lay near a fire, passed out after the earlier trauma. Doc was dressed in a dark cloak and sitting on a log near a fire, hand on his pipe and staff lying over his lap in the early evening. He used his staff to play with the red coals, although it never caught itself alight. This was the same staff that had been used to slice up soldiers the night before. Two shoulder bags sat near his feet. Under them lay a long sword and a bow with a quiver full of arrows.

"You two boys, okay?" he asked.

Both jumped back from where they'd passed out.

Angus stood, stumbling a bit, attempting to get his bearings, meat cleaver and knife in hand. "You—what in Hades is going on?" he asked.

"Relax there, you hairy little biscuit. I'm here to help, not hinder. You think I may be the cause of this, and I owe you for dinners and such. I'll pay up. Believe me, I will pay. However, let us all talk and eat. Problems are easier to fix on a full stomach. I owe you for a few meals, and I'll triple what I owe you. First, make do with this hog leg I procured as I left," said Maynard's mentor.

He reached behind the stump, producing a sizable, aged hog leg, and threw it at Angus, who stumbled with the size of it.

"Let's have a nice meal, Angus—is it not? Those boys will need nourishment for the traveling ahead," he said. "Now, all three of you listen up, and listen well. Wolf Hills is under the control of the Holy Imperium. Those soldiers numbered about fifty or so, including men at arms and archers in the town's center. There are more all about these troubled woods. The soldiers are clearing the nearby homes and leaving nothing in their wake. As you can see below, they're being thorough and nasty about the entire process."

Doc sighed and put up his hands to stop Angus, Maynard, and Runt from interrupting. His hands were callused and nicked up but healing. Angus moved about now, getting the hog leg cooking on his cast-iron skillet, putting his knife and cleaver to work.

"Please let me finish before you start pounding me with stupid questions. The Holy Imperium's soldiers took captives from the area. I guess they're heading toward Steelsburg under guard or back to Olde Ridgewatch or Hudson City. There's another group of prisoners headed toward the Erie Sea to a backwater town out of reach of the Grimwood city-state." He waited for a second to let the news sink in.

"As you can see, one of the Holy Imperium's armies is marching on Grimwood, and from what I gather, the city doesn't know or is in trouble in its own way. It's possible Grimwood quarantined itself as the plague from the Battle of the Reaping made its way into the populace. The prince started to consolidate his grip on independent city-states, specifically those that didn't join him during the Crimson Struggle. From what I can see, it's miserable news for Grimwood and my beloved university. It looks like you must kneel and swear loyalty to Prince Damon or face slavery or death."

"How do you know all of this? I saw what happened in the tavern." Runt stood; fists balled up. Anger blew out with every breath he took.

Doc took a puff from his pipe and blew a purple cloud of reefer smoke off to the right side of Runt's face. It curled into the shape of a wolf and ran off as it dissipated.

"I've been called many names. Maynard calls me mentor, I am a doctor by trade, and technically I've been a duke of the Holy Imperium, but my title and military rank were taken from me. I am the last battlemage in this land. I fought in the Battle of the Reaping on the Plains of Ursula, killing more than you can count, and their ghosts live inside me. When I'm drunk, I can perform feats you can't even dream of, and right now, I am stone sober. So, when I speak, when I give you the facts, you listen to them as if your Gods wrote them on stone tablets." He took another pull from his pipe. "A wise man once said, 'Facts are not told during the day,' and as you can see, it is near evening, so before I get roaring stoned out of my gourd and drunk with young Angus here," he pointed at Angus, who was not young in the slightest, with the end of his pipe, "we are going to have a fine meal, and tomorrow we start a nice, long hike. Right now, I am going to continue to tell you what is happening and why I came to find you in your little, now-burned-down village."

"You are the reason my mother is dead, so you—"

The briar bushes behind Runt shifted, dry leaves and sticks started moving, and growls echoed from the woods behind them. Doc looked around, thinking the night was his, but realized he didn't control everything as he had believed.

"Calm yourself, Runt. I don't want to hurt your wolf out there. Don't think I would hesitate to do so, however. I have already broken my vow of non-violence twice in two days, and I will do so again," said Doc.

He stood now, staff in hand, and the air shimmered with a feeling of power. A sense of pressure forced its way around the group. Instantly, Runt sat, and Maynard recoiled toward Angus, who looked up at Doc with slight annoyance while still roasting the ham leg on the fire. The noise in the wood dissipated. Runt's face, which had been concentrating, went slack, and he looked tired. Doc relaxed, and the atmosphere calmed.

"Doc, you can scare the lads with your power, but I can't cook this shit if I'm dead, so chill out," said Angus.

Doc stopped and sat again. "Okay, okay, but I don't like to be threatened with old power," he said. The briars parted, and the wolf drifted away. "That's better. You do those things; you can call on them like pets?" he asked.

Runt hesitated and answered, "Yes and no. When I get angry, they may show up, but I can't command them. My sister could do it, too, but from what I remember, only when it was about to storm."

"That's a fine trick, now, isn't it?" Doc nodded his head toward Runt and over at Maynard and winked.

"I took the sword, bow, and arrows off two mangled corpses on my way. Looks like wolves attacked them as they were leaving your little valley here early in the morning. I guess you and your anger had something to do with it. Bet it happened when you got to the valley." Doc smiled. He puckered his lips, took a deep pull on his pipe, and blew out bright-yellow smoke in the shape of a knife.

"Ahh, fine stuff. Now, where was I? Indeed, where was I?" He stood, turned as if looking for a thought in the air, and sat back down. "Ah, yes, well, I've brought you their bags, water skins, and dried food. The food I procured from a pantry or two—no need to worry about where or how. I get what I need. Maynard knows that. There's coin in there from the independent cities and the Holy Imperium—not a fortune, but enough for a room or two. Nothing dwarven, though. I couldn't find any of that rubbish—not enough time—so it could be a problem later."

"Good. You owe me," said Angus. "Foods done. We got no plates, so grab with your knife."

"Oh, bugger off with the money I owe you, short shit," said Doc with a slight touch of hurt, but he smiled at the end. "And thank you kindly for cooking. I'm in your debt."

"Already established that. Don't want to be in too much debt to a dwarve, especially one not afraid of staying above ground," grumbled Angus through a bit of food.

Doc and Maynard looked on as Runt cut a piece off the leg with an old boot knife he carried.

"Mentor, may I suggest—" Maynard said, and Doc interrupted.

"What, yes, yes, of course. Young Angus, since you no longer have a job cooking, and you're aware of the family structure and the politics of where Runt and Maynard are to head, would you mind if I hire you as, say, a liaison and personal guard for these two fine boys?"

"For Vulcan's sake, are you serious? The boy's mother was murdered, and his sister sold into slavery if she's lucky, and you want to hire me?" asked Angus. "Of course, I'll do it; Runt's like a nephew to me."

Doc took out a medium-sized clear bottle and uncorked it. "Here, have a sip. Its vintage is unheard of up here. It's Riverclear's finest. You can get whiskey anywhere, but only Riverclear makes bourbon."

"I've not seen this in years," Angus said, his mouth open and thirsty. He took the bottle from the crazy mage and admired it in the light of the fire.

"As for the money owed, if all goes well, I should be able to pay you a full year's wages by this time in six months hence if you agree. Please understand what I have provided you here is free as well," said Doc. He pointed to the pile of food and necessities under the weapons.

Angus looked at the bottle, then at Runt and back at Doc, confused.

"And where," Angus drank a slug from the bottle, drinking it down. "Oh shit, that's excellent," he said, swallowing down the bourbon. "Where would that be?"

"Steelsburg, often called Coalsburg, up here it is called Shitsburg, ain't that right, Runt?" said Doc.

Runt nodded but said nothing. Angus passed the bottle to the boy and shook his head.

"Here, have a sip. It's been a shit day," said Angus. "And heading toward Steelsburg makes it much worse."

Runt took a sip and swallowed hard and fast. He coughed as the burn came on, and tears followed for what felt like the seventh time today.

"And what are we going there for?" Angus said.

"Young Runt here needs to find what's left of his family—his brother, father," said Doc. "And his sister if she lives."

"Alysha! She's not dead? But I thought she was in the house. I mean, I should've looked, I should have," said Runt as dread, hope, and anger mixed around inside his head.

"Relax, boy, she wasn't inside your house," Doc said. "I know a man who can help—my old squire. He should be able to track down your family, get you back together, and help set life to order as it were."

Runt thought for a moment as he chewed on the cooked hog leg. "If my sister isn't dead, she'd be sent up toward the Erie Sea, right? Why are we going away from the sea? We need to rescue her," demanded Runt.

"Yes, we do, but we can't. I'm not able to take on an entire army, at least not right now, even with Maynard's help. I don't know. I don't think—" He stopped and took a deep breath, considering. "I'm not up to it. And four

80

against thousands doesn't work. I tried at the Battle of the Reaping. No, if your sister is alive, and I'm a betting man and I believe she is, she'll take care of herself. We won't forget her, I promise. If you want to save her, you need to get to your father near the Atlantis Ocean. We all die if you go up now and try to release her from her bondage." He stood and looked at the night sky, deep in thought for a moment. "We all die."

Maynard glanced at Runt with a slight guilt of knowing more than he did and shifted his eyes over to Angus, and they all looked at Doc as if he had any real answers in a drug-smeared head of his.

"It's near wintertime, and we can't do this alone. You three can't do this alone, at least. You'll need a few moments of luck, along with some murderers and thieves, to help you. Right evil bastards to do the dirty work and keep you safe." The bottle passed to him after Maynard took a sip. Doc took a nip from the bottle, lit his pipe, sucked in a resounding hit, and blew red smoke into the firelight. The face of a goblin was shown in the smoke before it disappeared.

"It's not right. I should try to free her," said Runt, dejected.

Angus looked at Runt and knew he was right, but Doc, this mad wizard, was thinking more clearly than himself, Runt, or Maynard. "Runt, I'm sorry to say, but Doc is right. Trying to save your Alysha would get us all killed."

Runt's mood and demeanor dropped even lower.

"It's all happening faster already than intended, and the treaty's ink is still wet. The war's over between the Holy Imperium, the Legion of Carigreed, and the Nation of Stouya in Vineland. Life in Vineland has changed more than when King Christopher and Erica the Red conquered these lands back in antiquity. What I accomplished above the Erie Sea on the fields of Ursula caused the Holy Imperium to lay claim to all of Vineland. There's not much to stop Prince Damon from doing whatever he wants. The elves of this land are no threat. Sickness and internal strife leave them weak, at least on this side of the Stagger Wall. They hide in the deep wilds and mountains, and rebel in the swamps in the south. Vineland is undergoing a perilous change, and your family has a part in saving it from becoming an ink stain in the book of history." Doc stopped and mumbled to himself: "Three to a family, three

81

sisters, be, and a love triangle or some such . . . I can't remember the rhyme, dammit. Whatever, whatever." He looked at Runt. "Anyway, I, being a grand and amazing mage, although debilitated and in need of a warm bath, can help. I'll try to make sure nobody else in your family dies. I make no guarantee, and I do believe more will die for your sake and the land we stand on. I do know if we reunite you with your father, we can save lives and maybe make Vineland something remarkable."

"Mentor, you're preaching again. You told me to tell you," Maynard said.

"I know, sweet servant's tits, I know! Fine, fine, I will get to the point. The Holy Imperium needs to pay its debts after the Crimson Struggle. To do so, those in charge are plundering what they can, like Wolf Hills. Your hometown, Maynard, Grimwood, will be taken by fire and stone, and places like Steelsburg, the Holy Imperium will attempt to persuade into submission. They want to control all of Vineland—the coal, the trees, the land, and the air itself. They want money, power, dammit, they want it all!" He spat with anger. "After I won the Battle of the Reaping—I did it, not that poser Blackheart or Flint or Casting . . . me, I did! I demoralized two armies. Those bastards are using my win to do what they please. I thought it was all over—no more bloodshed. We need no more bloodshed. We deserve peace. We all deserve peace and prosperity for Vineland, not just the nobles." Doc's anger changed. He turned quieter, sadder. "They'll use force, religion, and lies, and they'll use worse to get control because Prince Damon believes he was born to lead, to be sovereign over this land. For good or ill, your father, sister, and brother are part of this now, and you are, too."

Doc stopped, took his shaded glasses off his face, and looked directly into Runt's eyes. "Follow my lead and my directions, and we'll find your father and brother so you can decide what you want to do with yourself. If you want, you can throw your body on a sword seeking revenge or join your dad and kill babies for the prince and country. I think there's more to you," Doc finished and looked away from the three of them and into the fire.

Runt looked at him and on into the darkness, wondering what he was to do and where he was to go.

"What was the damn rhyme she whispered into my ear, that sweet minx?"

Doc whispered to himself.

Hudson City - A Council of Crows

General Casting peered through the window, lost in thoughts of previous events when his sword had run through soldiers' bodies. He tasted the air of battle, and the cries of those who had perished echoed in his ears. He lost himself for a moment, thinking of the end of the Crimson Struggle and the Battle of the Reaping.

The window was one of the largest in the city. It spanned three times the space of a woman and twice a woman's height, giving the few fortunate enough to get to this height a view of the city. Most windows in the capital were painted or stained and held together by mortar or pieces of wood, but this one was large, clear, and breathtaking. *The window is priceless and one of a kind, just like me*, Casting thought.

The higher the tower, the colder the room, but today, the fire across the window roared with life. Prince Damon's chair stood empty near the fire, its opulence sucking the very air from the room, showing the prince's status. Members of the leadership council would soon join Casting, with or without Prince Damon's presence. The General considered Hudson City beneath his feet, and city-states not yet under the yoke of the Holy Imperium as a scholar considers an assignment.

* * *

The Battle of the Reaping, the last major battle in the Crimson Struggle, had left thousands dead, and livelihoods stood broken. The madness had lasted into the night, ending when three unholy mages threw lightning, fire, and other forces of nature at one another. The battle broke the Nation of Stouya and the Legion of Carigreed's hold on Vineland, and now Casting was responsible for consolidating Prince Damon's hold on Vineland.

Magic was one of the few disciplines General Casting couldn't understand, and he feared it. Casting was glad magical bindings existed so the chaos of magic could be controlled and tempered. Without the binding rings, magic would rule overall, and sovereign nations like the Holy Imperium wouldn't even exist. A ring specifically forged for obedience and placed on a magic user's finger rendered them impotent, unable to perform dangerous spells and powerless to remove the ring without a painful death. They were practical and required to maintain an environment of control.

The few witnesses to the mage battle had barely survived to tell their stories. Most of those stories were hard to believe or justify. However, in the end, the Holy Imperium was victorious. General Casting lost his father and siblings during the battle, giving him his ancestral home, a small tower north of Trinity Cloudreach. He could look upon his home through the giant window, lost in the shadow of Prince Damon's tower and the seat of all of Vineland.

The Plains of Ursula became a scar of land where no one walked after the Battle of the Reaping. Those looking for loot and treasures soon died of an internal plague. The witnesses of the mage battle were the first. They started to urinate and cry blood. Shortly after, breathing became difficult as they spewed blood from both ends of their bodies until they died. Scholars recommended a quarantine for any participants of the Battle of the Reaping, but it was impossible to implement. General Casting feared the sickness called the Smoldering Plague could spread, but Prince Damon's personal physician said it was not likely, and thus, no steps were taken.

Before the Crimson Struggle ended, all three nations clung to any desperate notion to win the war and establish dominance. There were rumors of warriors carrying holy artifacts, a family heirloom, or a good-luck charm from antiquity, giving each person exceptional powers in battle. Those stories made their way to Prince Damon's court, where they took on a life of their own. Rumor became truth, and soon, those stories became fact. Casting even heard Gaston's staff had been used by the Holy Imperium's battlemage

Hunter Young before his embarrassing exile to an asylum. Unfortunately, Casting couldn't verify the fact, as now Hunter Young had escaped and was roaming the Blightbriar Mountains.

* * *

He sighed and moved closer to the window—yet another problem he needed to resolve. He stood, hands grasping each other as he gazed down on the smoke and movement of the people's little lives. Victor Parish remained in the room, serving as the cup bearer. He poured wine—after testing it for safety's sake, of course—and provided any documents requested during the Royal Council, or as Victor put it late one night after Casting had drunk too much, the Council of Crows. Victor had whispered that the most powerful and distinguished beings in the world sounded like a bunch of cackling crows picking at the body of a newly born nation. He apologized shortly and sharply the following day, and Casting had accepted it with a nod, saying it was accurate but to keep those thoughts to himself.

Casting thought Victor Parish was thirty years old, but he looked ageless with strong cheekbones angled toward lips. His gray-blue eyes were sharp and circled slightly with darkness, framed by a messy yet well-kept head of dark hair. He wore a well-fitted suit similar to what butlers from Great Brightland wore. He was more than a footman or butler to General Casting; he was a confidant, servant, and overall fixer of problems.

The council sat at a rectangular table of black oak felled after a lightning strike, its creation and painting completed by an artisan and native slave to Vineland. Casting often wondered why the natives here were called elves, yet in Great Brightland, they were known as fey. The painting on the table was of the continent's geography created in expert detail. After its completion, Prince Damon remarked on the table's beauty until he heard an elve had painted it. A day after, the slave disappeared under Prince Damon's orders. Later, after calming down, Prince Damon changed his mind, and the table remained in the tower to show soldiers' movements or trade like a real-life chess game, only with every move, thousands could die. Casting smirked at this, even with a bit of disgust at himself. It was funny, knowing people below him took part in a foolish game and didn't realize their lives could be snuffed by an angry man-child like Prince Damon.

The other chairs were made of black oak and featured red cushions. However, the prince's chair was more ornate, with his two dueling wildcats at the top carved into the wood. He was Prince Damon of the House of Farover, but unlike his father's coat of arms of a lion and unicorn crossed on a field of red, Damon had chosen two wildcats because there were no real lions on this side of the Atlantis Ocean. Damon had said it would help the peasants better understand him and his new family when he got around to marrying and creating one.

"Sir, Madam Diana Thompson is here," Victor said as he opened the door for her.

She walked quickly and with grace, bearing a binder and small satchel with writing implements. Her gown accentuated her hair, revealing her neck, which would cause alarm and awe if worn in the Holy Church, but it was trendy in the lands of Carigreed, and she remained aware of the latest fashions, like Casting himself. Her hair was a restless dark-chocolate color, spun and crimped so it stood out like giant brown ears on top of her head. As the leader of the Merchant's Guild in Hudson City, she was the director of trade for most of the Holy Imperium. She knew what stock was coming in and what was going out, keeping up on the trade from Hudson City to Steelsburg to Grimwood and cities in the south like Crescent City. She was loyal to the Holy Imperium because the Holy Imperium protected her and the merchants. She controlled the merchants of Hudson City, making her wealthy beyond anything she had ever imagined. She was an ex-slave from the land of the Yellow Grass. Diana Thompson used her substantial money to build capital and alliances, helping her erase the time before she was free as if it didn't exist.

"Diana, please sit anywhere. It is good to see you," Casting said as he kissed both of her cheeks. "We are glad you could make it so soon after your husband's unexpected accident and passing."

"Yes, of course. Business does not stop, as you know. How's the cleanup going up north?" Madam Diana Thompson questioned.

"Reports show most northern cities are swearing alliance to the prince and the Holy Imperium, but you may know better due to your business connections," answered Casting.

"Well, in the south, I hear we're faring well. The Holy Imperium only had some issues with Crescent City because of its importance in trade with surrounding islands, even with the Legion's loose grip on the city," she said. "They are complicated."

"We may be able to remedy the issue, though. More on that shortly. There's still the swampland in the Forsaken Peninsula near the gulf controlled by elves. Neither of the three—and I use the term loosely here— 'nations' have conquered those lands. The orcs and goblins in the Blightbriar Mountains are still openly hostile but scarce, but other than that, things should be back to normal or even better after spring," Casting said.

"Glad to hear. I have tidings as well, of course," she said, brushing imaginary dust off her bare shoulder.

Casting thought, *What a wonderfully enchanting woman.* He moved closer to her, but Victor interrupted.

"Bishop Devon of the Holy Church is here, accompanying our royal scholar, Victoria Parish of House Parish, and Charles Leadwall is here in place of Madam Hammer Clinton," said Victor.

Casting was a bit startled, but only for a moment. He moved toward the door. Victor nodded to Victoria as she walked by.

"Ladies and gentlemen, we were discussing the south. Sir Leadwall, welcome and come in," Casting said.

The formality of the situation made the meetings take too long. The bishop, wearing his vestments of tarnished white with gold and crimson threading, walked in, still talking to Victoria Parish, who barely engaged the oaf of a man. She looked at Casting and indicated with her eyes that she needed separation from Bishop Devon immediately. She stood tall in heels, wearing a dress fitted tight to her body, showing a long slit up to her knee, along with a man's white tunic and dress vest. Her dusky hair was tightly pulled into a bun. She carried a book and purse with her writing tools.

"Victor, wine me, please." She looked at him.

He nodded and poured. She took it, looked at Victor, nodded at Casting, and smiled with contentment as the bishop continued mumbling about the Order of the Blue Rose. She drank deeply, trying to ignore him. Her lips were a deep and enticing red, contrasting against her dull skin, which was similar to Victor's. Her eyes drank in the room as she sipped from her cup, sucking down the rest of the wine.

"Again, and thank you, my dear," Victoria said.

She moved her hips with authority— men's and women's eyes always followed as she walked— yet it was graceful, as if each step were planned and welcomed. The bishop plodded like a drunk plow horse next to Victoria Parish. Bishop Devon should have been appalled by Victoria's and Diana's outfits, which were against the High Church's conservative teachings, but he continued to speak to Victoria as if no religious rules were broken by their style. Casting knew he was an old pervert. The whispers of his affairs with young children followed him around holiday celebrations like a shadow. Bishop Devon was over sixty summers old, and the lines of his face told stories of his past sins. His hair was short and stuck out at every angle. He kept his face closely shaven while his smile veiled some of the liver spots splotched throughout his profile. His vestments were simple if not for the currency of gold and rubies on his hands and around his neck to honor the Maker, Child, and Servant.

Casting understood the look Victoria gave off. It meant to rid her of this aggressive pervert, or she would do so in an inappropriate fashion in front of everyone. Or he would disappear privately, and nobody may ever see the poor old fool again.

Victor Parish interjected, maneuvered between them, and showed the old coot to his chair while pouring a drink. Victoria's hair was pitch-black and fell to her shoulders when not up in a bun. Her brown eyes and lips resonated with General Casting as if they were Victor's, only slightly more curved and a lust to them, along with their distinct color pigment. She was younger than Victor, but her exact age was hard for Casting to place. The two confused him when seen together.

"Well, yes, thank you for having me as part of this little club, this council today. I shall do my best to provide all with sufficient information about the Hammer's work in the south and take notes, and I await any orders from the prince and his council," said Sir Leadwall. The man had nerves like a ferret. General Casting still could not believe the man was a full-blooded Redcloak.

Born of lesser noble blood than most, Lord Leadwall was competent in battle, using the environment and keeping meticulous control of his holdings and command. General Casting thought it would be interesting to see how he managed the crows today as they picked, plucked, and screeched their way through the meeting.

General Hammer Clinton had picked up Lord Leadwall early in her career. She was a fierce warrior, ever the underdog, and Leadwall had managed small successful battles when others failed around him. The two had met and became an unstoppable command structure. They'd dispatched slave revolts and fought entrenched Stouya in the Southern Campaign during the late Crimson Struggle.

Sir Leadwall had a beaky-looking nose compared to Victoria Parish's, and his ears felt a bit too much for his egg-shaped head. He wore short, grayish hair; a small mouth; and a slightly curved smile. He dressed in light armor, forgoing knights' arm and leg guards while in the field.

"Glad you could make it, sir. I hope the city has treated you well," said Casting. "Victor will assist in providing refreshments, Bishop. I must personally apologize for missing last feast night's sermon on the trials of the Holy Church in Great Brightland. I heard you slaying the crowd with your oration."

Bishop Devon dragged his eyes from Victoria at the sound of praise like a puppy hearing its name from its master. The lines on his face grew deeper and stretched as he smiled after hearing the compliments. The bishop, the oldest at the council, also stood as the shortest. His comments during the council were mindful yet cumbersome at times, and at least once every meeting, he attempted to drum up support for the causes of the Holy Church and himself.

"It was an amazing sermon. I had the women moaning and the men groaning," he said in a smoker's voice. When delivering a sermon, he carried emotion across the room and caught his congregation's attention, even if they were deaf.

"I'm sure I'll relish it even more come the next feast day. Now we are almost ready, missing a few more. There is no Lord of the North since we're still picking up the pieces after the Battle of the Reaping, but we hope to have that figured out by the end of winter. We're waiting on Admiral Lord Howl, Judge Sternball, and Joseph of the Blackheart family, who is sitting in for his father, Jacob, and who I have been informed will be here shortly."

Victor walked to the door, gliding like a poltergeist, put his hand on it, walked back, and whispered into Casting's ear, causing him to tense for a moment while the moment gave way to silence. "Thank you, Victor," said General Casting.

Those in attendance sat, enjoying mild small conversation, when both doors opened. The stunning and ever-dominating Joseph Blackheart, known to all as Brokenheart, walked into the room. Sir Joseph Blackheart carried the legendary sword, Twilight. He was clad in his house colors of white and red, donning his court armor, and walked with High Judge Sternball on one side and Admiral Lord Howl on his other side. Joseph Blackheart tried to show he had powerful friends and was prepared to move into a more prominent court. Casting thought that after the Battle of the Reaping, Joseph would request to be seated as lord protector of the north while his father sat as lord protector of the west. The Blackheart family was favored in court, ripe for picking up the pieces of General Flint's and Benedict Ashburn's absence.

"Good to see you all!" Joseph said. His hair was light brown, meticulously combed back into a ponytail. He carried a luminous smile and dark eyes, tall as his father but not the same build, leaner and more delicate. Nevertheless, where his father, Jacob, was quiet and followed when he should, Joseph was young and loud and didn't know he was not in charge, nor did he follow as well as he should. Jacob Blackheart, his father, was an ox in human form as Joseph was a racehorse, and he could slay most with his smile. Men followed him, but he failed to think ahead, to know the landscape of more than just a battlefield. Joseph didn't hold any scars on his squared, stubbled face. The beard, a work in progress, looked sad, like all young men's beards tend to. He had the best of his mother and pieces of his father but not enough to make him a man. Still, many swooned for his attention and gawked at his lean figure.

He slapped both Admiral Lord Howl and Judge Sternball on their backs. "Are we having a drink before the prince shows or . . .?"

"You may have a drink. Victor, please. The prince will show up when he feels he should, as the burden of the crown is much. He put me in charge until then. We have several notes to address on the agenda today," said Casting.

"Well then," Joseph tipped his cup to his mouth and toasted Casting. "Let's do this," he said with a smile.

"Indeed." Casting paused, standing while the rest sat. "The situation stands that the Legion of Carigreed's remaining soldiers left through the Crescent City last month. There are reports of riots and fighting as soldiers from the Nation of Stouya leave through southern ports. There are small spots throughout the newly crowned Holy Imperium that are elusive to us, but the lord of the south, General Clinton, left the stronghold of Cinderpool and started to clean up the rabble. Correct, Sir Leadwall?"

"Yes, correct. General Clinton broke her army into two separate forces. The smaller portion came with me and winter at Castle Greenleaf in the Portsholm River while General Clinton moved toward Crescent City. With the secession of hostilities, the general and I felt you might have a use for a maneuverable, agile, and seasoned army. There are rumors of rebels in Olde Ridgewatch and worse rumblings of bands of orcs in the Blightbriar Wilds. I even heard the mumbling of goblins riding giant birds. Children's stories come to life. I wouldn't believe it myself, but I met an irate farmer complaining about his newborn child being taken off by the like, saw the marks on the ground, and everything myself," Leadwall said. "I'm here to help."

"We have heard the same here in the capital and from our dwarven sources in Steelsburg," Casting said. "Normally would take these mutterings as hearsay, but a highborn man's hunting mansion was raided and burned recently—a friend of my family, as it were. The incident was investigated and appeared creditable. A liaison of the king from across the sea, Stephanie

Shannon of House Breechrun, reaffirmed the rumors. We should take heed of it if the remnants of our enemies start to use the unholy creatures to terrorize our compatriots."

"Monsters, you say. Have you considered using the Order of the Blue Rose to investigate these matters?" The bishop smiled like an old sheep. "I could provide a squad or two commanded by my few inquisitors to assist your men in the field."

"I'll consider it. Thank you, Bishop Devon, and I may speak to you after winter ends. Not much can be done when half of Vineland falls under the bright-white snows from the skies above. Maker's will be done," Casting finished. "I have been in Hudson City for a while and could use a hike in the Blightbriar Wilds. A crisp run at slaughtering goblins and orcs scattered across the ridges and valleys would satisfy me greatly."

"Getting sentimental and poetic, Lord Casting," interrupted Joseph Blackheart. "I'm game to join if you are so obliged. I would love to see your sword work." He looked at Casting intently; his eyes gleamed as he spoke, as they so often did for ladies of the court.

"No, just lusting for battle as you do so often," finished Casting. "Bishop Devon and Sir Blackheart, I will keep you both in mind if I need to send men to root out monsters and brigadiers as the snow flies," he said and smiled. "Now, onto other, more important matters. A small insurrection of criminals is causing problems, and Prince Damon cannot stop obsessing over it. As ordered, the Holy Imperium is attempting to weed them out in Olde Ridgewatch. I have the city under martial law, members of the Red Army housed in every merchant house of renown in the entire pigsty of a city."

"Did you know they burned a likeness of the prince and myself this past month? It appears the citizens of Olde Ridgewatch do not wish to pay for the Crimson Struggle, a war in which the Holy Imperium saved the entire city from the prying grip of the Legion and the Nation," said Lord Admiral Howl. He was younger than Bishop Devon, but his face sagged from windy days and nights. His hair used to be luxurious but now was combed back and tied, showing an ever-growing forehead.

"Yes, we do, Admiral Howl. General Ashburn and his Second Army already hold Bawstone Keep and other strongholds arranged around the city. Unfortunately, fiscal cuts slowed recruiting for this army, and desertion after the war caused the Second Army's strength to wither. Mercenaries from the old country, members of the Brotherhood of Bitterleak, both foot and a small band of rangers—all bolstered it. This is not optimal but needed. Sir Fredrick Burrow of the Brotherhood of Bitterleak commands the mercenaries under General Ashburn. Sir Burrow is technically on equal footing with Sir Donald Williamson, Ashburn's second in command. It would be feasible to swap out your army, Sir Leadwall, with Ashburn, but because of the size, I don't think it would make much difference," Casting said. "If hostilities continue in Olde Ridgewatch, I will consider adding members of the Order of the Blue Rose if Prince Damon grants permission," said Casting.

"Lord Casting, you put foreign mercenaries like the Black Eagles in Olde Ridgewatch proper? Isn't that why the local population hates the rule of Prince Damon so much? They aren't even born here or members of Great Brightland. Some are from much farther east than the Bitterleak lands," Joseph Blackheart started.

"The Bitterleak Black Eagles have been a stern ally to Great Brightland and, thus, to the Holy Imperium for longer than your family has been in Vineland. Although you're young and used to battle on the field, keep quiet and realize this is bigger than one battle. We are uniting this land under one rule of law, one man, and one crown."

He looked down at Joseph Blackheart with his deep, sunken, mahogany eyes. Casting was in control and had rebuked the hero of the Battle of the Reaping in front of his peers. He didn't smile, and the look Joseph gave back was one of pure fury as his jaw clenched, yet he remained quiet. The young man had climbed too high for Casting's liking and needed to be put in his place.

"Do we have the money to pay these troops? The Bitterleak mercenaries are a fortune to keep armed, and with both the First and Third Armies in the field, this will cause a substantial strain on the prince's coffers," Diana Thompson attempted to continue, but Casting, ever sharp and prepared, cut her short.

"I have an idea of that. Some won't like it, but it's not going to affect only nobles, so the backlash won't be as negative. I am proposing taxes which will affect nearly every person. We shall impose new taxes on brothels, gambling halls, and all taverns, inns, and beer halls serving alcohol and selling tobacco," Casting said. "As you stated, Madam Thompson, financial needs must be met, and the crown must pay its debts. This tax seems fair. We struggled for years during the war. It's now time to rebuild and unify Vineland. Many noble houses have fallen, and noble bloodlines have suffered losses nearly uncountable, so not only will noble bloodlines pay these taxes, but the people sowing oats, planting corn, and protected by our grand armies will do so as well. Everyone drinks, smokes, and fucks, so let them give a small part of their indulgences back to Prince Damon for his and their protection."

"Cheers!" said Bishop Devon before drinking from his cup and hiccuping.

"I second that, and the prince may tax as he sees fit," said High Judge Sternball.

Victor poured them all more wine.

The Council of Crows is going splendidly, Casting thought.

"I'll start getting these papers written up with High Judge Sternball," Madam Thompson said.

High Judge Sternball smiled with an elongated face, wise ears, and a nose that seemed to move when he talked. He nodded at Madam Thompson. Getting both to work together would be an effort all on its own, considering Judge Sternball, a white-wig-wearing noble, thought Madam Thompson lower because of her blood and sex. An "elvish money whore," he'd said previously while deep in his cups.

Royal Scholar Victoria Parish sat taking notes for the council and provided educational contacts upon request. The College Commission of the Holy Imperium had appointed her to the prince's council to provide their perspective on academic matters and, as Casting surmised, to offer eyes and ears for the commission as well. The universities in Vineland were known as the Silver Ivy League, which supplied a formal education to nobles, merchants, knights, and anyone else with money. But, like religious institutions, these universities had become walled cities like Grimwood by the Erie Sea.

Victoria remained quiet and only offered knowledge when asked about issues. She was radiantly beautiful and a member of Victor Parish's family, but General Casting was unsure if they were brother and sister, man, and wife, or just cousins. They looked close enough to be related, with many of the same mannerisms. The Parishes were prompt, sharp, knowledgeable, and well mannered. The rumor was Prince Damon fancied Royal Scholar Parish when they attended school together, although she'd evaded his advances. He'd kept her close to win her over or force his way with her. Thus, her appointment to the Council of Crows by the Silver Ivy League. She was also the reason why two of Lord Casting's best men were now exiled.

"Lords and ladies, please rise. His Grace Prince Damon is here," said Victor.

The doors opened, and in walked the prince of the Holy Imperium, Damon of House Farover. At twenty-one summers, he wore all the confidence and guile of an educated man who received passing grades at Crimson Yard University. He graduated because even though the prince may have been bastard born, his father was still the king of Great Brightland. Prince Damon had received his education in the wine halls, inns, and taverns of Crimson Yard University. He'd never entered the melee or jousted in tournaments. However, he could assert himself sufficiently when needed with a sword and buckler. Prince Damon had never served in the military or even in a battle. He admired soldiers, war, and the lifestyle but not enough to bloody his sword on a dueling field. He proved sufficient when debating, but alas, as he liked to say, the one true prince could win most arguments because of his birthright as a bastard to the king of Great Brightland.

His retinue stayed outside the doors during the council. It included a four-person honor guard of Wildcats, his jester, and a cloak bearer. In as many years, his fourth cloak bearer, as he tired of them quickly. Most knew if you became a cloak bearer to Prince Damon, you would end up deflowered and embarrassing your family. His swagger and a basic grasp of the fundamental political language were an annoyance to all in the council, but he knew where the threats lay and what side each chose on a given subject. Prince Damon played favorites, kept track of slights, and did not show enough civility or decorum for most older families. The older families, known as noble houses, loved to trace their heritage and be treated a certain way. The prince's attempts to fit in and appease them failed to work, creating rifts where there were none and breaking ancient treaties due to his inability to properly give a speech in public.

"I see you've all started drinking without me. Victor, my royal goblet." The prince sat sideways on the chair, legs hanging over the armrests on one side, hand in the air, waiting for the royal goblet.

Victor placed the goblet in his hand, bedazzled with rubies and diamonds worth more than the treasury of a small town.

"Where are we at, my good man Casting?"

"Your Grace. We were discussing the new taxes you and I discussed earlier," Casting said.

"Oh yes, those—well, money needs to be made. The burning of towns, slaughtering of soldiers, and raping don't pay for themselves. The dividends of these taxes after a few months will be tremendous! Don't you think so, Madam Thompson?" demanded Prince Damon. His face was pale and reddish, and he had taken to wearing women's makeup to look more active as if he were frequently in sunlight. He was slightly out of shape but not gone too fat, and he had enticing cobalt-blue eyes. His hair was reddish-brown yet already thinning and combed over to the side.

"I just learned about these taxes, Your Grace, but I think if they don't cause any issues with the populace, it could benefit the Holy Imperium. Of course, it will take time to figure out what it will do to the economy," said Madam Diana Thompson, the minister of the treasury. She tipped her head slightly in a bow to Prince Damon.

"Well, I know it will not, *not* make the commoners happy, but those people are the losers in this. Nobody likes a loser," said Prince Damon. He was so out of tune with the sense of the meeting that everyone in the Council of Crows looked around, skittish and embarrassed. "Joseph, my friend, the hero of the reaping, they are calling you in the papers the Sword of the Crown, The Brokenhearted One! So good to see you at court, I see, and basking in the glow of the battle and victory. Service to this country, to the crown, and of course," the prince stood sharply, putting his hands on the table and staring at Joseph, "to me." He stared for a second longer and smiled, his thinning hair falling pitifully to the side.

"Of course, Your Grace, all I do, I do for you, for I am at your service," said Joseph Blackheart.

The prince laughed and smiled even larger as he sat. "I believe we have only a few matters left before tea. We've already put great, great people in place after the death and destruction at this last battle, which feels as if it were yesterday. But one spot remains unfilled, and there are so many noble knights, lords, and madams who want this spot."

"Your Grace, before we get to that, you wanted me to remind you of the artifacts," Casting interrupted.

"Oh yes, a little hobby of mine. If you would do me a favor and put the word out that the prince himself will be rewarding the man, woman, or child who provides an artifact of the Maker to my hand at court. If one of these legendary artifacts makes it to my hand, I will reward them generously," said Prince Damon.

"Your Grace, you are speaking of Gaston's staff lost after the Battle of the Reaping? Pardon me, Your Grace, but those are children's stories and folk songs," said Joseph. "The Maker's Gifts."

"Lord Joseph, you mean artifacts from the Holy Church," the bishop corrected him.

"Yes, of course, Bishop Devon. It's just that our family sword Twilight and shield Midnight's Veil are considered artifacts from the reign of the Red Queen and the Golden King, perhaps works from families of the Maker, but those are stories and half-truths," said Joseph.

"They are, I know, Sir Brokenheart. Your house will be rewarded for keeping your family sword and shield in my service. One of those rewards is that you will be joining my soon-to-be queen's Honor Guard once our engagement is announced," Prince Damon commanded.

"Your Grace, I am . . . words cannot say." Joseph stood, moving his chair behind him quickly, and kneeled, head bowed. "Thank you."

This is not what I had expected today, not at all, thought Casting. The prince had decidedly taken out the most famous man in the land and had made it look like it was a reward.

"You may rise, Joseph. It is not a big deal yet. Please rise and sit, for I don't even know who I am marrying. I have several to choose from, all of whom will be in court soon enough, which is in part why we need more," Damon paused, "money."

Joseph remained cowed and quiet, looking at his fingers as he sat.

"Now, before we leave, I would like to announce our new warden of the north. He marches already to the rude city of Grimwood along with your brother, Jared. This city by the Erie Sea refuses to become a member of the Holy Imperium, so they must be crushed. If General Robert Flint breaks Grimwood, he will become the new warden of the north. They don't know it yet, as winter is near, but by this summer, the city will be mine."

The room became quiet. Some were thrilled, and others crestfallen. Casting had known this was coming because he controlled the Council of Crows, he ran Hudson City, and now, with the prince, he ran the Holy Imperium.

Runt - A Dwarven Debt

As the sun rose, Runt, Maynard, Angus, and Doc walked deer paths along riverbeds, fleeing soldiers of the Holy Imperium. They left the skeletons of burned homesteads at Wolf Hills. Doc led the way, with Angus following and Runt and Maynard in the back. They cut the donkey loose as it slowed their progress. At night, their camps consisted of finding a dry area and staying warm as the fall nights grew chilly. In case soldiers remained in the region, Doc wouldn't allow fires. Runt was not sure if his paranoia was drug-induced or real. He was manic at times and other times completely normal and in control of the situation. He didn't trust Doc entirely, but Maynard seemed okay, and Angus went along with it, so he did as well. Angus was the closest family left right now. Runt's thoughts muddled and twisted as they walked, drifting from his mother's death to his sister's captivity and wondering if traveling to Olde Ridgewatch, where his father and brother were stationed, was even possible.

They stayed out of sight of other travelers the first few days. The city-state of Grimwood remained free of orc and goblin tribes, which Runt was grateful for, and elves remained in the deep woods, rarely trading with local townspeople.

Runt remembered hearing rumors of Gloomspire, built high in the mountains beyond the Commonwealth of Erieland in the Blightbriar Mountains. The stories of dwarven crusades, of a great orc knight and wrath filled goblin hoards all invariably changed depending on the one who spun the tale. Maybe if he were lucky enough, he would catch a glimpse of it on his journey toward the Atlantis Ocean. He listened to the crunch of leaves beneath his feet as they meandered through the riverbeds southeast toward Steelsburg and for a moment didn't feel as if his life was twisting out of control.

"You doing okay?" said Maynard.

"Good as I can, I guess. I mean, it's only been a few days since my mom being buried and all. Thanks again for helping. I've been in a daze for a bit. Everything sucks right now," said Runt.

"I can't even imagine." Maynard patted Runt on the back. "I mean, my life hasn't been great at times, but nothing like yours. I've been fortunate, I guess. Sorry again. Remind me when we stop tonight. I have a jar with sap you can rub on your feet. It will help with blisters."

"No need to apologize. You didn't kill her. I can't even blame Doc. Those men were going to burn the town whether you two showed up or not. I know now. . .." He stopped speaking for a moment. "Nothing feels right anymore. The prince's men were supposed to protect us. Hades, my father, and my brother are soldiers in Prince Damon's army. They had no right to do this to us. I will find who's responsible for this, and I'll kill them," Runt said. His teeth gritted while he squeezed his fingers into fists; his knuckles turned red to match the growing anger inside of him.

Angus looked back at him. "It's a heavy burden, boy. Let's take it one day at a time until we get to your pa."

"If it helps, my parents weren't murdered, but my dad left before I was born, and my mom died when I was ten. I escaped from the home for boys I was living at in Grimwood, and I was lucky enough to bump into Doc when he stumbled out of a bar early in the morning," Maynard said.

"I didn't know they had a home for orphans in Grimwood. I've only been in the outskirts of the city," said Runt.

"Yeah, it's more like . . . I wouldn't use the word home, but they make you work all day to keep your floor mat and a roof over your head. It was better than nothing. I liked the city once I got out of the orphan home. So, I was walking down an alley running a message, and out came this drunk from a bar." Maynard paused to think. "Very lubricated. He bumped into me and called me a foul name. Doc wore those odd glasses. He stopped swaying for a moment, looked at me, and gave a weird half smile. You've seen it once or twice, right? He said he was going to get me an education, and he bent rules to get me into Grimwood University. Ever since, I've lived at the university, taking classes and getting by hook and crook."

"Sounds pretty amazing. Lots to read there, I'm sure, wish we were heading there instead of Steelsburg. I read all of the books at my house before it was torched. We only owned three and two of Angus's books as well," Runt said. "Still nearly memorized them all."

"Hey, you hear! Doc, you owe me two books. Add those to my tab, you bastard!" Angus yelled.

"Wow, so you can read," Maynard said, impressed." Not many folk outside of the city or university can read. I mean, it's unexpected. I guess I should know better. With the dwarven invention of the printing press, more books, papers, and pamphlets are circulating, and more people are learning to read. I carry a novel or two with me. I'll let you take a look at one when we get a chance to rest," He shouldered his pack, which looked misshapen on his back.

The boys continued talking, and the cloud of mourning lying over Runt moved slightly. Angus was a small comfort, but the dwarve was gruff most of the time, having lived a solitary life as a bachelor. He checked in on Runt, showing an awkward form of parental care. Doc's paranoia disappeared, and fires were allowed a day later. Runt wasn't sure if it had been a legitimate concern earlier or if Doc was slowly sobering up. He asked Maynard what Doc put in his pipe, but he shook his head and said nothing. They caught rabbits and other small animals along with fish when they could. They lived off food preserves from the dead soldiers Doc came across earlier. Occasionally, Doc would see a farm or homestead and wander up and bargain for a meal. For as mad as the man seemed, Doc was resourceful. Runt could see why Maynard stayed with the man and why he chose to learn from him.

The night of the first frost forced an adjustment. They took turns keeping the fire going throughout the night. Angus and Doc thought it was prudent to form a watch as well. They were near the edge of the state of Grimwood and moving into the Commonwealth of Erieland. Runt hadn't recognized a landmark or trail in days now. They had been lucky so far to stay out of the wilder parts of the forests yet keeping away from travelers and the bandits that haunted the roads.

Later, Runt asked to be left alone; he walked away from the camp early in the evening, far enough from the fire to be with his thoughts. The dying grass was wet, and the leaves smelled of a now wilted summer. He fell to his knees facing back toward Wolf Hills and his burned home. He prayed not to the Holy Church's Maker, Child, and Servant but to Jupitor, the Guardian of Light; Sif, the Matron of the Harvest; Stribog, the Father of the Veil; and Judith, the Maiden of Storms. After a while, his knees started to hurt, and he opened his eyes and felt the stars shining down on him. He looked across from where he kneeled; he saw a dead deer in front of him and a solitary wolf looking over it. The wolf turned and walked away, back toward Grimwood. He bowed his head toward rose from his knees, and carried the fresh deer back to the camp.

The next day, the walk was manageable, and they stopped for a light lunch, resting on the edge of a large field with tall grass. As they walked on, Runt stopped. Doc looked back after Maynard tugged on his multi-colored traveling jacket.

"What, dammit, I'd like to get across this field and under trees sooner rather than later. I don't like being exposed unless I am in front of two ladies of ill repute and—" Doc looked back, past Maynard and at Angus. "Oh, oh, Runt, what's the matter there, little buddy?" Doc said and lifted his tinted glasses to scratch his eyes.

"They are no longer with me, my mom, and gods. We're too far from Wolf Hills, too far away," said Runt. His eyes were wet with tears, but he forced them back. "Stribog, the Father of the Veil, Friend of Wolves . . . it feels as if he forsakes me."

Angus walked over and hugged him. It was sweet and awkward because even though Angus had known Runt since he'd been born, he had never shown him affection like this before. Doc and Maynard looked on.

"You don't think your gods will help if you carry on toward Steelsburg and hopefully to Olde Ridgewatch?" said Doc.

"My dad worshiped in the Holy Church, and he raised us to read and write from the Bible. He taught us of the Maker, of the Servant and Child, but my mom—she's a . . ." He paused. "She's not for the Holy Church. My dad knows, doesn't mind. Folk of Wolf Hills worship as they please, and Grimwood didn't push the Holy Church as law like, say, Hudson City does. We worshiped Jupitor in the summer, Sif in the autumn, Father Stribog in the winter, and every spring, we watched Judith ride the lightning in the sky above the trees. I think the festivals are all celebrated the same as everyone else, but my gods are in the hills back there, not this way." He pointed on. "I'm sorry. I'm not usually like this; it's all so much," Runt said.

"Your gods know your heart, boy. They'll be there; they'll be with you and inside you, even when you travel. They know your heart. Reminds me of two close friends, Umar and Jezebel Everfall," Doc said but choked a little and looked up for a moment, then carried on, looking back at Angus, who placed his arm around Runt as they stood together. "Those two mages worshiped the Profane, your gods, when they left Wolf Hills years ago. I'm sure you have heard the legends of them. I knew of them, I knew them, and they were loyal to Sif, Jupitor, Judith, and Stribog, and each other, until the day they died. I think I could say they were loyal to them until the end," he said.

"You knew them? I mean, I heard stories of them. We still sing songs of them, but I never really thought they existed at all," said Runt as he walked toward Maynard and Doc.

"Yes, I did. We disagreed a lot, but they were fiercely loyal and worthy companions and, at other times, my bitterest of enemies. But they were faithful, probably too faithful." He stopped and used his hands to push away the memories.

"Me, myself, I am a member of the Divine Church and all its pomp and bluster. It's glittery shit. Considering their rules, I'm a heretic, a heathen piece of unrepentant swine. Know this about who you worship and your religion. It's a personal matter—whom you worship; how you worship; whom you fuck; and whom you consider your king, queen, or whatever. Don't let a boundary take that from you, and don't let a rule or law take that away from you either," Doc said. He paused, scratched at his heart, and brushed a tear away from his eyes.

"Let's go. I want a drink, and we're out of wine and whiskey. As Maynard can attest, it's grim news for me and worse news for all three of you." And he walked away, hands in the air as if ridding himself of emotions and fading memories.

Angus and Maynard raised their shoulders as if to ask where else they were going to go, and Runt thought for a moment. He looked back and moved into the field, away from the hills, leaving them behind. They moved on through the long grass, listening to it as it moved around them, lost in thoughts for a time. Deep in his thoughts, Doc heard the screams of the past, the loss of his friends, and the death of miracle whisper *retribution* in her ear.

***

The crows laughed in the sky as they circled the dead. Swords crossed, spears met shields, and screams of anguish danced across the ground. A battle of armies, meat, anger, steel, and ignorance met to end years of strife, now known as the Battle of the Reaping on the Plains of Ursula.

"The lightning is mine."

"And I command the wind."

"It's over, Hunter. You can't compete with our combined power."

Jezebel flung her arms up, creating a sphere of energy. Umar steadied himself and thrust his hands forward, pushing the sphere out with the force of the wind, protecting those inside from the clash of arms as three nations battled for supremacy on the plains of Ursula in northern Vineland above the Erie Sea.

The magic working created havoc on the battlefield as lightning, and small tornadoes dropped from the sky, pressing down on the soldiers from all directions. The sounds of the battle were hushed inside the sphere. The three battlemages looked at each other, unsure of how long they could continue this struggle. The smell of sizzling flesh lingered near the third mage.

Hunter slumped against a stone, propping his back up as his body shook from the agony of losing the one person in his life who mattered. He felt her life slip away as she lay in his hands. His darkened staff sat next to him. He slowly brushed her hair from her face as the last of her life drifted away.

"You killed her. You don't know what you've done."

"Hunter, you can't best us even with the staff of Gaston. Your apprentice is dead," said Jezebel.

"Give up, and we'll spare you. The combined mercy of Stouya and Carigreed will spare your life," Umar said and breathed in, preparing himself.

The gnashing wind dried Hunter's face as tears of blood stained his cheeks. His colored spectacles were tossed aside, and his clothes were shredded and burned from the lightning that shattered the battlefield. Jezebel, representing Stouya, and Umar, representing Carigreed, stood at a distance, watching their former best friend hold his apprentice. Hunter, part of the coalition known as the Holy Imperium, was near defeat. Outside, wild cries of agony continued. Blades clashed against shields, and those seeking freedom tasted human flesh. Three realms fought one another, and the elements battled themselves, thanks partly to the battlemages inside a sphere of wild energy and excess.

"You'll train another apprentice, this one was weak, and you know our abilities allow us to continue after others have passed, Hunter," Jezebel said. She struggled to maintain the sphere of energy yet not show it on her face. *"You know this. It's over. Give up and let the future of two united empires control Vineland."*

"There will never be another life like hers. You've destroyed a miracle, Jezebel," yelled Hunter, the Holy Imperium's last battlemage.

Jezebel took a step back.

"As much as you tried, Umar, you will never be a father with your lover, Jezebel, but my apprentice was my daughter, and you took fatherhood from me."

"That's not possible. Mages cannot birth children," Umar stuttered.

Jezebel looked at Umar in confusion. *"Lover, no, no, you lie,"* she whispered, then screamed, *"You lie!"*

"Yes, there was a simple reason why your friend left court and stopped speaking to both of you; you fools. Not only did you kill a child, but you also killed the only child born from two mages."

Jezebel and Umar watched as their former friend stood, dropping his daughter's body to the ground.

"You brought this on yourself, Hunter," said Umar. *"You knew what this battle would bring. That Wightland sage whispered it to you in some closet at court as she lapsed into a prophecy!"*

"Your fire skills are moot, Hunter. They have failed you so far. We didn't know about your daughter. How could you not tell us? Even as enemies, you know our friendship runs deeper," said Jezebel recovering some strength.

The battle outside shrank back from the sphere made of living lightning in fear, even as the three separate powers inside and out struggled in conflict.

"Would you tell the world of a miracle? Would you trust anyone with a secret as such?" The air around Hunter shimmered as he stood, grasping his staff. *"You know how our art works, and it has a price. How much do either of you have left after giving up your love for each other? Maybe enough to best me, sure, but my daughter wasn't dead after you struck her with wind and lightning. Judith, your goddess, has left you both now. My daughter had time enough."*

"To take from a living creature tears a piece of your soul away, but for one such as her to give it all to someone as close as you, her father," said Umar.

"No, to do so would kill you or drive you to madness!" Tears lined Jezebel's face as she guessed that none of the three would leave this battle alive.

Jezebel and Umar braced themselves as she let the electric sphere down and attempted to shield themselves from a wrath never witnessed in Vineland before.

"Yes, eventually." Hunter's hands glowed with an unnatural fire of purple and green, and the black tears around his eyes drifted up into the air, showing nothing but the madness deep inside. *"But you and the rest will die first."*

* * *

Doc stopped a moment, looked around, and took off his glasses. His child and two friends were now long dead, along with countless others, yet their screams, laughter, and anguish remained. He wiped his eyes, the tears streaking his face, and cursed himself, swallowing back the sorrows of the past. He watched Angus, Runt, and Maynard as they walked along the path before him and hoped he could make the future something better than what he'd done to destroy it.

Runt -Songs of Yesterday

Hallows Eve passed, and November lay on the ground like a warm blanket, the leaves fallen dead. They walked past farms, their fields harvested from tradition and feared early snow.

"I wonder how the other cities fared as the Holy Imperium moved across the Sword Belt," Runt asked.

The paths merchants, tinkers, and tradespeople used between the Grimwood state and the Commonwealth of Erieland were known as the Sword Belt. The Sword Belt included Grimwood by the Erie Sea, Steelsburg, located in a deep valley in the Commonwealth of Erieland, and the stronghold of Iron Valley. The infamous Gloomspire had initially been the fourth member of the Sword Belt but had fallen into despair due to infighting between dwarves, orcs, and goblins. The other three were renowned for producing Vineland's best steel and armor. Poets and minstrels said the Sword Belt smiths used the blood of warriors to cool their works at the forges.

Angus took a deep breath, shouldered his pack, and walked on. The four avoided towns, costing the group quality food and easy rest, which wore on all of them. Doc constantly ranted about the politics at Prince Damon's court and the need for a strong drink. Maynard wheezed on, breathing heavily. Runt continued with endless questions, which grated on Angus's nerves, which had been frayed since Doc mentioned Steelsburg.

"Take it from me, Runt, nothing pleasing comes from an army crossing over open country," said Doc, and they moved on.

They were in poor shape and needed to evaluate their situation. They passed around the hold of Iron Valley. Doc scouted the area when they first neared it and said it had seen better days—that the Holy Imperium occupied it. At a crossroads, he met a former guard from the stronghold while Maynard, Runt, and Angus remained hidden in a nearby ravine. The guard, relieved because of a past injury, headed home to his parent's farm, hoping it hadn't been destroyed and looted. Doc wondered how a one-legged man would help on a farm and politely gave way to him before making his way back to the others. The stronghold itself was now part of the Holy Imperium, and they taxed anyone wishing to enter. The Holy Imperium now controlled the Iron Valley.

"Do you think they will lay siege to Grimwood?" asked Maynard.

"Yes. It's absurd. I know this winter will be one Hades of a bitch, but I think Prince Damon, the little shit, has plans for Vineland." Doc scratched his chin. "He wants to reign in the independent city-states, bringing them to heel, as it were. Those who comply will become part of whatever they're creating, and the others torn down stone by stone, brick by brick, until they are dust. Do we have any more tobacco?" He began searching through every pocket of his multi-patched coat. Patting it down everywhere, he pulled out several pouches; they were all empty. "I'm fresh out of everything here, everything! That's it, we need civilization. We need an inn, and I need resources, dammit. I need sweet leaf, bitter leaf, reefer, and spirits—anything to keep the voices, the ghosts at bay. Angus, any idea where we are or how far we are from your clan?"

"We are three days hard walking or five days slow walking to Steelsburg. We should make suitable time if we get to a real road and off these rabbit paths. We could get lucky and join a caravan," said Angus. He pulled at his beard and spat.

"Well, let's get up and be on our way, move toward the road. Maybe I can find some mushrooms," said Doc. "Runt don't be too worried. If we hadn't been hunted by now, it was my paranoid thoughts and too much whiskey. It's not like there are wanted posters with your face on them all over the place. Surprising, thought there would be, like when I escaped the asylum. Glad most of those were torn down."

"What did you just mumble, Doc?" asked Angus.

Runt chimed in, "Something about an asylum, I think."

Maynard looked at Doc.

"Nothing, nothing, right this way." Doc motioned, and they marched on.

Doc stopped, stretched his back, shifted his coat around, and looked in his pockets again. He wore a medium-length coat patched and torn as if a drugged-up tailor had sewn it together from numerous military uniforms and dyed it in the dark, a near-blackish crimson color.

They walked on a worn road running north to south. Loyalists to the Holy Imperium called it the Queens Road while the Kings Roads ran east to west. After walking south for hours on compacted gravel, Maynard spotted smoke looming ahead of them above the tree line.

"That could be helpful. Maker's tits, I hope it's a tavern," said Doc.

"Mentor, we don't have much money to house the four of us," reminded Maynard.

"Shit, I know, I know. We'll come up with money somehow. I have credit at a lot of places. Full credit, as it were, for a room, food, drink. All of it. I'm a doctor, a scribe, and a journalist—don't forget it," said Doc.

Runt noticed the road was muddy in spots, with broken stone and sand in other places, worn down from wagon ruts and heavy foot traffic. Runt, Maynard, and Angus followed Doc as he quickly walked toward the smoke and what they hoped was a form of civilization.

They felt encouraged by the potential of an inn after traveling and living off what the land could offer. They found one by midday, passing travelers who gave a wide berth primarily out of fear of the road and the day's current affairs. Soldiers, both mounted and unmounted, meant looting, rape, and robbery justified by might, religion, or the prince's wants and needs.

"Here we are. You boys stay with Angus a moment. I'll go inside and secure a room. Maynard, where is our purse? Oh, here it is. Okay, okay, what do we have here." The mage looked in the purse and shook it, making a face as if Maynard had broken his favorite bottle of whiskey. "Shit on me and call me King Geordie. This doesn't bode well." He tied the purse up and tossed it in his hand. "I'll think of an idea on the way. You boys stay out of sight for a bit; I doubt there're wanted posters for anyone, but you never know." And with a small amount of money in hand, an odd smirk on his face, and potentially wanted for murder, Doc disappeared.

"We're good as dead, aren't we?" Runt looked at Maynard, bags under his eyes and hope slowly melting off his shoulders. They stood under a large oak tree's shadow.

"Truthfully, we've been in tighter spots, but not by much. We made it out without too many scratches. Except in Hudson City. We had a terrible time there—too many parties, too much to indulge in," Maynard said.

"I'm no babysitter, boys. Going to wander around the stables and see what I can see. You stay out of trouble." Angus wandered away hoping he could talk to a blacksmith and get a feel for the area.

The inn sat as if to say, "Welcome, we are here to serve all." Its bulky frame was well kept with two floors, a clay tile roof, and a deck surrounding both floors. No wall protected the area from grazing animals or marauding bandits. The sign hung loosely, stating, "The Greasy P," due to the large p standing at the building's front, which was used for some sport and gambling when the patrons got lively.

Doc walked toward the inn's front and looked at a few men sitting in rocking chairs on the deck. They looked as if they sat here every day chewing on the local gossip and complaining about the weather that was coming or that had just passed. "You fellas know of any good apothecaries around here, I could use some medicine?" Doc said quietly.

The chairs continued rocking and paid no attention to the burnt-out mage.

He tipped his large hat, mumbled, "Thanks for nothing," and walked in. When the doors opened, noise broke out, and then he was inside, and all the group's confidences were with him.

* * *

Maynard sat, put his head back to the large tree behind him, and closed his eyes. Runt glanced at him with a questionable look.

"He'll come back, right? Or are we sleeping under the stars again and hoping to catch fish in the river nearby?" Runt's stomach grumbled. "Do we have anything else to eat?"

"No, it's up to Mentor," said Maynard.

"Why do you call him that? I've heard stories of mages, warlocks, and wizards and heard the songs of the Battle of the Reaping, but how does it work? Can you throw fireballs or shoot lightning from a wand? I mean, where does it all come from?"

Runt was picking small stones off the ground and throwing them at another tree bored and frustrated.

"Warlocks hunt mages. They blunt the art of magic, using talismans or, in some cases, their blood," Maynard said, on the defense. "Don't call me or Doc a warlock. It's like getting called a hog lover." Maynard looked at Runt for a second. "Look, I can get hanged or burned for even talking about this. But you aren't a follower of the Holy Church, and after what happened back in the hills, I guess you deserve to know a little about Doc." He stopped for a moment to collect his thoughts. "Magic is not taught at any university, technically. Mages, sorcerers, witches, whatever you think of people with power or special abilities, it's considered evil by the Holy Church and its worshipers. The dwarves shun those born with gifts they consider unworthy of their blood. People like Doc and I are persecuted and killed because we have no binding." He held up his hand, showing his fake binding ring.

Maynard took off his spectacles and cleaned them.

"I can't speak for the societies of goblins, orcs, or elves. They are as variable as the weather itself. Some hold people born with the affluence of magic as special, even gods." Maynard took a deep breath while Runt looked on, wanting more. "Some people are born with a natural talent. They pick up a lute, a sword, or even a cooking pot and are naturally proficient at it. They become cooks for kings, heroes in books, and amazing minstrels with practice and luck. Others are born with an infinity into a deeper sense of nature. How can I explain it? You know the feeling you get, the place you enter right before you dream? People like Doc and I can touch it. The best of us can manipulate it and even take bits of it and use it. There are various ways to get there including prayer, alchemy, and studying ancient books.

"And others use blood sacrifices, talk to demons, and dance naked around bonfires," interrupted Runt. He said it with a smile and egged Maynard on for more.

"Blood magic is deeply potent, and it takes a toll on the user," Maynard said. He brushed the thought away. "When you use it, the art—magic, as you say—it takes its toll. You have to pay for it. Most don't understand, but it pulls at you from within, taking time off the length you live, or it gets you sick. Every time magic is performed, the cost is higher."

"Like crossing a bridge, you have to pay a toll," said Runt.

"Sort of, yeah, only you know the toll gives you a disease after you throw a fireball. Doc, he's paid a price by losing his sanity. The only time he's actually pretty normal now is when he's high, drunk, or drugged up. It's awful to think about."

"His price was sanity?"

"In a way, yes, but don't talk about it. He's pissed that nobody credits him with ending the war already. Anyway, the universities teach the basics of reading, writing, mathematics, science, different languages, histories, and manners. Universities are the children of monasteries. The overall ideas have been twisted and changed as time has passed. Most are boarding schools, and it's not cheap. I'm one of the poorest students at any of the universities. What the mentor now teaches me is off the books, as they say. We use the university's resources to learn, collect what he knows, and investigate more about wielding and controlling what we can do. In the Holy Church, when a person is special and isn't killed or tortured outright, they're given a binding for life, and it's not pleasant. Technically, nobody has ever broken a binding. At the end of the Purge of Thorns, both the ruling nobles and bishops of the Holy Church found anyone showing a sign of magical power and subjected them to the binding. If not, they were hanged, beheaded, or burned at the stake. The higher classes find the binding practice to be useful, while in most parts of the country, it's easier to kill if you're found to be special," said Maynard.

"No magic is taught at schools at all. I'm confused as to why you went to the University of Grimwood. I heard they have a library you can get lost in, and lawyers, doctors, and mages grow on trees," Runt said.

"There were classes dedicated to the study of magic during the Golden Age. When the last of the Goldthorns' bloodline thinned, a power struggle occurred between the two biggest families, the Ruinthorns and the Hawthorns. This power struggle created distrust and backlash against anyone born with the ability to use magic. The Purge of Thorns started the year of the Maker 1650 with the Melasum Witch Trials and ended with the culmination of the Thornbriar War," said Maynard. "You know of the Thornbriar War, right?"

"I know there was a large fight between two families which eventually started the Crimson Struggle, but it was almost one hundred years ago," said Runt.

"Correct. The Ruinthorns and Hawthorns clashed over the remains of the Goldthorns' empire. University buildings were locked, books burned, and teachers hung from bell towers. It was a terrible time. At the start, those in control executed criminals already in jail, but it got out of hand quickly. Nobles were executed as the price of the purge rose. It's why the binding was invented." Maynard touched his finger. "Anything considered magical is now reported to the nearest authority. Most times it's the local Holy Church. Even after the Order of the Inquisitor was disbanded. The Order of the Blue Rose now attempts to keep any magic items from falling into unknown hands and binds or kills anyone with known powers. There are witch hunters as well, but most are just thugs and cutthroats—nothing like the original warlocks. The Ruinthorn and Hawthorn families no longer exist. They killed each other off in the late sixteen hundreds, and their strong lines of magic users and hunters are gone forever," said Maynard.

"My dad mentioned it to Ben, my brother, when we were younger. The Thornbriar War ended but created more chaos and started the Crimson Struggle," said Runt. "Okay, I think I get it."

"So, Doc and I are wanted, him more so than me. We can perform magic, unchained by the binding. There are others, hedge witches and mages, but they keep to themselves in the shadows of society. I heard the prince has a new mage, but they're weak and nothing like before the Purge of Thorns," Maynard said. "Let's talk about something else. It brings me down."

"When is Doc getting back? I'm getting hungry," said Runt. The afternoon shifted into twilight. "Tell me about university. I mean, you are only a few years older than me, near my brother's age, I suppose. There wasn't a school in Wolf Hills. I was taught to read and write but feel stupid around you and Doc."

Maynard scratched his face a bit and pushed up his glasses. "University isn't easy. Besides classes, there are more treacherous lessons throughout a person's education. It's a struggle where students group in factions, trying to get one up on one another. I tried not to piss off any of the nobility, old and new blood, merchants' spoiled brats, and the few girls there. It's a remarkable and frustrating game of leering, prestige, and gossip," said Maynard.

"How many colleges are there? I've only heard of those in Grimwood, Hudson City, the Commonwealth of Erieland, and Olde Ridgewatch. Doesn't Crescent City have one?"

"Most independent city-states have a university. The size and curriculum vary, though. The universities in Hudson City and Olde Ridgewatch are the oldest and most prestigious. Still, Grimwood holds the curviest girls from what I've heard. The schools together are called the Silver Ivy League. They try to share ideas and knowledge, but they also occasionally argue and fight."

Runt smiled for the first time in a long time. "School fights sound better than what we've seen recently—less violent and more mysterious."

Maynard's face shifted, and he moved to change the subject. "Tell me of the books you read when you were at Wolf Hills?"

* * *

The sun drooped deeper into the horizon. Angus appeared at a slight jog.

"There you boys are. Come on, Doc has got you a stall in the stables for sleeping. We're staying for two days. I have to cook tomorrow, and you're both running dishes and mucking the stalls to help pay for food and a roof over our heads. Of course, Doc gets two nights in a bed and actual coin. He's working on a few sick townsfolk —setting a broken bone or two after a bar fight he may or may not have started himself. Anyway, come inside. We have a booth in the back," Angus said.

They walked past local townsfolk and other travelers sitting down as Doc finished off a large stein of beer. Runt and Maynard looked on, both thirsty and hungry.

"Rest up, boys, rest up. We'll take ease and then make our way to Steelsburg. I've heard pray tell there may even be lute play and a song or two. The innkeeper said a fellow from one of the universities was playing his way around the area, wandering, telling and taking tales. I have a mind to speak to him later and gather further news." Doc cleaned his mouth off with his jacket sleeve. "Right, well, you three stay here. Angus, I've ordered you a round and whatever stew they're cooking. Relax, we'll work off what we eat. Tonight, I'll stay relatively sober. I need news and to drum up more work to earn further money. Every town needs a healer. This area is short of them. The Red Army is taking what they can as they head toward Grimwood." He smiled at the three of them, picked up his tankard, and walked toward the bar.

All three sat, tired and mystified. Runt couldn't figure out how he was still standing and talking to everyone. It was as if the alcohol fueled him.

The food was delivered and tasted like horseshit. Angus grumbled, stating their cook needed to be replaced. The bread was okay, day-old at worst, but they ate it. It had been a long time since they could sit. The hearth fire warmed the room, and laughter at the bar relaxed everyone.

The night moved on, and the three were about to go to bed when a lute player started to strum. The sky outside lay in darkness, and candles and lanterns lit the walls. The lute player was of an ordinary size, well built with bright red hair. It was an accomplishment to have a player in your inn. A tavern could bring in significant money if the player were marginally talented. The musician started to play, and it was a slow roll at first, a song of a girl lost in a well. Runt had heard versions of this around his town before. This version was similar but much better, the rhyming crisper. There were no gaps during the chorus, and the lute man could play. After several songs, the red-haired man took a pull from his tankard and took in the audience as they sat with delight.

Runt looked around; the place was filled with patrons, so Angus ordered

116

another round for the three of them. A group of mercenaries stood at the bar, taking in the show. A pair of dwarves sat near the door in the corner, keeping to themselves. They looked like a married couple, though Runt thought it was hard to tell. Angus stood, went to speak to them, but returned shortly after.

"They weren't interested in speaking to a clanless dwarve," he mumbled.

The musician started in on a ballad about the Battle of the Reaping called "A Dwarven Debt." The lute player spoke, slowly strumming his instrument: "This is a story about a debt owed to an executioner." He started into the song, telling the story of Gray Jim, the hangman of Steelsburg.

* * *

1763, Gray Jim on the Plains of Ursula at the end of the Battle of the Reaping.
The crush of the shield wall and the pressure of the melee broke spears and spirits. Soldiers fell, pierced by a sword or bolt from a crossbow. Heads lay on the ground, blood filling in through the nose holes of their helmets with nothing but the ringing of the crash above. Small ponds of blood and gore grew near the middle of a flat field where lightning flashed from the sky, and the earth moaned. Two mages fought a third while three separate armies clashed around them, rendering the field a living nightmare. The toll of death was unbelievable. The struggle ended after all three mages shredded themselves and the battlefield apart.

Five races of Vineland struggled and died for each nation's cause. Those falling that day couldn't remember what was so important about the whole damned mess. They perished because the wealthy had ordered them to fight, and death was easier than starvation or slavery. Gray Jim sat against a dead horse, but it wasn't his horse any longer. Nothing within sight lived except the birds, and all they did was cackle, circling above.

"Why are you cursing? You're feasting today, probably for many days," he said to them, but they didn't listen.

"Caw, caw!" they screamed at one another.

"Shut up!" He threw someone's gauntlet at a plump bird. It wasn't his, so it didn't matter. After a battle like this, not much mattered at all. He lost his gauntlet beating

117

a fifteen-year-old squire to death with it. The horse smelled as its bloated stomach leaked juices from a spear wound. He wasn't sure of it, but his sense of smell had dulled after the vomit, tears, and screams of the battle. He looked at his hands and knew of the joy of life after surviving.

Maker's tits, he was tired, so he just sat and waited. There were no commanders, none he could see. There wasn't much of anything near where the mages fought as lightning continued to strike the ground, leaving circular burn marks and corpses. He had witnessed a tornado of flames and lightning at the end of the battle and took refuge behind the fallen horse, covering himself with a body like a shield as the heat seared above him.

Gray Jim reached over and grabbed at a body, found a flask, hoping for anything, and was pleasantly surprised to discover gin. He took a swig, and it burned his throat and brought feeling to his body for a moment. He took another swig.

"I'll need to get out of here soon," he said. He spoke to a dead goblin next to him. An arrow stuck through the goblin's right eye, and muck leaked from its mouth.

Birds continued to circle above, swooping down and grabbing dinner. "Don't fly over by the burn marks, birdy. Reckon not much goes in there comes out," Gray Jim said.

A few birds flew toward the burn marks on the ground at a distance from Gray Jim as he noticed small fires burning on the battlefield with unnatural blue and green flames. The lightning continued, but no rain fell or thunder sounded, only short bolts here and there. At first, it shook Gray Jim, but nothing could really move you after all this. He looked around. The dead lay everywhere, and it didn't matter the color of their skin, what country they represented, or the religion they worshiped. All were lifeless.

"What happened when those mages fought? This is why the Purge of Thorns occurred and why everyone wielding magic was killed outright or bound never to use their powers again," Gray Jim said.

He watched as the bird flew toward a circle with no natural flame. It immediately cawed and burst apart into pieces, little blue-and-white bird pieces burning, falling to the ground.

"Told you, stupid bastard," Gray Jim said with a laugh.

He took another sip and looked to his left. About a hundred feet from him was a bare tree, only twenty feet high. The pitiful thing was the only point on the battlefield. Everyone used it as a point on their maps, either an area to control or leave from, the only slight slope on a vast field, and hundreds died there. Gray Jim stood and stretched his back. He fought for the losing side but wore no colors indicating his side in this battle. Gray Jim had been a butcher before joining the military. Guess he was still one; his commander used him as an executioner and torturer, and he was good at it. He knew his way around killing and knew his way around meat; he could heal a fair share, too. Healing was more straightforward than struggling in battles like this, but nobody avoided this battle. What happened beyond civilization where powerful generals controlled the destinies of people could only be described as the demise of generations of families and friends.

He saw a few people moving about, but no fighting. The fighting was done, the bone pickers were coming, and the not dead were starting to moan. One in particular, he heard a gruff voice that sounded familiar.

He walked to the tree, toward the noise. The bodies were broken, slashed, and busted everywhere. They wore full plate armor, ore leather, and chainmail, none of which had saved any of them. Most were dead, while others made their way to the inevitable end. To the tree's right was what looked like dead children in spectacular armor. Gray Jim wasn't sure anymore. He saw dead ugly dogs and giant frogs with saddles strapped to them among the bodies. It smelled as it looked, like dead dwarves, dogs, and frogs.

Dwarves from Steelsburg were part of the Legion of Carigreed's army, known as the Legion, to most. All dead now, even as they'd fought brilliantly with their dwarven shield wall and magnificent armor. A large band of day-walking goblins bearing elvish weapons had clashed with the dwarven soldiers. How the Holy Imperium had managed to get goblins on their side and arm them with elvish blades could be anyone's guess, but they'd neutralized the small band of dwarves that covered a flank. The goblins used guile, ancient knowledge, and savagery to find a way to make it through or around superior dwarven armor and shield walls. The Crimson Struggle featured goblins and orcs fighting for the Holy Imperium while the Legion managed two forces of dwarves on their side. The Nation of Stouya used tribes of elves. Although all three sides managed to use elves as scouts, Stouya employed them in their vanguard with thousands of savages from various tribes on this side of the Grave Reach River. Gray Jim remembered seeing the dwarves and their wall of shields holding back waves of elves, their historic enemy.

He approached the sound and found a dwarven hand moving under lightly armored goblin bodies. The smell was caustic. To lie under so many bodies and the blood and gore falling into mouth or eyes would be enough to gag you to death. Gray Jim saw the hand moving and wondered if he should make an effort.

He pulled six goblin bodies off the pile, their skin varying from black to gray, green, and brown. They ranged in body, size, and skin color like any human in Vineland. They bled and died like everyone else. A spear had pushed through a stout-looking dwarve. It had punctured through his back into another dwarve. The one at the bottom was still alive, but for how long? Gray Jim grabbed the top dwarven breastplate, pulled, and managed to snap the spear off so he could get a better look at the last dwarve of the company that fought for the hill.

"Ugh, hurts something fierce there, sir." He spit blood. "You here to finish me off or to get me off this field and back home?" muttered the dwarve at the bottom of the pile.

"Shit, I don't know what I'm doing. I'm the same as you, and the Holy Imperium won, so I'm guessing you lost along with me."

"Vulcan's beard, the Legion failed. Never thought I would see the day. And you, you fought for the Nation of Stouya?"

"Yeah, they fell as well. The mage battle is what did it for the Legion and us." Gray Jim looked down and scratched his chin. "Spear got you good."

"It's only partway through; it's caught on my armor and pushing into me, a slight wound. It hurts to breathe. Is that water you have or something else?" asked the dwarve, breathing weakly as blood wept from the tear glands of his eyes.

"Something else." Gray Jim reached out, shaking it. "Want a sip?"

"Sweet Vulcan's fire, I would love a taste," said the dwarve.

"You look pretty important, having another take a spear for you. And your armor, I never seen its kind before," said Gray Jim.

"You could say I'm important," said the dwarve.

Gray Jim rubbed his chin again. "What's your life worth to you?"

"I won't say anything." The dwarve was in an abysmal state, blood coming from his eyes, ears, and mouth. Although he could move all four limbs, his body was in *near ruin, with a crushed breastplate and a spear protruding from the abdomen. If he did not leave this field soon, he would die. "But if you get me off this field on a dwarven shield and I survive, you won't have want for much of anything," he said.*

"I'll try; I could use a few favors after this mess. I am going to pull the spear, pour this into your wound, dress it best I can, and drag you onto a shield. If I can get out and you survive, we will talk. If not." And he sighed. "I can strip your body and sell this fancy-ass armor for a few coins." Gray Jim did not smile as he spoke.

"Deal, but if you must sell the armor, take it to Steelsburg. You'll get a better price. Give me a drink before you pull the spear."

* * *

The musician finished and set his lute down, and the inn remained quiet. The song and others like it reminded people of those terrible last moments on the Plains of Ursula above the Erie Sea's shores. The silence broke when Doc slowly started to clap. Soon everyone clapped and cheered. After the applause, Doc bought the lute player a drink. The crowd got louder, and the air inside turned thick with smoke, talk, and laughter. Maynard and Angus left off for the stables to sleep. Runt lingered, lost in the warmth of those inside the inn, not thinking of their problems outside the doors. He walked around, taking in the servers and listening to random conversations as he grew tired.

As he left, Runt saw Doc talking loudly with the lute player about the song. He gestured with his hands speaking with his mouth and hands. A rough-looking sellsword sat on the other side of Doc. The man bore a shield on his back with a red plow over a green background. The door closed, and they were gone. He trotted off to catch up to Maynard and sleep.

The Bastards - Morning Drink

A cold fall's breath blew into the morning alleys of Steelsburg. Most of the time, sleep eluded Gray Jim or, at least, a deep, steady sleep did. He wandered downstairs into the bar area after a piss to grab a drink before he put in a day's work. The work nobody else ever wanted to do. Most folks were asleep, and the few who weren't were leaving the taverns or bars. The Cracked Brick Tavern stood empty except for the owner's wife, cleaning up, checking stock, and prepping. Her husband would work along with a few servers later in the day. The tavern stood in the city's mixed burrow, where dwarves and humans mingled freely without sneering or vulgar comments. Dwarven clans controlled the town of Steelsburg, segregating non-dwarves to only certain parts of the city. It was also the principal city in the Commonwealth of Erieland; the elves called it Three Rivers, and in the north near Grimwood, they called it Shitsburg.

"You want the usual?" the owner's wife sounded sour as she looked at large, beefy Gray Jim. He looked like a well-fed farmer who slaughtered animals in the fields, cleaned them, and carried them back to a barn miles away. His face was long, rounded at the chin, and poorly shaved.

"If you don't mind, Betsy, I'd like to change it up a bit," he said. His dark hair felt tangled and a mess. At the end of each strand of hair, it grayed, giving him his namesake. His shirt was cut in a V shape. It used to be white and stain-free. He scratched at his britches while sitting on a stool in the corner. "If you have any coffee, I'll have a cup, along with a pint of dark beer. No bourbon or the devilish potato liquor the dwarves drink. Maker's sake, shit is evil. Oh, and sausage and eggs. I have city work to do today," he said.

"Oh, so that's why you're asking for coffee. You know that shit's expensive, right?" said Betsy.

Her hands were pink from washing dishes. She was common-born and would be common-dead when she passed, along with her husband and the customers who frequented the Cracked Brick Tavern. Her light-brown worn dress and faded yellow apron lay on her big arthritic frame full of knots, pain, and bitterness.

"Give me the bar settled." She poured a dark beer into a large mug from a wooden barrel shelved in a wall behind her. "Here's your beer while you wait."

"Thank you, Betsy, appreciate it." Gray Jim took a large pull from the mug, his first calories for the day. He stood and opened the tavern door to check the weather. Coal dust, dampness, and sweat from the city drifted into the tavern. Steelsburg bled smoke and coughed dust from mines and smith fires, constantly pulling and burning minerals from the ground and grinding them to manufacture everything, including candlestick holders, horseshoes, and weapons, of course. He looked across the broad expression of the city.

* * *

Riverstone Citadel stood at the tip of where the Soundless Run, Deerchurn, and Orcfeast Rivers met, and its high walls controlled the city and much of the Commonwealth's trade. Since recorded history, it had been owned and managed by dwarves, its flag was never lowered to surrender or siege.

The Clearstone family controlled the jewel and silver mines in Steelsburg, using their treasury to maintain and command Riverstone Citadel, and held sway to parts of the Commonwealth of Erieland and lower portions of Grimwood. They backed multiple crusades into the Blightbriar Mountains, slaying goblins, orcs, and elves trying to take back the Gloomspire. However, when the Thornbriar War had ended around the year of Vulcan 1694 and the Crimson Struggle commenced, the crusades slowed as the dwarves turned to more industry and materialism. Due to business needs, the Clearstone family had attempted to keep the United Clans from partaking in the Crimson

Struggle. Instead, the family chose to trade with all three warring nations to expand the city-state's treasury and, thus, the Clearstone family's power.

Riverstone Citadel flew the United Clan's flags for over a century, and the Clearstone family provided much of the power keeping everyone in the city and below it united. Still, time eroded even the most potent grips on power.

After the last failed crusade against the mountain stronghold the Gloomspire, the city-state of Steelsburg consolidated its rule through a vote of congress. Each head of the family held one vote for causes of war, blood justice, and any other significant disputes. In contrast, the ruling family of Riverstone Citadel received five votes and the ability to enact tiebreakers.

The Clearstone family had tried to reign in trade after the vote through bribes and hostage-taking known as "fostering gifts," straining relationships in the United Clans. It kept most dwarves from joining sides in the Crimson Struggle. Unfortunately, the dwarven people long argued over family and government rights, thus creating fissures over the years. The two most prominent families, the Clearstone family, who held Riverstone Citadel, and the Blitzsteel clan, a significant steel smith family, were constantly at odds as each struggled for control of the valley. Cormac Clearstone had allowed families to join the cause near the end of the Crimson Struggle, joining in the Battle of the Reaping.

The United Clans, the unified dwarven houses between the Grave Reach River and the Atlantis Ocean, placed themselves above other races. They didn't accept the Holy Church's opinions on the Maker, yet their view of the races was the same as the Holy Imperium's and Great Brightland's religion across the ocean. The Holy Imperium and, thus, the Holy Church believed humanity was first among the Maker, while the United Clans thought dwarves were first among Vulcan. They both worshiped in separate ways and used different names, yet their core beliefs remained the same. The only reason they worked or lived with other races was for profit or advantage. The Clearstone family was liberal in concessions, knowing humans were needed for healthy Steelsburg commerce and trade. Goblins and orcs were forbidden in the Commonwealth, race enemies to the dwarves like the elves before. Many made a living by collecting bounties for goblin and orc scalps, being paid less for teeth, ears, and fingers.

The dwarves' outlook of the natives, known in the old dwarven tongue as elves, adjusted over time. In antiquity, the two had fought to near extinction in battles now written in stone. As a result, the elvish population dwindled, and they fled deep inside the Blightbriar Wilds, the swamps in the south, or across the Stagger Wall. Now both sides treated each other with an understanding of respect.

The dwarves of the United Clans adamantly opposed slavery while other independent clans carried no misgivings about it. The Clearstone family tolerated clanless or exiled dwarves to perform base work in the city, including serving as caretakers to Riverstone Citadel, the bridge keeps, and main holds in the area for a right to earn membership back into a clan via marriage. This process usually took at least twenty-five years to transpire, but dwarven life spans allowed for such punishments or, as the United Clans called them, blessings to occur. If a clan did not have enough exiles to perform lower-end jobs, they hired humans to work inside the city and outside the licensed areas. There was moderate pay for this work, more than a farmer or laborer working the same hours.

* * *

Gray Jim breathed in deep, tasting the air as if it fell into his lungs. Living around Steelsburg caused a thin film of coal ash to find its way home, into skin and teeth. Those drinking enough potato liquor would retain an unnatural whiteness to their teeth. He watched smoke fall out of pipes drifting into the sky, creating a never-ending haze to the day.

The rock face of Riverstone Citadel peered out; its star shape intimidated the fiercest enemies. Gray Jim knew attacking this dwarven stronghold would be dangerous and foolish. Dwarves used molten metal, steam, burning oil, and other deadly substances to kill and maim their enemies. Riverstone Citadel's shape provided the dwarves with multiple angles for arrow attacks from compound bows and high-end crossbows. The crossbow was illegal to all but dwarves across Vineland; it was a sacred piece of machinery. A specific family constructed the tool, each instrument taking years to hewn and make. The dwarven culture drew on the ideas of duty, honor, and toil as a way of life, and it showed in each of the crossbows created. Those same ideas were the basis for their culture, religion, clan hierarchy, and dwarven laws.

The daily endeavors in jobs like working in a mine, making pottery, or creating glass provided clan prestige. Families specialized in iron, steel, copper, leather, or ceramics. The work each family specialized in was the origin of family names like Clearstone, Blitzsteel, Bitterspear, and Fellwater. The dwarven lifespan allowed for each family tradition and sacred techniques to pass from generation to generation.

Three main bridges spanned the area of the city, one across each of the major rivers. Each side of the bridge was a keep made of impenetrable poured stone. A tunnel underground also connected each keep. Thus, each keep could be supplied from below, withstanding a siege for years if necessary.

Gray Jim stood in the Cracked Brick Tavern's door near the Orcfeast River in a burrow called the Strip. The Strip, so named because the land consistently flooded and was destroyed by the river, was the only area in Steelsburg where human traders worked and lived. The other portions of the city remained for dwarves only. If a human in the city is without the correct paperwork or license, their punishment would be swift while elves, orcs, and goblins were forbidden.

"Food's done, and here's your coffee," Betsy said. "How are you paying today, Gray Jim?"

"Put it on my tab. I should be paid later today by the city," he said.

"By the city, you say? Nobody like us works for the city. They don't hire us except for base labor at best."

Gray Jim smiled and didn't say a word. Instead, he dug into his runny eggs, sausages, and potatoes. The holy potato of the dwarven culture was the most well-known food used at every meal and the main ingredient in their honed clear liquor called vodka. Gray Jim took a sip of his coffee, remembering a few nights before, and promised himself not to ingest the evil vodka for a while.

"Vulcan's beard! It's an expense I usually can't partake in. Not many places to find it," he said to Betsy. "Can get tea anywhere, but coffee from down south? You would be better off seeing a dragon than a cup of this amazing elixir." She looked at him, knowing he would go on for another minute. She was concerned about his tab. "Yes, my masters are the dwarves. One of them owed me, so I cashed it in. They made me the big sword I brought in earlier, and they also gave me a job."

"What did you do? Save one of the high nobles during the Crimson Struggle?" She laughed. "Heard a story about one of the Clearstone dwarves joining up and fighting on the Plains of Ursula up north a while back," said Betsy.

"Sounds familiar," Gray Jim said, sipping his coffee. "I'm no hero. Believe me, mostly luck and stubbornness are what got me a job with the dwarves. When I return, I'll indulge in some Riverclear bourbon. It's going to be a bloody day today."

"Well, it's good to know you'll be paying your tab. My husband vouched for you when you came in and got a room, said you were okay, but it's been so long and all," said Betsy.

Gray Jim looked at his hand that held the coffee. Betsy didn't think he would pay his entire tab before leaving. Gray Jim had joined the Nation of Stouya as a mercenary in the Crimson Struggle. He would get his hands dirty, torturing, hanging, and killing wherever the money would take him. Unclean hands in a long and dirty war—like everyone else's hands. It was where he'd met the Cracked Brick Tavern's owner, Dufin, one of the few human building owners in Steelsburg. As one of the Nation of Stouya executioners, Gray Jim had been assigned to torture Dufin for information on troop movements. Dufin had been the last of twenty men Gray Jim had tortured that night. He'd been tired, a leather apron stained with blood and his instruments dulled. Gray Jim set it to Dufin straight: talk now or there would be pain until he died. He had been about to break one of Dufin's fingers when the camp was ambushed. Gray Jim knew a bloodbath when he saw one. On the promise of owing him a favor, he'd let Dufin go, and they'd both skipped out.

"I'm good for it. They pay me by the job, and I'm good at what I do. And I'll be doing a lot today," he said.

Outside, dwarves yelled as they finished putting up large beams and cross pieces.

Betsy walked to the door. "It looks like they're building up near Riverstone Citadel."

"Yes, ma'am, they are—building a stock and setting up an execution block."

"So, you're an executioner," she said, "a hangman?" She blessed herself with the sign of the Maker to keep any curses off her, like the simple person she was.

Gray Jim chuckled to himself. People always acted funny when they found out he was a hangman.

"I'm all done here. Left a few marks to ease your mind and a few more so you could grab me a small sack of those coffee beans. Leave them in my room later," he said. "The big sword I received earlier ain't for carving butter; it's for cleaving heads."

Gray Jim walked to his room to put on suitable attire for the day's work, where he'd earn proper coin for him, and for the condemned, nothing but the edge of a blade.

Runt - The Bent Plow

Maynard and Runt mucked the stables and washed dishes for Angus as he worked in the kitchen for two days. Angus taught the cook of The Greasy Pole how to make a couple new dishes so his food wouldn't taste like shit. On the first night, Doc dropped off two sets of clothes for Runt and a backpack with winter clothes for the rest of their journey and spoke to Angus quietly before disappearing into the crowd of the tavern. He saw Doc indulging in a lengthy conversation with the mercenaries Runt observed earlier. Later, Runt, Maynard, and Angus began packing away their gear to start down to Steelsburg.

"Here we are, lads. Please stand up," said Doc.

"What? Oh yeah, I forgot. Boys, stand up. He's made another bargain," Angus said, not looking at either of the boys.

Doc stood with the rough-looking sellsword from the other night. "Boys, I've spoken to this fine fellow here and made a deal. You'll assist him in whatever chores and duties he asks, and in turn, he'll get you safely to Steelsburg. This is Gunther Wilmot, captain of the Bent Plow Company."

"Runt and Maynard, you may call me Gunny. Welcome to the Bent Plow," said the man.

Maynard and Runt looked at Doc with disgust. Gunny stood there smiling. He was a little under six feet tall with broad shoulders, wearing boiled leather and light chain mail with leather straps holding it all together. A sword and knife were attached to his belt. A hand sickle was attached to his back, along with a shield. His hands were knotty and worn, and his beard was uncombed but short. He looked forty autumns old with slight gray in his brown beard.

"You there, Maynard, the doctor says you're his apprentice. Said you're fairly sound at healing. We could use a medic. I've got a few people who will need to be attended to as we travel to Steelsburg, and from what I heard, we may need even more of your services once we get there. And you, boy, will be my servant, getting my wine, cleaning my gear, sharpening my weapons, and taking care of my horse. And you, dwarf," said Gunny.

"I know, I know, get to the cook wagon, and it's dwarve, you stain, not dwarf. Bit rude to call anyone a dwarf," said Angus.

"So, it's like calling Steelsburg something like Shitsburg to you there, dwarve. I get it; it's a slur. Let's change that immediately. I don't want any trouble as we move to the city's border," said Gunny.

Angus looked at the man called Gunny. "We've always called it Shitsburg by the sea. It's what they do, shit coal from holes. Ain't that right, Runt?" asked Angus.

Grimwood and Steelsburg held a rivalry older than the Ruinthorn and Hawthorn families. Warring and arguing over trade, failed noble marriages, and other political intrigues throughout the years. Still, Runt nodded, unsure of the correct response. Angus looked at Gunny, spat at the ground, turned, and walked away. Angus was an oddity. Any man could count on two thumbs the number of dwarves who sided with Grimwood over the dwarven-controlled Steelsburg, and Angus was one of those dwarves.

"I'll give you some time to speak to the doctor, but we need to be off. We leave shortly," said Gunny.

Doc raised an eyebrow as Gunny walked away. He smiled, lit his pipe, and raised both his hands as if he were a prophet while looking at Runt and Maynard.

"Boys, I sold you to Gunny for the duration of your trip to Steelsburg; he's a good man. I know of him from past adventures, as it were." He talked with his teeth clenching at the pipe, taking it out to make a point here and there. "He's fair, objectively honest, and used to have three sons, so having you lot around for a bit may be a positive thing. Anyway, I'm bound for Affectus, the city of neighbors. I'll meet you in Olde Ridgewatch once your little time spent in Shitsburg is up and you find my squire." He blew out

130

purple smoke from his mouth. "I mean Steelsburg—don't want to piss off Gunny. Seems he favors the city and not so much Grimwood. Best keep your preferences to yourself, Angus." Doc smiled, reached into his jacket, and drew out a generous, flat-shaped, glass bottle. "This should help keep your temper down for the duration of the trip. It's what I would call medicine, bourbon as it were. Take care of it, and don't drink it all in one night." Doc looked at Runt and Maynard. "Learn as much as you can from the Bent Plow Company. They are a suitable group of mercenaries."

"Fine, whatever," said Maynard. "Wait, how are we going to find this squire? I don't know what he looks like, and we have no money." He and Runt were visibly pissed off at this change of plans.

"Details, details, details. Maynard, use your head. I taught you to think, so use your head. Find the man as big as a house in a city full of dwarves. Not hard to miss," said Doc. "I have faith I will see you again in the graces of Duncan the Squire." Doc clambered onto his newly bought horse and moved off down the road.

"How the Hades did he buy a horse?" said Runt.

"He does that often. It's either stolen or loaned or who even knows," said Maynard.

"Well, Doc's gone, the asshole. Guess we're part of a mercenary group now." Angus turned and walked toward campfires off in the distance, taking his gear with him. "Come on, boys, might as well get settled."

The camp consisted of tents, three fires, a grouping of horses, and accompanying wagons. Maynard looked at Runt in a bit of shock. They were both coming to terms with their new position as indentured servants.

Gunny walked up behind them as they made their way to the fires. "Relax, we're going to make you work to help pay for your meals and to keep you safe as we travel to Steelsburg. You signed on to the end of a nice caravan. We're protecting it from thieves and bandits. It's a few covered wagons and merchandise they're attempting to sell to the dwarves or whoever down the road. I know the doctor from the war. He fixed my arm and leg after the Battle of Faults Bridge," Gunny said, like a father talking to his son after he'd whipped him. "Traffic on the road's been busy. We've had to get out of the way for groups of soldiers. Luckily, the Holy Imperium's soldiers haven't taken any interest in the caravan. Might have something to do with the direction we're going and who hired us—a rich merchant from Counselor City."

"If I may ask, who are you all?"

"Fair question, Runt, isn't it? The Bent Plow are trained farmers and veterans from the Crimson Struggle. We couldn't find jobs after the war ended, so us ex-soldiers banded together and used our resources to guard caravans and other businesses when the contract suits us. Bo is my second in command, and she could whip about anyone I know in a one-on-one fight. The others, mind you, take care of unfriendlies just as well. Runt, when you're done eating, find my tent. It'll have my shield outside of it."

Each wagon stood walled and roofed except for one, open and piled high with bear, deer, wildcat, and other skins. Runt and Maynard made their way to the fire with the pot over it, and a rough-looking older woman stirred a ladle.

"You two young fellas be joining us?" She smiled. "Oh, oh, Gunny said there would be new blood. Well, grab a bowl. There is a bit more left. Mutton stew, onion, and barley—it's not much, but it will do," said the rough-looking woman.

They took their bowls and sat near a fire. A fiddler played nearby, and groups of people laughed, paying no mind to the newcomers. The guards wore a mishmash of mail and boiled leather, but nobody looked like a hedge knight. The horses looked made to plow or pull wagons, not lead a charge into battle. The merchants stood or sat around in their own clusters.

"When you boys are done, take my lantern, wash the bowls and pot out, and bring them to me." The older woman mussed up Maynard's hair. "Thanks, yous both." And she walked away to one of the wagons.

Maynard and Runt started to eat.

"He does this often, doesn't he?" said Runt.

"Yeah, it can be pretty annoying. Brings you back to earth right quick. He eventually makes it up to me by teaching a new hex or getting me drunk, but yeah, it sucks shit overall. I was alone often before we started this." Maynard took a bite of his stew and looked across at another fire. "What he taught me wasn't school lessons; it was more about how to survive when you're alone, how to control some of the things I can do, and how to get about not causing trouble as he does." He stood and stretched. "Whatever, at least it's not all men on the caravan."

Maynard nodded his head over to one of the fires where a girl their age danced with an older guard, her hair flowing around her blouse and her legs kicked up enough to see her ankles. She was dressed like a wayfarer, clapping her hands as the music continued.

"I am tired. Tired of walking, tired of my anger, just tired. I should check and see if our commander needs anything from me before I pass out," Runt said as he stood, looking away from the girl and into the night.

"First, we wash dishes. Come on, let's go." Maynard grunted and stood, his robes falling over his trousers. He grabbed the lantern and headed toward the stream.

Runt followed, walking quickly as the darkness consumed them away from the inn. Runt looked at the river and up to the sky as the stars within oblivion went on forever.

The Bastards - Not Dead Yet

Those dumb enough to break the laws in Steelsburg, if not executed on the spot by the city guard, get to wear handcrafted dwarven jewelry. The inescapable chains—prepared by dwarven techniques using fire, steam, steel, and runes—stayed on until the guilty parties were executed.

The only light in Steelsburg prison cells was a dimmed everlasting torch sitting across the hall. A smokeless light barely flicked through the bars on the cell door. The criminals, Duncan, Sorella, Stitch, and Cordial, sat in a cell, chained to a ring on a wall, each chain interconnected. There were only two copies of the key that could open the chains. The hangman carried one, and the other was held by the lead jailer. Escape for these four failures was hopeless.

They all sat, smelling of shit and despair, waiting for one of the key holders to set them free through death.

"What were we thinking, attempting to rob a dwarven bank in the biggest dwarven city this side of the ocean? Gods, we're stupid," Sorella said, blood dripping from her wrists as she twisted and turned.

"Give it up. They constrict the more you try to get out. Their smiths make them this way—no escape except by noose, blade, or rock" said Duncan.

"This is the last time I let any of you get me drunk in a city full of people that hate my very existence. I can still taste the clear vile in my throat, and we've been here for days." Sorella shifted to loosen up her muscles. "This is pretty bad. I don't think we can all make it out of here," she said into the graying darkness toward Duncan.

"We'll figure it out," said Duncan with a slight bit of confidence.

Sorella wore a tunic barely covering her body, like the rest of the prisoners. Cordial stretched out and used his hand to lift the bottom of her tunic a bit more. She struggled and kicked at him but missed.

"If we get out of here, I swear, Cordial, I will bleed you for looking at me," Sorella said.

"Relax, lovely, just wanted a peek before I die," said Cordial. He was all cheekbones, brooding eyes. Ladies noticed when he looked at them with his half smile. Cordial had a knack for mixing poisons and other alchemy. Shadow and light fell on his face, showing his deep-brown eyes, which were filled with a mixture of danger and innocence. He breathed confidence and wealth, even if he were as dirt poor as his best friend, Stitch.

Stitch was the youngest one in the cell. His face was thinned, egg-shaped, with wrinkles around his eyes. He grew a barely visible beard, and his ears no longer stuck out in points, as he'd cut them off at the tip to look more human. Stitch was a freed elvish slave and consistently ran into trouble. But, free or not, he never forgot the time before Sorella bought his freedom. She had taught him to be more than merely a slave laborer. Before the dwarven cell and darkness, Stitch had typically carried a pair of keen stiletto blades, which kept him in trouble even if his freedom papers were in order. Normally he dressed as a mercenary in boiled leather and belts, bearing a healed cut from cheek to cheek, giving him his name. After Sorella bought his freedom, she realized his previous master had taken a knife to his face one night, slicing the edges of his mouth open further. Stitch said his master couldn't take the slight grin he wore even as he was whipped into submission. Stitch had sewn up the wound himself, leaving a scar for the world to see—smiling or not. Cordial and Stitch were best friends, dressing like a shadowy sneak thief and a foppish half pirate.

"We aren't going to die. Well, some of us won't." Duncan looked around at the others who were chained up down the wall. "When I get a chance, let me talk, and we'll all be drinking dwarven vodka and pale beer before sundown," he said.

Wyatt Duncan sat against the wall. His dirty-blond hair barely touched his shoulders. His arms, back, and chest bore scars, telling stories about his life nobody cared to know about anymore. His face was thick and squared, aged from battle and weather. Duncan was the bastard son to nobody, always the squire, never the knight. The rumor was every time he was up to finally becoming a knight, the noble he squired died mysteriously. He failed to protect his knight in battle three times, resulting in their death at each instance. An honorable squire would fall with his knight and mentor.

Cordial and Stitch were known in the darker circles of several cities, and Duncan had known Sorella since he'd first bloodied a knife a lifetime ago with her and her sister. It had been a stupid idea to take the bank, especially in Steelsburg, the above ground capital of the dwarven clans. Still, an old friend provided him with reliable information, and they'd all been desperate for funds. It would have worked if the last member of the band hadn't died during the break-in. He thought about what had gone wrong.

The flameless light called owl lamps by commoners flickered, and the steel door down the hall creaked open. They smelled of shit and piss, as the drain in the middle of the cell had become clogged after several days packed together. The bells along the city's storied bridges started to ring. The noise echoed down into the cells. The criminals all looked up toward the cell door. It sounded like a church holiday started with all the bells ringing.

The door opened, and the light flickered. "Well, everyone, time to die!" a bearded face said. A dwarve stood in full armor with two short swords in his hands; several others were behind him, but the prisoners couldn't see them, squinting from the torchlight reflecting off mirrors two of the dwarves carried. The door and chains should have made more noise, but the dwarves developed them to be weighty; they only made noise when an attempted escape occurred. The guards stood about five feet high but were by no means diminutive. On the contrary, they looked mean and dangerous.

The dwarves of Steelsburg and the Commonwealth of Erie were thickly set and well-muscled. Other dwarves, depending on the area, could be a bit shorter and thinner. Most male dwarves wore their hair longer and beards cut in various shapes, but this was not true for all male dwarves. Recently, in the streets of Steelsburg, gangs of clanless dwarves roamed around in short haircuts and cleanly shaven, rebelling against their betters. Female dwarves varied from a petite status to nearer to a warrior status of mass and muscle. The dwarven people were as varied in shape, color, and size as orcs, elves, humans, and even goblins.

The chain pulled, and they stood as best they could in a stooped position, as dwarven cells meant dwarven heights. They stumbled toward the door, all wearing long tunics and nothing else, all cold, bitter, broken, and smelling of the dregs of a garbage heap in a busy city.

They moved in a bent walk through the keep, into a courtyard, and out into the streets of Steelsburg, the bells ever tolling as they moved.

Duncan's eyes adjusted and saw smoke looming from stone stacks in the distance. The smoke was the byproduct of numerous metals smelted into household items or instruments of war. The parade of criminals walked on paved streets shaped by the dwarven technique of frozen liquid stone. Duncan had walked on streets similar in Hudson City, but they were not as plentiful as they were in Steelsburg. The city was a marvel with nearly no rival. Duncan pushed on. The smell of the three rivers, the coal, and the steel mills mingled through the air.

They walked toward the Orcfeast River, the streets crowded with locals jeering, spitting, and screaming. Executions in the dwarven capital were unusual due to the low crime rate in the city. The atmosphere felt as if the city were on holiday.

They walked one by one inline, with Cordial, Stitch, Sorella, and Duncan at the tail. They were special. It was not very often a group attempted to rob the largest above ground bank in the city. Coal, moldy vegetables, and manure pelted them as they walked. Most of the vegetables were carrots or radishes because the potato was sacred to the dwarves.

After stooping for so long in the short cells, each step was a painful stumble. The guards wore full plate and chainmail, carrying a formidable shield and sword. They surrounded the chained-up criminals to make sure nobody escaped before execution.

Stitch looked ahead and saw the freshly built stocks and a headsman's stone. "We are so doomed. Sorry, guys, we should have planned it better. We should have," he said.

"Shut up, Stitch. I told you—I'll handle this!" Duncan argued.

"Duncan, this is getting pretty serious here. If you're getting us out of this, do it now, not later." Sorella sneered at Duncan. She was not one to lose her shit, and she was losing her shit. "No damned prophecy can get us out of here; these shackles don't come off our wrists until we die!"

The bells stopped along with the chained criminals. The convicts consisted of two dwarves, eight humans, and two elves: Stitch and Sorella. Near the water, they stood at the base of a half coliseum, which was used for plays or small concerts. A crowd of onlookers peered down at the prisoners. Stitch noticed below their feet lay a drain. The stocks and stone sat up against the river with a stone seating area around it. On the other side of the river, the dwarven towers and buildings stood with people looking out at the scene, watching the show.

Cordial said, "The drain is for the overflow of the river, so any blood falling below into the earth mingles with coal and whatnot. 'Tis sacred, I hear."

"Makes sense," said Stitch. He looked around in amazement. They had studied the bank and several escape routes before the robbery but had failed to study the city's jails or execution areas. They shivered due to their lack of clothes on the autumn day.

The guilty stood, somber and sober, as the crowd filled in a ring formation in the short-stepped theater. They were loud and abusive toward the prisoners. The throng drank hard, and it showed. At the top of the theater was a cask of ale and brown bottles of the dwarven liquor vodka, put to heavy use throughout the crowd. There were beards in a multitude of shapes and sizes as the crowd cheered and chewed on legs of turkey, throwing the remains toward the guilty. Horns, steins, and copper cups of ale sloshed about, continually filled by half-dressed servers who paid no attention to the drunks as they fondled and fiddled them while they poured. Several servers partook in festivities while others attempted to do their job.

"This was to be a hanging and beheading, not an orgy," said Stitch. "Wish I was out there in the crowd."

"I'd like them to use my blood in the ale they make. Gods, I'll miss their red ale here," Cordial said and laughed a little.

At the base of the seating area sat Cormac Clearstone, head of the Clearstone family for nearly three hundred years and one of the oldest dwarves above land. He wore a black-and-purple tunic of silk—his house colors. A necklace made of tightly woven chain lay beneath his white beard, bejeweled with two stones. An obsidian stone, the symbol of Riverstone Citadel, and a large clear stone, the family namesake connected to it. The Clearstone family emblem adorned a black patch with a purple sword crossed with pickaxes on the tunic's shoulder. The symbol was well known across Vineland, as it was on all dwarven marks of gold, silver, and copper in circulation. He sat regal but deflated for a dwarve his age, using a large horn for hearing and consistently chomping at his gums, making his large beard wobble.

His honor guard, adorned in the same colors but wearing full plate and mail, stood at his side, each with a sword and pickaxe in hand. First among Cormac Clearstone's honor guards was Gwawl Blitzsteel, renowned for his ability to break shield walls in pitched battles. The pickaxe held by the honor guard was not used in mines but more like a war hammer suited nicely with a short sword. The guards at the front of the line brought two dwarven criminals to a stone twice the height of a human and longer than a horse. The other humans were led to the stocks, where their heads fit into nooses. Stitch, Duncan, Sorella, and Cordial were led to a rectangular stone with an indentation and a bleed hole.

"Anytime now, Duncan. This is starting to get pretty serious here," said Sorella.

"We'll get there in a moment," Duncan said.

Other members of dwarven noble families sat, including Rodric Blitzsteel, head of the Blitzsteel clan, his family renowned for its swordsmiths, maker of several legendary named swords, including one owned by Lord Protector of the East Thomas Casting of the Longview. Rodric's son Gruff stood beside him, clad in the family armor—black on black—his tunic with the family seal of a black anvil with three yellow stars over it surrounded in white. Noticeably absent was Rodric's beloved daughter, Ella.

On Cormac Clearstone's left side sat his son, Heddwyn, heir to the

Clearstone family, and daughter, Morrin Clearstone. Gwawl Blitzsteel, a personal bodyguard to Cormac and his family, stood behind the three. He was sworn by blood and oath to protect them to his death. Other families in the presence of the Clearstones included a member of the Arrowstone family, two members of the Wateraxe family, and members of the Fellwater family. Rodric Blitzsteel sat on the right side of Cormac Clearstone with a member of the Bitterspear family, Smeltmaul family, and Copperswivel family.

By dwarven rights passing the death sentence on humans, a jury of the city families must be present at the sentencing and execution. The dwarves enjoyed an execution, almost more so than a wedding.

The executioner, a human, stood dressed in black leather pants, a large belt, and no shirt; he carried a substantial two-handed sword strapped to his back. The man wore his black hair pulled back, and his face, poorly shaven, looked out of place in all of the beards and braids the older generation of dwarves wore. He was a pale-skinned, large piece of meat, well-worn and muscled. His eyes showed an ability to cause harm and death without remorse. When he turned his head, it showed hair pulled back and tied, dark with gray tips.

"They say he doesn't use a hood like other hangmen because he is dead inside. Don't look at his eyes or he'll kill you with them," said Stitch.

"Seriously, will you shut your hole? I don't want the last thing I remember hearing to be you braying silly myths to me," Cordial said.

Stitch snickered a little and frowned.

Two dwarven jailers with short spears did most of the hangman's work, ensuring everyone stood in place. Finally, the executioner checked the nooses, moving the knot to stay in the proper position before the drop. Stitch noticed he did his duty well; the convicted would receive a hasty drop and, thus, a quick death.

The jovial crowd gasped at the sight of death before them and cheered for more. The jeers and shouts became yells of death, threats, and other gruesome, offensive speech toward the convicted. The guards at the bottom turned their backs from their captives and formed a shield wall; their blades remained sheathed.

"If I wasn't going to die shortly, I would make a joke about how I thought this city was the cradle of civilization," Cordial said.

"Now who's talking shit to who?" Stitch laughed.

Cormac of Clearstone raised a horn to his ear and, upon hearing the crowd, stood from his seat, turned, placed another horn to his mouth, and blew into it, releasing a deep and hearty bellow that sounded like a mule being raped by a mountain lion.

The crowd quieted. Cormac Clearstone blew into the horn again and spoke: "My fellow comrades, I beseech you to be quiet as we read out the death sentences for two of the stone's beloved children. Fredrick Bitterspear and Lawrence Bitterspear have been sentenced to death for conspiracy to murder a member of the Clearstone family and have been found guilty by tortured confession. Do you have anything to say for yourselves or to your family?"

The two men were stripped naked and chained to a circular rock at the shore's top. The hangman, Gray Jim, walked over to them, ready to do his duty.

One spat toward Cormac. The other shook his head.

"As brothers of the stone, if you can lift the stone off the ground or stop it before it rolls into the river, you are free of your burden of guilt. If not, to the stone, and may the river wash away your family shame," Cormac Clearstone finished.

"What are they doing, Cordial? This is barbaric," said Stitch.

"This is the dwarven way, right, Duncan?" said Sorella.

They talked in hushed tones as the head of the dwarves, Cormac Clearstone, spoke.

"Ah, it is. Even sentenced to death, the dwarves provide a way out to honor for your family. It's a proper sentence for those two. They came into a Clearstone home, murdered a child and wife due to a dispute between the Bitterspear and the Clearstone families. They are both lucky to be treated this way by the Clearstone clan. It's a privilege," said Duncan.

"Honor looks brutal," moaned Stitch.

"I would have given them less and tortured them more, but Cormac has recently been attempting to end any bad blood between the two families.

He's getting push back from the Blitzsteel family, who appear to back the Bitterspear family."

"Right, but umm, how are we going to get out of this again?" Cordial said, a look of worry in his eyes.

"We may not, but I am going to try my damnedest to do so," Duncan said. "Wait until we're up."

Each of the convicted dwarves lay chained across a large boulder. Both boulders stood at the top of a small hill with the river running below. The shoreline before the water was mud and broken stone, nothing like the sandy ocean shores. There was little to no sand or sun in Steelsburg, and the river water ran dark gray to green at times with spells of black from the soot. A chained net held the two stones across beams, allowing each stone to be released separately down the hill into the river. The two members of the Bitterspear family hung on their stones, faces showing anger and anguish. Two other stones stood empty, waiting for future use.

"Do the families have any objections?"

None of the Bitterspear family showed any remorse for their convicted family members, only strict, unreadable faces.

"So says the family, so ends their lives—to the stone!"

"To the stone!" yelled the crowd.

Gray Jim pulled on the mechanism, and the chain nets released. The convicts screamed for a moment, flipped up and over, and smashed immediately into the ground. The boulders continued to roll down the hill, showing bits of smashed dwarve and red smears to all as they rolled into the water. A cheer of jubilation carried up throughout the crowd from all except for those of the Bitterspear and Blitzsteel families. A few clapped politely, showing their favor, but with no real emotion.

"Oh shit," said Cordial, whose face turned green.

"Yeah, I'd rather lose my head," said Stitch.

"It doesn't matter either way. You're still dead at the end," Sorella said quietly. Even her unshakable, emotionless face showed anxiety.

"Next! You six are convicted in Steelsburg city, a free dwarven city," said Cormac Clearstone, his voice not as strong as before.

"The greatest dwarven city," yelled Rodric Blitzsteel.

"The greatest dwarven city, yes, yes, the greatest. Before falling to your death at the gallows, we must have a human representative to witness and hear out the convictions," said Cormac Clearstone.

"I shall hear them out!" shouted Gray Jim, the executioner.

The crowd laughed and cheered at the man.

"Mr. Gray Jim, these six felons were found guilty of the following crimes, tried by a dwarven court, and sentenced to death by the gallows for murder, slander of the high king, public buggery with a horse and mule, and cheating at games of chance in a dwarven brothel and inn. Do you feel they have been unjustly found guilty?" said Cormac. He was finding his voice again, even in his old age.

"No, sir!" said Gray Jim.

"Hang the mongrels," said Cormac as he performed a dramatic bow to the audience.

No sooner did Cormac finish his sentence than Gray Jim pulled the lever, and out dropped the floor for all six convicts with no last words, shouts of anger, or prayers. Their feet shot down, kicked, and dangled, and the smell of shit and piss soon followed.

Guards led Cordial, Stitch, Sorella, and Duncan to the stone used for beheading.

"Oh shit, oh shit, oh shit, Sorella, Sorella," Stitch whined.

"Stitch, keep your cool, kid. It's not over," said Sorella, but even she was not sure what to think anymore.

Cordial, the cockiest of the group, looked sick and pale.

"Mr. Gray Jim, these humans were tried by a dwarven court, found guilty, and sentenced to death by beheading. They are guilty of the high crime of attempted robbery of a dwarven bank, public drunkenness, and possessing dwarven mechanical weapons. Do you feel they have been unjustly found guilty?" said Cormac.

"I would speak to my king!" said Duncan. His voice was loud, and he was sure of himself. It echoed over the crowd and brought the orgy of yelling to a halt.

"Your king, you say? You have no rights here, human. You shall not speak. You have been found guilty," Heddwyn Clearstone said, speaking for his father.

Cormac Clearstone looked at his son, who shifted in his seat.

"I have my dwarven rights to choose my death!" bellowed Duncan, and at this, the crowd became uncontrollable, throwing feces and beer steins and, in some cases, spears and axes toward the four remaining convicts. The guards drew their swords and beat in unison onto their shields, making a thunderous noise.

"Mr. Gray Jim, do you feel they have been unjustly found guilty?" Cormac said weakly.

Gray Jim looked at the crowd, sensed violence, and saw Duncan standing proud, letting the refuse hit him. "Your Grace, at this time, I would ask for one moment to hear this man's plea, for what is one minute to a dwarve who lives an infinitely long life such as yourself?" Gray Jim said, looking oddly at Duncan as if he knew him.

"Very well, sir. Prove your dwarven ancestry and be quick about it," said Heddwyn Clearstone.

"I am Wyatt Duncan, also known as Duncan the Squire. I fought in the first campaign in the Crimson Struggle one hundred years ago and many since, fighting on several sides throughout. I am the son of a human mother who has long since passed. My father was Bearfric the Righteous Hand of the Gloomspire, who served in the Broken Flowers mercenary company in the southern Blightbriar Wilds. By this, I claim my right to die as my dwarven brothers do, and if I survive, I beg for the lives of my three comrades as a token of my king's generosity and kindness."

The crowd's response was a mix of questions and shouts of justice. Cormac Clearstone looked at the group. His daughter, Morrin, whispered into his better ear through the noise, stepped back, and respectfully bowed to Cormac.

"I say, Cormac, let us have some sport. I shall see if the man is a far-off bastard of my bloodline!" Rodric Blitzsteel said, attempting to weaken the leader and head of the Clearstone family.

The sitting jury nodded in agreement to Rodric, some out of drunkenness and others out of amusement at seeing another crushed by a giant boulder. The severely drunk crowd sensed another entertaining execution and cheered at the suggestion. The mob ruled Steelsburg.

The old king looked around at his family and the crowd, knowing he had lost the power of the mob at this human's suggestion and, thus, his authority. He looked again at his son and his daughter and nodded. "Chain him to the stone, and let the stone take him," said Cormac. He sat, puckered his lips a bit, and wiped his brow, disturbed by what should have been a simple execution. He grasped his chest slightly.

"All right, let's go," said Gray Jim, standing next to Duncan. He shoved Duncan toward the stone, using the back of his hangman's sword. "Face against or back against?"

"Does it matter? Shit, I'm strong, but shit. . .. Back against, I suppose."

"All right. Strip," Gray Jim said as he took the fetters off Duncan. This would be his moment to escape. He looked around, running his hands over his arms and legs to loosen them up as he stripped naked.

The crowd made lewd suggestions about his manhood, stating he didn't have a dwarven drop of blood in him. His body showed a menagerie of scars from endless duels, battles, and back-alley scraps. Others looked more purposeful, as if created through torture or self-inflicted.

The stone stood larger than him still, granite but darker and nearly round with only indention from the chains—not much to grab on to. He was chained with his face to the crowd uphill, the net holding the boulder behind it. It didn't feel like hope was anywhere near the stone he was strapped to now. Duncan took a deep breath and blew out, trying to calm his nerves and thoughts.

The crowd started chanting, "To the stone! To the stone! To the stone!" Their arms shook in the air to the beat of the chant.

"To the stone!" yelled Cormac.

Gray Jim pulled on the mechanism, and the chain net released. At the release of the net, Duncan managed to push off the ground with his legs to change the direction of the stone, shifting him as he rose off the soil. The speed and rotation of the stone picked up, and the rock hit a dent in the earth, giving Duncan a chance to shift his weight as he shoved and screamed, forcing his body in one direction. The stone's trajectory off, Duncan found he was now facing the river as the stone's weight fell onto his shoulders. His feet hit the bank and sank into the mud. Duncan groaned in agony as the stone settled onto his shoulders, and he bent down. The muscles in his back tore, and his arms gave out, pushing against the gravity of stone, the force of it wanting to roll. Duncan's will still unbroken, his feet sank into the muddy stone riverbank. He crouched, chest touching his thighs. He breathed in one last time as the final crush came. He slid into the mud, toward the rushing water of the river. The boulder looked as if it smothered him, but it slowed as Duncan disappeared into the muck near the water's edge.

The audience ceased to jeer and cheer as the stone stopped rolling, and for a moment, there was the sound of the water running past the rock.

"What, what, what has happened? Executioner, see why the stone has stopped. Verify the dead so we can take the other three heads," Cormac said in a huff.

"Yes, Your Honor," said Gray Jim. He slowly walked down the muddy bank, looking at the smears on the ground where the stone rolled and spun down the hill. Gray Jim hadn't witnessed a stone roll in such a manner, where the man chained to the stone had missed the crush of the boulder by the earth as it rolled. Executing a man with a rolling stone was not a typical affair. He came closer to the boulder at the base of the river. The other two stones, before long, had disappeared into the water.

Gray Jim sank his feet into the dirty water to get a more precise look. In the shadow of the large boulder, Duncan waited, bent, teeth clenched in an unspoken fight with the stone, chest-deep in the river and holding up the boulder.

"He lives. He is not dead as of yet!"

Hudson City - Half-Crooked Crown

P rince Damon perched sideways on the throne in Hudson City, the capital of the Holy Imperium, his crown half cocked to the side, impatient, bored, and horny. The throne room sat in the middle of Trinity Cloudreach's second floor, the tallest tower in Vineland. Dwarven-made columns surrounded the circular walls, stretching floor to ceiling. It was a wonder of poured stone, metal, and runes keeping the structure up, impressive from afar and awe-inspiring up close. The prince loved his tower and his position as ruler, controlling almost as much land as Great Brightland owned. It made him necessary, and he liked being important. He enjoyed this portion of his life, sitting and answering minor disputes between nobles and merchants until he became bored. A few common folks dared to come to his court with demands and requests, the worst of them begging for their "rights," which drove him to depression and anger. He wanted their *admiration*, not their *complaints*. Overall, he liked the idea of leading but hated actually having to do anything in his royal position.

Today he issued a death sentence to a minor aristocrat, a divorce including a wink and smile to the wife as she left, and other matters that he couldn't remember. The court scribe, Victoria Parish, recorded the prince's conversations, taking it all down with her long and sharp fingers and nimble quill. If he ever wanted to know what he'd said, he could ask her, but he didn't give a shit. The prince sat on his throne, which was made of redwood shipped from lands out west and decorated with two wildcats painted navy blue and with deep gold inlays. Dwarves had built his tower, his chair had been created by the savage elves of the west, and here he sat, thinking, *I am a man of the people,*

147

and, *Boy, do my balls ache.*

Behind him stood two personal guards, tied to him until death. One was Jasper Pinehard, the prince's best friend and captain of the Wildcats. The other was Austin Casting, newly sworn-in knight and cousin to General Thomas Casting. Austin lived in the shadow of his cousin Thomas, who was lord protector of the east and minister to the house of lords, which existed on paper but not in reality. Both Jasper and Austin wore half helms and light armor and carried a sword and rectangular shield bathed in the prince's colors of dark blue and gold. In addition, two guards stood at each exit with the same large shields to block an assassin's arrow or spear.

The marshal announced, "Murrow Edward, the editor of *The Post Enquirer*, Your Grace."

Murrow Edward bowed and presented himself at the foot of the stairs. The prince looked down from his chair and yawned loudly. Those petitioning the crown prince were forced to speak in clean, short bursts so Prince Damon could hear from above while he sat. If performed incorrectly, it could cost a petitioner their home, a finger, an ear, or their life. Murrow bowed. He was a man of average size with thinning hair and stress lines around his eyes from overwork and lack of sleep. He did not wear a wig, which was popular among specific merchants and members of nobility. His fingers showed ink stains.

"Your Grace, I request recompense for last week's Sunday paper from *The Post Enquirer*. Several thugs from the *Hudson City Journal* harassed my reporters outside our office. There was blood and nearly a riot. Please know, I request this from the dastardly *Hudson City Journal*, not from the crown. I beseech you directly because, Your Grace, the local sheriff did nothing to stop the desecration of our newspapers," Murrow spoke loudly and quickly, as he knew the prince was prone to boredom and could supply unfair justice at times.

The prince looked down, held up his hand, his palm toward the man, sucked in, closed his eyes, and waited. Then he smiled. He sniffed hard and checked his nose. Did Murrow just see him sniff wizard salt off his hand? He looked down at the floor.

The prince's eyes opened. "I call my own shots here, for I am the prince. I've heard of your paper; it's lively and full of gracious tales of the city and myself. You said you brought this incident up to the sheriff, and he did nothing, so you went around them and came to me. Takes guts, I would say, especially because you are the last to call for my charitable deeds on a long and trying day." He smiled and looked around at the court. "But this *Hudson City Journal*, I haven't heard of, unless . . . does it have a writer named Franklin or some such working for this rag?" the prince asked, using his hand to indicate Murrow was allowed to speak.

"Um, Your Grace, I believe it does. *Hudson City Journal* is a new paper dealing in fabrications. These lies about taxes, rumors about the nobles—they write like children," said Murrow. He pushed down his mustache with his hand, his body nearly shaking.

"So, you're telling me that this newspaper is disrespecting me, the crown, this very city!" He stood. "Stop, just stop, I say. I pronounce, *pronounce* this paper as fake. Yes, that is it—*fake news*, null and void and no longer allowed to print!" Prince Damon demanded this from the air inside Trinity Cloudreach.

"Thank you, Your Grace, you are too kind," said Murrow. The man backed away.

"See the registrar at the end of the hall. I'll now make your paper, the people's paper, *my* paper," the prince commanded.

Prince Damon shifted and scratched his trousers while looking at Victoria Parish. His head turned away when she looked at him. The woman's beauty and coldness enticed him, but she eluded his advances, making him frustrated and angry.

The prince thought for a moment, and it was an outstanding thought. It wasn't the first time he'd considered this, and he may have already enacted it. It wasn't even his original idea, but it sounded good now, and he was in charge. The royal treasury was empty. Money was needed to pay soldiers and levee back pay from years of war and keep several standing armies, as Prince Damon wished to crush any of the remaining independent city-states not yielding to the Holy Imperium.

He stood, having dismissed Murrow. "I propose an act of justice, an act for prince and country, an act to aid in helping our veterans, the soldiers keeping us safe in our beds and homes, the warriors who keep the savages at bay and the goblins and orcs away from our homes and keeps. There has been a rumor of goblin and orc hordes laying waste to homes and strongholds in the forests of Hudson. It's awful what they are doing. Even in Grimwood, there are riots in the streets and talk of rebellion in Olde Ridgewatch, and we must act. We have the soldiers, but we need . . . we need true patriots to the crown, oath keepers, proud men, and boys to protect us. To pay for these forces, I propose a Patriot Stamp Act. A stamp must accompany all paper goods used throughout the Holy Imperium. We will have officials to aid in the creation of these stamps for a small price. The price of safety for the prince and Vineland, for are we not all patriots to country and crown?" he said to everyone in attendance. Prince Damon heard a roar from the crowd below. The rest in attendance remarked as murmured agreement at best with a shaking of heads and a pattering of palms.

The prince looked back to his stooges as Victoria wrote out every word that had been muttered, and servants waited on him at his command. "Make this happen, and make this happen now," he spoke with a whiny authority. He stood, hands above his head, and the people in attendance began clapping and cheering. It was a modest crowd and a muted response. Still, Prince Damon heard a roar and saw thousands of his subjects applauding him, yelling his name, and crying tears of love for him and only him. He was brilliant, he thought.

The room was half empty.

After moments, he said, "Bring out the fool!" The day felt over. His jester juggled a live kitten, two knives, and a bottle of half-drunk wine at the base of the stairs to the enjoyment of those remaining at court. The prince let most of the court leave, and he noted the ones leaving first; others remained, and he noted those as well. He felt he was a man of the people.

"I think I am bored of all of this. Aren't you?" he said, looking in the direction of Victoria. He was talking to himself, but it was a matter of court record because he was on the throne. "I think a party is in order, a massive party with half-naked women and a slave orgy and masks and fireworks.

Hmm." He put his hands together and sat up. "Yes, that's it! A massive party here in the tower. I need a good time, and so does this town. The war is over, and we have a new land to celebrate. It will be *huge*, massive, the best ever. The papers love a grand party. They will love this. Victoria, remind me to get the Master of the Ceremonies after this sitting. We have planning to do."

He stood, whipped his shoulders around, adjusted himself, looked around and down at those still in attendance, and they bowed.

"Henceforth we are planning a party. The crowds will be huge; everyone will come, or at least the important people will come. Yes, all is well here in the Holy Imperium, for I am the prince, the one and only. Let us celebrate the end of hostilities, my victory at the Battle of the Reaping!"

The people continued to bow and remained silent, Victoria scribbled, and the hall was quiet.

Murrow Edward walked in the shadow of Trinity Cloudreach after dismissal from court, shaking his head. Two staff writers followed him. They started asking him questions.

"What did he say, what news, did he compensate us or provide us with guards?" said one of the writers.

"No, no, he said the *Hudson City Journal* was an illegal paper, that it was no longer able to print. As I left, a clerk provided me this scroll with the court and prince's stamps on it. It reads the paper is illegal now, but it also says our paper is now owned by Prince Damon," Murrow sputtered.

"What? Let me see." The second writer reviewed the scroll aloud. "It states anyone writing for the *Hudson Journal* is automatically guilty of libel, slander, defamation, and buggery and will be immediately thrown in jail. Well, shit, and henceforth *The Post Enquirer* will be the crown's paper from this day forward."

"What does that mean? Also, who writes henceforth and this day forward? I thought the prince was an educated man," said the other staff writer.

"It means Prince Damon has censored an entire paper, and we're bound to the crown prince for good or ill. At least we are on the right side of the stamp business. This could put a paper out of publishing. If you don't have a stamp, it's illegal." Murrow Edward wiped his prominent forehead, fixed his faltering mustache, and walked on.

"Come now, both of you. We've work to do. If we are going to be the crown's paper, we will do so with gusto. It's time to end the *Hudson City Journal* and any other paper getting in our way," said Murrow.

Hudson City breathed out merchants and tradespeople like cattle moving slowly across one side of the city to the next; the city guards walked in pairs through alleys and streets of mud and muck. The streets consisted of cobblestone or poured dwarven stone acting as veins, pouring people into shops and stores. Each burrow of Hudson City was under the control of a local sheriff. The city guards, called Copperheads, reported to a local sheriff. The sheriffs reported to the head of the guards, Sir Brock Rustblade.

The towers cast shade like giants over the private mansions and businesses of the city. The city constantly grew and changed—a disorganized mess of commerce and construction. There were no walls to hold back invaders. Instead, there were towers in strategic points, making it a headache for any force invading land or water. The sewers were a disaster, and slaves used dwarven tunnels to bring food and supplies into the city's heart during poor weather or the occasional riots. Certain sections were unsafe and under the control of local street gangs, which fought other gangs block by block to see who could extort the local merchants and shop owners.

"Conway, get your brother. He's part of the city guard. See if he can round up a few Copperheads or a drunken sheriff, and I'll hire a few sailors from the port. Meet me in my office in about two hours. We'll take our paperwork to the *Hudson City Journal*, boot them out of their offices, and with any luck, we'll have two papers by the end of the night," Murrow said.

After two hours and a glass of spiced rum, Murrow, Conway, and the other writer, Winston, walked up to the *Hudson City Journal* offices. With the help of a handful of mouth-breathing sailors and Copperheads, they tossed out writers, stock boys, and a clerk from their offices. The *Hudson City Journal* editor fought a sailor and tossed them out into the mud.

A crowd of onlookers heckled him, and a bottle of ink was warmed up and poured over his unconscious head. However, Murrow didn't capture Olivia Franklin, of the *Hudson City Journal* and the paper's mastermind. During the initial start of the fight, Olivia ducked out the back after blinding everyone using her quill. Murrow was appalled by their blatant use of outlawed magic. It would've been nice to send them shackled to the Prince's Court, but Murrow won either way.

After the paper's purge, Murrow cracked open a cask of wine for his colleagues and henchmen. The toast became a proper sloppy drunk with prostitutes called in and toasts given. They made their way from the new office to their old office and finished a twenty-year-old whiskey bottle from upper Great Brightland.

The next afternoon, a hungover Murrow walked back to check out the printing press he'd acquired in the bowels of the *Hudson City Journal* offices. He walked in, eyes deep and bloodshot, painfully aware he should never drink again. Murrow looked about; there was paper everywhere and a midget—not a dwarve, but a real midget—asleep on the floor, naked, ink poured over his body. The place was a mess, smelling of booze, vomit, sex, and animals.

The printing press was supposed to be in the basement, but it was gone. The only remaining items were a few scuff marks and one leaded letter from the press lying on the ground. It was the letter Z, one of the most unused letters in the alphabet.

"Now what?" Murrow said to himself. He ran his fingers through his hair, an action he took while under a deadline. "I should get a drink and start writing that the *Hudson City Journal* was robbed."

In another part of the city, inside Prince Damon's chambers, Austin Casting stood against the wall, silent and watching. As a member of Prince Damon's guard, he remained quiet, sober, and watchful during his shifts guarding Prince Damon. Austin Casting had given up his private life, religion, and family to serve as the royal bloodline's shield. Along with the other guards, he received one weekend off a month in revolving shifts. He was only allowed to go to certain city corners to avoid the lower masses' corruption. The Wildcats trained, slept, and took notes on Prince Damon's upcoming appointments and events when not guarding the prince. Lately, due partly to Austin's prowess in one of the last tournaments he'd entered, his assignments had improved. His last name helped as well. He was the cousin to the second most powerful man in the Holy Imperium, Thomas Casting of Longview.

This morning, the prince was getting drunk on bubbly wine and eating pheasant eggs and fruits from the south while he talked and laughed with a minor baron's now-ex-wife. The baron was off on campaign down in the south; the baron's ex-wife had brought the wine and fruit to celebrate her ex-husband's new commission fighting the elves down in the marshlands.

Along with Jasper Pinehard, Austin checked the room thoroughly, leaving Prince Damon and the baron's ex-wife to dine on breakfast.

Alysha - Fresh Stone, Old Wood

"See the woodpile out there? Grab an axe and get splittin'. Once you're done, get it stacked and covered against the wind there," said Hob.

It was near winter, and Alysha knew the wood wasn't suitable for an indoor fire, at least not for a few months. It needed to dry and age so it wouldn't cause a chimney fire. She nodded and dressed in warmer clothes for a day of demanding work. She walked toward the woodpile and looked at the axe, picking it up. It had a dulled, light blade not suitable for this work. She walked around the yard and found a large, flat piece of wood; rolled it near the pile of logs; with a huff, she dropped it flat and placed a log on top of it. She picked up the axe and walked it back inside, where Hob and Bob worked.

"This is shit. Where are the rest of your tools?"

Hob didn't say anything. Bob pointed to the corner near the back door. She walked over and found a mess of rakes, hoes, and other farm tools; near the bottom of the pile, she found a maul. It was made of metal, with a weighted head like an axe—but meaner and heavier. She picked it up and walked out the door.

That had been her first test. Hob looked at Bob and nodded.

Alysha set to work, cleaving the logs in two and then again into quarters, letting the weight of the maul do part of the work. With every swing, she thought of Jared Blackheart's face.

Alysha's first days working at Hob and Bob's smithy became a mixture of worry and stress. At night, she thought of death, lightning, and the thunder of war. She was of noble blood but was fearful of telling anyone. Maybe it was how the Holy Imperium soldiers had decimated her homestead and neighbors. It felt as if her family was targeted, but she didn't know. She wished death to Jared Blackheart and anyone affiliated with him. Everything she did, every movement and thought, was to make herself strong enough to kill Jared Blackheart. She breathed with one goal—his death—and the fire consumed her. If she swept up a mess inside the smithy and split wood, it was to gain strength. She worked to survive long enough to find a way to kill that bear of a man, who took orders from Prince Damon.

Although Hob and Bob worked for the First Army of the Holy Imperium stationed in and around Counselor City, she didn't hold any hate in her heart for them. If they got in the way, she *would* kill them, but they were a means to an end for now. Their contract was up with the First Army, and they continued to work for the army as freemen. They were known around the area as fair smiths, working on military orders and if a farmer needed assistance, they helped as well. Early on, she saw a destitute farmer asking about harness repair. Both smiths nodded and performed the work, sending the farmer on his way, free of charge. Hob said it was a form of free advertising and would bring in more work. Several smiths worked in the city, but most folks knew Bob and Hob were the next best smiths if they couldn't find a dwarve to do the work.

After days of toil, it seemed like the men were glad to have her; they could trust her work.

After two weeks of drudgery, Hob and Bob showed her around to actual smith work, providing her small tasks at first. She picked up the labor quickly, which surprised both men. Alysha began understanding heating, bending, sharpening, and other forging techniques. She protected her ears with candle wax and cloth as she produced horseshoes, kitchen knives, and prepared and fixed armor. Her days were busy, but she occasionally wondered how her best friend, Helena, fared.

"Put on warmer clothes, Alysha. We are heading out for more wood. Need to prep for the winter a bit more," said Bob, who covered his shiny bald head with a knit hat. He twisted his long, grayed mustache. "Hob left a thicker cloak with your boots."

Bob and Hob kept a reasonable supply of firewood and coal for their work, but Hob was paranoid that the winter would worsen every year, so he wanted to collect another cart full of deadwood from the region. They'd dry it inside while they worked if they needed to use it. She looked on as she moved outside the city for the first time since being forced into servitude by the Holy Imperium. Eventually, they climbed a hill, and Alysha looked back at Counselor City. She saw the smithy, where she now slept and lived, an obedient captive.

Bob and Hob let her walk by the cart, almost daring her to run. Bob carried a hunting bow, but the thought lingered in Alysha's mind. She could run, but with winter clouds coming from the north, she would be dead in a day— maybe two. And for what? Her mother was gone. She considered her younger brother, most likely dead, and her older brother and father were stationed near the Atlantis Ocean, perhaps never to return. Her entire town had been burned to the ground, and the remaining inhabitants were forced to make Counselor City a military base for the First Army. She looked out away from the city.

"I know what you're thinking," said Hob. "Believe me, believe Bob: it's better what you got with us. You're as near free as you can get. There ain't nothing out there but death and grisly memories. We're teaching you a trade, giving you a purpose and a reason to continue moving forward. Going out there ain't going to get you anything but dead."

She heard Hob and wished what he said was untrue. She looked at the city and saw a large ditch dug and other fortifications newly built; makeshift houses dotted the area as well, used by either the army or workers. Spiked posts to stop a formal attack from a horse or an ambush from unknown forces covered the top of the ditch surrounding the city. Nobles in the army billeted in city houses, causing uneasiness among the townsfolk.

She turned and walked next to the cart. She wore knee-high boots over wool stockings, a wool dress, and an overcoat. She left her cloak hanging over the side of the cart. It was not snowing yet, but the air was right for it. A knit hat kept her head warm.

Hob had given her gloves as they'd started that morning, "A proper smith needs all of their fingers and needs to stay warm at all times. So here, don't be stupid with them. Gloves cost a fortune."

The city had cleared the surrounding area of dead wood for burning and cooking, and most trees had been removed to make fortifications and new log cabins. So, they ventured away from the city farther than any of the three should have this time of the year. Both Bob and Hob carried axes and belt knives. Even Alysha had been given two knives.

"For cooking," Bob had said as he'd sharpened a foot-and-half-long "cooking knife" beforehand.

They traveled with a horse and cart, pulling up to a crossroads.

"Well, we go right. Looks to be fine wood over there," said Hob as he scratched at his head and ran fingers through his hair.

The men argued over which heated steel better, wood or coal. Neither won the argument, but there was plenty of yelling. Alysha didn't say a word. She didn't know which side was better. It was better to sit and wait out their arguments. They passed a bottle of hard cider around to keep themselves warm.

Looking at the road, she realized she'd been here previously. She spoke up before even realizing it: "We go left, we could find ash and oak trees and a few maples as well. I know the area. I'm from around here." She pointed left. "We were all forced through this area. We should find a hill with an altar and, near it, a cluster of trees.

Bob and Hob looked at her.

"You think it's a good idea, Alysha?" said Hob. "If so, we won't stop you. I won't, at least. You'll find nothing but ghosts and pain, though." He looked at her and nodded to where she was pointing.

Bob was more direct. "You aren't a slave. You work for us and earn your keep. We do our best to provide for you. We never asked about your past, and you didn't say anything. If your home is where you're pointing, it ain't there, and nobody is left where your home used to be. You'll find a burned-out shell if you make it back. That's if you aren't robbed and killed on the road or eaten by wolves before you get there. Hob and I both heard there are highwaymen where Wolf Hills used to be, and the forest is full of wolves, and they ain't discriminating against anyone," he said.

"I know," Alysha said, trying to remain stoic. "Look, there's quality lumber this way. My home, where I grew up, it's gone. If you head this way, we'll see a hill, mostly tall grass and a wood near it. Should be able to clear further dead logs out of it." She brushed her hair back and wiped an eye, not wanting to show emotions in front of the two men.

Hob jumped down from the wagon. "Your turn to ride, Alysha. Hop on up. We'll head left for a bit to see what we can see," he said. "Come on now, lass."

She got up on the wagon.

"It's okay to talk to us. We ain't going to bite, and we ain't going to lay a hand on you nor let anyone hurt you. Hob and I guessed you were from one of the towns. The Red Army put to flame most small towns in the area, and Grimwood has done shit to stop them. We try not to think about it because it brings us business. A bit harder, though, when your apprentice is from one of the towns," Bob said. "If we can, after winter is over and it's safer, we'll head on back to where you're from. Don't think we'll find much, really, but we can. Not a good time to do it yet—it's going to snow soon, and it may not stop for months."

"Okay. Thanks, Bob. Means a lot," Alysha said.

"Sure, lass, sure. Now let's get wood before this wind picks up," said Bob.

They worked hard into the morning and through lunch, filling the wagon with as many dead and aged tree limbs and logs as they could manage. They used metal pry bars to move the larger logs and dead fall branches into their horse-drawn cart. Alysha saw a clearing in the woods and wandered over to it, passing several blue spruce pine trees that grew tightly together. She squeezed past them into an almost small-framed area and stepped into a clearing. The location was barren of tree growth. The trees surrounding the area looked wilted, as if they'd burned years ago. A large stone lay broken in two. Alysha paused and heard a noise, and her anxiety rose.

"Hob, you scared me." She grabbed at her chest. "Look what I found!" She moved aside, and Hob looked into the clearing.

"Bob, bring the pry bar here. I think Alysha found something."

Alysha walked toward the stone. Trees surrounded the clearing as if they guarded the area. As she neared the stone, she saw it held a crisp, dark-gray color with a matte finish. The inside was glossy black. The stone together was the size of a beer barrel but was now in two pieces.

She heard Hob and Bob speaking but didn't catch what they said.

"It's star stone. You found one of the most precious metals in all of Vineland. Vulcan's beard, it's from the sky. Grab that cloak of yours. We're taking this baby home with us," said Hob.

She looked at him. "What can we do with this stone? I mean, it's not metal. Is it even okay to take it if it's from the sky?"

"As long as you respect the material, it can be molded into whatever you wish. This could be special. Technically, you found it, so we're going to help you create something new. We'll pry this stone out of the ground."

They spent several hours dragging and pushing the cracked stone to the cart, removing wood to make room for it on the back. Finally, they covered it with the cloak and dried wood.

"Not a word of this to anyone, you hear me?" ordered Bob.

"You talking to me?" said Alysha. "You two are the only contact I have with the outside world!"

Bob smiled, moving his mustache up. "Yes, and no talking to Hob as well, and to myself. We're going to make magic with the star stone."

"I don't know what to say," she waited a moment. "Thank you," and she looked up and away, breathing in deeply. "Would either of you mind if I walked up that hill there to the altar?" asked Alysha.

"Sure, lass, but let's hurry back. I don't like these parts," said Hob.

Alysha hiked up the hill to the altar where the old woman had been struck by lightning. Upon reaching the top, she found a bare stone altar. The waist-high, weathered gray stone lay on the ground, solid and marked up from numerous uses. Burned grass circled the altar. It held carvings at the base which Alysha could not read. However, she made out the name Judith on one side and old etchings of lightning, wind, storm clouds, and flowers around it. On top of the altar lay the set of chains the old woman had worn before lightning had struck her. Alysha thought she'd find a skeleton, but the only remains were burned and broken shackles. She pushed them off the altar as if they didn't belong and extended a prayer to Judith. Alysha cut her hand, smeared it onto the stone, and looked to the sky. When she finished, she ran down toward Hob and Bob. She felt ten years younger for a fleeting moment; she smiled.

They made their way back to Counselor City. They carried on as if she hadn't gone up to the altar.

On the way back, Bob and Hob traded off what they knew about the burning of the towns and the Red Army. The conversation felt natural. They didn't steer away from the nastiness they'd taken part in during the Crimson Struggle years back.

Alysha's mother, who had not been of noble birth, had educated Alysha and her two brothers. Her father, Benedict, wanted his children to read, write, perform basic math, and work with their hands. She knew of the military and even a few tactics her father taught her on maps when at home several years ago. The stories Hob and Bob spoke of made sense. She realized an invading force now occupied Grimwood and its surrounding territories but did not control the city yet. The Holy Imperium took control of critical points, killed any resistance, and prepared for a siege of Grimwood by the Erie Sea. The oddness of all the events was that the city of Grimwood remained quiet; no news flowed from the city. Nobody had heard of the renowned knights of the Grimwood known as the Grim Vultures making their way toward Counselor City or other towns since before early autumn.

She looked toward Grimwood and saw the dark clouds rolling in, giant waves bringing cold snow to blanket both the castle city of Grimwood and surrounding areas. Once the snow lifted, the First Army of the Holy Imperium would roll up to Grimwood and lay siege, using stone and fire to bring the city under its yoke.

Runt - Medium Rare

"Full stop!" Bo, the lead rider, screamed as the caravan stumbled toward the bottom of a hill.

The wagons rattled and shook until they slowed on the road. After passing several travelers, the Bent Plow Company moved under heightened alert. Rumors spread of goblins near the waterways, unheard-of animals creeping out of the deep woods and mountains. Gunny, captain of the Bent Plow, became more uneasy after this bit of news. No more sentries at night falling asleep, no more drinking. Everyone stayed near the wagons as they moved during the day.

The group lost a young boy of three summers to a fever several days back, but the boy had been sick since the start of the trip, before Runt, Angus, and Maynard joined up. Maynard had tried what little knowledge he knew of healing but couldn't break his fever. Doc had exaggerated Maynard's healing abilities as he'd attempted to sell Maynard, Runt, and Angus into servitude to the Bent Plow Company. The boy's parents buried their child by the road, and thoughts and prayers had been murmured as the dirt spilled on top of his body. When everyone walked away, Runt stood and said a prayer to his gods so no one could hear. The family of traders muttered that they didn't trust Maynard to cure a toothache, and he did his best to keep a distance from them after the burial.

"Boys, we're getting closer to the dwarven passes of Steelsburg. If my directions are right, we should come up to the pass guarded by the Bitterspear family," Gunny said. "Once we see them, we should be safe, but I want to take precautions. The words from those we have seen have been worrying, even if

I think most of it is horseshit. Goblins, ugh, doubt it; they haven't been seen in over twenty winters in this part of the Commonwealth of Erieland. Still, though, walk with Angus and the ladies when they get water, grab as many large pieces as possible of driftwood for torches. I'll try to have our camp lit for most of the night moving forward. I want you both to make another two fires outside the circle of wagons to provide better sight." Runt nodded, acknowledging the work assigned to him.

Gunny did his best to speak to Runt and Maynard as equals and less like servants or slaves. Maynard disliked him and said as much to Angus and Runt when either would listen; he didn't mind being in the caravan, but the idea of being indebted to another person went against his personal beliefs. Maynard wanted to choose whom to follow, not be forced into it, which ran against the fact that he was an apprentice to a battlemage and a student at university.

Runt took the opportunity as a chance to learn about cleaning and repairing armor. He kept Gunny's personal effects and routine in place and looked at himself as a squire to the commander. He wished he could have done something for his father like his older brother had done before him.

"Understood, Gunny," said Runt.

"Gotcha, boss," Maynard said flippantly.

"Watch yourself, Maynard. Don't want to fall in and get wet in that pretty robe you wear," Gunny said, walking away, hands in the air. "You would freeze to death on a night like this, you worthless healer."

"Ass, what an ass," said Maynard under his breath.

"I know, but he's teaching us how to care for our equipment, keep our tents dry, and general defense using staves and swords. It's useful," said Runt.

"Whatever. He's a nobody. Come on, let's go grab this wood. I got another card game in a bit with Hilda and the others."

"Yeah, you do." Runt smirked.

"What? I do!" Maynard said.

"Sure, sure. I'm sure you'd like to show her your ace up your pants."

"Shut it, Runt, or I'll . . . I'll—"

"What? Turn me into a toad? Get off it, Maynard. You are so hard up on her. You can't even stand in her presence, your boner sticks out your robes."

"Does not!"

"Does too!" Runt tapped him in his crotch, making Maynard double over, and ran toward the river with a rope and cloak to pull driftwood.

"Dick!" Maynard squealed as he fell to his knees in embarrassment and pain.

Twilight faded as they passed Angus and others coming the opposite way with kettles full of water, a few carried fish, and crawdaddies in pots.

"Good eatin' tonight, boys, good eatin'! Don't be late. It's getting dark too quick for you all to be out by the river."

"Just following orders, Angus. See you in a few," said Runt as he jogged past.

"Yeah, orders. I'm going to kill Runt, the little shit!" Maynard said as he half ran after him.

Angus laughed a bit and walked back toward the covered wagons.

Two fires were lit inside the circle of wagons as the mercenaries and merchants prepped for a late dinner. The boys made it to the bank of the stream and started to pile wood on top of the old cloak.

"You're an ass, you know. Lucky I even let you hang out with me," Maynard said. "You know I got to brush against her the other day. When I was pulling a box down from the cart, she bent over. On purpose, I swear."

"Yeah, I bet that was nice," said Runt.

"Oh, it was. It was," said a voice.

Both boys jumped.

"Oh shit, you scared me!" said Maynard.

"Me too," Runt said.

"Chill, Runt! Maynard, Gunny said to hurry up with the driftwood," Hilda said.

"We're almost done." Runt dropped another pile of sticks onto a tattered old cloak. "Maynard, grab a side. I'll grab the other."

"I'll help," Hilda said. She looked at both boys.

Hilda grabbed the front, bending down slowly. Maynard and Runt stared down at her blouse, cut in the Bitterleak style, a white blouse over a woolen over shift, showing enough cleavage to entice any teenage boy.

"Ready?" she said. "One, two, three, lift." She lifted, but the other two didn't.

164

Hilda dropped the cloak. "Boys, if you're going to stare at my—"

"Runt, give me your . . . give me your boot knife now! Hilda, move toward us slowly. We don't want to spook and anger it," said Maynard.

"Anger what?" asked Hilda with a bit of frustration.

"I can't remember the scientific term, but it's—it's a—"

"It's a spider," Runt said.

Hilda put a hand to her mouth but didn't make a sound.

Runt fumbled the knife over to Maynard. Maynard took it in his left hand and cut his palm, pulling down toward his elbow enough to draw blood but not cut too deeply. He dropped the knife. Maynard took his other hand, smeared the blood on his fingers, licked it, and started speaking quietly to himself. He placed his bloodstained finger on his temple and moved it around in circles. Runt grabbed a stick from the pile.

"What the—what are you doing, Maynard? It's a spider. No need to cut yourself." She turned, and about fifteen feet up the bank was a spider the size of a wagon wheel crawling toward them with black eyes and a dark body, making a chattering sound like a pack of squirrels fighting. She instantly jumped over the woodpile, stumbled, and fell, knocking Runt over. The spider moved in a jittery fashion, its size and movement terrifying them all.

"Runt! Do you have your flint on you?" said Maynard.

"Yeah, shit, what are we going to do?" Runt said.

"Grab the knife. Strike a spark; try to start a fire."

Runt grabbed his boot knife, cleaned off the blood, bent over, and tried to spark a piece of wood. The spider crawled faster toward them. They walked away slowly, toward the river.

"Gunny said this was a stream. This isn't a stream. We can't swim for it," said Hilda.

"It's not working, Maynard. It's not working!" Runt yelled.

The spider drew closer, lifting its head, white slime dropping from its fanged face.

"Don't stop. I nearly have it," Maynard said. "Aim the sparks you're making toward the spider."

A significant spark popped as Runt scraped the knife against the stone, and

Maynard moved his bloody hand in a motion toward the spider, which now stood on the other end of the cloak full of wood. The spark traveled, growing as large as a stone, and hit the spider like a flaming fist. Hilda screamed, and Runt swung and threw the stick overhand at the spider in desperation. Maynard's small ball of fire and the stick stunned the spider, and it started to shuffle back and forth, its head now ablaze. The spider stumbled and fell, catching the cloak and the wood on fire. Runt grabbed a stick as the spider spun in agony and kicked a leg away. He took the burning bit, jabbed at it, and stuck it through the middle section of its body, burning his hand in the process.

"Let's go, Maynard. Hilda, let's go!" Runt grabbed Hilda by the hand and shoved Maynard, holding his cut hand, and they half jogged up the bank and back toward the camp. They were shaken and out of breath.

"Hilda don't say anything about what I did. Don't tell them about the spark," Maynard said. He looked sick, sweat all over his face.

"What? I didn't see—I didn't see anything, and you both managed to hurt that thing after it attacked me. I don't know what I saw," Hilda breathed out. "Good gods. Thank you both."

"What is going on?" asked Ralph, one of the sentries this evening. He looked at the group. "Gunny, I need you! Shit, everyone, stay alert. We got problems."

The camp moved from a slightly guarded atmosphere to the likes of a threatened animal.

"Come on, you three, let's get you within the wagon circle," said Ralph. He was a bigger man, grayed on his beard, rounded on his belly. He was an old farmhand who'd learned to use a bow and axes to defend himself and was now a company member. He wore wool, boiled leather, and a green knit cap to keep his hair out of his face.

As they made their way to the fire, Gunny came up to them. "You sots all right? Did you get in a fight over the girl?"

"Spider, a giant spider, sir, by the river. We hurt it, but I don't know if there're more," Runt panted.

Gunny looked at Maynard, pale and bleeding, and Runt and Hilda, out of breath. All three were fearful, and he decided. "I've seen and heard worse;

glad you're all right. Elegantly done with the fire down there. Guess we won't be getting any more torch wood tonight. Double the guards up. The young'uns reported a giant spider," he said, rubbing his jaw with his hand. "Ralph, grab two men with torches, go down to the bank, and check it out. You three, go get cleaned up." He spat when he finished and waited at the edge of the wagon circle for Ralph and the two others to return.

Maynard and Runt walked toward Angus quietly. Hilda made her way to her mother's wagon. Men and women of the camp looked at them with fear, annoyance, and questions in their eyes.

"Angus, can you help me bind up Maynard? He got a cut that needs tending to," Runt said.

"Sure thing. Tell me, boys, what was it? What did you see?"

The boys retold the story and didn't leave out Maynard's magic usage. Angus listened quietly and attentively, putting fresh dressing on Maynard's hand.

"You should be fine. Make sure to wash it out and keep the dressing clean 'cause some of those things will lay eggs in you. You'll be eaten alive from the inside out while you sleep."

Runt and Maynard looked at each other with worry in their eyes and disgust welling in their stomachs.

"If it wasn't gray or white, you should be fine. I know my kin in the caves deal with them all the time, among other creatures, but cave spiders don't venture out too often—at least not outside of caves and deep woods. Humph, maybe it was hungry, I dunno, or it was forced out. We're getting into the hills now. It could be dwarven hunters who pushed it out hunting. Hard to know. Odd, very odd," said Angus.

"You know, if we found the cave or hole where the spider came from, we could crawl down and find the nest. Bet I could get spider poison or eggs to use for potions I've been working on," said Maynard.

"You can go into a cave or hole if you want—not me," said Angus. "You won't catch me near a cave or hole anytime soon."

"But you're a dwarve; aren't all dwarves supposed to love deep and dark places? You folk are made for it," said Maynard.

"Look, saying all dwarves like caves and darkness is like saying all elves love trees and gardens."

"Wait, they don't?" said Runt with a smile.

"Vulcan's beard, no! You need to grow up, Runt. I thought you and Maynard were intelligent. Dwarves and the natives—the elves, I mean—they're like you and me. Not everyone is the same. Everyone worships different gods all over Vineland, with different manners and customs. There're all types of dwarves, elves, humans, and other beings in this world."

"Can I ask, what do other dwarves think of your," Maynard paused, "tendencies?"

"They don't very much like it, think I'm insane. It's why I don't stay near others, their clans, or their towns. Makes me a bit of an outcast, not going underground or whatever. Sorry, I get a bit touchy about it. I don't like dark places like a cave unless I can pound an ale or two, and by that, I mean a quarter barrel of beer."

"I gotta piss. Be back in a second." Angus walked away from the fire.

Maynard whispered, "Does Angus worship the dwarven gods Vulcan and Maia, Runt?"

"I mean, I guess so. He doesn't talk about religion. He preferred to come to our celebrations more so," said Runt. "Most dwarves worship the god Vulcan and his wife, Maia. Vulcan, the god of the smiths—the smith, as it is, of working with metal, steel, and jewel, the creator and the destroyer of all. His wife is Maia of the ground and stone; through her, everything grows," he said. "Never heard him mention Maia in the past, only the god Vulcan."

"Bit of a theory," said Maynard, pushing his spectacles up. "I think Angus not liking the caves, the ground, the darkness means he doesn't like his mother. You know?"

"I know Angus never speaks about his mother or much anything else," Runt said. "I know he likes fire, and he swore to Vulcan, so he knows of him. I mean, he's a cook, so yeah, he still worships in his way, I guess," said Runt. He thought for a moment. "Wow, I've known him all my life; I should've asked. I know he'd join us for our bonfires, always loved our fires and our dances, but my family doesn't worship in the way the Holy Church does."

The dwarven creation story believed in Vulcan, the creator and destroyer, falling in love with Maia of the earth, thus creating the five races. The dwarves were their first children, for they loved fire and earth.

Angus approached the fire.

"Angus, you never talk about the times before you were in Wolf Hills. How do you know this shit 'bout hunting spiders?" asked Runt. "I mean, who were you before you called yourself Angus?"

He looked at Runt and Maynard and sighed. "I guess . . ." He waited a moment. "I guess I can give you a brief history." He scratched his face. "You're going to need to get me a bottle of hooch to drink, though."

"I might be able to grab a bottle of spirits," said Runt as he got up and looked around, thinking. He snapped his fingers, walked to where the cooking supplies were held, and spoke to the wagon driver.

Maynard watched Angus, standing over him. Runt shook hands with the older women and walked back with a bottle of clear spirits. When he got closer, he threw it toward Angus.

"Here, it's made from juniper and eagle nectar. They said the dwarve would like it," said Runt.

"How much it cost?" asked Angus.

"Gave her one of the knives Doc gave us at the start of this mess," said Runt. "It held a fine edge, and I still have my boot knife for eating and defending myself."

Angus looked at the bottle and opened it. "Here's to Vulcan, the bloody fool." And he took a drink. "Wow, burns." He sat next to Maynard on a tree stump rolled over from the brush near their camp.

"I know about the spiders because they're hunted like human's hunt deer. You know, we can live three hundred to four hundred years. My name's been Angus for as long as most can remember, longer than both of you've been alive. No family name, just Angus. I did have a family, but they are long gone. Before I was Angus, I had friends and comrades, but they're gone, too. Before I—" He stopped for a moment and took a slow sip from the bottle. "Before I got my name, I was young and stupid. Like you two, no tragedy had befallen me. No harm or demanding work touched these hands. I enjoyed cooking, but it was frowned on by my mother. She wanted me to be a leader and warrior and command other dwarves in battle and politics." He took another swig and closed his eyes. Tears welled up, and he looked away.

"Dwarves in certain communities send out platoons of soldiers to clear caves and walkways less traveled to keep the orc, spider, and goblin populations down and away from our cities and mines. They're a strike force, on guard in the wilderness and wildness below your feet. A well-off family will commission soldiers for periods to go into the deep and the dark, making certain passages clear and safe. Parents tell stories of baby snatchers, bloodsuckers, and beasties to scare their children into behaving. These soldiers are the ones who kept those monsters away."

"Like the old bog queen of the Litchbury Mire. Mom told us stories of her and the native slave queen and orc king of the Gloomspire," interrupted Runt, and there was a ripple of pain as the memory of his mother crossed over his heart.

"You better have a sniff of this, Runt. You, too, Maynard, and if you're done, I will go on," said Angus, a bit disturbed. "Remember, all stories have lines of truth." He looked at Maynard and Runt. "Well, my mother was a strong woman, sought after for her family name and money. My father died, assaulted, and ambushed during a skirmish against a group of orcs. She knew she would have to remarry, and in doing so, I would move into a better position in the clans. She met suitors and soon ordered me to command a group of soldiers and go out on patrol for a fortnight. I didn't want to, but she canceled a date I had with a woman dear to me and marched me on my way. I gathered twelve of my closest friends and one or two old hands with a sword and axe. We set off to bring home orc and goblin scalps and clear the dark roads of spiders. I'd never commanded men before and was too ignorant and stupid to know what I was doing. We all were, really. We all were." Angus took a deep pull from the bottle. "I'd heard a story something akin to your orc king, Runt, that you mentioned a second ago. Young, brash, and ignorant, we searched for a rumor like trying to find a fart in the fog. We killed a couple of ragged spiders and a handful of goblins the first few nights. Nothing heroic, but it was a start. For days, we found nothing and hiked northeast, off the beaten track. One night, I cooked for everyone, and we passed around the cooking wine and another bottle of the smith's best friend."

He stopped and took a long swig after mumbling to himself for a second as if it were a prayer. He poured a bit out and passed the bottle to the boys.

"When I woke up, I was under my closest friend's body, blood trickling into my eyes and mouth. The bodies of my friends stacked on top of me like a cord of wood. Not sure what was in the alcohol we took with us on the trip, but it knocked all of us out. I could barely breathe from the weight of the bodies. We were all naked at this point, and my friends and mercenaries were all dead. I don't know how I survived. I think about it every day."

"Angus, I didn't know," said Runt. "I'm sorry."

"It's not easy to talk about; I haven't spoken about it in years. Let me finish," said Angus. He took another slug from the bottle. It was half gone now. He handed it back to Runt, who took a swig.

"I slipped out from under the two bodies on top of me, not trying to make a racket. After clearing the blood from my eyes, I looked around and found myself in a kitchen. Those brute orcs were prepping my platoon to cook us. I looked around; found a heap of clothes; put on a pair of ripped-up pants, a long shirt, and boots; and searched around for a weapon. Anything, really. I should have been pissed, ready to die with my brothers and sisters in a kitchen where they planned to butcher us like hogs. I wasn't, though. I was scared and tired, and I wanted to get out. The smell of cooked dwarve made me silently vomit and heave. There was gore everywhere, and when I looked around, I realized only three complete bodies were left, as they had already cooked and eaten the rest of us. Like my friend's scalp, other bits and pieces lay around, and eight ears sat in a pan, soaking in orc-made liquor. I went to the door and found it locked. I glanced around and found a rope and a large pan." Angus picked up the pan he'd carried from Wolf Hills. It was large cast steel with a pour spout on each end sharpened to a knife's edge. "This pan. I took and tried to find another exit. All kitchens have chimneys, so I found a large, crudely built oven and looked at the chimney opening. I wasn't sure if I could make it, but I had to try. I didn't want to die butchered and devoured by orcs. I started shimmying up the chimney of the stove, which had been used recently. It seared my face and hands, and my boots slowly melted." He touched his pitted face with his hand.

"I eventually found a shaft leading out at an angle, making it out of the orc kitchen and outside, near the top of a mountain. As I crawled out of the chimney, crying, weak, burned, and broken, I collapsed onto the pan and passed out. The pan and I slid and drifted down the mountain. I was lucky and was found by a trapper from the Legion of Carigreed. When I finally woke, I was in a camp, covered in furs. The trapper asked me what happened, and I couldn't explain it. He asked my name, and I didn't speak. I couldn't speak. He said I smelled like burned angus under all the animal pelts. I laughed, tears in my eyes from the strain of escaping a kitchen where my friends were cooked."

"You never went back to see your family, never said who you were, and moved on?" asked Maynard.

"Bout right," finished Angus. "Dwarves can drink a lot. None of us should have passed out like that. Never really considered it, but the more I thought, the more it was likely the booze we took was spiked. Didn't think I was welcome back. I took the name Angus, a cruel joke to myself, to remember what happens when you don't follow your heart." The dwarve finished with a cough.

Maynard and Runt remained quiet for the rest of the night. Finally, after Ralph and the others returned, there was a hushed conversation about the camp security and the rest of the journey to Steelsburg. The area around the camp stayed on edge. Silence blanketed the wild night near the stream, past the cook fires.

The guards changed, and the night faded to morning, but nothing more occurred, and the wagon convoy got an early start.

They picked up the pace and rolled through a pass, weaving in and out of pine and oak trees until the packed trail broke and the ground cleared further onto a road clearly made by dwarves. Each side of the road held cuts or shallow trenches to grade the water away from the center. A blend of broken stone, sand, and brick pushed into the ground made it easier for the wagons to roll over. They walked on as the sun shined down between the pine branches, hoping for a safer day than the night just passed.

Jasper -The Party Plans

"What do you think, Jasper? Should I go as a stag or a horse?" Prince Damon placed one mask in front of his face and then the other. He stood considering masks and costumes for the masquerade he wished to hold, having taken over Trinity Cloudreach's upper west wing for the day, pushing government personnel into a different area to the annoyance of staff trying to keep the country together.

Jasper Pinehard, Prince Damon's closest friend, attended to him as a liaison and one of his guards, keeping the prince safe and content for the day. There was wine nearby for all in attendance, and a great mirror hung on one side of the wall. A violin played in the background, and Austin Casting stood as the other half of the prince's personal guard near the door, a breath of armored silence.

"I think both look fully adequate, but it doesn't speak to your position in this wonderful new land you're creating. May I recommend, your grace, the black raven? Or . . . oh, I've found it!"

"Excellent choice, Jasper. This is tremendous, a real winner," said Prince Damon. He picked up a molded wildcat mask. "I shall wear this, and those of my Wildcats not working shall wear similar ones, to confuse any who wish to speak directly to me. This is tremendous; so many people will be talking about this party for years. This party is going to be huge, spectacular. I will show the Nation of Stouya and the Legion who the Holy Imperium is!"

The entire affair with masks and costumes was loud and unbecoming. Several court ladies giggled nearby, and Jasper and Prince Damon looked over at them.

"Austin, please step outside with the musician for, let's say, an hour," Prince Damon commanded.

"Yes, my prince." Austin moved as ordered, letting the violinist leave first and closing the door behind him. The violinist started playing again, mostly so others couldn't hear what occurred behind the closed door.

After a few minutes, Austin heard boots walking up the stairs to the west wing. He put his hand on his sword but did not say a word. Then, Austin's older cousin, and Lord Protector of the East, Thomas Casting, a Redcloak of the first order, walked toward them. He was everything Austin yearned to achieve. The man controlled his sword, a battlefield, a strategy meeting, and even the prince as he wished.

"Austin, nice to see you," said Casting.

Behind Thomas Casting stood his shadow, Victor Parish, dressed sharply in a fine-cut suit, and another—Brock Rustblade, head of security for Hudson City. Both Casting and Rustblade wore weapons, but Austin noted Victor Parish, looking pale and tired, did not. Yet, out of the three, he felt most threatened by Victor Parish. His training prepared him for situations like this—handling one, two, or three threats in a hallway, allowing the prince to escape while holding them off. The whole thought game was unneeded, but it came to his mind, nonetheless.

"Good to see you, sir. The prince has asked not to be disturbed for the next hour while he tries on masks for the party."

"Does he now? And Pinehard is inside, correct?"

"Yes, he is. He's protecting the prince in person, as the prince requested," replied Austin.

"All while you stand out here and listen to music and guard the door. I can see the disappointment on your face—not to worry, I will get you on the field soon enough," remarked Thomas Casting as he reached to knock on the door.

Austin moved in front of him. "Sir, I must persist, the prince has ordered."

"Gentlemen, please look away for a moment," interrupted Thomas Casting as he peered back at Victor Parish and Brock Rustblade. Both turned their faces as suggested.

Casting turned back to Austin. Casting's eyes burned into Austin's, and

Austin held his breath. Casting's cheeks narrowed, and his nostrils flared as time dimmed. Austin recognized the moment. Thomas was frustrated and pissed off, calculating his next action.

Thomas slowly raised his left hand, moved it away from his body, pointed at the man playing the violin, and frowned as he continued looking at Austin, whose eyes quickly moved toward Thomas's pointing finger. In a moment, Casting grabbed Austin below his breastplate and pushed him, placing his foot behind Austin and seizing his sword from his belt. In a moment, the scuffle was over. Casting presented Austin with his sword pointed directly at his neck. Austin was pushed against the wall, frustrated but in awe of how quickly his older cousin moved against him.

"I've engaged you, taken your weapon, and embarrassed you, so please," and Casting paused for a moment, looked down, and smiled, "step to the left. I need to speak to the prince about a matter that cannot wait."

The conversation was as if Casting were talking to a stranger and not a family member. Austin did as requested, and Thomas presented his sword, hilt first, which Austin sheathed. Casting knocked loudly and kicked in the door with force.

"What the shit? You better have a solid reason for—oh, it's you, Thomas. And your man Victor." The prince was busy with two women, all three-half undressed and sweating.

"My prince, please finish up. We have an urgent matter to discuss," Casting said, looking on, not the least bit embarrassed.

"As you can see, Thomas, I am a bit busy—deep into personal matters of court. Tell you what, I'll continue, you fill me in, and we'll see where the matters play out." He blew up at his hair, which was long and getting into his eyes a bit, as he continued his motions.

"You there, continue. Eat! Eat!" the prince said.

"As you wish, your grace. Rustblade here said you plan on throwing a large party with members of court and civilians in and around Trinity Cloudreach, and you've already ordered wine, beer, and spirits, not to mention food and several pyrotechnic mages, the like of which this city has never seen," said Thomas Casting.

Prince Damon and the ladies of the court were moaning and gyrating, half-clothed. Casting turned away, and Victor did so as well. Brock looked on, a bit unsteady.

"Brock, you want in on this when I'm finished. Royal seconds from the ladies." Prince Damon waggled his eyebrows.

Doing his best not to offend Prince Damon, Brock Rustblade turned his head and attempted to answer. "No, Your Grace, I am unfit to address the ladies even with your approval," he said.

"Wait, Prince Damon, where is Jasper? He is supposed to be guarding you along with Austin," said Casting.

Jasper walked out from a dressing stand on the other side of the wing, fully dressed. His hair was a bit tousled, and his pants were not entirely in place. "Well, this area is clean, chaps. So good to see you. I see Prince Damon has asked you to join us as we try on masks."

"Jasper, you are supposed to be on duty, not frolicking with tarts and trying on masks," said Casting, frustration showing on his face.

"Thomas, please, Jasper was ordered to attend to me, so don't reprimand him. Besides, I don't know who sits higher, the captain of my guards or lord protector of the east. Hmmm," said the prince. He moaned for a moment and finished while Casting spoke to Jasper.

Behind Jasper, two bodies moved behind the curtain but remained covered. Thomas made a note to find out who they were in case he ever needed an advantage over Jasper. Casting knew Prince Damon played favorites. He also noted the women the prince was spending time with today. They would also need to be addressed if a royal bastard were created. Casting nodded at Victor, who immediately understood. As lord commander of the east and appointed not by Prince Damon but by King Geordie across the ocean, it was his responsibility to make sure illegitimate heirs were not born. If this were to occur, they would be dealt with quickly and quietly.

"My prince, Sir Rustblade and I have reservations about this party," said Casting.

"You'd better not! You're off duty and coming to the masquerade. It will be a festival of peace, a celebration of a new nation, a coming together of new families. It will be wonderful!" said Prince Damon. "Fix your reservations, get the party security settled, and prepare to get smashed with me and the rest of our gallant nobles for a night to remember. I'll have no more excuses. Make it happen," he ordered.

"The security, your highness, we have reports that the writer and reluctant mage Olivia Franklin was enraged when they lost the *Hudson City Journal*. There are rumors of a sect of followers, the Bastards of Liberty, planning protests. There've been a few unsolved murders of minor nobles. One Jessie Stainfurd married the owner of *The Post Enquirer News* and drowned in her bathtub, and Nicholas Firemane, the fourth son of the mayor of Hudson City, was found dead outside a high-end brothel. We believe they're connected to Olivia Franklin. In addition, sir, we cannot afford a party of this size. The pay for the Copperheads will exceed our yearly expenditures," Rustblade implored, his voice deep and calm. He was a professional man and knew how to present himself to the prince, who was sharp yet emotional.

"I'm making this new country *great*, and to do so, we must show we are great, with large gatherings of my people, both peasants and nobles." Prince Damon ignored Rustblade. "My people!" His mood turned. He didn't like power struggles, especially with lesser men, yet he feared Casting and knew Casting held the country together even though he was the prince and bastard son to King Geordie of Great Brightland.

"Yes, of course, but I have concerns for your safety, your legacy. I want you and this land to be the most magnificent and powerful in the world, but we need to take specific steps to achieve this, and this may not be a step in the right direction," Casting said.

"Thomas, this party will occur on my order, your rightful ruler and hand of the Maker himself," Prince Damon commanded. "Now, if you have suggestions on how to handle the finances. . . "

"I have a few ideas, Your Grace, when you have time to speak on such matters," Thomas replied.

"Now you're getting there. Please go on," the prince said.

Rustblade stood next to Victor Parish, listening, and standing still.

"Your Grace, may I take a moment?" Thomas said.

"Of course. I do need to dress now." And Prince Damon threw on his robe.

"Thank you, Victor. See the ladies out and clear the room of any guests. Jasper? Please step out and stand with Austin for the moment. And send off the musician," said Casting.

Jasper looked at Prince Damon, who made a motion with his hand, advising him to do as commanded. Casting made a mental note of Jasper's loyalty to Prince Damon. He needed a contact on the inside of Prince Damon's Wildcats soon, if nothing else, to keep an eye on Jasper.

Victor looked at Thomas Casting, nodded, and moved toward the curtains quickly while the prince's back was turned.

Brock Rustblade was the second son from a merchant family, old blood from across the ocean. A stout man with a shrewd bald head and an unappealing mustache, his dark eyes showed the confidence of a pit wrestler, and he took his job seriously. His job was challenging because he commanded the city's sheriffs and lieutenants, locally called Copperheads, a mixture of corrupt thugs and mercenaries. He also navigated nobles in the capital, militant orders like the Order of the Blue Rose, fraternities, merchants, guilds, and the often-foreign dignitaries claiming diplomatic immunity.

Those moving pieces influenced the city's economy like a bear slowly roaring inside its cave, causing panic and disgust from unknown dark places. Brock did his best to remain above any party and, in doing so, was almost helpless in keeping any of his Copperheads clean of corruption. He went to Thomas Casting, whom he knew from previous campaigns during the Crimson Struggle when working with the crown prince himself.

Each neighborhood of Hudson City had a local sheriff, and each sheriff controlled numerous lieutenants or Copperheads who would work street blocks of the city. Some portions of the city ran cleanly and efficiently, at least by the looks of those city blocks. Sheriffs and Copperheads walked the streets, handled minor disruptions and crimes, and kept neighborhoods calm. In other parts of Hudson City, Copperheads would not venture out by themselves unless they numbered in groups of five to ten due to the street gangs or guilds controlling certain areas openly.

Jasper Pinehard was the head of Prince Damon's guard, the Wildcats. Each wore blue, gold, and red on their surcoat, and they were named after Price Damon's family coat of arms. The Wildcats was an extension of the royal guard called the Red Guard, which numbered about two hundred. Their only job was the personal protection of the prince and the royal estates housed throughout the Holy Imperium. Near the end of the Crimson Struggle, the Red Guard, led by members of the Wildcats, had been used as shock troops to bring glory to Prince Damon. If one guard member fell in action, the prince himself would elect his replacement.

Jasper Pinehard was tall and built to mount a horse or whomever he deemed his entertainment for the night. They were near opposites. Brock was built for bar or prison fights, while Jasper was made for fencing and cavalry. Jasper dressed finely and fought melee in tournaments, often falling into orgies afterward, covered in mud and blood and devouring men and women in the darkened corners of brothels. He wore his hair long but kept it tied together; with a sharp-angled blond beard that showed his old-world heritage. As one of Prince Damon's closest friends, Jasper constantly provided Damon with a sense of calmness and security. After guard duty, he showed his true self, often joining the prince for wine or sport.

Brock thought Jasper to be a drunken, rash man with an affinity to wine, women, and blood, and Jasper thought Brock was a strong-armed pimp trying to hustle Prince Damon for power and money.

The Wildcats loved to compare themselves to the prestige of the Redcloaks, a knightly order formed over two hundred years ago in Great Brightland. Many an older family of Vineland remained loyal to Prince Damon due to their love of King Geordie and Queen Layla of House Troulbuss across the sea. Each member of the Redcloaks was highly trained in feats of arms along with music, painting, poetry, and diplomacy. All knights enrolled to become a Redcloak spent two years serving the king of Great Brightland at his leisure. The minstrels sang legends of Redcloaks and their prowess in battle, as their tales were written into books to withstand the turning of time.

Casting discussed paying for the party first. The prince liked the ideas and approved further taxes. Prince Damon also said he would let Casting review the attendance to ensure only the appropriate people showed up inside the tower, allowing the public to gather outside. Casting noted the prince was still single, and a powerful marriage could shore up his princedom if done correctly. The party would allow Casting to find Prince Damon a wife.

"On to security," said Prince Damon.

"Brock, it's not that I don't trust your guards, but other than the Red Guards and my Wildcats, well, I don't trust your guards," Casting said "Certain parts of the city are not even passable. We really must do something."

Brock nodded. "I agree, sir. There was a slave riot in one of the lower neighborhoods; we are still recovering. It involved savages, sir, and—"

"Natives, you say, and slaves? This disgusts me. I want to hear no more. I thought the Stagger Wall built out west kept those mangy, thieving bastards out of our lands," spat Prince Damon.

"Sir, I believe they built the wall to keep us out of their lands," said Casting, and then he thought better of himself. "No, no, you're right. Certain households use savages for labor, cooking, and cleaning. Most of the time, they are well behaved, but one of the neighborhoods nearly burned down a few days ago."

"We understand fighting broke out over a trifling thing about a newspaper," Brock said.

"Well, I want it addressed. Slaves and servants documented. They all should have proper documents from their owners. If they don't, I want them rounded up. If they have cause to resist, we will burn them or hang them. If they don't, we will use them to start cleaning up the streets around the city. It's time this city became proper, civilized, not just a series of towers and holds and bricked-over mud paths. If this is to be the seat of power for the entire Holy Imperium, we need to start enforcing the laws. Brock, set your men to it!"

"As you command, sir." Brock was flushed with anger but hid it well.

"Brock, you do adequate work—thank you—but please don't fail me. I would hate to have to let one of Stephanie Shannon's ticklers work on you. They can be impatient with a man your shape," said Prince Damon. "Your girth intrigues the torturers, I hear."

"I will not fail you, sir," said Brock.

Thomas said nothing, knowing the prince would carry on like this and nothing could stop him. The prince was a bully, and he would demean you until you knew Prince Damon was above you by a large measure and that you were just a toy to him.

Stephanie Shannon of House Breechrun was part of Prince Damon's council as the minister of letters. She was a paunchy elder woman who had known Prince Damon's father before settling in Hudson City; she regularly corresponded with King Geordie of House Troulbuss. Stephanie handled the executioners of the city, royal communications, writs, the flow of information, and censorship throughout the country, controlling a vast spy network. She was unpopular at court. Rumor followed her as fear followed a plague.

"My Wildcats will be inside the tower. I will have six with me; they will be masked and close by, and the rest will remain unmasked to show their presence. The Red Guard will protect the outskirts of the palace. I'll request a few sheriffs attend and do their best to make sure these slaves, savages, and servants behave inside the palace. The others can piss off for all I care. But, Brock, I leave any other security matters to you. Do as you will under my orders. Is that sufficient to calm your fears?" Prince Damon stared down the two men, daring Thomas Casting or Brock Rustblade to question his thoughts.

"Yes, sir, excellent. Thank you for allowing me to interrupt and use your precious time," said Casting.

Brock nodded as well.

"Now, go. And make sure your man Parish brings me my jester, for I grow bored of this talk," finished Prince Damon of the House of Farover.

Casting bowed and exited, nodding to Jasper and Austin who were standing at attention at the doorway, and walked down the stairs, Brock Rustblade and Victor Parish behind him. After several flights, Thomas stopped and whispered a hurried message to Victor, who disappeared shortly in the other direction while Brock and Thomas continued down the stairs.

"This request of the prince will do more harm than good. I dislike the pointed ears creeping in the woods and bloody grass, but the city's entire economy runs on their backs. We breed them to keep our economy running. This place will become a bloody mess without them. Nobody does the work they do in Hudson City or any other major city in the Holy Imperium," said Brock.

"I understand. I treat my servants and slaves fairly, but even I can't remember where all the papers are located. Do what you can. Make a few shows of force, get rid of your most corrupt men, call a brute squad, clean up the worst neighborhoods, and buy off a few criminals and gang leaders to keep quiet during this masquerade. Also, ensure the appropriate owners have the papers they need to keep their servants secured. We need laws followed and nobles on our side, not at our throats begging and threatening another war because of a stupid party," said Casting.

Brock nodded, saluted, and walked away.

"Brock, wait. I have an idea," said Casting.

Brock's boots scraped against the floor as he stopped.

"The brute squad and guards—we'll need more men to keep the order. Do we still have contacts with the special forces used in the Battle of the Reaping?" asked Casting.

"Yes, sir, I know a few I can rustle up out of the dark," said Brock.

"Bring their highest officer to me later tonight. This presents an opportunity," finished Casting.

Runt - The Gates of Steelsburg

The head of the wagon train progressed toward a large archway of gray stone with the captain, Gunny of the Bent Plow, on the lead covered wagon. Runt sat next to him as black metal gates lay open, each built three times higher than the wagons and as wide as four horses. Gunny pulled up on his horse team and put his hand up to stop the other wagons. He spat and scratched at his chin, which was a tendency Runt had noticed Gunny did when he worried.

"Bit odd being at the front of the first Bitterspear gate and not a single dwarve to stop us or ask questions," he said, more to himself than to anyone else.

Runt stayed on the wagon. Gunny hopped down and called for his second in command, a gruff female named Bo, mother to Hilda. Both kept their hands on the hilts of their swords as they spoke in hushed tones. They walked around, looking for signs of life near the gate opening. Towering pines, mostly blue spruce, stood around them; their branches swayed like giant umbrellas above the gate. It smelled almost minty due to the trees. Pine needles spread over the ground under the horses' hooves.

Bo was younger than Gunny but just as worn down. She carried a bow on her back, arrows at the hip, and a short sword. Medium height and muscled, she took no shit and dealt it out when needed. She wore baggy cloth pants popular with some folks with pockets sewn into each side.

"Seen anything like this before in your travels?"

"Nope." Bo spat a large puddle of tobacco juice; the black, brown liquid dribbled down her chin. "Never. It's Bitterspear's gate, been in the family for ages, and to leave it unguarded is disrespectful to the family. Brings dishonor to them."

"Warn the crew. I expect the travel to be quicker since the road is in better shape, but I want our guard up. Have everyone stay close and report anything odd up the chain of command. The spider shit back there and no guards for the first time in how long?" Gunny said. "It's messed up. I just want to get to Steelsburg without losing any cargo or people."

The group rolled under the archway of the gate. Everyone felt insecure, as if an ambush from highwaymen or worse were around the corner. It smelled of damp pine and cold mist after a soft rain.

The caravan moved through the hills. The climb graded up, but the road was quality, so there was no worry of stumbling or an animal breaking a leg or ankle. Finally, near the summit, they came to another gate, this one like the last, a stone-built arch with a sturdy steel gate wedged between stone cliffs, looking intimidating, with gates closed and locked in place.

"Stand down, strangers," a voice hollered from inside the gate.

Runt held the horses' reins. Gunny sat next to him, one hand on his sword and the other on his knee. Bo was at the side of the wagon, bow strung but down, several arrows stuck in the ground at the ready. Angus and Maynard were in a wagon near the back with most of the kitchen supplies and food. Angus became fidgety and nervous the closer they moved toward the city.

Gunny advised everyone to stand down with a hand gesture.

"Welcome to Bitterspear Gate. What we can we do for you?" asked a voice from inside the gate.

"Not much of a welcome, I'd say. We've got a few wagons with supplies meant for trade. We're merchants. There are a few men and women here hired to keep them safe. We mean no harm," said Gunny.

"Whom do you wish to trade with? Which family?"

Angus whispered to Maynard, "This is a test. Something's wrong." He took a slug from a tin flask. "They're trying to see if we favor a specific family in Steelsburg. Hate this place, man, as Vulcan hates the sky."

"How do you know?" asked Maynard.

"Do I look like an elve or goblin to you? I'm a dwarve, and my family guards each gate. We're being tested here. Something's going on in the city, and it's big. Dwarves live and die by their families and extended families. The Clearstone family runs Steelsburg, but the Bitterspear family is sworn to the Blitzsteel family, and they've no love for the Clearstone clan. If any clan heard of what happened back, there . . ." Angus hiccuped a bit. "Heads would roll—or worse."

"Worse? What's worse than death?" whispered Maynard.

"To a dwarve?" Angus looked at Maynard, his eyes deep, darkened, and bloodshot as if sleep alluded him last night. "Why, exile, of course."

Gunny spoke at the front wagon: "We claim neutrality, but because this is your gate and run by the Bitterspear family for years, we will give you first right to trade with us. What say you, fine gentle dwarves?"

"Who leads this outfit?" asked the voice behind the gate.

There was a rustling of bodies and movement, but nobody could see. Cut pine branches woven between the gates metal concealed whoever made the noise.

"Name's Gunny; I am the leader of the Bent Plow. The merchants here say they've got forms letting them have open trade with all dwarven families of Steelsburg. Is something amiss in this grand city?"

With no sound, the gate opened, showing the magnificent dwarven metalwork the pride it deserved.

"Yes and no," said the lead dwarve. He carried a two-headed axe, one side with a blade and the other side pointed for punching holes in armor. He wore mail and plate and moved about with ease, looking like a small metal boulder the size of a human hitting manhood.

"Runt, stick with me. Bo, lead them on. We will catch up shortly," Gunny commanded.

The wagons moved on, and Runt made eye contact with Maynard and Angus as they passed. Angus nodded to Runt and took a big swig from his tin flask. Gunny and the leader of the guards shook hands.

There were four dwarven guards, including the one speaking to Gunny. Runt moved closer.

"This is my ward, Runt. Pay him no mind; I'm teaching him proper manners

186

and such. Here is your border fee, of course. If you could provide further news to help my small company and the merchants, I am sure we would all appreciate it," Gunny said as money exchanged hands.

The dwarve nodded. He wore an open-faced helm, showing his black, finely combed beard. He wore the Bitterspear emblem of three black spears over a white circle; the middle spearhead was gold in color, standing out on his short black surcoat. The dwarve weighed the coin purse in his hand and quickly put it into his armor.

"There is a . . .," he paused for a moment. "How should I put it? A family squabble between the two biggest families in Steelsburg. An execution went array, and sides were drawn. Enter the city from the north; come straight down into the valley to remain on the Blitzsteel side. The Bitterspear are bannermen to the Blitzsteel family and back them. The Clearstone family stands disgraced, and members of multiple families have asked them to stand down as city leaders. They have decried afoul to this and have locked themselves up in Riverstone Citadel at the mouth of the three rivers. The Clearstone family holds the river towers in the south as well, and the Blitzsteel family holds the towers in the north. There have been clashes, and parts of the city are unassailable. This is all topside news, as you know. I won't speak of below side, as it's dwarven business," said the dwarve.

"I am Toplin Bitterspear." The dwarve shifted his belt a bit and grasped his beard. "Most dwarves have been drawn to the city, leaving the initial gates empty, as you all could see. The secondary gates remain well guarded, but mining and smith work have stopped, and so have the mills. I am not sure about the prices you'll get. Life is difficult and not looking at getting better. It's near winter, and if this gets any worse, I dare say it could get ugly. There have been skirmishes, mostly on the bridges, but now all normal work has slowed to a standstill. If your company is looking for business after this caravan, you may be able to find work. Stay true to the Blitzsteel family, and you may all have a few gemstones in your pockets before you know it."

"Thank you kindly, cousin dwarve," said Gunny. He handed the dwarve another small purse and asked, "Shall we room anywhere specific or ask to speak to anyone in particular?"

"You won't be making it over to the main part of the city until this is settled. Try the Fearless Pig Tavern and Inn. Tell them Toplin Bitterspear sent you."

"Thank you. I will let my men know to be on their guard and to be extra patient and well-mannered while in your city." Gunny nodded and walked off.

Runt followed, ingesting all the news.

After a moment, Gunny started speaking to Runt as he walked at his side, "Your service, along with Angus and that lazy bastard Maynard, is nearly done. We'll give you three a tiny share of any profits made. We may be hard soldiers, but we aren't total assholes. I saw you training with Bo when time allowed. She knows her shit. I can't say the same for Maynard, constantly hanging around Hilda like a dog in heat. I'll be glad to see him go, but if you or Angus want to sign on for another tour, we'll be here through the winter, it looks like. Money to be made, and in a city with this much political turmoil," Gunny said, "we could be very useful to a dwarven family in need of protection."

"Sir, I will have to discuss it with the others, if you don't mind. I am still hoping to reconnect with my family, who is out near the ocean in Olde Ridgewatch. Maynard is supposed to help, and Angus, I think he's coming along as well. He's the closest family I have at this point. Besides, I don't think he wants to be here long," Runt said.

"I know as much. Well, you are all welcome in the Bent Plow—even Maynard, I guess, the fool. After we unload the wagons into a warehouse, come see me, and we'll square up," said Gunny.

* * *

They walked on, meeting up with the back of the caravan as it slowly rolled into the valley of Steelsburg. As the valley broke into sight, Runt saw stone-made homes built circling each side of the river's valley cliffs and bluffs. The stones were a mixture of white, gray, and black. Some buildings had been made with poured and hardened stone, a dwarven invention, and stonemasons had stacked others with wooden support beams and tiled roofs. The northern parts held houses carved into the side of the cliffs, and at the base of the river were short and hardy stone docks. It looked as if the area flooded often. The pillars held up the docks, standing higher than a typical house. Warehouses were on timbers as well to stay above flood height.

"It's built this way so when the three rivers flood, ramps are put in place, and the second and third floors of the warehouses handle the excess merchandise. Dwarven engineering at its best keeping the upper Orcfeast River and lower Deerchurn River in check as they connect, creating the Soundless Run," said Angus, who then took a pull from a flask and hiccuped. "Let's find this squire and get out of here."

Ropes and pulleys filled every corner of the docks, and although the dwarve Toplin Bitterspear had said the mills were closed, smoke still spewed from multiple chimneys throughout the city. Each smokestack was brick in large circular formations, reaching higher than buildings. Murky smoke loomed in the air, creating a constant haze at the tip of land where the two rivers met, and the fortress known as Riverstone Citadel stood.

"There's the citadel. It's not hanging the united flag of the clans anymore—only the Clearstone banners. What a sight to see," said Angus. "See the five-pointed star shape of Riverstone Citadel? It's never been taken by an invading army. It's all dwarven-poured stone and the best stone cutting work ever completed. It's older than the Golden Age is long. They say Erica, the Red Queen, and King Christopher came into the valley to conquer the dwarves. Upon finding Riverstone Citadel, they lowered their banners and asked for a parlay with the Clearstone family, knowing war against the mighty Riverstone Citadel would be futile. The star shape provides vantage points for attacks and leaves less space for enemies to hide. The bridge towers, this valley, and all trade coming down the rivers keep the city rich in commerce. Not many other cities can contend with it when it comes to commerce except Crescent City, Hudson City, and Olde Ridgewatch," Angus spat. "It's why Grimwood and Steelsburg constantly squabble over trade. Don't get me started, though," he said. He tugged his mustache. "I'm too sober to be here. I hate this place."

Runt tried changing the subject: "This is going to make finding the squire difficult. Whatever he's called."

"You got a name at least, Runt?" said Angus.

"Doc, he told me to look for a man named Duncan. Maynard may know a bit more, I guess. I still don't understand Doc. He's a bit loony," sighed Runt.

"Let's unload the caravan wagons, get the pay Gunny was talking about, and grab a beer. I might hate this place, but I still love dwarven red ale. We can plot out our next steps over a nice pint of beer."

The trio helped unload the wagons and said their farewells. Angus and Runt waited while Maynard said goodbye to Hilda. She grasped his hand and kissed him on the cheek. Maynard walked back up, a big grin on his face.

"Well, guys, let's find a tavern. I'm hungry," said Maynard.

"Did she say you could call on her or write her?" asked Runt.

"What? No, no, no. She let me put my hand up her shirt a little bit ago when we were kissing while you all were unloading wagons, though," said Maynard. "She can't read, so there will be no writing."

"What? I call bullshit," said Runt.

Maynard grinned, and Angus shook his head.

"Maynard, you wouldn't know what to do with a woman if she were naked on a soft feather bed. Let's go, boys. This place is alive with violence and malice. I'm going to need another drink and a warm meal before we find this squire," said Angus.

The Bastards - Games of Chance

Duncan lay on a soft bed and hardly moved, as the pain made it difficult to breathe or think. All he remembered was a large stone and dirty water as he tried to hold it all back. He wanted to save himself, his friends, and her. But she was gone, leaving nothing but a shadow deep inside him. His dreams tasted like wet ash and blood as he ran his tongue along the roof of his mouth. The crushing of shields, the cries for help, the whirlwind of death, and the guilt of living through battles remained when his eyes flickered open. These moments mingled with the reminder of a pressing stone and dark water, beckoning him back into oblivion. He pulled away and drifted back into harsh reality and the senseless pain of the living.

"Hey there, stranger. Glad to see you with your eyes open finally. Gave the boys and me a bit of a tough time getting you up here, and you slept for I don't know how long," she said.

Victoria, Duncan thought and then shook the thought away. No, she was dead, long dead now. Her sister looked upon him with green eyes, a pale face, and short dark hair framing a look of concern. Duncan didn't smile. He should have fallen for her, married, and started a farm. Instead, he'd made all the wrong choices, and fate or shit luck had led him to this bed and longing for the love of another. This beautiful creature had stuck with him while they'd loved each other's siblings, who were no longer in this world.

"Well, I don't like to lie—told you all we'd get out of it. Looked the Maker in its eyes and spit right at them." said Duncan. "Shit, I hurt." He coughed, pain searing his torso.

"Yeah, you did. Here, drink this." said Sorella, handing him a bowl. "It's a dwarven spirit with herbs added. It's going to burn, but it should take the pain and swelling away. You're in shit shape right now and shouldn't be moving for a bit,"

Duncan drank from the clay bowl, transparent liquid with flakes of herbs rolling around in it. The dwarves pronounced the liquid "vodka," but others called it "berserk drink" or "stone sweat." It burned going down and then cooled.

"Better. Now water, clean water, and tell me more. Where are we? What happened?" he asked.

"As you can see, you lived and so proved you're innocence. The Blitzsteel family took you as one of their own because they hate the Clearstone family. I thought the other dwarven families would consider the Blitzsteel clan blood traitors to have a half human as part of their family. Either way, Rodric Blitzsteel used the moment that you stopped the stone to seize power from Cormac Clearstone." Sorella stopped and looked at him. "You saved our lives but started a civil war between the dwarves of Steelsburg. Lines have been drawn, Duncan, and we're on a specific side on this one."

"Maker's tits, tell me more. I don't remember anything after my feet hit the water and I felt every muscle in my back strain and give out," said Duncan.

"After the initial chaos, Rodric Blitzsteel freed us, and we carried you away. I don't know what happened after we left. The three of us just wanted to get you somewhere safe and find a healer. The hangman stabilized you so you wouldn't die and recommended this tavern. We're in a mixed-race building called the Fearless Pig on the northern side of the city. The Blitzsteel clan controls above the Orcfeast River; the Clearstone family controls below the Deerchurn River and Riverstone Citadel. The land between the two rivers is unsafe at best. Murder, rape, fighting, and looting take place day and night. Tower gates to all bridges are shuttered, and ways in and out of the city around Riverstone Citadel are not easily accessible. That's above the ground, from what the rumors at the bar suggest. It's worse below ground. It may be an all-out war," Sorella said.

"Well, I'm alive for now. Shit, anyone know where we are? Like, members of the Clearstone family or their allies?" Duncan asked, trying to think ahead.

"We moved you under as much cover as possible, and it was anarchy after you were declared innocent. We think only the main members of the Blitzsteel family know where you are resting," Sorella said. "Both Cordial and Stitch are in the bar below, trying to be inconspicuous. Considering how those two are, I'm sure everyone knows. What can you move at this point?"

"Everything aches. How are my legs?" Duncan said to himself. He moved his knees slowly, and then his toes. "They work, but there's pain. I guess I can't ask for much more," he said. He moved his fingers and arms and adjusted his head. Again, there was discomfort but no lasting damage.

"I mended what I could, and you should be able to walk if you can move all your body parts. I repaired the broken bones with my abilities, but they are weak, like your back. It will take more time to heal back to the head-cleaving monster you were before," she said. "Your dwarven blood helped the healing process. You're in better shape than any other person I know could be in."

She turned her head as he stared at her. The unspoken thoughts passing between them were enough. She didn't want them to go any further, at least not now.

"Thank you. I know you don't like to . . ." He paused. "I know you prefer not to . . .," Duncan said quietly.

"It's fine. You're better." She stood and, with a smile, changed her attitude and adjusted her thoughts to other matters. "What should we do now? I don't know how long the Blitzsteel family will endure us here in Steelsburg. The Clearstone family has a bounty on your head and ours as well. Also, we're low on funds."

"Let's find a way out of here. Go get the other two. We can put them to work, if necessary," said Duncan, looking at Sorella Silvercrow as she stood firm and inexpressive.

"Okay, stay here and don't get up. I'll be back in a bit." She turned and walked away without looking at him again.

* * *

Duncan and Sorella were on the third above-the-ground floor of the Fearless

Pig Tavern and Inn, a sizable stone building with ten floors below ground. There was a communal bar on the main ground level and another bar below ground for dwarves only. This feature occurred in most mixed-race bars and taverns in Steelsburg. If a dwarve didn't wish to drink above, they would walk below ground. Other races weren't allowed to walk below ground without written permission from a dwarven family and were then escorted by a dwarve. There were also entire clans of dwarves that never set foot above the ground, using couriers or extended family to conduct their business.

With Sorella tending to him, Duncan had recovered in fits and unconscious spasms. While he stabilized, Cordial and Stitch got drunk on vodka mixed with a bubbly strawberry water mixture in the bar below known as witch pepper. The Blitzsteel family had supplied them with their old clothes and weapons but not their burglary tools used at the initial bank heist. The instruments were one of a kind, magical, or illegal. Whatever was in their drinks made them feel glorious, so they snuck into the jail armory, grabbed a few irreplaceable items, and slipped back with only wet feet as an afterthought. They were professional, limiting their sins to grabbing their items and pinching a repeating short-shot crossbow. The compact weapon could shoot four bolts without reloading, just a quick pull on a back piece of metal.

Now Cordial sat with Stitch in the back corner of the first floor, drinking dark ale from a stein. He snickered to himself and burped at the memory of the theft. They enjoyed the reprieve after the bank robbery, trial, and immaculate save by their friend Duncan. They were content to do nothing while their comrade healed up.

There were others in the bar: traders, merchants, and general drunks mixed in. To the patrons' displeasure, armed dwarves stood guard outside the front above-ground and below-ground entrances since the open feud started between the Blitzsteel and Clearstone families. Blades, axes, and knives remained in plain sight, and the atmosphere felt tense. Rumors of the open rebellion floated through the air. Stitch and Cordial did their best to listen and gather as much information as possible.

"Man, this place is a sausage fest," said Stitch. His face, ordinarily clean shaven, had stubble on it; he carried more grittiness after Steelsburg's torture and dungeon. At eighteen summers, he was one of the youngest in the bar. "I mean, even the barmaids look manly in this town. You think Sorella would be pissed if I spent a coin or two on a friend for a few hours?"

Cordial was freshly shaven and as hard up for a companion as Stitch. "No, she wouldn't be happy. We have enough coin to get us out of here if a bribe or two is needed and to travel by, but if you were to use your magic fingers to find another purse to cut, then guilt-free fun could be had, Maker save us," Cordial said. He smiled, teeth white, hair long with the ashy-blond hue so many ladies loved. His voice slinked its way through the conversation. "I mean, really, I'm itching—itching to stretch my legs. The run across the river a few days ago was nice, and I'm glad for it, but my blood is running now, and I need the arms of a passionate woman . . . or reefer smoke," he said.

"Hey, Cord, did you get my deck of cards? I need to keep my hands busy." Stitch's hands were visibly antsy. One scratched at his side, and the other held his ale, his thumb tapping on the grip of it, his eyes bouncing around.

"Drink your ale down. It should get you where you need to be. Then we find a mark, walk over, hit 'em, and move to a house of ill repute," said Cordial.

"Sounds perfect." Stitch pushed his mop of ash-brown hair off to the side, a slight smirk settled on his slender, scarred face.

Cordial liberated a smoke from his jacket pocket, lit up, and tossed Stitch another along with his deck of cards. The smoke was a finely ground tobacco and other herbs rolled neatly into a thin sheet of newspaper shorter than a finger; a small copper tube served as the filter. He lit it, using a candle. He sucked smoke in and breathed it out his nose.

"Now, don't make attention with those cards," said Cordial. "Low profile. We need to get out of here clean. Remember, the society has no bureaus in this city."

Both Stitch and Cordial were loosely affiliated with a gentle person's club called The Society of Shadows. According to rumors, they were like-minded people performing odd jobs that ordinary people wouldn't even consider. The Society of Shadows placed bureaus in most major cities and outposts. In these places, job contracts were posted with details on how to pick up payment once completed. The jobs ranged from simple errands to bodyguard duties, while other accommodations including theft, extortion, and assassination were available as well.

Stitch went to shuffle his cards. He was manic about them or anything touching his hands. His two stilettos were on his sides, and they were sharp and deadly. He also hid a knife in each coat sleeve for cutting purses.

Cordial carried knives and a pouch with a glass jar; if thrown, it caused a considerable amount of smoke to appear. He now also had a nice, small, highly illegal crossbow. Both men wore military-cut coats, dyed black from their original crimson red and stolen off corpses years back.

As his name implied, Cordial carried agents used in rudimentary alchemy, lock-picking, and poison. The pair was a formidable team in minor pieces of crime—until they'd met Duncan and Sorella.

The tavern's front door opened, and a dwarve walked in with two younger men. One wore a scholar's robes while the other looked worn and shabby. The youngest jingled around a small leather purse.

Stitch looked and smiled while Cordial stood and took a long swig of beer, placing it down on the table. Stitch did the same, leaving a coin for the barmaid walking by.

"Bump and run," they said together and walked toward the three newcomers.

* * *

The bar was busy enough; a fiddler played off to the side, and tobacco smoke floated in the air. The dwarve walked toward the bar, held up his hand for three drinks, and used his other hand to call for three dinners.

"Whatever is in the pot there," said Angus.

Runt and Maynard waited by the door while Angus ordered drinks and dinner.

Stitch walked by, bumped into Runt hard, and both fell over.

"Oh no, come on now, friend. You must be drunk," Cordial said as he reached out and grabbed at Stitch, lying on the ground. Cordial placed his hand on Maynard as he dragged Stitch up.

"Sorry, buddy. Let me help you up, and look here." He grabbed at Runt's money pouch. "You lost this." He handed the pouch back to Runt. "Gentlemen, if you will excuse me, I'm going to go take my friend outside so he can piss and throw up in the gutter." Cordial shoved Stitch out the door in a stumble.

"Isn't that nice of him," said Runt.

"Nice? Runt, he took your money and a pouch of herbs from me."

"What do you mean? He gave me my money back. Oh, wait," Runt slapped his pocket. "Maker's tits!"

Runt bolted out the door, failed to see either man, and sniffed the air like an angry dog.

Inside, Angus turned with three mugs of beer and, to his surprise, saw neither Runt nor Maynard. Angus looked for a moment, saw the table where Stitch and Cordial had been sitting only minutes ago, and sat. "Well, the boys will come back—or they won't. Hate this town and can't be a moment sober here." He started drinking, his hands shaking slightly.

Maynard came behind Runt as he looked around in amazement and annoyance outside the tavern. "Give me a second, Runt. Doc will be pissed I did this but damn it all. Runt, go get that large stick by the barrel over there," said Maynard.

Runt went and grabbed it.

Maynard looked around, grabbed a human hair from the purse Runt held in his hand, and took his knife out. "Give me your leg." Runt looked at him. "Just do it. Trust me," said Maynard.

Runt pulled up his trouser leg, and Maynard sliced a small cut into him.

"Ahh, that hurt, you bastard! What's your deal?" yelled Runt.

Muttering to himself, Maynard started rubbing his bloody fingers together.

Runt felt a little sick and light-headed. "What are you doing? Feel a bit off," he said.

"Getting your money back. When you hear screaming, run toward it. It will be a pair of men. And hit them in the head. I'll come around and get them from behind." Maynard continued to mutter to himself.

"They were both bigger than me. There's no way we're getting it back," said Runt, dejected.

197

"Stop being such a whiny baby, Runt. Be more than your name. Your home's burned down, your mother is dead, your sister sold into slavery, and the very government—the very lords sworn to protect you and your family— did it. Stop letting people get away with shit, and start doing something about it. You can't petition the prince to save you. You can't even get people together in protest. You can't write an angry letter and get it in the newspaper. Those shits stole your money—our money—so we gotta take it back. All of it," Maynard said.

He started chanting again quietly, eyes closed, and teeth bared. The chanting rhythm almost sounded as if it were from an elvish tongue.

Runt's face changed from annoyance to righteous anger. There was a scream and then another. The streets were dark except for lights coming through the windows and lamps here and there. The lamps outside were flameless dwarven owl lamps created with etched runes and crystals, expensive outside Steelsburg. Runt spun around, trying to figure out which road or alley to go down.

"There!" he yelled, running into the darkness, away from Maynard, who jogged after Runt, sliding into the shadows.

The two men were in an alley off a street near the river. Stitch lay on the ground, holding his leg near the same area where Maynard had cut Runt. Cordial hunched over Stitch, looking at his friend's leg, trying to figure out what happened.

Hudson City - Outbursts and Conspiracies

"Dammit, why does everything have to be complicated?" Prince Damon bellowed to everyone, but nobody dared reply. Austin Casting and Jasper Pinehard, his guards for the day, stood at attention a short distance away. The prince was suited for training, standing in the dueling circle with blunted steel in his hand. Stephanie Shannon of House Breechrun, counselor to the king, attended with Murrow Edward, editor of *The Post Enquirer*. They stood off to the side, away from Prince Damon's guards and the prince's ear for the moment. Stephanie Shannon's hair ran to gray and white, combed back with a slight part. She looked on at the prince, her face full and her jowls overhung, making her frown deeply. Her face was splotchy from excessive drinking, but her eyes were sharp as she listened to the prince.

Prince Damon was trained in using a two-handed great sword and waited for his sparring partner to come at him. Today it was Brock Rustblade. Brock was an old hand with a vicious cut with the blade. It would be exciting to see an aged, neckless brute like Rustblade tussle with Prince Damon, so young, spry, and overconfident. Unfortunately, the prince's royal blood would not allow for it. Rustblade would not win in the face of Prince Damon and risk losing his job or his life. The crossed swords separated and met again. The prince swung his blade, hitting Rustblade's sword arm at the elbow.

"One touch for me! Rustblade, your age is catching up on you," Prince Damon said without losing his breath, his mood changed, and he looked at Stephanie Shannon. "I want to throw a party—a huge party—because we won! We're winners, I'm a winner, and we kicked Stouya and the Legion's asses all over the battlefield. The Red Army beat them so hard the history book is still being written." He threw his sword at Shannon like a toy, as if he were an angry child. "They signed it! They both signed for peace here in Hudson City, creating the Holy Imperium. We are no longer part of my father's Great Brightland. This is our country now! Vineland no more; this is the Holy Imperium. But *no*, people have to tell me we have no money, security is a problem, there could be a slave revolt—it's all bullshit, capital grade-A bullshit. Rustblade, you served. You know how much we suffered. You bloodied your blade and fought for us. Why all the excuses from everyone when it comes to making the Holy Imperium great!"

"My prince," said Stephanie Shannon, attempting to deflect his anger. "The Crimson Struggle did end three years ago, but the reconstruction has taken a tremendous amount of time and money. There are still pockets of resistance in the independent city-states from the Grave Reach River to the Atlantis Ocean. This country you have so heroically fought to create is still not purified of the threats from Stouya and the Legion. Not to mention, as you said yourself, savages hide in the forests and there is the looming threat of armed slave revolts. Goblins, orcs, and those forsaken heathen elves bite at the ankles of the empire you wish to create."

The prince screamed at everyone as Stephanie Shannon looked on. It wasn't pleasant to be yelled at—not by a noble, not by a young man, not by a would-be king. Prince Damon needed to eat or bed someone, potentially both, after which talking about policy matters would be easier. Stephanie knew the prince enjoyed Bitterleak burgers and wondered if his favorite tavern could have lunch made and delivered to the dueling circle. It seemed odd, yet an interesting idea. Have the sandwiches made, wrapped in butcher paper along with fresh chips, and have someone use a horse to spring up to the circle, where they could be enjoyed as if they'd just been made.

"We've had to pay out a lot from our treasury, and there're been raids on the Kings and Queens Roads, stopping taxes and hostage ransoms from making it into our—I mean, your—coffers," Shannon said, still staring at Prince Damon with a lack of respect. She wore a look of pity on her fat face, almost willing to say she could run the country better. Stephanie Shannon was Prince

Damon's minister of letters. She helped control newspapers, the mail system, entertainment, and the prince's spy network inside and outside of Hudson City. It had been Stephanie's idea to bring Murrow Edward along for this conversation so she could deflect the prince's anger off onto him.

"And this dreadful, horrid paper, the *New Hudson Journal*, keeps telling lies about me. I'm tired of it, so tired of it! I don't pay for whores! I do not. How do they even print? I thought I put them out of business!" he yelled to the sky and stared at Stephanie and Murrow. The stories angered the prince because they were true. He screwed other people's wives, used church funds to build an estate north of Hudson City, and enjoyed torturing dogs and playing sports instead of attending social functions. He didn't use loftier words when speaking in public or in private. His royal blood allowed him to do whatever he wanted. Scoundrels in back alleys, nobles in tea shops, merchants in taverns, and slaves in underground cellars heard or read stories, laughing and judging Prince Damon as less than royal.

Stephanie motioned for a servant and whispered into their ear with precise instructions. Prince Damon looked at her for a moment.

"My prince, I will have a small lunch delivered to us—a snack I think you will enjoy, my grace. My apologies for interrupting, but I just thought it up and believe it will bring you a small moment of delight," said Stephanie.

"It better. I don't like being let down," huffed the prince. "I need to kill something." He took up his sword again and motioned Rustblade to another round. "One more, and put your back into it," he said.

Rustblade was in sketchy territory, as he couldn't win but had to show he was trying enough. He knew practice dueling was not even close to a fight. Having survived the war and several attempted robberies, he knew how to handle himself.

"It can't be that bad in the slums of Hudson City for there to be threat of another riot," Prince Damon complained.

Hudson City had dealt with a minor slave revolt that killed a minor lord, a sheriff, and three Copperheads before it had been put down. Overall, the revolt had ended up burning down several businesses, including Prince Damon's favorite tailor and brothel, a few weeks ago. There was a rumor of the Smoldering Plague from the north making its way down and killing off small towns and farmsteads, and with no war, well-trained soldiers—suddenly with no jobs—were idle and ready to cause trouble with local lords and madams. There was murmuring of dissension in Hudson City and other cities at late-night bonfires and taverns down the Atlantis Sea coast and into the hinterlands of the Blightbriar Mountains, where most news broke and died. Austin Casting thought this as he stood next to Jasper, looking past Prince Damon, Brock Rustblade, Stephanie Shannon, and Murrow Edward as they spoke about party plans.

The duel ended with Prince Damon winning, four touches to Brock Rustblade's one touch. Prince Damon was visibly sweating, and Brock Rustblade sucked in air but looked ready to go another round.

"Had enough, you old dog?" he motioned toward Rustblade.

"I'm defeated, my lord, but if you wish for another round, I'm happy to oblige."

"No, you've had enough, I think. I don't want to wear you out for your rounds and work this afternoon." Prince Damon took a deep breath and drank a tall glass of watered wine.

A horse ran toward the dueling circle, stopping at the gate, and a delivery girl hopped off the saddle, carrying a satchel. A guard let them in, and they rushed toward the group. The prince failed to notice, which was not uncommon.

"Nothing is right. Why don't they listen? Why is nobody happy? What is wrong with this land?" said Prince Damon. "We'll open Hudson City to all and show them something positive, something special. They deserve to have a party."

Jasper thought, *Nothing is wrong, you shit. You have all the power in the world. You don't pay attention to what's happening around you. This delivery girl could walk up and stab the prince, and he wouldn't even realize until the dagger's hilt stuck out of his rib cage.* Jasper moved in front of the prince in short order, putting himself between the prince and the delivery girl. She collapsed on her knees.

"Look at me, Stephanie. No one of royal blood has ever had it this bad. I want this mage Olivia Franklin caught and burned at the stake like the heretic they are! If there are any witch hunters worth a shit, send one after this witch. You hear me, Shannon? Whatever it takes—get those measly Templar involved if needed. And you, Edward, find this wretched bloody rag of a paper and shut it down. And bring me the fingers of any of the writers of this trash!" ordered Prince Damon of House Farover. He looked wide-eyed at the people, surrounded by so many, yet he remained alone.

"My prince, I present to you Bitterleak burgers from Old McRaffle's tavern down the main causeway. Freshly made and ready for you to enjoy." Stephanie bowed and presented the satchel to Prince Damon.

"Yes, brilliant. I'm glad I thought of this. Let's all eat standing like peasants, for I am a man of the people." And Prince Damon took a bite of his Bitterleak burger and smiled as he chewed, swallowing the meat down.

The delivery girl continued to kneel, having not been acknowledged. Jasper and Austin looked down on her, a little annoyed that neither Prince Damon nor Stephanie Shannon had released them from their service.

Runt - The Bastards Assemble

"Give me my money back!" shouted Runt at the front of the alley, silhouetted against the light, long, wooden stave in his hand.

"You want your money back?" Stitch said as he rolled and hopped up, limping visibly. He was pale and sneering from the pain shooting through his leg. "Come and get it." And he grabbed for his stilettos. "Cordial, what happened to the twins? Cordial!"

"Found them, Stitch," Cordial said. He had indeed found Stitch's favorite weapons. One was pointed right at Cordial's throat; the other Maynard had pointed up under Cordial's armpit. Each dagger was eleven inches long. Seven of those inches were the blades, each double-edged. The stilettos bore ringed grips used by mariners in Great Brightland. Stitch cherished them, making sure they were sharp and oiled so no rust would tarnish their surface. The stilettos were meant for stabbing or puncturing light armor yet remained edged enough to cut if needed.

"You, the skinny one, give my friend his money back and kneel on the ground," said Maynard, who shifted behind Stitch and Cordial.

"Sure thing, kid, sure thing," said Stitch. He looked at Maynard and back at Runt. "Here you go, kid. Here you go. Fair and square is what I always say, fair and square."

Stitch looked at Maynard, knowing he was the bigger problem, not the snot-nosed kid with the big stick in his hand. He reached for the knife hidden in the sleeve of his coat. There was a quick movement from where Runt stood, and then blinding raw pain radiated from Stitch's crotch.

"Ahh, my nuts—the kid hit me in the nuts!" Stitch fell back down.

"You aren't ever going to try to take anything from me or anyone else again," said Runt as fury blossomed in his chest. He swung his stick down on Stitch's head.

"Excuse me," said a female voice from behind.

Runt stopped his swing and looked back to see a woman standing, dressed chiefly in men's clothes: tight black leather armor strapped together with belts and buckles, faded black leather coat, and tighter aged leather and cloth pants. Her belt held two savage-looking tomahawks and a hunting knife. She carried a long dagger in her hand, bladed on one side and serrated on the other. She stood, foot up on a turned-over barrel, wearing a leather archer's hat over her murky hair. Runt looked on, unsure of what to expect from a person dressed like a landlocked pirate.

"Yes, yes—I mean, what?" Runt said, confused, his voice dropping.

"My two friends seem to have made an unfortunate mistake. If you would be so kind as to ease up on them, I'm sure a proper apology could be made, and all pieces of merchandise returned." She smiled for a moment. "Ain't that right, Cord?"

"Hi, Sorella. Yes, of course. I was telling this young man behind me the same thing," he said with a smile. It was the best he could do with a knife to his throat.

"See now, lads, it looks like you showed them up. So do me a favor—let up on them, and all will be returned," said Sorella, the woman in the hat. She walked toward them, hips swaying. "These two friends of mine; I use the term loosely. You see, they are needed to help our comrade get out of this forsaken city," said Sorella Silvercrow.

The adrenaline faded from Maynard's body. He was starting to weaken after what he'd done with the blood magic minutes ago. "Yeah, okay, fine. Sure enough," said Maynard.

Runt looked at the man on the ground, who was breathing hard. He looked at the woman with green eyes, pale skin, and lips painted as red as a rose. He lowered the stick and shoved the man to the ground with his boot. "Money. All of it."

"Sure, sure, here you go," Stitch said and tossed the small bag to Runt.

"All of it."

"That is all of it, you little shit."

"Stitch, you and Cordial got your asses handed to you by two boys. Give them a few coins for the trouble. They found you, hamstrung you, and beat you down, and you're giving them guff—a bunch of softies, as near as I can tell. You're both lucky I don't cut your tongues out for such ignorance," Sorella said.

"Right here you are, chap. Few coins for your trouble." Stitch flipped Runt two more coins.

Maynard pushed Cordial toward Stitch and tossed his two blades in a gutter full of the night's refuse.

"Fine, now we leave. You pray our dwarven friend doesn't hear about this, or his clan will be after your heads," lied Runt.

"Nothing new to us," said Stitch as Sorella picked him off the ground.

* * *

Runt and Maynard backed out of the alley and headed toward the Fearless Pig Tavern, taking a street near the river to look at Riverstone Citadel. The Orcfeast River flowed by, and across the Brothers Bridge lay the star-shaped citadel, controlled by the Clearstone family. To the east of Riverstone Citadel, a few coal stacks and steel forges spewed smoke into the air in the middle of the city. The northern side of the Brothers Bridge was controlled by the Blitzsteel family, along with the northern part of the valley. The Brothers Bridge spanned the Orcfeast River, connecting the north shore to the middle of the city, called the Strip. This was next to downtown Steelsburg, a contested area, before it butted up against Riverstone Citadel. The bridge's stone archways anchored ancient iron gates featuring runes carved into the stones on each end; the carvings had been done by dwarven families. Most bridges controlled by dwarves were set up this way. The classical runes would not allow access unless the heads of each gate permitted the gates to open.

"How are we supposed to find this squire in this mess? We can't even cross into parts of the city. The whole place is openly hostile at this point," said

Runt. He spat into the river and gazed out at Riverstone Citadel's walls across the river.

"I know. Let's go back and get food. I'm hungry and weak. We'll talk to Angus about it. He'll have a better idea of what to do," said Maynard. His face looked haggard; his eyes sunken. He needed a drink and a night's worth of sleep.

They slowly walked back, Runt with a minor limp and Maynard feeling completely drained. They opened the door and came into laughter as a fiddler played in a far corner, smoke danced throughout the ceiling, and tankards of dwarven lager kissed patrons' lips.

"Over here, boys, over here. Barmaid, another round of fine dark beer," Angus barked. His face was red and plastered with a smile. "Boys, meet Cordial, Stitch, and Lady Sorella. They were speaking to me about a little dust-up with goons in an alley, said two orc-sized men jumped them. They fought them off best they could and only lost a few coins to boot. Said they nearly lost their legs due to a special orc curse cast on them." Angus took a deep sip of his tankard, foam dripping from his beard, and turned it over. "I tried to tell them you won't find an orc or goblin within fifty miles of the nearest smokestack in this area. Since the Golden Age, orcs haven't been spotted in the Commonwealth of Erieland." Angus burped. "Where you boys been to anyway?"

Angus was playing a card game with Cordial, Stitch, and Sorella, and it looked pretty even, not much money lay on the table. Runt and Maynard looked at each other, not sure what to do.

"Well, sit. I ordered you both a drink and a bowl of mystery stew. Bloody dicks, I would love to get my hands on the server." Angus was feeling splendid. He laughed and threw down his cards. "I hate this town but glad to be around my people again. Great lady folk, and the beer here is excellent. Ha! Oops, I win!"

Cordial gave Stitch a look of "what the Hades?"—one that would be given to a cheating friend who is still losing.

"Boys, you look confused. What's wrong?" asked Angus.

"No, no, you had a winning hand there, sir—that's all. Didn't expect you to pull those cards," said Stitch, clearly flustered.

"Hey, Cordial, isn't it? And you, Stitch, how's the leg and bruised balls?" said Runt.

"Son of a—" Stitch bumped the table as he leaped for Runt.

"Oh, shut up! Stitch." Sorella pushed the bench out with her leg. She smiled, her face showing the sharp lines of an elve. "Sit, the lot of you. I think we all need to have a chat," she said.

"I will not sit. Your pals, Stitch and Cordial—whatever kind of name that is—tried to rob us!" Runt retorted.

Angus's eyebrows rose, and his right hand moved to his side. His other hand stayed near the turned-over tankard.

The bar was loud, full of dwarves, humans, and business.

"You boys said these two men tried to rob you in an alley?" Angus said. suddenly stone sober. He stood. "You, Cordial, were accosted by these two," and he smiled, "orcs?"

"Well, I wouldn't say that just now," said Cordial.

Angus laughed even louder, placing his hand on his stomach, near the giant carving knife he carried. Quickly, he yanked out a meat cleaver and slammed it between the fingers of Stitch's left hand. The bar stayed loud and busy, but the table was silent except for Angus's laughter. Stitch looked at his hand and up at Angus, who held his other knife out near Cordial's throat. Finally, the dwarve's laughter stopped, and he glanced at Sorella, who, like the other two, did nothing but stare in amazement.

"You silly cave pigeons," said Angus.

The barmaid showed up, the top of her breasts showing all their glory, and looked at the scene: dwarve, hatchet, knife, and nobody moving. She walked over and placed a beer down to the left of Angus and whispered in his ear. Angus's eye twitched, and his hands fidgeted.

"Right, I'll be back with the bowls for the boys, sweetie," she said and walked away.

Angus laughed, again from his belly. He put his hand down and knife away, grabbed the cleaver, yanked it from the table, and snatched the beer mug. Stitch lifted his hand, untouched, and looked at it, feeling it up and down.

No fingers scratched, not a slice of skin missing. Angus looked into the scoundrels' faces, his eyes deep, bloodshot, and full of alcohol and a righteous kind of anger.

"If you try that shit again on my two boys here—or any other card tricks—I won't fucking miss your hand, nor your apple under your chin, you piece of shit. You try sleight of hand in this town, and I will watch the city guard fuck you with a broken bottle the length of your whore mother's arm. Is that clear?" Angus didn't wait for either of the two men to speak. "I apologize for my harsh tongue. I do beg your pardon," he said to Sorella and bowed his head. "I have no problem carving you up as well if need be."

"It's okay, Angus; we have broken bread with you. I expect a little bit better from both of my men. Boys, will you please sit down? If we have not gathered enough attention, you standing there gaping at a little bar skirmish isn't helping," she said.

"Right, well, I don't expect much hospitality from the Society of Shadows these days. You lot have fallen on tough times after the Crimson Struggle ended," said Angus as he shuffled the cards.

The boys sat, and Angus dealt them into the hand.

"Sorry. Sorry about this, Mr. Angus. It won't happen again. How did you know we were affiliated with the club?" Said Cordial.

"I took a wild guess at seeing the small crossbow hanging inside your coat on a rope. Might take care to stow it away, or you'll be arrested and executed," said the dwarve. "As your caretaker Sorella advised, we've broken bread, so let's carry on as if we aren't a bunch of thieves, drunks, and maniacs." He burped, and the entire table smelled of beer and sausage.

"Okay, boys," said Sorella. She put her hand on Stitch's shoulder in a sisterly way. "Runt and Maynard, tell us a little about yourselves; your drunk friend said you are in town after finishing a run as caravan security for the Bent Plow."

They ate and drank, exchanging their most recent stories. Sorella spoke of the past months leading up to the botched bank job in Steelsburg. Runt felt more like a man than he had in the past month. At fifteen summers, he was still short, and this woman speaking to him showed a sharp wit, laughed loudly, and kept up drinking with Angus, who held his drink better than most. Angus provided their new friends with an abridged version of why they were in Steelsburg, looking for "The Squire" or a family member of Runt.

Sorella mentioned another member of what she called "the gang" during the swapping of stories. Runt could see that Sorella kept everything under control. A linchpin for Stitch and Cordial, keeping them from ending up dead. She could be loud but let Cordial and Stitch talk while scanning the room and taking in her surroundings.

The night grew late. Angus stood and said he was off to piss and to bed.

Maynard got up, too. "Runt, you coming? We should get some rest. I'm beat from taking care of these two." He pointed his mug to Cordial and Stitch. "Cheers, chaps." He pounded the last of his beer and burped, pushing his spectacles back onto his nose before departing..

"Yeah, we can search for this squire tomorrow, although I have no idea how, considering half of the city is cut off to us," Runt said as he stood, legs wobbly.

"A man called squire, huh? Any particular house or family you are inquiring about?" Stitch said. "Best be careful—say the wrong thing in the wrong part of Steelsburg, and you'll lose your tongue, or worse."

"Truthfully, no. Maynard's mentor said we're to look for a squire called Duncan. I think he mentioned another name—can't remember which, and that's bad considering he's supposed to help get us to Olde Ridgewatch." Runt was not feeling well now. The table spun a bit.

Cordial looked sideways at Stitch, and they both turned toward Sorella.

"We'll see you at breakfast tomorrow. Good evening," Sorella said a little sharply.

The boys turned and stumbled up the stairs. Sorella, the soberest, watched as Stitch and Cordial played a two-person game of cards.

* * *

Runt didn't sleep well. He kept seeing his mother's mutilated corpse, his friends, and neighbors long dead, and the Holy Imperium soldiers who performed the slaughter. He remembered the enormous spider on the road to Steelsburg and drinking with scoundrels who tried to rob him of his only worldly money mere hours ago. Time slipped forward as his head spun upside down into a muddled fog.

The room shook slightly, and Runt awoke, his head pounding behind his eyeballs. He fell out of bed, pulled his pants over his small clothes. His head spun, and he nearly threw up. Maynard was up, putting on his glasses and pushing his hair over so he could see better.

"Did you fall out of bed?" Maynard mumbled.

"What? No. Yes, I did, but the noise wasn't me. Wake up Angus. There's a situation. I don't know, but it could be trouble." Runt started buckling on his sword from earlier in the trip. He went downstairs dressed in a light tunic, leather vest, a short-cut wool coat, trousers, and an ill-fitting pair of boots.

Stitch, Cordial, and a large man stood near the door. There were shouts of "fire" and other rumblings coming from outside as the door continued to open and close with dwarves and humans leaving and coming in.

"What's happening?" Runt said, scratching at his eyes, trying to think clearly.

Stitch looked at him. "We dunno but should know more shortly. Sorella went out early this morning to gather news."

"I heard someone from the bar say there was a fire across the Orcfeast river," Cordial said.

Angus walked down the stairs, scratching his crotch, looked at the people standing by the door, paid no attention to them, and made his way to the bar. He was still dressed from last night, knife and hatchet at his belt, his hair askew. No barkeep around, so Angus reached over the bar. Cordial watched him before joining him by the bar. Angus poured a beer for himself, saw Cordial, and poured one for him. The scoundrel nodded and took a pull from his mug.

"Well, shit." Stitch slid over the top of the bar and grabbed an entire bottle of whiskey and several empty bottles from behind the bar. He whipped out a bag from nowhere and placed them all inside, fumbling with them so they wouldn't make noise. "Just doing the laundry. It needs to get done. Right?" Stitch said to himself, looking around with a half-smile. "Going to be a long day." "The laundry" appeared to be stealing anything he could put in his burlap bag.

Angus smiled, drank his beer down, and slid the mug back. Patrons at the corner tables lay with heads down, passed out. The door swung open. It was morning, but no light came through the door. Only a fine fog-like mist lingered in. Sorella walked in. She wore a scarf on her face, and her head was covered by a leather helmet typically worn by archers from yesterday. It looked worn and patched. She pushed down her scarf. Runt noticed she was armed and looked dangerous.

"You're all here. Perfect. If we want to leave, we should do so now. Money or no money, we should go. Things are about to go to shit in this city. Cordial, Stitch, a horse, and wagon are outside, along with two lanterns. Stay by them and kill anyone who even thinks about taking them." She looked fierce with a quiver of arrows slung low on her hip and a bow near, strung and ready to go. "Duncan, you okay to ride and fight if need be?" she said.

"Ride, if need be, but fight, you said? Sure, if it comes to it," the man named Duncan said in a baritone voice. He wavered a bit as if standing for the first time. He was broad-shouldered and muscled, but he looked beaten down and weary. He reminded Runt of a bear in human form. He scratched his face and ran his fingers through his hair. "I'll go grab all of our gear," he said through a partial beard and full mustache.

Runt looked up at the grizzly bear masquerading as a man. His hair hung around his face, framing a broken nose and healed scars. He slowly lumbered up past Runt and toward the stairs.

"Duncan, do you know a man called Doctor Young?" the boy asked. He was taking a wild guess, but his gut told him to do it. Duncan stood on the stairs and looked down at Runt. "He sent me to you. Doc said you would help me. Do you know him? He's a bit loony, not all there."

Duncan's sloped eyes examined him. Runt felt wrath resonate from the man's breathing. He looked beaten down, like a dog who had seen too many fights in a pit, as he lumbered back down the stairs, reached over, and picked Runt up, holding him by both arms. "What did that lunatic say about me?" He spoke through his teeth.

Runt could see the man's nose hairs, which were black, not white. His scruff was primarily black as well. Runt placed him in his thirties, but he was unsure. He was supposed to be intimidated by this large man picking him up—he could be crushed. But Runt wasn't threatened at all. He was relieved.

"He said you would help me find my father, brother, and maybe my sister. He said you would help," Runt said, looking directly into Duncan's eyes.

"I'm Maynard, Doctor Young's apprentice. Please put him down. My mentor said to give you this—said you lost it. He also said he knows he owes you money, and your payment is coming." Maynard handed Duncan a small rectangular box.

Duncan smiled as he looked inside the box. He took out the chained locket and put it over his head. "Let's get going."

Sorella turned her head and started tapping her foot. "Duncan, we got to go. The whole city is at war or on fire. Come on, come on—those bells ringing are not for religious services," she said.

Duncan looked at the two boys and Angus, whose hands were on the handle of a hatchet and knife stuck into his belt. "Sorella, they come with us. We got room?"

"Figured as much. Yes—you three, get your gear. You have two seconds; there may be two major coal mines on fire below the city, and an all-out battle is taking place in the Strip. I don't know what's happening exactly, but nobody is happy," said Sorella. She pointed her finger at the barkeep. "You! Get us a small keg of beer and as many wineskins as you can spare." She flicked the man a gold coin and then another.

"Also, a tea kettle and food fit for traveling. No questions, or I'll tell the Blitzsteel city guards you are Clearstone sympathizers," said Angus with a burp. The barkeep shuffled away into his pantry, shaken at the orders provided. Angus smiled. "The adventure continues. Boys, get our shit. I'm having another beer."

Cordial looked at Sorella in surprise. "I thought we didn't have any money?"

"We didn't, but there is a battle going on out there, so I procured it off a body or two. It's how I bought the wagon and horse," she said.

"You sly crow, you are," said Cordial, wagging his finger and smiling with

213

white teeth.

"Get outside now. Go! We need to move!" She clapped her hands at him and Stitch.

Stitch looked at the bar again. The barkeep was in the back storeroom. He gingerly moved his sack so the barkeep wouldn't hear its contents and moved out the door with Cordial.

"Duncan, I dunno how you can be half dwarve if you're the largest person I've ever met," said Stitch as he walked by.

Sorella hit him in the back of the head. "Get going, you idiot, or I'll put my foot in your ass," she growled.

A few minutes later, they stepped outside. Maynard immediately coughed. There was hazy smoke everywhere, like a lingering, visible, wet fart.

"Is it day or night?" said Runt, waving his hand back and forth over his mouth and face.

Cordial and Stitch stood in a side alley around a large cart hitched to a mangy horse.

Sorella put her scarf on her face and started giving short orders as she walked toward Stitch and Cordial. She hopped up on the cart's front seat. "You, dwarve, get up here and sit with me. We'll need your help getting out," she said.

A dark shade of smoke glided across the river, filling the morning sky. There was a battle at the Brothers Bridge. Both gates lay open as bridge towers blazed aflame, arrows and rocks flung about. A small shield wall from both sides met in the middle with a crushing roar of metal and meat grinding together. Runt watched at a distance, amazed for a moment. The battle felt remarkably close. Smoke wafted from another point across Riverstone Citadel on the other side of the valley. Runt saw further ahead that smoke streamed from another mine shaft above the valley. They were witnesses to history as the city battled for its very soul. The ground rumbled.

"You boys get to each side of the cart. Let's try to get out of here in one piece," said Sorella. "It looks like the families mutually agreed to kill each other on the bridge."

Duncan tied his hair back with a small leather strap, dipped his hands in

214

coal dust from the ground, and smeared the ends, making his hair darker in case the Clearstone family recognized him. There was a large shield in the cart along with other gear. Angus tossed his belongings into the back, including a sack of food and a medium-sized kettle. He then climbed up next to Sorella.

"Stitch, in the front. Guide the horse by the reins. Cordial, in the back in case you need to assist in us leaving," Sorella commanded.

They set off away from the bridge, now set in a pitched battle, and let the chaos flow behind them. There were screams and the sound of metal hitting metal.

"Keep your eyes open," Duncan said to Runt and Maynard. "Report anything you see to Sorella. I'll watch the back with Cordial. I'm still not fully healed— don't know how much damage I can do if one of the big families wants to stop us. Considering I may be a reason why they're killing each other and leveling the city, it will be a miracle if we get out of here."

The cart headed northeast along a red brick road with the river to its right and hopefully away from a feud that could go on for years. Duncan smeared his face with more grime, trying to make sure he did not look like the man who had nearly been executed weeks ago. Cordial smiled slightly as he walked alongside and looked around, almost enjoying it all. They came to no resistance as they neared the end of the Blitzsteel side of the city. They slowed as a platoon of well-armored dwarves marched quickly, but they didn't pay any attention to the group. The dwarves were loud as they moved in a military-like cadence, shields and short spears swaying in sync. It was like watching highly organized children moving toward war.

The wagon proceeded to where the street ended, and they had to choose a direction. They could move toward a gate controlled by an unknown family or straight onto a bridge held by the Blitzsteel family on both ends. The group stood quietly, waiting for Sorella to decide. Finally, she snapped the reins and followed refugees leaving the city—small packs of dwarves, human merchants, and others—out of the center of Steelsburg and hopefully to safety.

City guards stopped and questioned refugees as they walked toward the bridge's gates. One guard bore three yellow stars over a black anvil with a white background on his surcoat, indicating his loyalty to the Blitzsteel family. Stitch greased the leader's palm with some coin, and the guards appeared appeased. One of the younger guards looked strangely at Angus. The dwarve wore his black hair parted over with shaved sides; he looked arrogant and ready for a fight.

"Potential blood traitor, I says of this fool on the cart. Don't let the traitor leave," said the guard.

"You aren't in charge now, are you? Relax, kid. There's a whole line of people, and these losers have nothing in their cart except for a few meager possessions. We can rob another with a bit higher living standard in a few turns," the leader said.

The young dwarve looked at Angus and spat at the ground toward him, aching for a fight. Angus tipped his wine bag, took a long pull, turned forward, and moved on. Runt let out a deep sigh as he passed, and Duncan hopped up on the back of the wagon.

"We haven't made it halfway out of the city, and a quarter of our money is gone," said Sorella.

"Give me the rest of our money, Sorella," said Cordial.

"What? I barely trust you to be alone with yourself, you pervert, why would I give you the rest of our money?"

"Trust me, love, I'll get us out of here, or you can cut off my fishing pole and tackle," said Cordial. He looked at her with a sheepish smile. Finally, she relented and gave him a purse full of coins. He weighed it in his hand and took half the money out, giving her the loose change. "Stitch and I'll take care of this and come out on top. Promise," said Cordial.

The line moved forward. Cordial led the horse onward. Sorella blew the air out of her mouth, stressed, and looked at Angus, who said nothing but took another drink of wine and passed it to Sorella.

"We'll be out of money and wine before we get out of this city. Then we are truly bent over," she said and took a drink. Angus laughed a little. "Never thought I would try to escape a city full of dwarves with a dwarve who looks like he hates his comrades."

After the initial exchange with the guards, they waited in the queue to reach the first gate of the bridge, leaving Steelsburg behind them. Runt watched, standing at the back end of the cart while Cordial argued with the gate guard. He put his hands up; said, "This is robbery," in a huff; gave the lead guard with a heavy axe a handful of money; and walked back, shaking his head. Stitch snickered and shook his head with a dour smile while talking to two other guards off to the side. Gentle laughter came from them. Runt watched Stitch pass a tin flask to one of the dwarves, who took a deep pull from an ex-slave bullshitting with a dwarven guard. Vineland had right and genuinely changed.

Sorella said, "How'd it go?"

"Splendid, and by that, I mean terrible. Gave them all our money to cross the bridge," said Cordial.

The gates opened, and they started moving.

"You said we would break even," said Sorella, angry.

"Oh, we will, we will," Cordial said and grabbed the reins, pulling the horse onto the bridge.

Stitch continued to have a lively discussion and waved the buggy on as he finished his conversation. He put his hands on the shoulder of one of the dwarves, slid it down, laughed, and repeated the same while taking a pull from the flask they passed around. The head dwarve came over, and Stitch nodded and asked to see the man's large axes. The dwarve waited a moment and gave it to him; Stitch fell with it due to its weight. There was more laughter, and the flask passed around again. He got up, looked back, realized it was time to go, bowed, said good day, and ran toward the wagon as it crossed the bridge, which spanned a river gorge below. Runt saw him stuffing his left hand into his pocket.

"That was fun. Never stolen three purses in a row before. I hope they're not too cross," said Stitch.

The cart continued over the bridge.

"You get enough?" asked Cordial.

"Yes, I think so." Stitch weighed each bag in his hand, opened the smallest one, took half the contents out, and gave them to Cordial. "Here you go, for the other gate. Let them know one of the other guards back there dropped it."

Cordial did the talking again, pushed on past the gate, and they officially moved out of the city. Cordial walked up to the cart after they were safely away and offered two-coin purses to Sorella. Runt saw Stitch pocket two gold coins but didn't say anything.

"This should cover the nut for the horse, wagon, and more." She smiled. "Nice work, you bastards. I know now why Duncan and I kept you two around."

"Thanks, Sorella. Stitch and I also snagged a flint, a nice knife, and other trinkets. They didn't know what hit them," Stitch said.

They moved out of the valley as refugees kept a distance from one another best they could as fear and paranoia spread like the fires in the caves behind them.

"So, you managed to steal from one of the guards?" Runt said as Stitch walked by.

"Stealing involves theft. I found these items, my friend, and they ended up in my pockets." Stitch laughed. He tossed a flint box to Angus. "Here, I bet you need this. Also, Runt, I stole from all three of them, not just one." He winked and stuck his tongue out.

Runt laughed a little but felt dejected. He looked around again at this strange band and wasn't sure what to feel. He, Maynard, and Angus had managed to find the squire he'd been looking for and now walked among thieves, bank robbers, and rogues. Smoke rolled up from the valley behind, trailing them as they left Steelsburg, burning under the veil of battle.

"It may burn forever. A coal mine set on fire could set the entire valley aflame," Sorella stated, guiding the horse on.

"Whoever started fires in those mines . . ." Angus paused for a moment, almost choked up. "It's a terrible thing to do to the ground and a family. Such a terrible thing. I pity the young dwarve back there who wanted to fight me. After this civil war, there will be no pride left for dwarves in Steelsburg. Not with the bloodshed, destruction, and disgrace happening. It's unholy and a curse against those that brought it on." He took another swig of wine and passed the skin to Sorella.

"True words, dwarve, true words," she said.

They sat quietly as the wagon moved back and forth, knowing they'd left a moment in history behind. Day moved into early evening, and the winds kicked up, blowing soot and coal dust everywhere. The smoke continued to filter out of the valley. Angus looked back at the city as it slowly shrank away from them.

"Where are we headed, Mr. Duncan?" asked Runt as they walked.

"Yeah, where to?" piped in Maynard.

"Well, Sorella figures we head toward Olde Ridgewatch, and we see what we can see. Your mentor—as you call him, Maynard—has contacts there. Maybe we visit them," Duncan said.

"How long to Olde Ridgewatch?" asked Runt.

"Two to two and a half weeks on during the summer, but now, three weeks at best and conceivably longer," Duncan said. "If we get hit with a snowstorm, we may need to winter at the nearest town and earn a living."

"We should make our way to Hagarville Valley and Mount Nittany University. We can find work near the university and an inn to stay at for some time." Maynard said. "I may be able to scrounge up news as well, due to my status as a student at the University of Grimwood."

Sorella looked at the mage-apprentice thoughtfully. "Marvelous idea, Maynard. What do you think, Duncan?"

He walked with Cordial. "I think we camp off the road at the next hill, and yeah, heading to the university is the responsible thing to do. It's hard to tell what the weather is with all this smoke, but I don't think we'll last too long if we don't make it there soon."

The wind continued to move the gray and black smoke throughout the night, bringing colder weather and the darkness of snow pressing from the west.

Runt- A Raven's Dinner

The bastards passed a few small shacks in the hills near Hagarville Valley. One of the problems with heading into Hagarville Valley involved the mountain cougars. At night, Duncan built fires to keep the animals away. Occasionally, Runt heard the large cats roaming in the shadows, crying out in the darkness, reminding everyone who owned the night. Runt spent half an hour on his knees in deep concentration, reaching out to the animals, trying to befriend them like the wolves in Wolf Hills, and failing as he had done nearly every night. Maynard and Angus knew he tried to reach out to the animals but never mentioned it to the others.

They were a day out from Mount Nittany University.

"What the Hades?" Runt said, standing on the wagon's front seat as Stitch managed the reins next to him. He pointed toward the edge of a clearing near where two roads crossed. A half score of child-like bodies hung from one of the lowest branches.

"Vulcan's beard," Angus said as he walked by Maynard's side.

The entire group instantly became more alert. They loosened swords, and Sorella strung her compound bow. She hopped down from the back of the wagon, nodded to Duncan, and slipped into the woods, heading toward the swinging corpses via a circular route. Stitch slowly moved the cart ahead, toward the crossroads. All conversation stopped. Duncan got out and slung his massive round shield on his left arm. Several ravens picked at the hanging bodies, fighting over scraps of flesh and not caring about the new arrivals to their feast.

"They don't look human," said Runt. "They look like green children."

"Goblins," said Maynard. "I dissected one in Grimwood."

A look of shock fell on both Stitch's and Cordial's faces.

"Aren't you perceptive, my spectacle-wearing friend? Here I thought you were an old-fashioned healer, but you have the look of sorcery on you if I don't say so myself. Let me see your hand."

"Touch me, and I will fucking burn you," Maynard said.

"S'all right, s'all right. Just giving you a hard time. So you're a hedge mage?" Cordial asked as he scratched at the side of his face.

Sorella appeared by the bodies and poked at one with her bow. The cart and the rest of the band were still a distance away. She didn't frighten the birds away, which seemed odd to Runt. Sorella waved them forward. Stitch moved the horse on a bit faster now. The ravens left except for the largest, which pecked at the face of the last hanging goblin. The bird looked up, squawked at Sorella, and returned to eating.

"It looks like a proper butchery of woodland ghouls and goblins," Duncan said. There were two orc heads on spikes below the hanging goblin bodies. "Looks like the local sentries for the Queens and Kings Roads are active in this area. They took their time to hang them. I bet they ambushed the group. These little assholes don't leave the caves too often. Mostly a dwarven problem. Shit, I haven't seen their kind since the Plains of Ursula, and only during the night battles."

"I don't know if it was a local road patrol either," said Sorella. "Found pieces of broken glass in the trees and burn marks. It could be staff from the university."

"Anyone check them for gold and such?" Stitch walked toward the hanging ones. He got close and vomited. It had caught him off guard. "Shit, they stink," he spat and coughed.

"Did you know goblins hoard everything? If they can't carry something valuable back with them, they sometimes swallow it and hope to throw it up or crap it out later. I've never seen it, but Doc said he found a small fortune in a goblin one time," Maynard said.

Stitch poked one of the goblins' bloated stomachs with a knife. Bile and intestines fell out, spreading the smell of decay and rotting food over the entire area. Runt almost vomited, and Cordial had tears in his eyes.

"So gross, Stitch. So gross," said Runt.

"You find anything," asked Maynard.

"No, just a few lucky stones and a copper ring," Stitch said as he examined the ground under the goblin's body.

"From what I know, they don't come out too often in more than a pack of six. Goblins get too aggressive and end up fighting one another," Angus said. "When I was younger, they would get hungry and agitated and try to take dwarven gates underground. Could be a real nuisance. In the tunnels, a stupid kid wanders off, and the family would later find their bones—if they were lucky. The little mongrels would eat everything and loot the armor and weapons. Living above the ground, we never heard of any coming around." He spat at one of the corpses.

"With the local wild cat population, you'd think they wouldn't dare come about," observed Maynard.

The wind picked up a bit. It was nearly lunchtime, but the smell was terrible. They all made faces of disgust and covered their noses.

"Let's get out of here. Don't want to be around here at dark," Sorella said. She looked to the sky as if she felt something. Her eyes filled with worry and stress of the unknown.

They moved forward as Sorella waited for the cart to pass. She walked behind them into the next section of overhanging trees, moving into the woods and toward the university. The last raven finished supper, squawked, and flew eastward.

She quietly sang to herself as she followed behind the cart. Duncan walked at the front, tense and alert. Angus sat in the back, twirling a stick in his left hand, keeping his mind busy. Maynard sat with him and watched Sorella as she sang. She looked to be in a trance.

"How'd you do it?" Cordial asked.

Maynard rubbed his right ring finger and looked away.

"Maynard, it's okay. Stitch, and I are wanted in several free city-states. Shit, Sorella and Stitch are considered fair game to bounty hunters, as they're half breeds, although it's hard to tell. So, give us your story. How did it happen?"

The cart rolled on for a moment, going uphill through the ruts toward the university.

"My mentor helped me break it. Songs call him the 'First to Break the Binding,' which is one of his names. He's got many names. Duncan knows him by a few as well. He's brilliant and powerful but a bit insane and rotten with money. I think what he did above the Erie Sea haunts him. He doesn't sleep much, and when he does, he has nightmares. I think some of his past power has taken a toll on him, including when he helped break my binding." Maynard paused for a moment to get his bearing.

"If it's found you have special abilities, like you can talk to sheep with your mind or freeze water in the summer, the Holy Church may take the time to bind you, so you don't become too powerful . . . or they burn you at the stake. The binding controls what you can and can't do. It stops you from intentionally harming other living beings. The process of binding is painful. It feels as if a piece of yourself is ripped out." Maynard looked away for a moment.

"If I was bound, you would see a ring on my right ring finger, silver in color but permanently on my skin. The binding stops people with power from performing demonic and blood magic, and although the Holy Church doesn't tell you, it limits your progress in the other schools of magic.

"Doc, my mentor, found me and took me in, seeing my potential, I guess. He was back from the war and working at the University of Grimwood. That's the short end of it." Maynard looked at Cordial. "You want more, don't you?"

Cordial nodded. "I tell you what. After we get Runt to his dad, Stitch and I will get you enrolled in the little club we're part of. There are business opportunities available for a person of your status."

"I've heard stories about the Society of Shadows. I'd rather not. I could end up like those goblins behind us just for talking about them." Maynard paused, smiled, pushed up his spectacles, and went on, "The first thing Doc did was show me how to remove the binding. If not for him, I could have lost my hand, gone insane, or worse. Doc helped me through it, and it was my first big lesson. It wasn't easy. It took me two weeks to figure it out, and I'm still forever marked."

"And now you're an all-powerful hedge mage!" commented Cordial.

"No, not really. Still learning." Maynard shivered visibly. "You don't just get power. Most people learn to find it and take it, like finding grains of salt in a handful of sand. The truly powerful, if done right, are given it, which doesn't happen often, if ever."

Cordial put his hand on Maynard's shoulder. "It's all right, mate. It's not the same, but when you join the Society of Shadows, they brand you. It hurts, and nobody likes to smell their burned flesh. We have mages in our group, but they are mostly shit, unlike what you did in the alley. That's right—evil shit. Sorry if I brought up old wounds. Meant no harm. I was trying to get to know you fellas 'cause you look to be joining our little band of misfits and bastards."

"Bastards, ha! So, you don't know your parents either?" Maynard asked.

"Yeah, I guess so. We're a bunch of bastards and criminal deviants in the eyes of the Holy Imperium. Duncan is a lifelong squire, bound to knights who die before knighting him. He knew of his father but never met him. Sorella is a disgraced half-blood native, Stitch is a half-blood native and a petty sneak thief, and I'm their fearless, attractive, and penniless noble leader. I'm sure you'll hear about it over a fire one day. We need to get safely to the university." Cordial blew on his hands.

Sorella looked at Maynard. "Don't believe half of what Cordial spits out of his mouth. He speaks, and shit falls out," she said and started singing quietly to herself again.

"Bastards!" Stitch laughed. "Never knew my old man, and I was sold away from my mom as soon as her milk ran dry. Either our parents live long enough to disappoint us, die too soon to teach us, or never know our names, and we live as their mistakes." He spat on the ground in anger. "It's probably why we're helping you, Runt. You still have a semblance of a family, even if it's a bit broken up. You deserve a shot at it—or justice for what's been done to you."

Angus scratched his beard in acknowledgment, and Cordial shook his head, thinking of his only sister. Runt looked back at them and then toward the sky, lost in memories.

"Cordial said you're elvish. Means you know the high art?" Maynard said.

Sorella looked at him and nodded. She took off her hat and pulled back her hair. Her ears were human-shaped, not pointed like elves'. "I took the time to look like you so I would be freer to move about in cities and castles, but if you stare at me and know your way around us savages, you can tell I'm one. I know about the ancient ways, but I'm not trained like your fold, and it's a bit more natural to me," she said, putting her archer hat back on.

"The bird," he said. "You saw through its eyes? Runt said he can do something similar with the wolves where he lived."

"I didn't know," she said. "Explains why Runt prays nightly, ever since we got into the area where mountain cougars live. I haven't been able to reach out to cats, either. When I jump, even for a minute or two, it makes me a bit sick afterward."

"I can show you how to stop it if you want. It's not too hard. Just takes a bit of training," said Maynard.

"Are you a skin jumper?" she asked.

"No, but I've read enough, and there are steps you can take before you jump to limit the dizziness and weakness after," he said.

"I'd like that, but later. Let's keep moving," she said. "It's easier to talk to the birds than to jump into them. All you have to do is listen to them, and they will sing to you. Get to know them enough, and they'll whisper to you even."

Maynard had noticed that two crows always seemed to be around Sorella, but he'd never caught her speaking to them.

The late afternoon got colder as they made their way up the pass, walking the roads of set stones toward Hagarville Valley. Finally, they hit the peak and looked upon Mount Nittany University and its buildings in the twilight. A large tower sat opposite the valley, providing a vantage point across the area.

Upon seeing an inn, they stabled the horse cart and went inside for food and sleep, glad to feel safe for a moment.

* * *

The bastards settled in for the winter. Maynard managed to get a room in the university dorms. Runt had no idea how Maynard had connived his way into school lodging. Maynard checked in once every few days at the Red Horse Tavern, where Sorella and Duncan took rooms. Cordial and Stitch said they would be back in two weeks, promising they would not get into trouble, indicating they would find lodging and check in with old acquaintances in the area. Runt and Angus found housing at an inn called McMaster's Pour House. Runt washed dishes, prepped food, and cleaned tables, and Angus cooked for several teachers during the winter break. Most students left to return to their respective families, waiting to come back when spring rolled in. Several poorer students stayed around, working odd jobs in Hagarville Valley. Everything became snowbound and windswept soon after they arrived.

Runt started training daily with Duncan in the horse stalls of the Red Horse Tavern. They practiced sword and shield work for two hours every morning, and Sorella taught Runt forestry and other survival skills until lunch. After that, Runt followed up with Angus, who worked in the kitchen at the university and cleaned up dishes after the lunch rush. Runt worked with two first-year students from the eastern part of the Commonwealth of Erieland. They were an okay company, but their religious views kept Runt at a distance. They were pacifists wishing to become monks for the Holy Church, and they looked down on Runt for his military training with Duncan.

The weather turned to bitter winds and heavy snow. The cold seeped inside from the cracks of doors and loose cobblestone walls, and wind wormed its way through poorly assembled windows. The snow fell as large flakes, coating fences and the roofs of inns, homes, and hovels without discrimination. On other days, the snow fell as small specks spitting horizontally from the surrounding woods and deep forests. If the fires didn't stay stoked, frost would form inside the walls and windows. Animals, both wanted and unwanted, sought warmth inside well-heated buildings. Mount Nittany University's buildings used vents made from tin or copper to bring warm air from large dwarven-built fireplaces.

Winter settled into the valley, and the cold became a constant concern for those staying at the college and in the surrounding town. Outer body parts never felt warm enough as ears, fingers, and toes were at continual risk of frostbite. The larger halls at the college remained empty, as the heat was closed off until classes resumed. Winter's stench lingered near every fire through the short days and long nights. A mixture of wood, coal, and other heat sources attempted to keep the season of Stribog from consuming the entire valley. Everyone waited, hoping the winter god, Stribog, would leave soon, and Judith, Maiden of Storms, rode through, wailing thunder and lightning while bringing spring rain to melt the snow and end the darkness and cold that seeped through the walls.

Duncan worked as a door attendant and bodyguard for the Red Horse Tavern, located outside the university. The establishment was named after the legendary horse of a hero from a far-off land. He worked the door taking money while the Red Horse played live music and was called upon if a drunken patron or student could not pay their tab or got too handsy with a barmaid. He wore a large overcoat, a hat, and fingered gloves, and carried a cudgel the size of a mace. Inside his coat, he donned several knives.

The three sides of the university and surrounding town were isolated from the rest of the Commonwealth of Erieland. Travelers could reach the valley only by the road near the crossroads where the goblins hung from the tree.

Outside of the sheriff, the rule of law came from Mount Nittany University and its staff. The townsfolk all considered themselves as working for the college and, thus, under the school's rules. They called it "the Lions' rule," and the school prefects, upper-level students, kept the law. If the breaking of a rule became severe enough, a magistrate of the school took over the proceedings. The sheriff used the prefects as well and reported them to the school magistrates.

Maynard mentioned this while they wandered about the basement of the school library one night. He'd provided a reading list for Runt to start on over the snowy days of winter. It was Monday, so Runt didn't work this afternoon. The basement venting inside the library worked enough to keep frost off the books but not enough to be comfortable, so Runt and Maynard bundled up before heading into the stacks. They carried tin-roofed lamps with green glass sides, giving the shadows a spring-like glow.

"Finding a book is exorbitantly difficult. The entire system is unclear on purpose," said Maynard. "It keeps everyone on their toes and the power in the hands of one or two librarians. Libraries are even more confusing in bigger universities."

While Runt hunted for the suggested books, Maynard searched for two his mentor was interested in procuring. If anything, he believed they would be in the basement or even in the sub-level below the basement.

"Did you ever find out what happened to the goblins outside of town from anyone at the university?" Runt asked.

"One of the librarians, Hattie, told me a bit—said there was trouble on the road, so the teachers and a few prefects set about taking care of business. I guess the teachers took several of the school's best archers; a few alchemists, not true mages; and a few of the prefects out near the road where we found the bodies hanging. It was during the day, and they came upon a nest of goblins out in plain sight at the top of a hill overlooking the valley. They got them to fall into an ambush, and they lay waste to them," said Maynard.

"Wow!" said Runt. "Professors and students did that?"

"Wow is right. Don't piss off the enlightened and highly educated," said Maynard. "Here we are."

"Damn, it's cold," Runt said. He wore fingerless gloves like Duncan's to help him grip a sword better, even though he didn't have one. He wanted to impress the man; he looked up to him. Duncan said if you lost your sword, you'd better have lost your hand because without it, you were dead.

"It is, but this will be worth it," said Maynard.

They moved further from the stairs, bringing them to the basement and deeper into the stacks of bookshelves. The books were covered with dust. Some held mold and smelled of decay. The cold kept most critters out, but the dampness ruined the texts. Runt stared at the books and scrolls, wondering at the knowledge and stories kept inside. Their shoes and breathing were the only noises made for several minutes. They walked quickly, looking at the spines of books in languages long dead and unknown to any living person. They came to a stop after a while.

"I've never seen so many books in my life," Runt said, eyes wide in delight.

Maynard raised the lamp as it flickered, swayed a bit, and placed it on a shelf of books. "We're looking for a book with a black spine and red lettering marked *Gaston's Chronicle of Weapons*. You'll know it when you see it."

"What's so important about it?" said Runt.

"Doc said to find and procure the book if I can. I'm sure it's a bit of heavy reading, but if he wants it, it's important."

"It's not this?" Runt grabbed a book with a handle on its spine about eight inches in length. "I can't even pronounce the words on this one." He blew off the dust on the spine and coughed.

"Me either—could be fun. Keep it. We'll take it upstairs after we look a little more," Maynard said.

A screech came from the end of the row of shelves, echoing over their heads in the large empty room. The door to the stairs and out of the basement was a long way off.

"Yeah, we should head back, Maynard. I don't have anything except my boot knife."

"I know, I know, but we haven't found the book. Besides, it's probably a hall cat trapped down here after the last time the door was opened, and its half-starved, I bet."

Maynard continued to look at the spines of books. Runt raised his lantern to light the area as worry filled his face. The lantern shined a foggy green around them. They moved down the lengthy bookshelves, listening to their breathing and footfalls. Runt thought he heard humming or music coming from the darkness. He didn't mention it to Maynard, not wanting to act weird in front of him. They shift to another shelf toward the back.

"The university has no idea what they have here. I should talk to Hattie at the librarian's desk. Maybe a professor can help them get these books out of the basement and into a better place, with more space and less wetness. This place needs to put the library in the tower."

"Maynard, we need to make it through winter and get to Olde Ridgewatch alive," said Runt. "Starting a library—a book-organizing project might seem like paradise to you, but I want to see my family. We can come back and spend years doing it when we're old farts with nothing to do."

"There's so much knowledge in here, and it's being ruined." Maynard pushed up his spectacles and brushed his hair away.

A book fell from far off to the left as Runt turned.

"What was that?" he said in a hushed voice.

"I dunno, but yeah, it might be time to go," Maynard said in a muted tone.

He pocketed a few books inside his robe, and they started heading back. As they neared the end of the bookshelf Runt heard the singing again. He was unsure whether it was in his head or coming from the books.

"Do you hear . . .?" whispered Runt.

"Music, yes. It's not just you; it's a finding song. Someone else is in here looking for a book. Most everyone is on break, so perhaps it's a professor," Maynard said.

They tried to block their lights. Runt stopped talking and listened while he drew out his boot knife. Maynard did the same.

Each bookshelf almost touched the ceiling, stacked tightly with scrolls, pamphlets, and letters, creating an excellent wall for every row of shelves. Unfortunately, their green lamp light did not penetrate to the other side of the shelves. Although alarmed, both Runt and Maynard were curious about the song's origin. They moved to the end of the bookshelf. The music continued faintly. They turned the corner and peered down the next row, looking far down the line of books.

"Holy shit, it's a—" said Maynard.

"Goblin," Runt finished.

Doc -The Lost Staff

Doc stopped walking as he neared the edge of a bridge, his horse long dead behind him. Across lay the future of Vineland, and behind, his friends. The ghosts of those he took remained deep inside, pestering what was left of his soul. He found the solitude pleasing, but a small part of him craved the joy of telling stories and the laughter of people no longer of this world. They haunted him when sober, and the one who gave up everything for him remained like a ghost even when he numbed himself with drugs and alcohol. He tried to erase all the battles, lessons, and losing two close friends by his hand, and it all slowly broke him down as he teetered the fine line between genius and madness.

He patted his worn coat, snagged a small tobacco tin, packed his clay pipe, and lit it with nearly his last bit of power. Doc was out of reefer and whiskey, which didn't suit his thoughts as the voices whispered and laughed at him from the cobwebs of his darkest thoughts. Across the bridge lay the city-state of Affectus, the so-called city of neighbors. If he walked over the bridge crossing Blue Hen River events would take place changing the closest people left in his life, and Doc wasn't sure he could subject them to that. He could turn back and meet up with his apprentice and the motley crew of thieves and failures, reunite Runt with his father, and perhaps save Runt's sister, Alysha.

One of the three siblings was the key to creating—dare he think it? One of them could birth a new nation. Which one the witch had said, it didn't matter . . . or maybe he couldn't remember.

Doc brushed away the thought. He held the pipe in his teeth, breathed in deeply, and cleaned his shaded spectacles, trying to shut the voices out of his head. Coughing, he dropped his staff. It spun around several times unnaturally, the blade facing the city and the head of the staff pointing behind him. The staff's name was Gaston's Beard, one of the most powerful tools ever created, and it often acted on its own accord. It was one of the Paragons, forgotten by most and sought after by those who knew of their power, often called Maker's Gifts.

"Well, shit. Bleak omens all around," he mumbled.

Doc leaned down and picked it up, cleaning the head of the staff with his cloak. He was due to meet a peer soon. They would be waiting and hated when he was late.

He plodded over the bridge, its wood and metal creaking with each step. Two hungry squirrels capered by, and he made a clicking noise, holding out pieces of dry apple for them. They perked their heads up.

Doc was weak, and he could use the energy. He hadn't taken from an animal or human in so long. Finally, they came close enough, and he lunged at both.

He left his past behind and moved toward the future, leaving two bloody squirrel carcasses on the bridge. He licked his fingers clean of his and the animals' blood. He felt a slight surge of power and guilt run through his veins. Soon he came across his destination.

It was a manor house on the outskirts of the city, found down a long horse path through a field, two floors high with a cellar in the back. A large front porch wrapped around the house, and a barn sat nearby. Three horses were tied to the front porch. He patted one on its rump. "You are a fine specimen, aren't you?" It looked at him with the slight fear and timidness all animals gave to Doc. He could pull from this animal and be that much stronger but decided against it.

Candles lit up a kitchen off the main dining room. Doc walked in and turned left, toward the light, with hesitancy.

"Bout time you got here. I nearly headed into town and found more pleasurable company. Better than sitting here reading and waiting for the likes of you, old man," Olivia Franklin said. She put down a book. She sat with her feet on the kitchen table, the chair tipped back, dangerously close to falling over. Yet she was entirely in control of the room. Her eyes almost shimmered, and her long, straight, dark hair was soaked by the candlelight. "Thirsty?" she asked.

Doc was parched. Sucking the energy from a creature of Vineland against their will provided Doc with the power he needed and created shame deep inside him. When he took power, a small piece of him drifted into oblivion. It was like losing a tooth or fingernail. There was still blood caked under his nails.

"You've been abusing the art, haven't you? I get the idea of blood magic, Doc. I don't like what it could do to you permanently." She slid a glass of whiskey across the table to him.

"All forms of the art scar the user in unique ways. I choose to know what it's taken from me," Doc muttered. "Thanks." He nearly drained his glass. "I haven't taken anyone or anything in since before the battle." He smiled slightly and relaxed. "Getting here has not been easy. Is anyone else coming?

"Yes, a few more, I expect," she said and took a drink, putting her feet down. "Sorella will not be showing. She is otherwise engaged."

"Hmph, I will miss her," Olivia paused, "company. The three sisters will not be making it for many reasons, mostly to do with you and Prince Damon. I saw you didn't bring any bodyguards. Where is the husky brute Duncan?"

"He's performing a task for me," mumbled Doc.

"He's a quality man, and people follow and look up to him. Keep him close if you can. No bodyguards either shows a boatload of trust or pure stupidity. I mean, you're weak. I can tell. Maybe I'll slap you and take the staff out of your hands."

Doc gripped the staff. "I think you know I have a few tricks up my sleeves, Olivia."

"True. I would not want to get burned."

"Where are your guards? I wouldn't want a knife to meet my throat tonight."

"They're minding themselves in the back room. Neither mingles with humans unless they have to."

"You always did like them big and stupid," Doc said.

"Don't underestimate orcs and goblins. They're just as civilized as humans, Doc. You know that. I know you keep several elves close, including Sorella and her cohort Stitch."

"The elves of this land got a raw deal and are the purest beings in Midgard, Olivia. Hades, they taught us all about the art and its different forms before any humans could practice it."

"Same could be said of orcs and goblins, Doc."

He paused at this and took another drink. "I suppose you're right. Hades. You're right way more than me." He smiled and looked directly at her.

"You're asking who else would show. I think we'll see the general and the traitor tonight, and I believe a new player will surprise us in a matter of moments."

"Your powers are not like the three sisters', Olivia, and it frightens me to my bones," Doc said gruffly.

There was a sudden rattle and two hard thumps as bodies hit the floor in the room behind them. Doc stood, his chair tipping over. He moved quickly to the door. Olivia stood and moved to the kitchen fire.

"Show yourself, Samuel. You know we can't practice the art around you. We're barely armed," said Olivia.

"Oh, I do, I do. Hello, Doc, you have something of mine. Olivia Franklin, I do believe you have a bounty on your head, too. I must have the Maker on my side tonight," said Samuel as he walked in, brash and confident, short sword pointed at Doc and a ball and chain ready in the other hand. He looked prepared to whip out and crush heads.

Doc gripped his staff and attempted to call up a defensive hex using fire, but nothing happened. He grasped for power but felt uncomfortably numb. "Olivia, he's a Templar," said Doc.

"I'm a *Hawthorn*, Doc, not a damn Templar. We didn't all die during the Thornbriar War," he said. "Well, most did, but some of the bloodlines managed to leave before we were all slaughtered. Both of you are old enough to have bloodied your hands during those years. I should cut you down for your past sins right now." Samuel pointed his short sword at both of them.

"Fucking warlock scum, you hunt us instead of leading the country and taking the throne here in Vineland," Doc said and spat in his direction. "Don't you have a sense of duty to your people?"

"My sense of duty was lost when my mother and father were killed while they slept, and they weren't even in blessed Vineland. We're hunted as much as you are by Great Brightland and the Holy Imperium. Now give me your wand and staff," ordered Samuel Hawthorn. His ancient blood from King Christopher and Erica the Red blunted the two mages' powers.

"Men behaving as men with the yelling and bravado. Samuel Hawthorn, you have us at an advantage. All we have is this staff, and this fine tea kettle. Say, Samuel, may I ask how you care for a tree you wish to grow?" asked Olivia as if what was occurring was as common as slipping on a pair of boots.

He looked at Doc and Olivia and said quietly, "You water it with blood and give it freedom."

"Would you like tea?" she asked politely.

Samuel looked at Olivia—who stood near the stove wearing a dark robe, a fitted bodice, and men's trousers—and at Doc, who was stooped and holding his staff like a child holds a stuffed bear before bed. "I would, actually. Please, both of you, sit."

Doc looked surprised by his response. "A Hawthorn that believes in liberty, Maker's tits! Never thought I would see the day," he said under his breath as his shoulders relaxed.

Samuel didn't sheathe his short sword, but he eased up and moved away from the kitchen door. Olivia bowed, put the kettle on a warming pad on the table, and sat without effort.

"At last, civility. You know, Doc, it was impossible to track you down. Your buddy General Flint has it out for you and your friends. I got mixed up near Steelsburg and followed the easier of the two trails. I wandered around for a long time until I realized I was chasing you and your staff, not Rhett Ashburn."

"Is that what you want—the boy Runt?" Doc asked.

"Couldn't care less. I just need one of those weapons to pay a large debt. It could be the dagger, wand, or staff. You can give me one, or I leave you with throats slit and bodies hanging from a tree. Choose wisely, please."

"Maker's tits, a warlock with manners. The world changes," said Doc, still feeling uneasy and still unarmed.

Samuel Hawthorn stood just under six feet tall, wearing a mixture of light armor and boiled studded leather which allowed for mild protection and ease of movement. His fingers were free of gloves, and his wrists were wrapped tightly with light chains and amulets. Several amulets were tucked around his throat inside his armor as well. He was muscled but not in a heavy bruiser way, more in line with the distant elvish heritage from Erica the Red.

"Sit, Doc," said Olivia. "As you can see, Samuel has affairs to discuss. You came alone, like Doc. Welcome to our small gathering," she said, acting as if she still controlled the room. She pushed an empty chair toward Samuel with her foot. Doc plopped down. Olivia poured tea from the kettle into three cups. One cup had a small chip, the other multicolored, and the last cup's handle was wrapped in a strand of silk. Samuel continued to stand.

"Shit, well. You have me. Nice sword, my friend. Do you happen to have any reefer on you?" Doc asked as if Samuel were a known dealer. Doc took the chipped cup and sucked up the steam into his face, fogging his colored spectacles.

"Let me guess—others are coming as well, and I will be outnumbered shortly. Can't wait to meet them."

"My bodyguards—are they . . .?"

"One forced my hand, and I took his life, the asshole. He was vicious; the other one, the orc, I knocked out."

Olivia shifted, feeling the pain of losing a close friend.

"Biggest goblin I've ever seen, and yet he still looked small next to the orc," said Samuel. "Unlucky for her, she got the sword. The other got the ball and chain."

"They wouldn't have harmed you, fool. I was expecting you."

"You were? How is that possible?" said Samuel.

"Olivia may not be able to perform her art now, but as you know, some of our kind read the stars and taste dreams, Samuel," Doc said tartly.

"Fortune-telling and mysticism, sure, sure. You can tell the future to piss right off," Samuel said. "Is that why you let me kill one of your guards?"

"What I do is not exact, as what Doc has learned is not exact. We came here to plan the future," she replied, looking at the Hawthorn cooly. "Not gaze into its clouds with ignorance."

"The future of this country, of this land from the Stagger Wall to the Atlantis Ocean," said Samuel. "One, a deranged and haggard battlemage, and the other, a petty fraud who won't die. Yeah, I see greatness ahead for all of us."

"It appears you are part of this now," said Olivia.

"An old mage and witch planning the future of Vineland," said Samuel as he shifted into a more defensive position.

"As I've said, others are coming."

The back door of the house slammed open.

"And here they are now. Hello, General Benedict Ashburn."

Doc smiled and didn't move from his seat. Instead, he gripped his staff more tightly, adjusting his posture. Olivia shifted and raised her cup of tea. Samuel quickly kicked over a chair, blocking a direct path to himself.

"Witch, I hate your damned games!" he said, putting his sword to Olivia's throat. The further movement came from behind him, from a younger man with a drawn crossbow.

"This is not what I was hoping for, but it seems I have the better of you three," Benedict Ashburn said. "Keep the crossbow pointed at the man with the sword. The other two don't seem to be threats, Benjamin."

The front door opened, and a tall man with a dangerous-looking spear pushed through. "Doc, Olivia, a pleasure, and it looks as if we have a mysterious guest. And ahh, the Holy Imperium has graced our presence. So good to see you again, Benedict."

"Lord Washcreek, you know this lot?"

"I can speak for the two sitting, but the jittery fellow, I don't know," said Lord Washcreek.

"My name is Samuel."

Washcreek poked Samuel's back with his spear. "Put the sword down, boy, or I will run you through, and there will be nothing but your blood and shit left before your blade touches her neck."

"Samuel is deciding if he wishes to join our tribe, Washcreek, and Benedict is searching for his pride or—" said Olivia.

"His son Runt," finished Doc. "Solid lad. I saved him from an unfortunate event a few months back."

237

Samuel made a calculated decision, moving his sword away from Olivia's neck and down to his side. He remained tense but still.

"My son, where is he? And why has he left his mother and sister!" yelled Benedict Ashburn.

"Your son is seeking the same answers you seek for yourself, General," advised Doc.

"Careful, Benedict, I've dealt with Doc and Olivia before, and they shape the reality around them with words and more. Half the time, Doc doesn't make sense until it's too late, and the other half, he's out of his mind with the purest form of truth. Olivia is a lovely companion until she tires of you," said Washcreek with a smile as he slowly moved his spear between the three of them. Lord Washcreek was six feet tall and past fifty springs old with a slim, muscular build and an ability to command all those who encountered him. His hair, mostly silver and gray with delicate pieces of black mingled in, was pulled tightly and tied in the back.

"That must be young Benjamin. He's the spitting image of you, except he's got a bit of his mother in him. A little wildness in those eyes. He looks like a real soldier now—full uniform, crossbow, short sword, and knife," Doc said. He nodded at Benjamin, shooting a wink at Olivia.

Samuel looked around and noticed the soldier to the right of General Benedict Ashburn carried a knife with an elegant bone handle like the one he was supposed to find for General Flint. It was supposed to be in the Ashburn house, but he hadn't discovered it on Mira Ashburn's corpse or in the remains of the house. Alysha Ashburn's remains hadn't been found. Samuel had been tasked with retrieving the blade or any other named weapon. He knew Doc held the Maker's Gift named Gaston's Beard, and there were rumors this Olivia witch carried the wand called the Maker's Quill. Four true Paragons in one place.

Four stood, and two sat.

"My footman is ready with our horses. There are two bodies on the floor in the back of this house, and everyone is agitated. We came to talk of the Holy Imperium, the crisis of the free city-states, and the yoke Prince Damon is attempting to place onto them," said Lord Washcreek. "And I walked into this calamity."

"Bold words, comrade, to speak them loudly, or someone may call you a traitor to the crown prince," said Benedict. "I came looking for my son Runt."

"And you brought your other son as well," said Olivia. "What of your wife and daughter? Do you not care for their well-being?"

"My wife, I know of where she is and her safety," Benedict angrily said. He grimaced, and then he composed himself.

"Well," Samuel said with a smile, "my tea is getting cold." He grabbed his chair, stood it up, and sat. "Let's get it all out—no need for bloodshed or use of the arts. It's up to you. No one wants a blade when offered a warm drink on a frosty night. Would anyone else care for a bit of tea?"

Olivia spoke with calmness and authority: "I'm glad everyone made it tonight, whether you intended to or not. We all came for selfish reasons, yet they align for a better purpose. Samuel will not draw blood tonight against us, nor will General Washcreek. The only concern is the young man pointing the crossbow. There is a mystery in his actions I have not tasted before. It's fuzzy because of Samuel's presence. Please put your finger away from the trigger and point the crossbow at the floor. Wretched machines, those dwarven weapons."

Benedict nodded, and his son did as ask. He stood; arms crossed.

"Benedict came looking for his youngest son and wants change. Samuel is here to pay a debt and seek revenge for those who harmed his heritage, Lord Washcreek seeks liberty, Doc seeks penance and power, and I . . . well . . . I am here to serve tea and bring unity," said Olivia.

"You are the newspaper writer from Hudson City," said Benedict Ashburn.

"I've read your stories—outstanding work," said Samuel. He shifted his hand toward his belt.

Doc lit his pipe and burped. "Let's get to the meat of it. Enough already. Whether you believe it or not, we hold here pieces of history which could change the fabric of Vineland," he said. "Go ahead, look around. General Washcreek has severed countless heads and legs with his spear. He carries the Holy Truth even if he worships no gods. The boy over there carries Dawn's Breath, a knife not seen in years. I went looking for it and found the wrong son. Runt didn't have it, the bastard." Doc pointed a wagging finger at the father and son. "Olivia writes so well because she carries the Maker's Quill, and I have this old thing." He placed his hand on his staff, which lay on the table, blade pointed toward Samuel.

"Ahh, Doc, trying to get to the truth of the matter," said Olivia. "I have missed this."

"What are you speaking about, old man? Old tales like the Makers Gifts? Those are myths and stories," Samuel said.

"So naïve, yet you're similar. The first items created may be the best, as the gods themselves used them and, thus, made them more powerful than those following them. Your blood reeks of the same, and your blood blunts my ability to burn you to a crisp. Which is an indication that long-told stories reek of truths forgotten. The Paragons are real, and I hope to verify my research soon," Doc said.

Samuel didn't believe, yet the old man carried a whiff of honesty as he spoke.

"True, absolutely true. They could change Vineland for the worse or for the better. We all can agree that nobody would want these in the hands of Prince Damon," Olivia said.

They all looked at one another and shook their heads, even Benedict Ashburn, not sure what to think.

"Too much power here. I wish all these blessed tools destroyed," said Lord Washcreek. "Whether you believe it or not, Samuel, I have never been bested with this spear, and I have seen both those mages work with staff and quill to create unholy madness. They have done things unheard of." Washcreek looked at Benedict. "Your family held a specific knife for generations, Benedict. Have you ever wondered why fortune continues to smile on you even when you constantly push against it?"

Benedict Ashburn looked ashamed for a moment. "What you believe is up to you." He turned to Doc. "Where is Runt, old man?"

"He's trying not to get killed by Prince Damon, General Flint, and the bounty hunters searching for him." Doc tossed a scroll at Benedict Ashburn.

It fell to the floor, and Benedict slowly bent over to pick it up. He unrolled it as he stood. "What is this? Why is Runt wanted for witchcraft and murder?"

"This isn't how we unite Vineland, Doc," whispered Olivia.

"I think it is," Doc said bluntly. "Your son is searching for you right now, Benedict. He's walking his way toward Olde Ridgewatch, where you're stationed. Your youngest son, hunted by the Holy Imperium for doing nothing but trying to save his mother. He's now one of the most wanted people in Vineland. He's no mage and no murderer, yet one of the noblest families in the Holy Imperium accuses your very son of such things." Doc sipped his tea. "Best get back to Olde Ridgewatch. Don't want him to end up like your wife."

"Wait, what's wrong with my mom?" whimpered Benjamin. He moved in front of his father and pointed the crossbow at Doc and Olivia.

"Ask your father," Olivia said. She ignored the crossbow and the boy, as if he were no more than a fly. "So, we'll have chaos and hope through war we unite? Is that it, Doc?

"What are these two mumbling about?" Samuel asked Lord Washcreek.

"Prince Damon lowers himself to self-righteous murder and slaughter. Is this not enough? I asked for help, and all I got were riddles and madness from you. I'm leaving. Find me in Affectus if you want a civilized conversation," Lord Washcreek said.

"I'm leaving as well. Benjamin, put your crossbow up," General Ashburn snapped. "We are heading back to the barracks. Your mother and Alysha are fine. Runt has gone adventuring like those books he loves and caused your family hardship and embarrassment. Now the nobles of the Holy Imperium have gotten involved and attempted to ruin our family name. Get the horses."

Lord Washcreek and Benedict Ashburn started to leave in opposite directions until several glass bottles shattered on the manor's roof and smoke filtered inside.

"What was that?" said Samuel.

Everyone looked up as green flame licked down from above.

"Holy fire, Templar, we must go!" yelled Olivia. "This was not supposed to happen tonight!"

Samuel lunged at the table, grabbing the staff.

"You goat-sucking coward!" Doc screamed, his teeth gnashing. He grabbed the other end of the staff. Samuel's hands slipped, cutting them both on the blade as he let go. Doc's inertia pushed back, staff in hand for a moment, but he stumbled into a chair, falling onto his back.

Another bottle slammed through the window and hit the stove. Green fire splashed everywhere.

Gaston's Beard, the staff Doc had used in the battle at the Plains of Ursula, spun out of his hand and landed with a thud next to Benedict Ashburn as he left through the back door. Benedict looked back quickly and picked up the item as he hurried out of the burning building.

Samuel kicked Olivia in the stomach; she fell to her knees, cursing him. Olivia's hand hit the top of the iron stove, causing her to drop her wand. Samuel grabbed her head and smashed it against the hot stove, knocking her out.

"I'll take that," grunted Samuel.

A Templar in full armor kicked in the door, mace in hand. "Comply with Prince Damon's orders. All witchery and mage work are to cease. Drop your weapons, and nobody will be hurt immediately."

"Screw this guy," said Samuel as he drew his short sword and grasped for his ball and chain, dropping the wand.

Lord Washcreek thrust his spear in line and quickly stabbed it through the metal and into the meat inside the armor. The Blue Templar tried to adjust his mace to block and slumped over the spear in a rapid death rattle. Lord Washcreek drew his spear back. "We can't extinguish the fire. We must flee," he said as he looked through the door. "There are more coming. The Templar don't care who's in here. They want us all dead, Samuel. Leave with us and stop fighting the two mages," he ordered.

Doc was on his back. He sat up, placing his hand on Olivia's wand. "Shit, this isn't mine, but I'll take it for now. Olivia, we must go!" he pleaded. "Well, I best play the part of the noble knight." He pocketed the wand and drew a nasty, rusty boning knife from inside his coat. "Samuel, move toward me, and I will blind you. Washcreek, cover our exit. I'm getting Olivia out back and on a horse. Once I'm not around Samuel I can distract the Templar with smoke." He grabbed Olivia under the arms and dragged her to the back. As he neared the orc in the back room, he kicked the brute. "Wake up, you beast. Your master needs you."

Samuel and Washcreek engaged two more Templar. Their armor shined with silver and blue tints as their blood splashed across the armor plates.

The orc bodyguard stood, shook his head, and looked at Doc with hazy eyes.

"What happened? Someone smashed my head in," the orc said, not to clearly.

"I didn't do this shit. Protect Olivia, damn it to Hades. Grab her and drag her out. I'll get the horses," Doc said and lumbered out through the back door. Smoke from the fire followed him.

"He's not coming back. Let's go," Samuel said, still inside the house, fending off another attacker.

"Doc is a survivor, but he'll come back," said Washcreek.

The fire and smoke consumed the house. Washcreek and Samuel killed two lightly armed Holy Imperium foot soldiers. Blood caked the table, oven, and walls as the smell of shit and pain rose from the bodies.

"Get down!" Washcreek pushed Samuel to the floor as arrows and bolts splintered the kitchen wall behind the table. "Move now before they fire again!" Washcreek commanded.

Samuel, impressed by Washcreek commanding the situation, followed as they pushed through smoke, tears in their eyes, coughing and spitting, and tumbled out the back just as Doc rode up with two more horses.

"Members of the Order of the Blue Rose and monks are chasing ghosts in the fog," Doc said as his pipe reeked out plumes of oily smoke. "It's disappearing now because of Samuel." He tossed the horses' reins to Samuel and Lord Washcreek. "Strap Olivia to my horse. I'll get her away safe," Doc said to the orc.

"My name is Paul. Please tell Olivia I'll miss our long talks," the orc said. He grabbed a slab of fence, broke it in two, and headed into the smoke.

"That is dedication. Washcreek, Samuel, we will meet again soon," said Doc as he rode away from yet another burning building.

Runt - Smile Like You Mean It

The goblin hunched over near a bookshelf, looked at the book spines, flipped through some, and then placed them back onto the shelf while humming and singing. It looked awkward to Runt, as he expected most goblins to be like a man-child in both thought and action. The nearly five-foot-tall goblin's back was crooked in shape. The spine showed large bumps poking up from its dark, green-tinted skin. It wore a poorly made shawl over its shoulders, rusty scaled armor, and a cloth around its genitals that was pinned up by bone. The fabric was darker than its skin. Runt realized he could smell it from book stacks away, damp and foul like a well with rotting food floating in it. Small bent horns circled the goblin's head. Each horn placed the goblin higher in its clan's hierarchy. This beast was not just a lonely foot soldier or cook.

The goblin continued to sing, a light chant with a beat, but it hit different notes at odd times as it faced away from Runt. Maynard leaned as if his legs were going to give out. The song sounded almost natural, like a lullaby in another language.

Effortlessly, the creature turned to look at the both of them and smiled, showing crooked and sharp front teeth with sizable back choppers meant for chewing and grinding. It wore a beak from a large predator bird on its nose like a mask, drooping over its nose with a string wrapped around its head to keep the beak propped in place, which brought attention to its yellow cat-like eyes. It had large ears thinned to points near its scalp and spotty portions of dark and bristly hair. The goblin carried a book in its hands and continued to sing. Its overall affect was full of sorrow. The music slithered from the goblin's beak mask, which muffled the words.

Maynard slumped slowly to the ground as if falling drunk. He lost control of his legs and hands. Runt felt weak at the knees but didn't fall, managing to stand. The goblin continued to sing, putting its last book away. It stepped toward Runt, pulling a curved dagger from its belt. Runt was starting to feel exhausted; he just wanted to take a nap.

"Maynard, are you okay? Oh shit, oh shit." Runt felt queasy. It was as if time slowed as his thoughts muddled. He dropped the book he was carrying, grabbed Maynard's lantern, and raised it higher to see more of the area and blind the beak-wearing goblin as it moved toward them.

The goblin hissed and leaned back like a rat caught out in the open at night as the light neared it. It stopped singing. Maynard started to stir. The goblin screeched at Maynard and Runt like an angry raven, making a weird bird-like moan. It slashed out with the knife but didn't move into the green hue of lantern light.

"Get back, you freak! Move," said Runt, emboldened now, using the light as a protective shield. He moved toward the goblin, and it shuffled back, staying out of the light, hissing in a deep phlegmy tone. Runt used the light to push the goblin away so Maynard could recover from whatever was wrong with him.

"Enough of this," Runt said and threw the odd-shaped lamp at the goblin, hoping to scare it off. The thing lurched away from the light as the lantern sailed through the air. As the green light hit the goblin, it screeched and ran into the darkness, away from the two boys, dropping a book before scurrying off. It howled down the stacks.

Runt jogged over to the broken lantern, which was out, and collected its contents. He investigated the darkness, holding his working lamp, and listened. He thought the goblin might be gone. His lantern held several etches of runes and writings on it. The candle changed from green to white, as an ordinary candle would shine. He walked back, wondering if the lamp's etchings changed the light inside when a goblin neared.

Maynard stumbled over, visibly shaken, as he dusted off his clothes and drew his hair away from his sweat-covered face. He picked up the book the goblin flung to the ground and put it inside a robe pocket. "Thanks, man. The goblin, is it gone?"

"Yeah, I think so. The light from the lamp scared it away, I think. It freaked out when I tossed the other lamp at it. Busted the lamp though. I think it's gone. You got all weird and fell when the goblin saw us," said Runt.

"I feel like shit, but I can walk. Can't think right. Let's get out of here before it comes back. We'll tell the librarian what happened." Maynard looked pale and haggard. "I think the singing made me fuzzy, man. I feel like I need to be sick, but I can't throw up."

The boys walked rapidly up the stairs, making sure the door locked on their way out. Maynard stumbled most of the way. They spoke in hushed tones to the student in charge of the library for the day as she stamped her feet near a large hearth, trying to stay warm with the meager fire inside it. Runt did his best not to sound like a manic, letting the librarian know what they encountered.

"So, you found a goblin in a lower section of the library, searching for books, and scared it off but broke one of the library lamps in doing so." The librarian, a college student named Hattie, shook her head. She was older than both Maynard and Runt. "Not sure what's going on with this school this year, with random goblins on the road and now this? I'll let the magistrates know, and they'll take care of it." She continued to stamp her feet, reading her book as if nothing had happened. "You two, head on back home. I'll check the door to make sure it's locked." She moved them away with her hand.

* * *

They walked back to the Red Horse Tavern through frigid wind and light snow. Runt realized he still carried a large book in his satchel, and Maynard had slipped three books in his robe pockets, each of varied sizes. The wind blew from the north as the pair walked, reminding Runt of home and the remaining nothingness of his burned house. He could almost taste the ash lingering in his throat. It'd be covered now, as if it hadn't even existed. The snow crunched under their feet, the temperature dropping as the day drifted into twilight. Deep gray clouds would bring cold, snow, and further wind to Hagarville Valley for the next several days.

They opened the door to the Red Horse Tavern, shivering from the walk.

Duncan sat inside near the door on a stool, talking to a man in a bunched-up jacket of white cow skin. He wore a tarnished white hood over his head, and neither of the boys could see his face.

"Come on in, boys. I'll catch up in a moment. Grab a seat. I'm not sure how busy it will be tonight. Bit nasty out even for the drunks." Duncan motioned for them to sit as he continued to talk to the hooded man.

The bar was half full of patrons, students, professors, and laborers, mingling as they drank and ate supper. Runt and Maynard sat, exhausted from their odd meeting in the basement. A circular dwarven fire pit with a suspended chimney sat in the center of the room with stools and chairs set around the warmth. Another fire was in the back by the kitchen, and the other light came from the owl lamps, a specific lighting fixture created by dwarves or elves, hung around the tavern. The windows were stained glass and framed by iron. Runt felt as if he could sleep at the table, the warmth finally making its way into his bones.

Duncan walked over shortly after the boys sat down. "You look like you saw a vampire in the night. Let's get you drinks and dinner." He placed his hand on Runt's shoulder with care for a brief moment and walked to the bar.

The man dressed in white cow skin now stood at the bar, taking a long pull from a beer stein. Duncan greeted him quickly and raised his hand to the bartender, pointing at the man. They spoke for a moment again.

Maynard cleaned his glasses, squinting at the two men. "What do you think that's all about? Duncan isn't really the super-friendly type to buy another man a drink," he said as he put his spectacles back on.

"I dunno. We could ask him when he gets back," said Runt.

"Before or after we tell him we saw a goblin in the basement of the school's library?" Maynard said.

"After, definitely after. Here he comes."

Duncan nodded at the server, and they came back with two short warm ciders for the boys and a large stein like what the tall man in white drank at the bar. Duncan moved the chair and sat down.

"Now tell me, other than this Maker's forsaken weather, what troubles you?" Duncan took a long pull from his stein of dark beer.

"Well, we were on the lower floor of the basement, looking for a book, a particular book, and we saw—" Maynard began.

"A goblin attacked us," Runt said, interrupting. He took a considerable swallow of cider.

Duncan looked at them for a moment. First, with the same face you would give your best friend when they tried to bluff you at cards, but then he realized the story may be true.

"I read about them in books, even cut one up once, but it was dead already. This one, I couldn't defend myself. I couldn't do anything," Maynard followed up.

Runt cut in, "We fended him off, this goblin, and locked the door behind us. Told the closest librarian to alert members of the college and the town."

Duncan's eyebrow rose a bit, and he ground his hands together. "Interesting. You boys weren't drinking a weird potion from an alchemy professor and passing out in the library?" He looked at the two boys. "No, no, I guess not. Well, I was getting a bit bored here anyway. Working at the door and training has started to become a bit monotonous. 'Sides, my friend there could use a job. You boys stay here. I'm heading to speak to the dean at the university, real plain-like, let them know what I can do for them," he said.

Supper arrived for the boys, and they dug in quickly but quietly.

"When we saw the goblin, did you hear singing or humming?" Runt asked through a mouthful of chili. "Did it mess with you?"

"I don't know. I heard the goblin singing like it was coming through my head. I couldn't think straight; it was more like an odd mumbling. I think it may have been a," and Maynard whispered toward Runt, "a casting song, like a finding spell." He continued in hushed tones, "It messed me up, like my head was underwater. The goblin may have altered the spell into a sleeping spell. Singing magic isn't unheard of."

"We should get our gear and head back with Duncan. Why not help with this goblin thing? And we could find the book you were looking for," Runt said.

The apprentice-mage nodded. They went upstairs to grab Runt's sword and Maynard's walking stick and knife and before heading out to join Duncan.

The boys arrived at the desk where Hattie had sat, only their footsteps making noise. The librarian nowhere to be seen. The room was warmer than the outside but not exceedingly so. They hung their cloaks and mittens on hooks near the door. They remained quiet and walked down the stairs to the lower portion of the library. The door stood closed, but torches were lit on either side, indicating a presence inside. They took two library lamps nearby and continued.

Maynard opened the door, the hinges creaking and echoing through the stacks. Runt gritted his teeth at the noise, and Maynard smiled sheepishly. He held up his lamp, peered down the stairs, and listened but heard nothing. They crept into the darkness. As they neared the bottom of the stairs they saw the stacks lit up by several lamps scattered throughout.

"Place looks different now, all lit up," whispered Maynard.

"Yeah, not as creepy as before," Runt said as he spun around. "Or even creepier—your call."

They heard a faint noise from the back. Neither Runt nor Maynard could make out what it was.

"Well, no Duncan yet, but someone has been here. Shall we carry on?" said Maynard. He pushed up his spectacles and slowly moved on, his staff clicking softly against the floor.

"Yeah, I guess so," replied Runt.

They walked through the stacks, now lit with the faint odd green glow of the lamps.

"The lamp's dwarven runes carved into them seemed to provide protection against the last goblin. I hope they do the same now. Runes aren't my thing. I know a smattering of languages, but these lamps are old, and I can't read the ones on them," Maynard said. Runt could tell he was nervous, and so was he.

Maynard's staff tapped lightly on the floor. The wood from the staff was wind-worn with a dark maple finish. It was lighter than expected, yet still felt strong enough to use for defense in a fight.

"Your walking stick. Does it shoot lightning or fireballs?"

"No," Maynard said. "I mean, I guess it could help if needed."

They were past where they'd met the goblin and followed sets of footprints through the dust to the last lit lamp at the end of the stacks. Unfortunately, the books in the stacks in this area were moldy, and Runt could hardly read the names on the spines.

"All of these books are near ruin," Maynard said with annoyance at Mount Nittany University. "I should talk to the dean."

Runt grabbed a book and looked at it. "This, Maynard, is an exceptional magical text." He handed the book to him.

"The title says *The Long Lonely Nights of a Milkmaid*. What the Hades is this?" Maynard asked.

"I bet it's the confiscated shelf from years back," said Runt.

"Ha! I bet it is. We'll have to come back here." Maynard slipped the book into his robe pocket.

The boys made it to the last lamp. In front of them was a large hole a little taller than they were, and light from inside was faintly visible.

"Well, here we go adventuring," said Maynard.

"Yeah," Runt nodded. He drew his short sword and marched into the large hole in the wall, stooping slightly.

They made their way through the darkness, following the light that began to grow. The cave smelled of mold and stale water. They heard boots scuffing the hardened ground. They came out of the dark cave into a vaster opening where they saw two torches far off and another lamp like the one, they carried.

"You boys, what are you doing?" yell-whispered Hattie, the librarian with rounded spectacles and a scar across her right eye. She carried an oversized lamp like theirs with the green shaded light and stomped toward them.

"We came to help!" yell-whispered Runt.

"Oh, okay, well, come now. You can assist us. We found an opening in this dwarven crossroads."

"I'm Hattie," the older girl said briskly. "We met earlier. The dean, although concerned, sent me back to investigate and seal up the hole if I could and if not, report back to him. These two men asked to accompany me for a small exchange of funds from the dean."

"Why did the dean send only you?" asked Maynard. "I mean, it's a goblin. They usually hunt in packs and can see in the dark. Shouldn't we be worried they could overwhelm us?"

"Not really. I'm capable of addressing this problem. I have permission to use alchemy to stop any further goblin incursions," she said. She wore her robe over a gray sweater, white collared shirt, and tie. Her hair was longer and mussed up as if she had just rolled out of bed. She wore a large leather belt around her robe, from which hung another dwarven lamp.

Maynard was in a similar robe, with a leather vest and woolen shirt underneath. "Ingenious to hook the lamp to the belt, Hattie," he said.

"Thanks, it helps when you're roaming the stacks during the school year down here, and I guess when it comes to finding and fighting random goblins." Hattie smiled, a bit manic, a bit spooked.

Duncan walked back toward them. "Boys? Shit, I guess you came at the right time. Could use a few more hands if this gets messy. Don't want to be outnumbered down here in these dwarven crossroads. Did you bring Angus by chance? He might be able to let us know if we should be worried about other doors in a crossroad like this."

"No, he wouldn't come, and I'll try to explain later. Did you say you found an opening?" asked Runt.

Everything felt tense.

"Right, yes, my friend is near the opening in case anything comes up. I was about to ask Hattie if she had any ideas on closing it. We figure if we can close it up, the university wouldn't have to worry about random goblins coming out of the dark and interfering with students' studies."

"No sign of the singing goblin with a beak mask?" wondered Maynard.

"No. We heard scratching from the opening back there, so I want to take care of this quickly. No telling what's down there. Get it done, get paid, and get out of here," Duncan said.

Maynard looked down at Hattie's right hand and saw a ring. If the robe did not give it away, the ring sure did. Hattie knew the high art and was bound by the ring.

"I should be able to put something together. Dean Slither gave me permission and all. Let's see what we're dealing with," Hattie said, excited.

They moved forward.

"What discipline are you, Hattie?" Maynard asked.

Hattie was frantically messing with pockets inside her robe. "Me? Oh, I'm part of the alchemists, you know, the corruption of science and whatnot, and ahh, I can do other tricks as well."

Maynard felt her nervous energy. "It's okay, Hattie. Runt knows I work in the arts as well. I doubt I'm as strong as you. I study mostly the philosophy of it," he said.

"Oh, yeah, right, right. I see your finger there."

Maynard slipped on a ring he kept in his pocket. It wasn't an anchor ring like Hattie wore, which bound Hattie's power and kept her under control, but the false ring looked close enough. While Hattie studied alchemy, Maynard dabbled in blood, nature, and manipulation magic.

"If you're wondering, I'm apprenticed but on sabbatical. I'm running errands for my mentor, actually. Runt and Duncan are along for the ride," he said.

"Oh, cool. Well, if you see I need assistance, please feel free to jump in. I think I'm going to try a potion or two to bring down the opening, and we'll sprint back the way we came and hope it doesn't collapse on us before we get there."

"Sounds reassuring," Runt said with concern, glancing at Maynard. "We're all going to die down here."

Duncan shot Runt a look, shutting him up for a moment.

"Duncan, who's the other big guy?" Runt asked.

"Old friend of mine. Last we met was in Steelsburg." Duncan stopped for a moment. "He was my executioner."

Runt stared at Duncan in confusion.

"Gray Jim, what's the word?" Duncan asked the other brute.

Gray Jim leaned over, looking into the dark area where doors used to stand. A vast door lay broken about the ground, metal and stone, massive pieces everywhere. "They're coming. Everyone, weapons at the ready," said the large

252

man.

Cackling laughter and scratching came from the dark hole. Duncan loosened the sizable round shield from his back and pulled a half and hand sword from its sheath over his head. Gray Jim pulled out short swords. Runt also noted the large two-handed sword he carried on his back.

Maynard held two medium-sized beakers as Hattie quietly spoke to him, pouring liquids back and forth into each. Hattie placed two stoppered beakers into her belt, near where her lamp hung, and stopped whispering.

"Duncan, Gray Jim, sirs, please step back, behind me, into the middle of the room, and take your torches with you. Runt, could you take your lamp and go with the two gentlemen? Place the large lamp in the middle of the room," she said.

Runt felt odd taking orders from Hattie, who didn't hold the same authority Sorella, or Duncan possessed. Both Duncan and Gray Jim gave Hattie a strange look.

"Your funeral, kid," Gray Jim said, and he walked toward the back of the room, where they'd entered from.

Duncan joined him with a shrug.

"Goblins and other creatures will be crawling out of this door soon; can't you hear the scraping? Do you hear laughter or singing?" Runt asked Hattie.

"Unless you want to end up burned crisp and breathing in rubble, do as I say!" she yelled.

Runt decided it would be best to avoid the dark hole with the creepy noises.

"Okay, I'll take care of the door here. Hopefully, the first potions work and collapse the dwarven work, but destroying ancient dwarven masonry and rune work is no easy task," she said.

The laughter continued to get louder, and soon screeching came like angry cats. The sound of armor and screams moaned from the dark, slowly reaching the crossroads opening where the band stood.

"If any get past my works, Duncan and Gray Jim, take them down as we back away and up the stairs. We'll close the basement door on them until we figure out what to do," the librarian said as she pushed her brown hair back, visibly sweating now. "We'll leave the big lamp in the middle of the room.

Dean Slither might get upset because it's irreplaceable, but it will keep most creatures away from this place after the collapse. The runes should keep the candles burning for an exceedingly long time. Okay, Maynard, follow my lead."

Creatures were starting to move in the near dark at the hole's edge. Runt squinted but could not see clearly. Moments later, yellow and green blinked through the hole. The darkness moved forward, fading to a murky green. Hands and feet emerged as a goblin—a short, stooped, humanoid creature— peeked through the darkness with dozens moving behind it.

"Now!" Hattie yelled.

Maynard tossed the two vials at the top of the broken door. They flew without sound and looked pathetic and weak as they soared toward the top of the hole where the goblins had started to come out. They both hit and broke; a dark yet shimmering liquid spread over the pitch of the hole. Hattie pointed a wand and muttered under her breath. Red and blue sparks shot toward where the beakers lay broken. The sparks flew like lobbed snowballs thrown by young children.

She turned and ran. Maynard realized he should run as well.

Runt, Duncan, and Gray Jim watched as Maynard and Hattie ran toward them. There was an explosion of blue and red light. The air was sucked out of the room for a moment. The blast pushed Maynard down onto his chest; Hattie grabbed him, and they rushed past the lamp in the middle of the crossroads.

"Get up the stairs now," she demanded.

The area by the blast started to break apart around the hole. There were sounds of rage and pain, making Maynard's ears ring. Duncan and Gray Jim ran up the stairs with Runt.

Hattie turned around. "I forgot the words—shit, shit, shit. Right, got it!" She said the words, and the lamp lit up the entire crossroads. "Let's get out of here."

Maynard gave Hattie the two other vials. She placed them in the dirt at the opening of the stairs leading to the library.

"Maybe not as big this time," said Maynard.

"Right. Everyone up and out," Hattie said.

She glanced around, standing at the base of the stairs. Maynard was behind her on the first few steps; Duncan, Runt, and Gray Jim stood above, looking on in astonishment.

"Let's go!" Hattie flicked her wand again and tried to light the two vials up. They fizzled and sparked but didn't explode. "Run up the stairs! Go, go, go," she said. "They'll blow soon."

Hattie tripped and stood with Maynard's help, moving as quickly as possible in the dark. There was nothing but breathing, swearing, and a flash of light as the air pushed out from behind them followed by fire and the crashing of the stone above the stairs, blocking the way down. Dust and debris followed and pushed out into the stacks, covering the books as well as Hattie and Maynard. They both fell, exhausted.

"Well, that was fun. The first time I got to evaluate my experiments." Hattie coughed, tears running down her smiling face as she looked at Runt, Duncan, and Gray Jim in satisfied shock.

* * *

An hour later, Maynard and Runt sat on a bench outside the office of Rickman Slither, the dean of Mount Nittany, while Hattie, Duncan, and Gray Jim talked inside the dean's office. First, they heard yelling, primarily from who they thought was Dean Slither, then, for a brief period, laughter, but the boys couldn't make any specific words out.

"Below the basement library stacks was a sub-floor containing a dwarven crossroads in which a cave's sealed door was broken open. A goblin—or many goblins—broke one of the crossroads chamber doors open and made its way into the library," Maynard said to Runt.

"Yeah, where we saw a goblin with the beak, singing and acting like a creepy librarian," Runt said. "And you shat your pants and passed out."

"No, I didn't shit my pants, man. It was madness, but I didn't shit my pants."

"Right, well, what were the vials Hattie made?" asked Runt.

"No idea." Maynard shrugged. "Nearly killed us all."

"That ball of fire was insane. It knocked over bookcases in the basement and first floor. Glad I don't have to clean up the mess." Runt laughed, and Maynard smiled. "Hey, did you snag anything on the way out?"

"Yeah, I grabbed a few books—nothing Doc was looking for, but he might like the pieces for his new collection. If we take any more, we'll never make it to Olde Ridgewatch, though," said Maynard. "Oh, look, it started snowing again. This place is going to bury us in the white shit."

The door opened, and the laughter from inside suddenly stopped. A woman walked out. She was tall, in her forties, with long, dark hair and a hooked nose. She smiled like a cat who had eaten a house bird.

"Stand up," Dean Slither said, her voice nasally as if she had previously broken her nose and healed wrong. "Please come into my office." She swiped her hand over to show them the way. She wore long, dark robes over her bird-like frame, a wool vest, trousers, a buttoned-up shirt, and a green and sable silk tie. "Your associates were just leaving. Thank you again for your assistance; Hattie, thank you as well. I will see you in the stacks. Excellent job."

The two men and Hattie, the librarian, shook hands with Dean Slither and walked out.

"Boys, we'll see you at the Red Horse and catch up. The dean would like to speak to you both personally," Duncan said. "Be on your best manners, please. Remember, Runt, you represent me now as well, boy." Duncan put his pointer finger to the tip of his nose, brought it out, and pointed at Runt, as a father would do to a younger son. He put his other hand on the boy's shoulder, tapped him, and nodded at Maynard. "You too, boy-o." And he walked out.

The other man, Gray Jim, looked them both up and down, eyes deep and hollow, and before departing.

"Please sit."

Dean Slither stood behind her desk, one arm crossed over the other, holding her elbow while her other hand propped up her chin as she thought. It took more than a few moments, as if she had done this before with her students or her children, playing the moment, making an appeal, showing them who was

256

in charge, who was waiting for whom.

"Our school motto is 'Make the Day Better,' and today, you both have done so for our school, the town, and me. I thank you," she said.

"You're welcome," said Maynard with gratitude.

"Maynard, please wait a moment." Dean Slither held her hand out to acknowledge that Maynard and Runt were not to talk.

"First off, I know you, Maynard. You are an apprentice to Doctor Young, and you have stolen a few books. Your mentor and I go back and are on speaking terms when we cross paths. He is my superior in the arts we practice, but this does not give you the right to steal from underneath my nose. I expect those books to be returned eventually by you or him. Please let him know this when you next speak.

"And Runt, you're currently under the keep of the dwarve named Angus and are being taught by Wyatt Duncan in the matters of war. It's a holiday here at school, so most students and staff are returning to their warm, happy homes. You may continue to work in your feet of arms—but under the care of Mr. Duncan and nowhere else. Do not draw blood here on campus, or it will mean your life, no matter whose fault it may be. We're a peaceful institution," she said, then took a breath as she walked toward a bookshelf.

"Hattie said you were instrumental in aiding us with our little singing-goblin problem, but you left a mess below. I want you both to work in the basement, cleaning up the fallen bookshelves after the cave-in." She picked up a book, looked at the spine, opened it, closed it, and put it back. "This will pay for the rental of the books you pinched from our shelves." Dean Slither smiled for a moment and then frowned, looking out the window of her office. She stood in profile and acted as if others were watching, but it was only the boys and herself.

"Yes, ma'am," they said together.

"One last thing: From my understanding, Mr. Runt here is wanted. Did you know there's a small price on your head? Yes, or no? No, from the looks of it. Either way, there are posters for a boy your age and likeness, so people are hunting for you. The Holy Imperium wants you, dead or alive. I would guess your father is searching for you as well. He's a high-ranking officer in the Holy Imperium Army, and yet you don't turn yourself in. I'm sure officers of the Red Army would be able to assist you," Dean Slither said, looking at Runt as if she could pry more from him simply by staring. "Yet you do not, and you resort to mercenaries and criminals as companions."

Runt only felt irritation and resentment toward her. He took a deep breath before speaking.

"I can't trust soldiers of the Holy Imperium. At this point, the Holy Imperium and the Red Army would help me like they helped my mother and my town. They butchered her and burned the rest down. I don't know why they did this. I hope to get to my father, but I'd like to do so alive and on my terms. I don't rightly trust many people and turning myself into the group that killed my family doesn't seem like the smartest thing to do, does it?"

Dean Slither looked down. "For now, I haven't seen anything, but due to the nature of Mount Nittany University and the current political problems at the prince's court, please do not become a nuisance, or you will be reported to the authorities. Thank you both. Now, please leave," she said curtly. She walked to the door, gesturing them out.

Runt and Maynard left the office, startled. Because of his schooling, Maynard was used to getting lectures from adults, and Runt had been dressed down enough by Gunny and Duncan, but this felt different. The Holy Imperium officially wanted Runt Ashburn, and it felt unusual to hear it aloud from an authority figure like Dean Slither of Mount Nittany University.

The boys grabbed their cloaks from hooks and waded outside into the snow, hoofing it back to the tavern. The air chilled them, and they both shivered after a minute of walking. Runt couldn't wait to relax by a fire and drink warm cider or wine.

They opened the door and found Duncan and Gray Jim speaking at a table near the tavern's hearth. Runt and Maynard trudged in, kicking snow off their leather boots.

"Come now, boys, grab a chair. Johnny, please bring two more for these young men," Duncan said to the man behind the bar.

The bartender brought over a round of drinks. Runt and Maynard sat and began to warm themselves.

"Runt, Maynard, this is Gray Jim. He was the Steelsburg hangman."

The boys nodded and said their hellos.

"As I said earlier, he recently attempted to execute me before you both met me. Tried to crush me with a giant sodding stone and drown me, you bastard."

Gray Jim nodded, smiled, took a deep pull, and looked away.

"Oh, come off it—not your fault. Nobody knew I came from a famous line of dwarves, and I don't look at all like one. I just age slower and heal a bit better than humans. Nearly died anyway," Duncan said.

"You didn't, though, and you ruined my reputation and caused a dwarven civil war. Never good to have a botched execution," Gray Jim said. His voice sounded like chewing freshly chipped coal from the hills. "I nearly lost everything, Duncan, except my kit and execution sword. I have nothing. My savings and everything is gone, along with a few people owing me life favors. Now I'm stuck here in this shithole, helping the man who ruined it all."

"Yes, but we'll put it right if we can. This fucking Prince Damon caused your issues, and you know it. He's got his hooks in everything now, from the civil war in Steelsburg shattering the Clearstone family to problems up by the Erie Sea in Grimwood to the rumors of civil unrest in Olde Ridgewatch. He threw his weight behind the Blitzsteel and Bitterspear families by funding them. We stole the coin purses off Bitterspear and Blitzsteel guards, and they carried all newly minted coins from Hudson City, not Steelsburg. The Clearstones never favored trading with Prince Damon. This land is a mess— not to mention orcs and goblins being spotted outside where they normally hunt, according to rumors coming from the Stagger Wall."

"Lucky I'm a man of honor. I lost it all because—"

"Stop wallowing in it. We found work until the snows break, at least. You can get coin in your pocket and follow us to Olde Ridgewatch, and we'll see what we can see. I'm sure heads will need to be taken in some capacity, and those religious bastards hate to do it themselves," Duncan finished.

"Thank you for the drinks, sir," said Runt.

"It's no problem. You had a long day. As I was saying, we spoke to Dean Slither, and she'll pay us to be available while we're here if there's another goblin or orc problem, or any other problem. So, on top of the bar work here, we get to go on patrols. Guess who's doing those patrols?" asked Duncan.

"Me, sir," Runt answered.

"Correct! Gray Jim here volunteered to spar with you on occasion. You could turn into a better fighter than your dad," Duncan said. "We can try, at least."

"Do you think there will be any more openings in basements like what we saw down there?" Maynard asked.

"Kid, that was crazy shit," Gray Jim whistled. "I know dwarves and their ways well, but those crossroads were not on any map. To see it breached by goblins is unheard of. The dwarves of Steelsburg put two or three groups of bug hunters out—goblin hunters to us normal folk—about this time of the year to kill anything they find in caverns or caves."

"Wonder what those little bastards wanted in the crossroads?" said Duncan. "I know Angus doesn't like to talk about his kind, but maybe he'll open up about what we went through, shed a small light on it for us humans." He scratched at his beard.

"With two major families in a civil war, all eyes are on the city of Steelsburg. It looks like other dwarven affairs are falling to the side. You lot left at the right time. It was chaos when I got out of there. Steelsburg and the surrounding area will not be the same. The local economy ground to a halt. As you said, Duncan, this country is a mess, and you all," Gray Jim looked at Duncan, Maynard, and Runt, "along with me, are in the middle. Maker, take us all."

"The dean said Runt's got a problem now. More so than what we thought when we left Wolf Hills," Maynard said.

"I heard Dean Slither laugh about it, didn't I?" said Runt.

Duncan froze for a moment, realizing Runt was a very sharp young man. "It was an odd conversation. I didn't feel like myself in there. It was strangely comfortable, and she got weird for a bit, and then Dean Slither said frankly to get out of her office. She wanted our help, sure as Hades, and the coin is good, but she doesn't want to be seen with us—said the rest of the coin will come from a third party."

"Who is the third party? Why do I have a price on my head? This is stupid.

I worked in a tavern in Wolf Hills," Runt said.

"I'm guessing Dean Slither used a charm on you guys from what you're explaining," said Maynard. "If Hattie is an alchemist, it would make sense that Dean Slither also knows the high art. I didn't see a ring on her finger, but she said she knew my mentor."

"Sorella and I were talking about this before she left," Duncan said. "Most likely, your father has pissed off a court member in the Holy Imperium, and they're trying to get revenge or use his family as leverage, Runt. I don't think it's anything you did. For now, stay away from travelers until you don't look like your poster's likeness. Might want to call you a different name. I'd guess they'll try to look for you by your father's name if anything, but we don't know the extent of what's going on. We may know more when we next see Stitch and Cordial, or when Sorella returns."

"What third party, and what poster?" Runt became frustrated and worried.

"I'll take care of it. Don't worry about it," Duncan said.

"But you're not telling me anything!" Runt spat.

"The Maker's tits, man!" said Gray Jim. "Tell the boy. He deserves to know."

Duncan sighed. "We weren't laughing at you, Runt. You have to understand, with the charm Maynard spoke about and the ridiculous nature of the lie, it's the only thing to do, but unfortunately, it's pretty serious, I guess. There's a bounty on your head for burning down a tavern, witchery, and the murder of your mother and others. The Holy Imperium blamed you for the entire thing. You're wanted now. Your likeness is making its way to every outpost on the Kings and Queens Roads."

"So, this third party is . . . let me guess—we know them?" said Maynard.

"Right, dumb and dumber," Duncan smiled.

"I don't follow," said Runt. "You mean Stitch and Cordial?"

"Wait, from my understanding," Maynard spoke more quietly now, "the Society of Shadows is not an institution to be trifled with by anyone."

"Thing is," said Duncan, "we know two of the boys at the local branch, so if it gets dicey, we'll be on top of any odd plays by Dean Slither."

"Interesting," said Gray Jim. He slowly chewed his food while scanning the tavern.

Austin - A Knight Out

J asper poked his head out of his room, bare-chested, and yelled to Austin as he walked through the Wildcats' common room, "Hey, baby face, you wanna go slumming with me tonight? I'm going to meet a friend, head out to a borough, and drink and whore until I'm blind."

"You think it's a good idea?" Austin asked. "We aren't supposed to go to certain parts of Hudson City. I don't want to get demoted."

"Who do you think gave me permission, *Sir Austin?*" Jasper rolled his eyes. "Nobody but the prince himself. Besides, the chap showing me around tonight assured me he would remain sober as a stone. He's a dwarve, for Maker's sake, a sober dwarve."

Austin felt the exhaustion from guard duty on his bones and saw the dark lines under his eyes. He was so tired he felt drunk and lusted for a good night's sleep, but saying no would disappoint the guard captain. So, he reasoned with himself for a moment longer, knowing he'd say yes.

"When shall we leave?" huffed Austin, breathing in the energy and ignorance of youth and pushing past his fatigue.

"That's my baby face! In two hours. I need to freshen up with a bath, and you need a nap," Jasper said.

Overall, Austin was honored to be a Wildcat and personal guard to Prince Damon. After Prince Damon ordained him into the Knighthood of the Wildcats, the air tasted fresher, the sky felt clearer, and he felt alive, standing guard duty for twelve hours to near exhaustion. Even as fatigued as Austin was, his simple life was satisfying, and he relished guarding the most important person in Vineland.

He worked his guard shift for over two days straight with only six hours of sleep. He wished for nothing but rest. Austin's status as personal guard to Prince Damon afforded him a room barely larger than a closet, which housed his bed, a place to store his weapons and armor, and a small dresser to hold what little clothes he needed outside of work. It was a little better than soldier's barracks, as he shared a common room where the other Wildcats relaxed and talked. The common room hosted card games, strategy sessions, and late-night sparring or wrestling bouts. The Wildcats ranged from as young as eighteen to as old as forty-five summers. Pap was a veteran of more duels and pitched battles than any other man Austin had met, the most senior member of the Wildcats.

Although Prince Damon named Jasper the captain of the Wild Cats at twenty summers old, Jasper was sharp enough to call Pap his second in command. He knew his age and inexperience hindered his decision-making and made sure Pap participated in any serious discussions.

Austin promptly turned into his room, fell into bed in his complete kit, and slept. He awoke to a splash of something cold dropping onto his face.

"Wakey, wakey! Sorry, you looked lovely sleeping there, but we must be off. It takes time to get to the Eastern Village near the city."

"What time is it?" Austin rubbed his eyes, trying to remove the wine Jasper had dripped on his face.

"Nearly dinnertime. Come, we must be going; an old buddy said there're strumpets to be bedded and wine to drink in the Eastern Village. I've heard we will witness sights never seen before. Put these on." Jasper helped unbuckle Austin from his armor and threw peasant clothes at him, accompanied by a bright cloak. "Wash off before we leave. I left a warm bath in my room."

"This looks awful," said Austin.

"Truly, it is, but I'd rather not be recognized as a court member in the Eastern Village. The locals reach to be like us but hate us all the same. They dress like a mismatch of rogues and actors when they go out as most are actually rogues, actors, and the like. Thus, the bright cloak, leather mail, and off-putting peasant clothes, and oh—sparkly feathers for our sword belts."

"I am not putting this on," said Austin.

"Oh, you will." Jasper barked. "I'm ordering you to after a bath."

"Right. Stay here. I don't need you watching me bathe," Austin said.

"No, don't be ashamed—I don't mind." Jasper sat on the bed and kicked his legs up to watch.

Austin sighed and walked toward Jasper's considerable room.

"Hurry up with the bath so we can be on our way!" Jasper yelled.

Austin finished bathing and started to dress. He left the weapons he used for guard duty in his room, put on a short sword, placed a dagger behind his back and under his cloak, and placed another knife in his boot along with a few coins in case things got out of hand and his purse was stolen. His hands felt odd with no gloves, but peasants couldn't afford such an extravagance.

"You do look smashing! Here, drink this. Our contact isn't far from the base of Trinity Cloudreach. We'll take a service dumbwaiter down. There will be a lot of walking, drinking, and humping tonight, and we must maintain our energy."

Austin yawned. The sleep had helped, but his body and mind needed more; two hours was not enough. Jasper's wine went down and felt strong, giving him a floaty feeling in his head. A pre-drunkenness settled into his stomach as they moved down through the tower. Dressed as fashionable rogues, they walked through a kitchen in the tower's basement and toward a cellar.

"Grab a lantern," Jasper said.

Austin snagged a piece of meat off a skewer from the fire and burned his hand, grabbing the lantern with his other hand. They entered the cellar and walked into a wine storage area to the back.

"Here we are, and follow me, please."

"Where are we going? I thought we were going to party?" Austin asked.

"We are, we are—trust me. We need a ride there," Jasper said.

It was dark except for the one lantern Austin held.

"Now, where is the latch?" Jasper groaned. He walked to the end of the wine cellar, looking at the floor. "Grab a bottle for the ride, please—red, not white. It's too dark for white wine. Found it!" He grasped a handle on a bottom wine shelf and pulled up. Dust flew everywhere, and they both coughed. "Sorry, haven't used this entrance in a while. Down we go." And he disappeared into the dark.

The stairs spun around in a circle of darkness as they descended. Neither spoke, but Jasper chuckled to himself. The stairs looked sharp and maintained. Austin thought it would be helpful to know about these stairs if he ever had to help Prince Damon get to safety.

"Here we are, and here is our contact," said Jasper.

They walked through an arched entrance leading into a spacious cavern carved from stone by the hands of slaves and dwarven craftspeople. White and blue owl lamps were mounted on the walls. Austin walked up to one. Each owl lamp was the length of a sword and gave off enough light to brighten the cavern.

"Austin, welcome to the dwarven tunnels under Hudson City. This is where the grand houses get food, supplies, and other necessities for their towers. It's a known secret, protected by a family of dwarves loyal to the crown."

"We are loyal to our own family, not to the crown. We have an accord with whoever rules Hudson City, 'tis all," said a dwarve walking toward Jasper.

"Ahh, yes, formalities," Jasper corrected himself. "This fine dwarve is our guide tonight. He'll take us away from our responsibilities and on an adventure."

The dwarve wore an impressive mustache and a little beard under his chin. He wore gray trousers with a dirty black jacket. Around his waist was a tool belt with pouches, hammers, tongs, a small rope, and a set of hand axes.

"Good day, sirs. Do you have my payment?" he asked.

"Austin, meet the dwarve of the hour, Bradley Railhead. Yes, one brick of tobacco and one brick of weed," said Jasper.

"Excellent. The wagon is over here. Right this way," Railhead said.

Jasper looked at Austin sternly, commanded, "Not a word, young man, not a word," and walked with Railhead.

The dwarve carried an owl lantern which glowed like the blue owl lamps hung on the shaft every two or three hundred feet.

"Watch your step. The rails are right here, and another cart will be along shortly," Railhead said.

"I had no idea this was here. This is simply stunning," said Austin. "Does this go under the river? Maker's breath." Austin was in awe of the lights without flame, the cavern's architecture, and the fact that Jasper used illegal reefer as currency.

"I got your payment from a mutual friend of ours. I believe we may see them out and about. Would you care to join us once we get to the village?" Jasper asked.

"I may, I may. This must be quality dope." The dwarve let out a low whistle of approval.

"I wouldn't know, but I'm sure we can try it out. Austin, hop in. Please don't touch the dwarven war dogs pulling the cart."

"Yes, okay." He was in childlike awe as he climbed into the large metal cart and sat, still looking around.

Two war dogs stood chained to the front of a large metal cast cart. The wagon was big enough to fit six stout men. The sides of the cart stood high and slowly tapered down to the front where the dogs stood. Its four wheels ran on rails and metal, so the cart would have trouble jumping the track. The war dogs were primarily black and brown, wearing horse-like harnesses to pull a chariot or wagon but dwarven-made in strength and artisanship. Two owl lanterns cast blue light on the front of the cart to show the way, and two similar white lights were on the back. They glowed brightly but did not hurt the eyes.

"You gents, get settled, and we will be off in a moment," Railhead said. He took a hand axe out and placed the hollow metal handle in his mouth, blade facing out on the other end, and sprinkled the dried leaves of the reefer into a small hollow area opposite the blade. He lit it like a pipe. It reminded Austin of a flute with a blade on the end. He made a spark using a metal gadget, and the dope caught alight for a moment. Austin thought it might be a dwarven tinder catch, but he'd only heard of one and had never seen its use. It reminded Austin of a tobacco pipe only in the form of a hand axe. The dwarve sucked in, held his breath, and blew smoke into the dogs' faces. The dogs looked at him the best they could, for each had blinders on; they moved their heads back and forth.

"Rat-chasing bastards, you love this shit." Railhead giggled. "One more hit."

He breathed in and blew a stream of colorful smoke into Jasper's and Austin's faces. "Good shit, Jasper, good shit."

The dwarve hopped up, pushed the two men aside, and took the reins. The war dogs stood, each obedient and oblivious to their plight in life. They jerked forward.

"You blow the smoke in their face, and it loosens up their muscles and joints, makes them last longer." The dwarve chuckled.

Austin looked around and noticed a total of six different sets of tracks heading in the same direction. As the dogs moved the mine cart, some tracks veered to the left while others shifted right into separate caverns.

"Each rail goes to various places in Hudson City and beyond. Our dwarven friends protect the entire underground. Not many folks from above come down through the tunnels. Most fear a collapse. Still, I find the travel easier to deal with—no crowds, and no worry about highwaymen, pickpockets, or any other trouble you can run into through the slums or central forest," Jasper said. He took a pull from the axe-pipe and blew smoke out. "Prince Damon visited once or twice, but now he's a bit too busy and all high and mighty with his plans to dominate all of Vineland."

"He's a halfwit if you ask me, a moron siding with the Blitzsteel family in the Steelsburg civil war," said Railhead.

Austin reached for his sword, but Jasper put his hand on Austin's. "You're not guarding anyone tonight, and people are allowed to have opinions, my dear friend," he whispered. "We're here to enjoy ourselves, not get into political arguments about matters we can't control."

Railhead was ahead of them and hadn't seen Austin's face of disgust at the comment about Prince Damon. They picked up speed. The dogs' mouths opened as they pulled, sucking in air, and sharp-fanged teeth glinted in the lantern light. As they moved, lights in the corridor whizzed past.

"Keep the coal burning, Jasper," Railhead said as he passed the axe-pipe.

Jasper put the handle to his mouth again, sucked in, coughed, and handed it to Austin.

"No, thank you." Austin tried to push away the axe-pipe.

"Don't deny this kind dwarve the pleasure of engaging in this holy ritual with you. It's blasphemy to his roots as a dwarve," Jasper said with a deep smile, eyes boring into Austin.

Railhead glanced over his shoulder, smiled, and nodded with a wink.

Austin hesitated before putting the pipe to his mouth. The smoke entered, and he tried to let it slip into his chest, holding it in and coughing it out. Rose and purple smoke came out of his nostrils, and soon he was chuckling. Jasper giggled and took the pipe, lit it, and put it to Railhead's mouth so he could finish it off. Railhead was too busy with the reins to hold it himself, and so it was as they made their way to the Eastern Village of Hudson City.

Railhead finally slowed the war dogs, letting Jasper and Austin out of the dwarven mine car. They made their way up cut stone steps, smiling and giggling, rubbing their eyes like newly awake children. They appeared behind the bar from a cellar where the barkeep kept barrels of ale and mead. Austin had no idea where he was on the island of Hudson City.

They obliged themselves to stay for a large tankard from the tavern's bar, listening to a singer and harpist belt their way through a rough and funny song. The song detailed Prince Damon's small cock and its ability to raise taxes. By the tune's end, they both sang along, yelling, "Down with the prince, up with our freedom!" while they grabbed at their crotches.

Austin would have previously drawn his weapons for a song disrespecting his prince, and now he was singing about Prince Damon's small cock and didn't give a shit.

The evening trailed on. Jasper took Austin to his first proper house of ill repute called The Delicate Pilgrim. Austin felt uncomfortable but a bit more courageous than expected, so he took a lady into a room. He left Jasper in the common room with a young man on his lap, feeding him grapes while a lady massaged his shoulders. Austin's strict and militant family upbringing provided a pang of lingering guilt only dulled by beer and dope. Sober Austin would be appalled with himself, but stoned on illegal dope, pints of ale, wine, and other spirits, he hardly knew up from down, a boy from a girl, or left from right. His confession at the Holy Church would be long and make him blush, and his knees would ache during penance if any madness remained in his memories.

Austin stumbled through a small affair of lovemaking under dim red candles and dressed, realizing he needed water and air.

The woman lay, now undressed from her doll-like clothes. She lazed about, smoking hash out of a pipe looking much older than the one Austin had smoked from earlier. "No need to rush off, honey. You paid for a full hour," she said. "Here, take this for a second while I clean up." She handed him the pipe and walked over to a washbasin. He watched her walk, admiring her shape, but he was still too shy even after finishing to say no to the pipe, so he took it and inhaled. She returned to him and took a hit, breathing deeply from it. He watched her lips pucker and relax as his eyes became hazy.

The second time lasted longer; afterward, they both lay sweating on the bed. As she cleaned up, he got dressed quickly, left a small tip, said "Thank you" loud enough for her to hear, and slipped out of the room.

Clouds of smoke from tobacco and dope mixed with wine and the stench of sex overwhelmed customers walking around The Delicate Pilgrim. Austin felt the spins as he looked for Jasper, using his hand to guide himself down the hallway, hearing laughter, moans of ecstasy, and the slapping sound of body on body through the thin walls. When Austin returned to the common room, Jasper was gone, likely entertaining in another room. Austin walked, mumbling quietly through a checklist of his belongings. He retained his clothes, a jacket for warmth, a cloak, a short sword, a knife, and money. He looked around, gave up on his search for Jasper, and stepped out of the house to get his bearings and clear his head.

Austin took a deep breath and looked around as every window lit up like a high noble's mansion, but it was a brothel, and he'd sinned. Across the street, an old church was now a gambling hall. Another door stood open, and music slipped out from inside. The streets contained jugglers, entertainers, drunkards, and those looking as if they'd never seen a bath. They all mingled and jawed at one another in different dialects, moving about to another party or vomit-filled beer hall. Originally a farming community, the East Village was now a series of brick buildings, hovels, gambling dens, brothels, and other businesses connected by semi-paved streets and courtyards. The shadows of towers controlled by nobles rested at a distance on the island of Hudson City.

"This is amazing," he said as he stumbled toward an alley to piss on the wall. He finished, pulled his pants up, and walked back to the brothel.

Jasper fell out the door as Austin opened it, laughing hysterically.

"We must be done with this place, dear brother in arms!" He clapped Austin's shoulders. "I will lose myself entirely in there with those barbarians. Come, let us mingle with the magical fae, people of orc blood, the heathen natives, and wondrous dwarves. Onward to the new and refreshing." He stood, drinking out of a jug of wine, somehow unspilled from his fall out the door. He leaned on Austin heavily. "Drink, drink! Come now, there are only so many hours in this evening. We are the eyes of the righteous and studious."

* * *

The madness of the decadent night consumed them both. They made their way down the alley Austin had pissed in, twisting and turning to another street. Austin lost his bearings, looking at three men playing cards on a building stoop. A lantern was lit above them. He thought they looked like humanoid weasels.

They moved down another road and turned into a densely packed alley, this one darker, and Jasper stopped. They looked foolish and lost in their floppy rogue's clothes.

"Where is this entrance? We should be looking for a shoemaker or a tinker's shop—or, shit. Where was . . . we should've taken a left," said Jasper, confirming Austin's thought that they were indeed lost in the East Village, far from any help from a Copperhead or sheriff.

They were among the dregs of society, pickpockets, trash burners, and the like. Austin was spinning drunk but considered himself better off than Jasper. He knew from the moving shadows in the corners and door frames it was hardly safe for either of them. Austin glimpsed a woman on her knees down the way with a vagrant and others drinking out of horns on a doorstep, talking and looking their way. Austin placed his hand on his sword pommel.

"Yes, I remember. Here we are, the local post office," Jasper said. He drooled, leaned a bit, took a deep breath, and stood straight, attempting to master himself and look less drunk, but his glassy, blood-strained eyes gave him away. "Do my eyes look as bad as yours? We're screwed if we don't pass the test—dare say, right truly screwed," he said.

"What do we have to do?" Austin replied.

They stood at the side building entrance.

"Just remember, they hate nobles, and we're outnumbered." And he knocked.

A slide at the top of the door opened, revealing yellow eyes surrounded by gray skin.

"Long live the prince," the owner of the eyes said.

The door was dark wood, painted green, with iron braiding up and down its surface.

Jasper looked at Austin and whispered loudly, "They want a pass code." Jasper looked at the eyes. "I don't remember," he slurred.

The door slid closed loudly.

Jasper frowned and thought for a moment. "One more time." And he knocked.

The door slid open. "Long live the prince."

"He's a fuck wit," said Jasper.

Austin's mouth dropped open, the door cracked open, and the guard smiled and opened his arms, admitting them both inside.

Jasper winked at Austin. "Follow now and behave, you scoundrel." He gazed at Austin with new hunger in his eyes. The man could go from maddening drunk to a severe amount of passion in a minute, making Austin feel awkward.

They walked in. The figure behind the door bowed and pointed down a barely lit hallway, music and the sound of laughter beckoning.

"Welcome to the Yellow Dragon," the door guard said.

Austin turned his head to look at the doorman. Jasper grabbed his arm and dragged him on toward the sounds coming from the end of the hallway. The hornless, gray-skinned orc was dressed in a lawyer's suit with dull yellow eyes and dangerously sharp teeth.

"Is that an orc?" Austin mumbled.

"Yes, the large fellow back there is an orc—a stout, strong one. Don't piss her off, or she'll rip off an arm. I've seen it happen to a third-degree noble. We blamed it on a horse-riding accident. What a bloody mess. Come now, I need to see a wizard and make a deal. One drink and we are off, back to where we belong. Keep your wits about you," blurted Jasper. "We will only be here for one drink, got it?"

"Sure, yeah, got it," said Austin.

They walked into the room connected to the hallway, which used to be a back office of a postmaster. A printing press sat in the middle of the room with bottles and candles draped over it. Most of the people in the room were in states of half dress, dancing to music provided by a small cluster of musicians in a corner. The rhythm of the music was new and enchanting to Austin. Most people danced and yelled over the music, a stark difference from a courtesan ball. Those dances involved rules, specific steps, bows, and acts with grace and manners—but not at this party. People touched one another with their legs, arms, and hips, coming together as they moved to the beat of drums. Their bodies shook and pulsated, moving in and out as if mimicking sex, both slowly and quickly.

The people wore a motley of clothing showing skin or a bright color, like half-cut open slips, revealing dresses, and leather chaps with no underclothes. Austin saw a woman wearing an officer's uniform but nothing under the coat. Laughter came from Austin's left; moans came from around the printing press. The room was a crush of bodies, and it was hard to concentrate on anyone. Groans and cries of happiness filtered over the music. A dwarve drank off a woman's buttocks—it was obscene, and Austin thirsted to join in. The band stood playing instruments loudly and poorly. If one of the musicians stopped to drink, smoke, or pleasure themselves, the rest kept playing a drum, flute, or whatever was at hand. Everyone intermingled with no chains, elves poured drinks with humans, and a few orcs and goblins in poorly lit corners gambled with dwarves.

Jasper grabbed Austin's hand and dragged him into the mass of people grinding together. He yelled, "No enemies here except for nobility and the prince. This place is sacred. No fighting, just pleasure. Come on, we must find the wizard."

They moved about. People grabbed at his head and pushed against his crotch, and Austin yielded himself to the sweet embrace of lust and freedom. He lost Jasper and continued with the smash of grinding bodies dancing and moving together to the music. Pipes were passed around, each admitting an assorted color of smoke when puffed on. There were few candles placed on the walls. The primary light source was an owl lamp emitting shades of light above them all, and a merrymaker would spin it, making the entire room feel as if it were moving to the music coming from the corner. He saw a large leaf with white powder known as wizard salt passed around, fingers running through the powder and shoving it into a mouth or nostril. He knew the wizard salt was used to help artists stay up late and bring other odd feelings to the front of their imagination but it also could kill if taken too much, was addictive if not used sparingly.

Austin's hips ground with a lean elven woman and her partner, whom he believed to be a tall male dwarve or a short human. He shifted between their bodies, but after moments, he caught himself and realized he needed to move on. "Thank you and excuse me," he said to them both. They heard or didn't—he couldn't tell. They continued to move to the music and dance with themselves.

Lost without Jasper, he pushed his way to the back, trying to be polite and make as much headway as possible. He thought he saw a court member but wasn't sure. He was long gone at this point, pointing toward a wall with a painting of a dragon, wolf, stag, sea creature, and lion in a fierce battle to the death. The music slowed for a moment, and he shifted away. He looked upon an area with two guards. They wore mail and leather, longer hair, and darker skin. Considering the rest of the post office was packed with people, he made his way toward them. This was where the wizard held court. Austin could feel it.

A dancer screamed from behind him in terror. Both guards tensed and drew swords. Another scream, nothing filled with joy or lust. This sounded of fear. The door Austin and Jasper had used earlier exploded from the force of a kick. The music floundered.

"Shit, Jasper!" Austin yelled toward the curtain where the guards stood.

Suddenly, the two guards moved past Austin and toward the source of the disturbance. He looked at the curtain and back toward the other side of the room, where he and Jasper had entered. Armored soldiers came through the opening. They wore enough metal to pose a threat to a commoner. The light in the center of the room continued to spin, making it hard to understand the commotion.

"Master, it's a raid!" one of the guards yelled back to the curtain. Another yelled, "Raid!" The room fell into a disaster of shadows and screams.

A large shield displaying a sword with a candle for the blade pushed through the front hallway door, followed by a man in full armor and helm; a tarnished white cape adorned his shoulders. The emblem represented the religious law of the Holy Church called the Path of the Blessed, the supreme religion of the Holy Imperium. The Templar's Genteel Monks fanned the knight's sides, carrying bludgeons, maces, and cudgels, ready to break heads and take prisoners. The monks wore robes and vests of scaled mail, while the rest of the room's inhabitants stood or slouched, drunk, wearing next to nothing. The knight, a member of the Order of the Blue Rose, also known as the Blue Templar, held a torch with a cross guard. The parties screamed and pushed to the opposite walls, moving toward a back exit.

The curtain near Austin parted, and out strode a person wearing a fine-cut man's suit, round spectacles over sculpted cheekbones. She stood at five feet five inches, was older at fifty-six winters, stately, and looked extremely pissed off. Her black suit was a fine woolen cut, and the top of her shirt and vest were left unbuttoned, giving her a slightly feminine look. She seemed imposing and intelligent, as if she could hold her own in a fight but would rather read a book and drink wine. Her eyes were youthful, bright in their blueness, but crow's feet had laid siege to them. Her hair was long and chestnut brown, and there were sharp pieces of gray and silver through it. She carried a walking cane, and each of her fingers held rings shining with different jewels. She looked around and pointed at Austin.

"You must be Austin. Go inside the curtain," Olivia Franklin said. "And you two," she pointed to the guards, "save as many as you can. Push the innocent toward the curtain. I'll provide the ability to see in the dark." She waved her hands at the two guards. "Close your eyes for a moment."

They did as she stated, and one of the rings on her hands dimmed in color. She pointed her cane to the dwarven light and with her other hand, in a grasping motion, pulled it toward her chest. The light from the candles on the wall, the dwarven light, and the Templar torch jumped toward Olivia's cane and into one of her rings. All went dark. There were screams and movement behind Austin as he moved through the curtain, leaving madness, violence, and blood behind.

Austin stumbled from the darkness into a hallway until he saw the light of an open door and an alley. He ran into the alleyway and breathed in, exhausted from the excitement and fear. Austin saw Jasper's arms locked together over his head with a thug who was trying to crush his head with a mace. Jasper drunkenly struggled, unaware of how much danger he was in. Austin ran over and stabbed the man under the armpit, pushing him into the corner of the alley, where the thug soon lay motionless.

Jasper put his arms down and yelled, "Why are people attacking me? I just want another drink! Piss off!" Clearly, he didn't understand the desperation of the situation. He spat at the corpse and kicked at its foot, slipping childishly.

"Jasper, get up." Austin grabbed him by his shirt. "The Blue Templar are here. We need to get the Hades out of this place now!"

Jasper's eyes were full of madness from whatever drugs he and Olivia Franklin had partaken in before the party broke up. Austin dragged him out of the alley as people flooded out of the door behind them. They moved from the path and away from the post office.

Jasper finally started to walk by himself as they lurched another street over. He stopped Austin from pushing him. "Hold up, hold up," Jasper said and retched into a horse trough. He cleaned his mouth with his hand. "What happened? I went to score and talk to the wizard, but shortly after, she rushed away and pushed me out the door."

"A Blue Templar raided the party," Austin said.

"Shit, I gave Olivia a lot of money!" Jasper hit his hands together and searched his person, looking for a small parcel, tapping his pockets as if he had lost a lucky charm. "Shit, oh, here it is." He produced a red velvet bag, investigated it, and smiled. "Spectacular," he said and looked up. "Okay, let's get out of here. No tunnels head toward the Midway Woods. We'll find a carriage, and I'll pay."

"What is going on?" Austin said.

The rush from a moment ago had sobered them up. They hailed a carriage away from the melee of the party.

A shambling homeless man stumbled toward them, smelling of decay and drink. He fell onto Jasper. "Spare change or bread? Do you have any spare change or bread for a soldier of Prince Damon and the Red Army? I served in the Battle of Reaping, I did. Spare change," he implored. He wore the rags of a soldier's uniform, tarred, ruined, and falling apart. The man's face looked like it was melting, and his mouth held very few teeth.

Jasper stared at the sick man. The man coughed and spewed out phlegm, spitting to the side of Jasper.

"I'm sorry, you fine people. Can't seem to kick this cough," said the beggar.

The carriage appeared; Jasper threw a few coins to the soldier, crawled into the carriage, and headed back to the barracks and Trinity Cloudreach.

Austin blurted out, "I thought . . . we're supposed to be righteous and the rulers—why . . . I mean, I guess I know why, but . . . does this often happen? Busts like this and the violence?"

Jasper looked at him in shock and tried to focus. "Look, our job is to protect the prince. Either of us could die at any time, so in my free time, I either train or obliterate my mind so as to not think about all the horrible shit we can't do anything about. Yes, shit like this happens, but not exactly like this. The Order of the Blue Rose showing up is shit news. They can do more than jail people and crack skulls. They ruin entire families," he said.

"So, I guess Prince Damon is collaborating with Bishop Devon and allowed the Order of the Blue Rose to start performing morality raids," Austin said.

"I didn't get to see the knight's face, but Bishop Devon usually has one or two large priests accompany him wherever he goes," said Jasper. "I may know the man you're talking about, but I'm not entirely sure." He put his hands to his face and tried to rub away the previous night. "I mean, the Holy Church outlawed all inter-species contact and mating in, what, 1650? Immediately after the last of the Goldthorn family died, which ended the Golden Age. It doesn't stop us from using other species as slaves or from using their wares and weapons. All great nobles use the owl lamps, created by dwarves or elves, and hunters and archers seek the elvish bows."

Jasper smacked his lips. "I need a jug of water and bacon or sausage." He looked at Austin and said, "Anyone caught tonight will be tortured and their families disgraced or blackmailed into submission by Bishop Devon." He started to talk lower for fear of someone overhearing. "I know Bishop Devon wants to be cardinal but can only do so with the high family's blessing. I bet Prince Damon borrowed money from the Holy Church to put on the masquerade party this summer. It's all anyone is talking about. He could've ordered Bishop Devon to expand the Order of the Blue Templar to lighten the debt. Unfortunately, they consider everyone else base and under themselves. The Maker gave dominion unto them, and they shall control and lead as the Maker's disciples." Jasper moved his hand away, indicating he did not agree with the Holy Church's teachings. "We should've paid better attention to what he's been doing."

"I go to mass regularly," Austin yawned, "and normally adhere to and follow the church's rules and the prince's laws, but this Order of the Blue Templar . . . they look and act like strict fundamentalists. I mean, do they think the Maker put us above all other species? Do they think the Path of the Blessed is the only way to live life? It's children's stories. We have to have relationships with all people. Half of the food we eat comes from elves born here in Vineland, not the old Holy Imperium. If we go by scripture, we will starve because elvish food is technically unholy and blasphemous to eat."

Jasper smiled at Austin and looked out the window as the carriage moved. "I hope people can get out of the mess back there. This city and this island are the most diverse areas in the world. Shit, humans mix with elves and dwarves in broad daylight with no issues, and it's easy to find civilized goblins and orcs in dark alleys and shitty taverns and beer gardens."

"Jasper, who is Olivia Franklin?" Austin asked.

The carriage shook as it moved over the streets and away from the East Village's haughty homes and sketchy apothecaries.

"They are whatever they want to be and are not to be trifled with in any manner," whispered Jasper with worry in his eyes.

Austin looked at his friend in silence and realized he knew nothing about this city or its court politics like Jasper did. He'd been brought up to believe in faith in your family, Prince Damon, and the Maker's righteousness. But, after tonight, he didn't feel so sure about religion or Prince Damon.

Jasper put his hand on Austin's leg in a friendly manner. His eyes darkened, and the smile from the night before was gone. "The night is over. We rest, we prepare, and we go about doing our job, which is protecting and, if need be, giving our lives for the royal family. This is our duty, and no matter what, we must keep our families' honor, you understand?"

"Yes, of course," said Austin.

Jasper smiled at his companion for a moment. "Now remember nothing and sleep. We still have a little way left to go." And he looked out the window with no smile, just a long stare into the morning gray.

Runt - Past Battles

"So, on top of the fencing, running, and lifting hay every day," Runt counted on his callused fingers. "Oh, and sharpening, oiling, and polishing your kit—I get to walk around a specific section of the town or university looking for goblins and orcs? All of this for free, mind you, not a single coin in my pocket for my time."

Duncan looked at Runt as he dipped his spoon into oatmeal, picked it up, and smiled. He took a bite and swallowed. "Yes, and every third day, you and Maynard do the night loop in the library, which Gray Jim and I do every other night."

Runt finished by swinging a heavy sword used to grow arm strength. He was tired and sore, yet he continued, "Fine, fine." He sighed. His body ached, and the weight of working out daily and the toll of the last few months lay across his shoulders, even if he didn't realize it.

"Stop your bitching. You sound like a hungry calf or annoying stray cat with your bleating and sighing. Look, you're training to get in shape. Nobody wants to use a weapon but move fast and strike to kill when you do. If you are in shape and can run, you have a better chance of not getting dead," Duncan said. "At this point, if we find your father, you'll most likely join the army. There isn't much else for you to do. I'm doing you a favor and preparing you for life."

Runt wasn't sure what to think. He didn't know what would happen once he met his father, once he explained what happened to their home. Runt pushed to learn as much as he could and get to Olde Ridgewatch and didn't consider the next steps in his life. But he was also tired of trying to do the right thing.

"I'm no hero, no knight, but I'm alive, and I survive. You want to be a knight, a member of the Wildcats for Prince Damon, go on, but you'll die by a sword, a bolt, or a spear quicker than you can piss yourself," Duncan said darkly. "There's no honor in a fight, a battle, a war—just the need to survive and live. You don't salute your sword in a fight. You smash their eyes in. You rip your fingers through their noses. You punch, pinch, scream, and bleed them until they stop fucking moving. Then you carry on, leaving the praying behind, and hope the only pain you feel after it's over is in your nightmares. That's why I'm training you—because people like me survive, and people like your *father* give orders to slaughter boys like you."

"Okay, okay. I get it; I understand."

"Not even close, Runt, but you'll get there." After sparring, Duncan toweled off. "Besides, your tavern work only pays you room and board; you need coin for food and to build up your armor kit. Most of the shit you have needs to be sold or traded in so you can get properly fitting gear. Now give me thirty laps around the barn and move the hay over from one side to the other."

Runt didn't say anything. He started running and considered what he would do once he met his father. The constant training and journey changed him. He wondered if his father would recognize him or believe his fantastic story. Duncan pushed Runt even further after the episode with the goblin in the library basement. He was determined to make Runt independent and decisive.

* * *

More snow fell in Hagarville Valley as preparations for winter parties began. Folk celebrated the old holiday of Yule, worshipers of the Holy Church observed the shortest day of the year, called the Day of Faint Light, while others found the time of the year another excuse to dance, drink, and argue about politics.

Maynard and Runt restocked the shelves in the library's basement after the explosion in the dwarven crossroads. No further incursions by goblins, or gossip spread about what had really happened in the library. Runt's patrols, both inside and outside, were quiet except for the occasional howl of a wildcat or dog. When Runt performed his guard duties inside, he found Maynard reading in the library with two lamps around him. Maynard now wore a dagger concealed on his hip and always kept his staff nearby.

"Just precautions, that's all, Runt, just precautions," Maynard said on his first patrol.

Runt would nod and walk on. The basement felt off to Runt, but Maynard said there were so many books to read and review, and he couldn't miss the opportunity.

This late afternoon, he finished his walk about the library and adjacent rooms and grabbed Maynard for a pint at the Red Horse Tavern.

Holly and mistletoe draped the doors and corners as they walked outside. They hoped to see Cordial and Stitch, back from adventures in the surrounding villages. Instead, they walked in to find Duncan and Angus as they finished their supper, the dwarve enjoying the night off from his cooking duties. Sorella was noticeably absent. She had been traveling around the area since the start of winter. Runt and Maynard sat and ordered dinner. They started into a hearty stew when Stitch and Cordial walked through the door, wind and cold following them.

"Look what the bloody snow blew in," Angus croaked.

"Hey, look, Cordial, they got us dinner. They must have known we were coming by," Stitch said. He grabbed Maynard's bowl from him. Cordial came up from behind Runt and snagged his stew.

Duncan signaled to the bartender for two more bowls.

"Dean Slither was in touch with us," Cordial whispered to the band. "She asked after Duncan, Runt, and Angus. We said we would let her know if we could provide any information. Which we didn't." He took a bite of the stew. "Oh, this is good. Thanks, boys." He wiped his chin on his sleeve. "Sorella wandered into the mountains again to see what can be seen?" he asked Duncan. He took a drink of warmed wine.

"She should have been back a few days ago, but with the weather as it's been, she could've been held up," Duncan said. He nodded and pushed Cordial to go on.

"In our work, we're able to glean info from a few Red Army soldiers heading through to Steelsburg. Three came into Hagarville Valley carrying mail, stopped at a friend's house for supplies, and moved on. After they left the university area, one slipped and went missing. I think it was a few miles off as they headed west, and the other two soldiers moved on, thinking their friend dead."

"We managed to find the missing soldier, and he talked a bit to us. He was grateful we showed up, or he would have frozen to death," said Stitch. "He was amiable. Sad, he died of natural causes soon after," he said as he smiled at Runt. "Couldn't keep the blood from naturally flowing out of the hole I gave him in his lung."

Angus burped and laughed a little. "Long as you don't bring any further heat to us." He took a sip of beer. "Fine by me."

"From what we heard, it sounds like the Red Army is moving to strangle cities and places that are refusing to join up with the prince and his pals in Hudson City and the Holy Imperium, as we suspected earlier." Cordial said. "Also heard there are no vagabonds or destitutes in Hudson City. They've been put to work rowing ships for the prince."

"Yeah, he confirmed there was a mixture of Red Army soldiers and mercenaries occupying Olde Ridgewatch, trying to keep the peace. The soldier knew all sorts of shit and talked our ears off," said Stitch. "Sounds like your father is there, Runt. At this point, it's pretty much confirmed."

"Means the Red Army and those mercenaries keep the peace by taking a mace to the face of the city. It's under martial law, and yet pamphlets screaming for freedom fly around the taverns and brothels, and street fights break out between locals and soldiers late in the night," Cordial said.

"At least—oh, that is so lovely. I missed warmed wine. At least that's what the soldier said. Poor bastard fell off a cliff after he died of natural causes. So sad," said Stitch. "Those wild critters need to eat, too."

Runt and Maynard sat and listened.

"You two are a few squirrels short of your nuts," said Angus.

Both Cordial and Stitch smiled at the dwarve.

"Hello fellas, sorry about the near execution back in Steelsburg—just business, you know," said Gray Jim as he walked toward the table.

Cordial stood and knocked over his chair.

Stitch pleaded with Duncan, "What is he doing here?" as if he were ten years younger. Runt noticed his hands moving down to his boot.

"Both of you chill, no knives or poison," Duncan said. "This is Gray Jim, the ex-hangman of Steelsburg and now a friend of ours."

"I bought you these. Please drink up. It's the only bourbon in the valley and cost me a day's wages," Gray Jim said, setting the cups in front of the two scoundrels.

Cordial and Stitch looked down at the drinks and sighed. They both thought for a moment, deciding on what to do next.

"Fine. Duncan approves," said Stitch as he eyed Gray Jim. "Cheers to old enemies and new friends."

Cordial picked up his chair. "Wow, Stitch, you're easier than a prepaid whore on summer solstice. Just like that," he snapped his finger, "you're friends with a guy who flayed your back?"

Gray Jim had tortured Duncan, Sorella, Stitch, and Cordial after their attempted bank robbery in Steelsburg. Stitch had been the first to be tortured, but Gray Jim had taken no heart in it and hadn't felt the torture was necessary. After only a few minutes with Stitch, he'd ordered the torture stopped, putting his career on the line. They had all admitted to their crimes earlier, after all.

"It was only one or two pieces of skin, and ladies don't care about my back." Stitch said, putting his hand to his back. "They prefer my front,"

"Nobody likes your front, Stitch," Maynard said.

"I should have done us all a favor and flayed your face," Gray Jim said.

Cordial snickered at this, and Duncan spat out his ale.

"Okay, Mr. Gray Jim, cheers to burying the hatchet. And," Stitch threw back the glass of whiskey, "if you ever betray my friends or me, I will bury the hatchet in your back." He pointed a dagger at executioner. Nobody knew when he had drawn the blade during the conversation.

"Fair enough, boy, fair enough."

Cordial, Stitch, and Gray Jim shook hands uneasily.

"What you all been up to since we last spoke?" Cordial asked, stretching and changing the direction of the conversation.

Duncan, Gray Jim, Maynard, and Runt gave him an odd look.

An old song played at the other end of the tavern, sung with enthusiasm and not a single ounce of talent, but it was lively, and everyone else came in during the chorus. Laughter spread throughout the night while glasses filled, and friends toasted away the darkness with songs and tears.

"Who's up for cards?" Angus croaked.

The night lingered on, and Runt and Maynard drank more alcohol than at any other time in their lives. Cordial and Stitch only cheated on one game until Gray Jim called them out. The rest of the games went well. Cordial and Stitch left to search for some older female students they had met previously. Maynard stumbled toward his sleeping quarters.

"I'll take Runt up to bed shortly," Duncan said to Maynard. "Don't have to worry about him."

Maynard smiled and nodded, his head fuzzy and eyes blurry.

"You don't have to take me to bed, Duncan. I can do it myself." Runt yawned. "Right after I—" And he promptly fell asleep.

Gray Jim looked at Runt. "Oh, to be so young," he said.

"You're telling me," said Duncan. He stretched his shoulder back and took a swig of ale.

"You know, Duncan, never seen anything like what you did in Steelsburg. Tell me, why were you trying to rob a bank? You knew you were going to fail. Nobody steals from the dwarven folk, especially in Steelsburg." Gray Jim poured himself more ale as the candles in the tavern burned lower.

"Human's right. There's no way to break into a dwarven bank and not get caught." Angus took a deep pull from his ale.

"Man named Doc," at this, Angus groaned, "hired me and the others. He hired us to break into the Crystal Trust Vault to acquire an item he'd previously owned. He knew of my ancestry and knew I was down on my luck, so we gave it our all. We tried to get it legally first, but they denied us. We tried another way, which technically wasn't stealing. Unfortunately, the safe cracker died before we could get close enough to get the item. Doc offered all of us pay enough where we would be set for our lives—and anything else we could take. Stitch and Cordial jumped at the chance, and Sorella followed me into the madness, leading us to the dwarven cells of Steelsburg."

"This Doc never got what he wanted?" asked Gray Jim.

"No, he didn't, but as it's been some time, I wonder if there was much more to it than theft. Like he knew we would get caught." Duncan fingered a locket and two metal tags that hung around his neck. "I still got paid what I wanted from him. Wasn't a lot of money, but it was important."

"Doc reminds me of a drunk fox. Can't trust him, and he's dangerous," said Angus. "I doubt we'll get any money he owes."

Runt started to snore.

"Kid's done for; I don't think he's ever been this drunk," Duncan said as he took another sip of ale. Gray Jim took a large swig.

"You trusted this Doc character enough to do a job where you and your friends could have died. The more I think about it, the more I think you may be the luckiest bastard ever. Sounds like a shit idea overall," Gray Jim said.

Duncan played with the thought for a moment, moving his tongue around his mouth, and then spat on the ground. "Doc's a battlemage, and what he did during the Battle of the Reaping was unspeakable. It's how the battle was named; after he finished off two other battlemages, he continued to slaughter, like reaping wheat at harvest. Anyway, one of the Blackheart brothers killed a hedge knight I squired for, cut the shit eater in two with his sword like it was nothing. His sword, Twilight, sliced through armor so quickly. He's not a talented swordsman, and I could have taken him." Duncan paused. "If things were even. Well, they weren't. I'm sure you were there—a pitched battle with three separate armies and those mages battling one another. After it was over, Doc found me, and that's how I ended up here, more or less."

"Yeah, the battle was abysmal. People ask me about it. It's hard to put into words. Things changed, though. Great Brightland sits across the sea, and we now bow to Prince Damon and the Holy Imperium. The last of the free city-states are falling. Steelsburg is in total disarray with a dwarven civil war." Gray Jim laughed with mirth. "Cheers to the Legion, the Holy Imperium, and the Nation," he said.

"Cheers to knowing who our enemies were and knowing who our friends are now," said Duncan.

"To knowing those in front of our blades, what's in our cups, and who's in a six-foot hole in the ground," said Angus.

They drank.

"We are one sorry morbid group of bastards, we are," Gray Jim said.

Duncan and Angus nodded. Runt slept at the table.

"This kid here and the other—you babysitting now?" asked Gray Jim.

"Runt's a good lad; so is Maynard. Taking Runt to see his dad in Olde Ridgewatch, and conceivably, he'll reward me with a job and a seat at the table. I don't know. I still long to be knighted, for Maker's sake. Plus, Maynard is Doc's apprentice, and one way or the other, I'd like further words with him," Duncan said with half a smile.

"Fair enough. Suppose I'll tag along. I'm sure you could use another sword on the road to Olde Ridgewatch. 'Sides, I ain't have a job anyway," said Gray Jim.

"Well, if you did, I wouldn't be here." Duncan stood. "I'm off to bed." He grabbed Runt. "Come on, boy, you too."

Duncan carried Runt to his bed, dropped him off, and headed to his room. He came down the hallway and saw a faint light coming from under the door. He tensed up, pulled a knife from his belt, and gently pushed the door open.

"I heard you stumbling up the stairs, you brute. Get inside and close the door," said a familiar woman.

He saw Sorella in his bed, furs wrapped around her, only her bare shoulders showing.

"I got in a few hours ago and have news from my friends in the area," she said.

"Sorella, for a moment there . . . " He paused, thinking of a memory about someone forever gone, and he grasped at his locket and tags. "I thought you were her."

"I know. Come in and get into bed, Duncan. Don't make me beg. It's a special night," she said, pulling at his shirt, the furs slipping off her shoulders. He moved toward her, wanting her, and trying not to think of his dead lover.

A lifetime of memories passed between them in a moment, and she blew out the candle.

The following day, Duncan woke up Runt, angrier than ever, and dragged him to the barn to train. Sword movements were first, followed by running and lifting weighted sandbags, broken up by Runt's vomit breaks.

Duncan pushed him and continued pushing him throughout the valley's winter storms. Runt's hands and body hardened, and he became more determined to make it to Olde Ridgewatch to confront his father and find out who had ravaged his home and so many others.

Alysha - Wind and Words

The wind pushed from the north and pulled water from the Erie Sea, covering Counselor City in ice sheets, causing only the brave or senseless to move outside during the winter. Work picked up at Bob and Hob's smithy. Alysha, Bob, and Hob spent their days and nights in the smithy for warmth, only leaving for a night or two to wash up and get away from one another. They were fulfilling contracts for General Flint's army, getting them ready for a siege on Grimwood, when winter finally broke.

Alysha was now their unnamed apprentice, learning the trade of making iron and steel into farm tools and blades. After each dinner, Hob dragged Alysha from her chair to train in sword and axe. They instructed her in blunt and bladed weapons, recommending she know how to protect herself and how the weapons worked in order to forge them properly. She ached every night before falling asleep and woke when either Hob or Bob shook her out of rest. They kept her so busy that mourning for her family and her previous life sank into memories as the day-to-day toils of servitude wiped her of energy. The smithing, the training in arms, and the harsh winter cut her figure lean and powerful.

Compared to most, Alysha was lucky. The Holy Imperium's soldiers and supporters initially camped outside the walls, but they started taking residence inside the city at the first sign of snowfall, causing overcrowding. Those outside the city walls lived in roughly built cabins with too many occupants, while others lived in tents not made to withstand a Grimwood winter.

With overcrowding came a sickness; the Smoldering Plague began as a cough, followed by fever, and finished with uncontrollable excrement and blood filling latrines, pits, and pots. The illness killed hundreds. The mayor asked Bob and Hob to assist the town hangman in removing bodies from the streets, so Alysha joined them. They used horses and a cart to pile the frozen bodies outside the city walls like lumber. The bodies were tarred and set on fire on the frozen Erie Sea. Later, Alysha saw the poor who lived outside the city warm themselves by the human bonfires.

The general forced his soldiers to be quartered in any house within the city limits. The city's leaders and merchants provided a civil and spirited rebuke. General Flint heard them out as they requested compensation for the time and food the soldiers ate out of their households. They met in a large town hall at the center of Counselor City.

Bob, Hob, and Alysha stood in the back. Bob put his hand on her shoulder. "Just watch. We aren't part of this," he said.

Alysha stood quietly. She watched General Flint's calculating eyes as he calmly listened to the complaints. His face showed hints of disgust at the entire situation. "We will wait out the winter here, and the city will be grateful for it in return. Any further complaints will be met with the harshest of reprisals."

The younger son of a merchant, overweight and full of himself, stood. "That is too long, and you and this army are too much. We deserve our freedom from you and Prince Damon!" he shouted. Other townsfolk cheered. Douglas Huber was nineteen summers at the most and was unfamiliar with the Holy Imperium's ways.

The boy's father, Thomas Huber, embarrassed and shaken, attempted to quiet the scoundrel. "Shut up, boy! Shut up!" he said in a loud whisper.

General Flint looked calmly at Douglas Huber, standing five feet away. The general was a member of noble blood and a Redcloak. Douglas Huber stood with an air of confidence and swagger only the young and naïve possessed as his friends patted him on his back, showing their support. Flint stood, walked over, and looked down at the boy. General Flint drew his dagger and stabbed Douglas Huber through the eye, pushing the blade to the end of the skull and out.

The shouting began, and a resident vomited.

Jared Blackheart walked in from the side of the assembly and pushed through the crowd. He pulled out the father, Thomas Huber, and choked him with one hand, lifting him off the ground. Other community members stopped arguing and yelling as life seeped out of the merchant.

General Flint was dangerous, and Jared frightened all that surrounded him.

"Your time of wallowing in the mud of so-called freedom is *over*, along with any rights from the Grimwood city-state," General Flint growled. "This is the Holy Imperium now, and you will live by our justice or perish like the Huber family line." He held Douglas's body by his fine merchant shirt, his head bent to the side as blood and brain dripped onto the floor.

Hob and Bob grabbed Alysha and pulled her through the back door. She shook in anger. The two smiths kept tight grips on her as they pulled her away, Hob whispering to calm her down all the way.

That ended the town meetings to provide grievances to General Flint in Counselor City. Later, General Flint ordered the merchant's entire family dragged from their house and hanged in the town square. Twenty-one people were hanged, from a three-month-old child to one of the town's elders. Jared Blackheart personally ended all the children's lives as he prayed to the Maker, Servant, and Child in all his righteous fever.

At Flint's command, the family's property fell into his hands, and soldiers made the family's ancestral home into barracks. The town guards fell under Jared Blackheart's control and became the second set of spies for the army stationed in the city. Conspirators, including those who backed the Huber family, disappeared or were hanged in the town square without trial. By mid-winter, Flint's army controlled the city and surrounding area through a series of executions and bribery. But, again, no threat from Grimwood came. Finally, a rumor spread that the Smoldering Plague had hit Grimwood so severely it had destabilized the government to the point where they had put themselves into a military quarantine.

General Flint performed all of this after burning Alysha's village, murdering her family, desolating the rest of Wolf Hills, and indenturing or enslaving anyone who survived. He was ruthless and calculated. From what she'd heard, this occurred in additional towns as Flint's army moved from east to west. The enslavement wore on the few Wolf Hills townsfolk she occasionally saw while working the smithy. Their pride ran through their veins, and now those enslaved barely hung on, their spirits crushed. Her family initially stayed in Wolf Hills because of the indomitable spirit of liberty Grimwood provided to those living in the hills and valleys.

* * *

Hob and Bob allowed Alysha to accompany them to a local tavern. She earned some money and used it tonight. Although technically not free from her position, she was better situated than when she'd first come into their service.

Alysha bathed at the Broom and Bustle for the first time in a month. She lay in a bath upstairs and was to meet Hob afterward for dinner. Before they'd separated, Hob had indicated that he needed to deal with some urgent business and left Alysha to her own devices. She knew Hob went to see a prostitute. He'd attempted to show manners to Alysha by trying to be discreet. She took her time in the bath, getting the grime off her hands and face. She admired the strength in her arms and legs and, for a moment, felt content. She could hammer for hours and not tire, and her body showed this fact. The moment passed, and she reminded herself she must grow stronger to endure and survive where her family had not.

Alysha dried off and dressed, thinking of her father and how to reach him. She contemplated a letter to her father or brother, both members of the Red Army. Her father's last letter had told of a change of command as he'd been moved to Olde Ridgewatch, a city-state near the Atlantis Ocean, away from the capital Hudson City—but this was before autumn. Her father and brother may know more about Wolf Hills. General Flint's First Army censored the mail leaving Counselor City. She wondered if Runt was dead or alive and dreaded the reality of the thought. She knew he'd worked at the Wayward Tavern and heard it had burned down after a barroom fight, along with other buildings in the central portion of Wolf Hills. Any survivors had ended up in Counselor City, and Alysha had neither heard nor seen anything of Runt. She kept her eyes out for him, but she suspected him dead after so long. It was hard to mourn when there was no proof, no funeral.

She remembered Miss Wightland speaking to her, telling her to stay quiet and grow strong. Alysha breathed in deeply. She let the anger of the past push down and take root deep in her heart. While working with Hob and Bob, she remained stoic and appreciative of their kindness. They treated her like an older daughter. Alysha accepted it with grace and the determination to not let them down, but a fury lay deep inside, waiting to escape.

Alysha walked down the stairs and ordered whatever was in the kettle by the fire at the bar. She sat, and Hob walked toward her as a waitress sat a bowl of a lamb stew with onions, carrots, and blood sausages in front of her. Hob wore a slight grin on his face. They sat in a corner and talked about the shop and local news. There was a large communal table in the middle of the tavern, and women made their rounds as laughter and smoke lingered in the night. Alysha sat with her back turned away from the crowd, ate, and drank the warmed wine Hob had bought. It was too cold even inside.

Hob looked up from his stew and said, "If I had seen her, I wouldn't have been so quick." He glanced at Alysha. His smile sank, and his face warmed from embarrassment. "Beg your pardon, Alysha. Sometimes forget you're a lass and not a lad."

Alysha smiled a little and spoke, "It's okay, Hob. We're only human. Besides, as long as you know I'm a woman and not an object, I will not be so easily offended. Remember, I'm attempting to become a real apprentice and, one day, a genuine blacksmith." She took a drink. He smirked a bit and nodded. "I hope you respect them and their work. They're performing a job as well. We work with iron and steel. They work in flesh and passion. So, which one were you looking at?"

It was bold of her to say, and she wouldn't have spoken of it to Bob, who was more militant, while Hob doted on Alysha when he could. Hob nodded. A strumpet walked by the edge of the bar. Alysha blew on her spoon and took a bite of stew. She moaned a little after getting a taste of tomato, lamb, and pepper as it lingered going down her throat and looked in the direction that

Hob nodded.

"Helena!" she exclaimed, not thinking.

Helena Catseye, her friend from Wolf Hills, stood holding a goblet of wine. Her kirtle pushed up her breasts until they nearly burst out, and her arms were bare, one draped over an older man. The dress color was deep green, and her hair was long and tied in places with red ribbon. Her face was now whiter and her lips redder than Alysha remembered. The makeup pulled out her features and gave Helena an exotic look but also aged her. She kissed the man on the neck as he ran his hand up her leg and under her skirt. She slapped him away, said she would be back in a moment, and walked over to their table. This wasn't the girl she'd spent summers with, giggling under a crab apple tree, dreaming of marrying knights under a star-kissed sky.

"Oh shit, you know her," whispered Hob as she came over.

"Yes, she's from my town," she said as worry and despair shivered up her spine.

"Alysha, is that you? Well, my, my, my," Helena said, sauntering over. She fell onto Alysha's lap and laughed. She was drunk and smelled of sweat, wine, and other men. "Look at you. Alysha, you got you an older man." Helena looked at Hob. "You there—buy me a drink. I am so thirsty."

Hob made a motion to the man behind the bar.

The man at the table Helena had visited looked flustered, but soon his eye came across another. He was not too meticulous.

"The Maker's tits, that was close. I totally didn't want another tonight. Thank you, honey." She tipped her cup to Hob and squeezed Alysha's hand. "Look at you. You're looking well, Alysha," Helena said. "Fit and strong, not an inch of fat on you. Is your husband even feeding you enough?"

"Not my husband. I'm indentured. How are you doing?" Alysha asked with apprehension. "I'm sorry. I wasn't allowed to look for you or anything when they placed me with the smithy. I couldn't get away."

"The lives we live now should all be so happy, even to be alive. I thought you dead." There was a pause. "Better than what I do now," she whispered. "Now me? I'm okay. We made it, Alysha, you, and I. Most of the survivors of Wolf Hills died before winter from digging trenches or the Smoldering

293

Plague. After the bonfire, Alysha, we were all thrown into a shit show on a wagon." Helena took a deep drink of her wine, pulled out a thin cigar, lifted a candle, and took a deep drag. "Mmmm, good." She breathed in the smoke from the cigar and slowly exhaled. "Alysha. Alysha, look at those arms. You know, my lady would pay to have you join us girls here." She motioned to the other girls walking and talking to customers around the tavern.

"What? No, I'm with Hob here. I'm his servant, his assistant. I frankly don't know what I am anymore," Alysha said. She pulled from her warmed wine and let the burn go down her throat, heating her stomach.

"It's fine. We're not who we were a year ago, so it goes. Hob, is it? What do you do to this pitiful thing that makes her arms so muscular and her face so thin? She barely has any curve to her, except for those perky tits. You are next to nothing, girl," Helena said. Her attention flicked between Hob, Alysha, and the rest of the guests like an animal on the prowl.

Alysha frowned in thought, not sure if she liked the new Helena.

"Miss Alysha helps with me at the smithy. Miss Helena, is it?" asked Hob.

"Why, yes. Look, a man in here with manners. That's too much." She laughed again. The laugh was nearly genuine as Helena attempted to keep her facade up. "You work for Hob here, at the smithy. Ain't that cute." She leaned toward Alysha, so they were barely a foot apart. "Least you aren't getting plowed by farmers, rode by soldiers, and sucking off sailors." A fit of anger flared in her eyes. She changed back to Helena again, calmer, making a fake face.

"I have to put up this smile, or the mistress will punish me," she whispered. "Look, I'm sorry. I'm drunk. It's all I ever am. I have to be; I have to have a grand time, serve those who pay, and have fun doing it, or I don't get a place to sleep. This is work, Alysha, so don't judge me. I make less than a quarter of what I earn, and this is my easy night. I'm at the tavern. I get to eat and drink for free as long as one of us girls sucks off the innkeeper before we leave tonight." She took a pull off her thin cigar. "He lets the mistress's ladies come in on the weekends to do our thing, not at the flophouse or out in the streets."

She drank from the goblet in her hand. It was a long pull, and her brief silence followed as if she were thinking of a time before, when she and Alysha had been friends and innocent. She burped a bit and looked at Alysha again.

"I earn enough money to stay in the flophouse, sleep on the floor, and not die from the cursed wind. My life sucks, and I have to suck to live. Could be worse, right?" She didn't wait for the answer. "Could be part of the labor pool, dying of the cough in tents and cabins along the wall. At least I get stew and whatever I can drink a few nights out of the week."

"Can we," said Alysha, "can I do anything to help, Helena? I don't know what to say."

Helena looked at Alysha, and a moment passing between the two of them that only they knew, that only they could believe ever existed. They were back home again and unbroken innocent before the sin of war and politics corrupted every moment of their existence, and then Helena blinked, and that moment was over.

"Can you help, honey? No, I don't think so—unless you can buy me out— but I doubt it." Helena sighed. "The mistress won't let me go. I'm too new, too fresh to be bought out for cheap. I guess if you can find me a soldier with enough coin to buy my freedom or take me as a wife. . . No, I think I'm stuck here." She took a drag from her cigar. "If it helps your feelings, I try to make sure the soldiers don't get handsy with me and make sure they finish quickly, the turds." She got quiet. "And if I see that pig Jared, higher-than-thou goblin sucker, I will saunter up to him and stab him in his dick." She pulled a short knife from her dress pocket. "But no help here. I'm a whore now, Alysha, so no pity. I'll find you if I need blacksmith work done. You need whoring done, look for me here," Helena said. She turned away, disgust flashing across her face, with herself and them.

"Buy me another drink there, Hob, or piss off with those eyes. You gotta pay for what your eyes are doing to me." She went from happy to angry so quickly. The drink, the men, and cold desperation had changed her in only a few short months.

"Let's go, Hob," Alysha said as she stood up, flinging her cloak over her shoulders.

"Sure thing, sure thing," Hob said, flustered.

"I'll see you around, Helena. Stay strong. We'll figure something out," Alysha said.

Hob stood and put on his coat. He grabbed Helena by the arm as she walked away.

"Hey, asshole," she slurred.

"Here, it's not much. Please stay warm, and don't get hurt," Hob said, giving her a few coins. He squeezed her hand and walked away to catch up to Alysha.

Helena looked at her hand, then watched Hob's and Alysha's backs as they walked out of the Broom and Bustle. She sniffed, frowning for a moment, wiped her eye, and then smiled. She turned back to the community table and laughed loudly in a fake manner to get a merchant's attention.

Outside, the wind blew the snow horizontally from the sea.

"Alysha, wait up. Wait up!" Hob jogged to catch up to Alysha.

She was walking quickly, trying to return to the smithy and its warmth. And maybe to put some distance between what she just discovered about her best friend.

"It's so cold. Fuck, it's cold." Alysha had developed a tongue like Hob and Bob, she realized.

They walked close together, Hob attempting to block the wind until they got to the gate nearest the smithy, on the other side of the wall. Alysha could deal with the snow at Wolf Hills, however, the wind pushing off the sea into Counselor City acted like another season itself. It continually changed and grew in coldness and strength without warning, moving piles of snow as it shifted the landscape in a matter of hours. Mothers didn't take newborns out at night for fear of the wind sucking their child's life from them. Birds, rats, and other animals sought shelter from the wind, but it found its way into everyone's homes. Tonight felt as if it were trying its worst to blind them both.

Hob and Alysha wore scarves around their faces; only their eyes showed. Alysha's hands were protected with gloves she'd made from used cloth and fur, both leftover from a knife sheath made for one of the smith's customers. Her boots, laced up to her knees, were the most expensive thing Alysha owned. Hob and Bob forced her to use her money responsibly. Alysha had yelled and fought them at first, arguing the money was hers and that she could do what she wanted. They let her rage, spit across the room, and throw a chair, but she calmed, saw the intelligence in their ideas, and suffered their punishments (mostly more manual labor) in silence.

She was indentured to the smithy for a year and was treated well. Hob and Bob attempted to teach her more than any previous servant. They helped her procure suitable tools or showed her how to make them herself. They made her buy her cloak and material to make a hat and scarf for herself. The winds picked up, and the snow didn't stop. She knew they'd been right, as they had been about everything else.

The city gates closed at dark, but Hob knew the guards, and they let them out through one of the side doors.

"Hello, Miss Alysha," said one of the guards that was frequently polite to her. Edwin Flatrock was a younger man with a wisp of a beard growing.

"Hello, Flatrock. Too cold to talk now—maybe another time," she said, and they half walked, half ran back to the warmth of the forge. They opened the door and jumped inside. Wind and snow followed them, blanketing the floor around the door.

"Close the door. I'm working here, and you're messing up my papers." Bob stood near the fire pit, working on a new sword for General Flint.

Hob and Alysha stomped their feet and started taking off their outerwear. Hob walked over to check on Bob's work. The weapon was a cavalry sword, and Bob took his time to make it right. Alysha walked over, thinking about the events from the night in her head one more time. She looked at the two men as they spoke about the sword. They were talking, but not loud enough for her to hear. They stopped and stared at her when she got closer.

"Hob says you met someone from your town, and she's a prostitute now. I'm sorry," Bob said frankly. He walked to a shelf, grabbing a bottle and three cups. He portioned out the brown liquor. "You have a fury deep inside you, Miss Alysha Wolfthorn. It's time we talked and figured out where you go after you're done here."

"You don't even have to say as much—it's not my place. I need to remember I'm nearly a slave, and if I don't work hard, I will remain as such," Alysha said.

"You are both fair to me, to have taught me as much as you have already."

"We respect you and others as much as possible. I don't know what we can do to help her, your friend. Buying out a servant or an enslaved person, even for us, it's hard to do. It took us years to buy ourselves out. You are lucky to be contracted to only a year," Bob said. "Although I don't think most of the servants and slaves from this area will make it through the entire year. General Flint and Jared Blackheart are hard on their labor force."

"What'll happen to me at the end of my contract? Where am I going to go, what am I going to do?" Alysha asked.

"Can't tell the future, Alysha. You have to work one job at a time," Bob said. "What would you do if you could?"

* * *

The following day hit her like a brick to the face. Nobody had died last night, though she felt she might have already. Everything hurt, and vomit lay in her hair. Hob slept at the table, and Bob lay curled up near the fire while Alysha lay under the table.

Last night they'd told her more than she'd wanted to know, and she had dreamed of the stories they'd woven and spun as they drank whiskey deep into the night. Alysha remembered talking to Hob and Bob about her darkest wishes of revenge and murder.

Popcorn lay on the floor along with broken mugs. Everything spun and hurt, and nothing would stop the beating of a hammer inside her head. A deep-seated painful moan rose from the bottom of her chest. There was a bottle next to her. Empty. Hob snored loudly, on the table she lay under.

Bob moved and stood, pushing his hair out of his face. "You okay, Alysha? We need breakfast and wine. Eggs, bacon, and a beer—then back to work."

"No, I'm dying here. I can't. I need water," Alysha said.

"Get up, get snow in a pitcher, melt it, and get hydrated," Bob said. He scratched at his magnificent white-and-gray beard.

Hob started to move, cleaning up the mess from last night. "We really got into it. You're right, eggs and bacon if we can manage. Need to eat and finish the polish on that sword for General Flint. He's to stop by later this evening to pick it up."

Alysha got to her senses quickly. General Flint was the man who ordered her town to be destroyed and who had ruined her family. She wanted him dead and facing him would help move this process forward. She moved, head throbbing as she scooped up snow to melt into clean water. As she came back into the smithy with a clay pitcher full of melting snow, she asked, "May I assist in the polish of the calvary sword, Hob?"

Hob tidied up the area, righting chairs and picking up debris. He gave her a curious look. "You may, but I expect your best, and I will scrutinize you after. This is a well-paying customer; his praise will get us a lot more business." He stopped and turned to Bob. "Bob, did I tell you part of the general's payment for his new cavalry sword was an old family heirloom he recently found? Said he'd bring it by upon his return."

"I'll do my best to exceed your expectations," she said, looking at the sword.

"No need to use fancy words. Just ensure you don't disrespect Flint, even if you dislike the man. Enemy or not, he worked to get to where he is and has the money and power to bury you and us with a wrong impression," Hob said. "Sides, we still have his contracts for those big pieces for the siege as soon as the weather breaks."

The night before, Hob and Bob asked her to stay on until she found other work. She felt like her life could be better. Alysha had been happy for a moment as they'd drank, laughed, and toasted to better days. Now reminded of her mother's death, of Ryan Purenut pressed into the Red Army, and Junior Wolfe killed at her feet, she knew an escape from Counselor City needed to occur. If not, she'd try to kill General Flint and Jared Blackheart. Or die trying.

She finished the polish on the cavalry sword. It was over thirty ounces of steel and nearly forty inches in length with a slight curve. She placed the blade in its sheath and left it on the workbench. She tied her hair back and brushed herself off, her apron still tied around her waist, her back to the sword.

The door opened, and the bell above the entrance dinged. Bob walked into the room with a smile, his bald head cleanly shaven and his mustache curled above a shaped beard. He looked tired but ready for the customer. "Welcome to our shop," Bob said.

Alysha stood, stoic.

"Bob, good to see you again," General Robert Flint said. He shook the snow off his heavy cloak.

Alysha glanced up at the man; his hair was short and parted on the side, dark blond to near brown. He wore a long mustache similar to Bob's, but his beard was trimmed short and close to the jaw. General Flint was tall and well built, with power in his eyes and a hungry, almost menacing manner of standing. He was capable of violence, both with his hands or his commands.

Behind General Flint came another person, shorter in stature. His face was covered with a scarf, but Alysha saw his nose and eyes, which looked sharp yet charming. He wore a knit sailor's cap to keep warm, a mix of Holy Imperium infantry uniforms, and leather pants worn by elves near the Erie Sea.

"This is my lead scout, Ian. He has business as well," General Flint said.

Alysha studied the general, trying to remember his face for future reference.

"Alysha will you take care of Ian while General Flint and I speak about his sword, please," Bob asked.

"As you wish," said Alysha, and she walked over to Ian, realizing he was elven. "How can I help you, sir?"

"Very kind to call me sir, but it's unnecessary. I have several blades that need touching up. Sharpened, and a few of the handles need to be reinforced," Ian said. He placed several knives of varying sizes onto the bench before him.

Alysha looked at the blades. "Well-worn, but all seem sturdy and of suitable weight. You take care of your blades, even with heavy use," she said. She noticed how adept she had become with her smithing knowledge. She realized Ian used these knives and daggers to kill people, maybe even her friends and family. "How do you want them sharpened? For cutting through leather, cloth, or for," she paused to look Ian in the eye, "closer work?"

Ian regarded her with a slight tilt of the head and broke a brief smile. "Bob, your apprentice knows her blades. My compliments," he said.

Bob nodded and smiled at Alysha. "She is talented. It doesn't hurt that she learns from the best," he said.

"Miss Alysha, this is for skinning game; this for work on the battlefield; and these two are for, as you say, closer work," Ian said, pointing at each knife in turn.

"Okay. I can have this done in about two days. I will check the handles and refit anything loose or off. Payment upon completion. Anything else?" Alysha asked.

"Yes, if you have any heavy game arrowheads, I could stand a dozen or so, please," he said. "The general has allowed me to go hunting for a wolf, a runt run astray."

Alysha glanced at him and felt sour. "Yes, of course. I will do my best to get several made," she finished and nodded, grabbing the blades from Ian. "Let me get you a receipt." She wrote up the receipt and placed it on the bench.

General Flint turned to her after she had finished with Ian. "Bob said you're one of our indentured servants, finishing up a year with them. I'm sorry for any difficulties you've had," he said. "We serve the prince, as you do. Please work hard. I hope your family is freed soon, and you come out of this with a new skill under your belt."

"As you command, sir." Alysha bowed her head as her mother had taught her.

He nodded and walked out, the elve following behind him.

She was pissed off. He didn't even know what her family had gone through or what had been done to her home. He was naïve and ignorant of her life's trauma and where she'd grown up. She tossed a knife at the door after it closed.

"Alysha!" yelled Bob.

"What?!" she screamed back. Her hands were in fists, and she breathed hard, in through her nose and out her mouth.

Bob glared for a moment and inhaled, trying to suck the anger and bitterness out of the room. "Come over here. I want to show you part of the payment. It reminds me of a weapon I've seen before," he said.

She walked over, angry yet curious.

Bob unrolled an old cloth, showing a broken sword.

"Flint gave you this? I've seen it before. It was broken in Wolf Hills," Alysha said. "It was Junior Wolfe's sword before Jared Blackheart killed him. But wait, where have you seen it before?"

"I know the sword because Hob's grandfather made it along with a tobacco pipe," Bob said. "Hate to see a sword like this broken, though."

Hob walked over and looked at it. "I dare say, given the right environment, we could make it a bit stronger this time. We have new metal to play with now, don't we?" He looked at the trunk, where the star metal lay inside, locked away. "Got enough to make a hammer and forge this sword anew."

Runt - Spring Break

"I can't take this anymore. I almost want to find another goblin down here," Runt complained. "This sucks."

He adjusted the straps of the leather harness he wore over a chain-mail shirt. It felt like his thousandth patrol, walking by shelves of books and scrolls, every corner memorized. In the past few days, the only positive was the return of students to Mount Nittany University. He hadn't made any headway in meeting a girl, but he saw plenty now, adding a little brightness to his otherwise drab days. The library was coed, which was a bonus, even if he were too shy to speak to any students. The students ignored him or walked away when he came near. Perhaps his armor kit and weapons put them off? When he entered the stacks tonight, he saw several students reading at a large group of tables near the door. He placed one of three lamps he'd brought down as his patrol started. Runt walked away from two girls, who laughed as he passed up and down the shelves. He had walked halfway through the room when he heard his name.

"Runt, Runt, I found it, I found it!"

Runt moved his lantern in the direction of the voice. It was Maynard. He wore a shirt and the tie of the school, a new robe fell on his body, wrinkled and misshapen. Even with new clothes, he looked like a poor copy of a university student.

"What did you find?" Runt asked.

Maynard had a small lantern strapped to his belt over his robes, making a mess of the wool vest he wore over his shirt and tie. "I know I'm supposed to be down here walking with you, but nothing is going to happen now. School is back in session. More teachers and students guard this place than when on break, anyway."

"So, you spend your time searching for books, taking naps, or trying to hit on girls that won't give you the time of day," Runt said in a teasing, brotherly way.

Their relationship had grown throughout the winter, akin to what Runt believed his relationship with his brother should be. Maynard was near Runt's brother's age. Runt and Maynard had much in common and taught each other about school, girls, and books.

"Yeah, of course." Maynard moved his hand as if he were pushing a spiderweb away from his face. He blew up, toward the hair falling over his glasses. "I found the book my mentor wants! It was near where we met our friend, the singing goblin, a few months back."

"How? You said the goblin used a form of," Runt paused and whispered, "a form of a song or spell to find it and couldn't."

"Truthfully, I wasn't even looking for the book. I was looking for a sequel to another book. Remember *The Long Lonely Nights of the Milkmaid*?" Maynard said.

Runt remembered the book. He had pored over it and its delicate writing style, finding it to be some of the most intimately profound erotica he'd ever read. It was smut of the lowest caliber, and Runt had read the book several times after Maynard handed it to him one night.

"Wait, you found a book concealed for ages, lost by your mentor and many other scholars while looking for a sequel to something people jerk off to?" questioned Runt.

"Well, yeah," Maynard said and smiled. "All because I feel like a dog in heat around all these girls."

"Let me see it," Runt demanded.

Maynard handed over the book. The cover read *The Early Mornings of the Lonely Milkmaid*, however, the cover fell off. Inside was a worn cover with red and gold lettering.

"I've looked through the library dozens of times but never thought to look for this book—not until I read *The Lonely Nights of the Milkmaid*, which, if I can say, is entirely underrated as a bastion of literature. I checked for another book by the same author and found what you're thumbing through instead."

"Yeah, it's very educational. Any idea why Doc really wanted it?" Runt flipped through the pages, finding the writing unreadable and in different languages. "What is this? Is it written in elvish, dwarven, or something else?"

"I think it's written in code—no idea, though." The fledgling mage shrugged. "I hope he can read it. I'll try to decipher it as we travel."

"It's a good thing you found it because we should be leaving soon. It hasn't snowed in two weeks. We need the snow to melt, and then Duncan says we'll be on our way. Mud or not, if the roads are passable. You still coming along?" Runt asked.

"Yeah, of course."

"It would suck if you didn't. I was worried you were getting too settled in and . . ." Runt trailed off.

"Relax. My allegiance is to Doc. As much as I love books and education, getting out in the real world is where you learn to become a real," Maynard glanced around, "mage."

Sorella sat at the tavern with Stitch and Cordial, talking and laughing later that evening. Duncan and Gray Jim sat at another table, mumbling, and drinking from large beer steins. Maynard and Runt walked in, saw the two separate tables, and immediately went to Sorella. She had just returned from her trip to the Blightbriar Wilds. Runt thought she was easier on the eyes than two old soldiers getting drunk.

"What news, Sorella? Where have you been?" Maynard asked.

Runt made a sign toward the bar for two drinks. "Warmed cider or wine? We'll take whatever is handy."

"Hi boys. Runt, put your hood up. You look cold still." She reached over, picked up his hood, and put it over his face.

"I'm not that cold, Sorella. What gives?" He pushed it back down.

"You've always had that hair color, right?" asked the elve.

"Yeah, why?"

"Stitch, can you see if the barkeep has raspberry or, better yet, blackberry preserves? I doubt they have any fruit other than that," Sorella ordered. "And grab a cup full of coal ash from the fire over there."

Runt could see this would be a serious conversation. Stitch moved toward the bar without saying a word.

"I have a feeling your news isn't good," Maynard grumbled.

"Cordial and Stitch came across some interesting information," she said.

"I thought you were part of the society, Sorella," Maynard said in a hushed tone.

"Yes and no. Anyway, it's pretty clear that members of the Holy Imperium want to find Runt and Maynard for what went down in Wolf Hills. Both are wanted for witchery and murder, judging from the wanted posters circling all over." She paused. "And your father has an order for you to be arrested. The Society of Shadows confirmed it again today via a letter on a billboard. There are descriptions and wanted posters out now at bureaus. It appears you're wanted, dead or alive. The likenesses are for both Runt and Maynard. You are wanted for murder, causing a riot, and witchcraft."

"Relax, mate. We aren't going to cut you or turn you in," Stitch said. "Money's all right, but we listen to Sorella, more so than the code of our little society. She has gotten us through scrapes like this, and we owe her a few."

"Screw the society's code. You're one of the bastards now," Cordial said.

"Yeah, of course. Plus, I think I could take at least one of you down if it came to a fight anyway," Runt said with a smirk.

"Ha, it would never come to that, mate. Instead, we'd cut your big toes off with chicken wire while you slept and watch you stumble around as you tried to walk, then knock you over the head and bugger you with a pool cue for fun," Stitch said.

"Vulcan's beard, Stitch, I believe in the Profane, and I think that's messed up," Runt said.

"You boys done with your jokes and chest-puffing so the adult can talk?" Sorella said.

Maynard laughed a bit, the others smiled but said nothing.

"Look, I haven't been out in the elements in the middle of winter just so you can get caught. Before heading east, I traveled north and looped back around here, searching for news. I spoke to my feathered friends as well. There has been a massive troop movement by the Erie Sea. It looks like Grimwood is in for a mess of a siege once the weather breaks. The Red Army's guarding the main passes over the Blightbriar Mountains and implementing new taxes." She paused for a second and drank her green tea. Her skin was worn out and more sallow than usual, and her eyes were tired and sunken.

"As the Red Army marched toward Grimwood, they either burned every town they crossed or demanded loyalty in the form of servants, slaves, money, or food. Counselor City has been garrisoned, forcing families to house soldiers. The loyalists don't mind, but there are pissed-off people. It was General Flint and the First Army all the way from Hudson City."

"Doc mentioned this when he first rescued me at Wolf Hills," Runt said. "but I don't think Maynard, Angus, or I believed him a hundred percent due to the drunken haze he lives in."

"The Queens Roads' strongholds may be more garrisoned now than in the last few years of the war, which could be a good or horrible thing," Sorella explained. "Most likely means fewer highwaymen and roaming bandits, but each garrison takes tolls and monitors mail, so uncensored news will be harder to come by. Plus, the wanted posters now cause issues. We should start preparing to leave, head to Olde Ridgewatch, and learn as much as possible. Hopefully, meet up with Doc. We may get a better idea as to what the fuck is happening. We will dye Runt's hair tonight, and I will work with Maynard so they both look slightly different. It should fool most idiots looking for them—unless we run into a professional hunter, or worse. If that happens, we'll handle them." She ran her fingers to the bridge of her nose, showing stress.

The group moved out of their chairs when the door swung open. Angus came in and hurried toward the group.

"News, everyone, we need to get moving. Dean Slither may be moving against us. She received word soldiers from the Red Army are coming to occupy the college and keep it in line with new laws and regulations from the prince." Angus breathed in hard.

"How did you hear of this?" Sorella asked.

"I cook for her and several professors once a week. I stayed around cleaning up and overheard them. It sounded like she wanted me to hear them talking," Angus said. "We should pack up and leave. I think the party will be coming from the Kings Road running from the north to here. I'd guess foot, archers, and a few knights. Enough to be a presence in the area and keep the place under control but not enough to sack and burn it."

"I have to run back to my dorm and get my bag," Maynard said.

"We'll go to the bureau, check for mail, and meet you on the Queens Road heading east outside of the college, but first we'll head west toward Steelsburg and circle, make sure we are seen heading the wrong way. Throw them off if they are looking for our special little boys," Stitch said.

"Everyone, dress warm. Looks like we leave before the area thaws. This could get treacherous," Sorella said. "I'll tell Duncan to pack up his gear." She moved to the other table.

Runt didn't say anything, only started moving and packing once he got to his room.

They left in the early morning by cart and packhorse. Duncan rode his horse, as did Gray Jim. Neither articulated how they'd come upon two horses and tack with the bit of money the group earned, but they were ready and moving as the sun rose. Angus sat with Maynard in the back of the cart, covered against the weather on three sides. Sorella guided the cart, and Runt sat next to her with darker hair after a quick dye job.

They walked on roads built hundreds of years ago by slaves and serfs using broken stone and rubble so armies could travel more quickly across the vast Blightbriar Mountains. The process of creating the Queen's and King's Roads had desecrated and destroyed elves', dwarves', orcs', and goblins' lands, all in the name of progress, which had led to unrest for hundreds of years. The Goldthorn family used lies, bribes, and treaties to connect strongholds and castles. Guile and brute force had been their tools to shape the roads. The building of the streets and the major construction of bridges and dams eventually bankrupted the Goldthorn family. It divided the family lines into the Ruinthorn and Hawthorn families as time passed. The two families had warred over the failed Goldthorn dynasty. Historians called it the Thornbriar

War. In the end, both family lines had nearly ceased to exist. This created the current environment of fiefdoms, strongholds, and city-states led by nobles. When the renowned Goldthorn dynasty had fallen, three realms had vied for control of Vineland: the Holy Imperium, the Nation of Stouya, and the Legion of Carigreed. They had fought for decades in the conflict known as the Crimson Struggle.

The Queen's Roads were major byways from east to west with focal points on key castles, cities, and keeps, and the King's Roads connected the north and south. Initially, nobility assisted in garrisoning the strongholds lining the roads. However, after the last of King Christopher and Erica the Red's family, the Goldthorns, died in the year of the Maker 1650, the strongholds had become tools between the warring factions vying for control of the crumbling dynasty. The techniques used to build the Queen's Roads allowed better drainage than other paths and walkways constructed just a few summers ago. Erica the Red and King Christopher's legacy connected the inner wildlands to the oceans.

"I wonder if my ancestors died and were buried under the stones we now walk on," Stitch said. He looked at his feet as they traveled east.

"This is going to be bad at best. I would have preferred to have a few more people and horses for this long trip, but we will have to make do. Gray Jim, do you want point or drag?"

"I'll take drag, Duncan. I prefer to see the ass-end of an ambush, not the glint of the arrow as it leaves the bow and ends up in my chest," Gray Jim said.

"I think we'll be okay on that front. Stitch and Cordial can smell ambushes out. Besides, the goblins and orcs will be less active. They hate the early spring. They don't start raiding for another month," Duncan said. "We must worry about other wild beasts among the trees and hope they are still hibernating."

The cart moved along on the road, still muddy from the melt of the snow. The weather, although warmer, still felt like winter, so they all wore warmer gear.

Each stronghold on the Queens Road was strategically placed to be a day's ride from each other if traveled on during clear weather. The more traveled areas held fully garrisoned forts which allowed for more growth. Thus, small towns dotted the lands between each garrisoned stronghold, allowing riders and travelers to take a day's lunch between rides, and providing news and messages. The forts offered protection or vengeance as needed if ill befell a town or hamlet.

Throughout the Crimson Struggle, the ongoing strife between the three nations caused strongholds to become great cities and city-states on their own. In contrast, others had become forgotten or dangerous nests for darker creatures. For example, the myth of the Gloomspire had come from a stronghold enveloped by an orc clan, never to be taken back.

The first night, the small group made it to a stronghold garrisoned by locals from the Commonwealth of Erieland. The group ate a hearty soup of meat and beans. Runt fell asleep soon after the meal ended as whispers of war, taxes, and rebellion floated through the room like smoke.

Runt - On the Road

They stopped near a crossroads, trying to decide on a direction after three days of difficult riding. The gang stood between Hagarville Valley and Olde Ridgewatch, lost in the fog of the Commonwealth of Erieland as a hazy sun attempted to break through the brisk, late-winter day.

Signposts nailed to a long-dead pine tree pointed in every direction. The tree's needles lay on the ground, with most branches bare from fire or rot. The failed pine tree stood alone in the middle of a field on the Queens Road, trying to help the lost and weary; a bare forest with a path leading toward it lurked in the distance. The area smelled of the decay of early spring, as the snow mingled with last year's thoughts and this year's growth. The signposts offered help like a mad joke. Bird feathers hung from deer sinew and sticks on branches tied together with young sapling bark jingled in the wind.

Runt looked at a pair of old, rotten boots hanging on a branch above a cruel-looking cage suspended by a chain, a lifeless elve inside it with its hands missing. The long-known punishment for thievery. He tried not to focus on the corpse.

Stitch observed the cage and glanced back at Sorella, providing a whole conversation in one moment. Sorella scratched her left ear.

The signs claimed city names, stating each distance for destinations like Hagarville Valley and Steelsburg. Others pointed to the north or east, toward Olde Ridgewatch via Shrewtuff's Pass and Rookgates Hold, and another to the southeast, toward Affectus, the city of neighbors.

Angus, Duncan, Sorella, Stitch, Cordial, Gray Jim, Maynard, and Runt stood on worn feet and frayed nerves. They longed for a restful night at an inn, but this area offered little except a deep forest which none wished to enter—except Sorella.

"We stay on the Queens Road; there are outposts for us to stop at, and it's safer and smarter," Gray Jim said. He knocked mud off his boots and scratched at his full white beard.

"I think south; it's better to stop in at Affectus to see what's what. We may be able to stay with friendlier faces sympathetic to Runt and those hurt by the Holy Imperium. Maybe even take passage by ship north to Olde Ridgewatch," Sorella said. "I hate boats, but they're safer than walking. Taking this portion of the Queens Road brings us too close to ground I don't wish to cross. Nearly all travelers turn away from the direction we're about to go. It's why the foot traffic and paths diverge so much here. The keeps nearby won't be guarded by friendly faces either."

She watched Gray Jim, the rest of them considering the options, waiting for a response. Ravens on the tree cackled and yelled at one another. Maynard shimmied up the pine tree, attempting to reach an area of the tree recently struck by lightning.

"Maynard, stay away from the corpse, you freak," Gray Jim said. "Duncan, what do you think?"

Duncan didn't say anything, only looked at the crossroads. Stitch and Cordial disagreed. Stitch said to head east still and stay on the Queens Road. Cordial agreed with Sorella.

Angus chimed in. "I'm with Sorella. Orcs and goblins took over the dwarven ruins near here during the Crimson Struggle, and dwarven families led crusades to retake them, only to have their names wiped from our histories." He paused. "So much blood spilled, fighting in the Blightbriar Wilds. Hades forge, they still fight over strongholds where our eyes can't reach, and the fog blurs more than a person's sight." He stopped again for a moment. "It's not a good idea to pass through the area, even if a Queens Road points in that direction. There are other places and passes to use."

"We stick to the road, and we'll be fine," Stitch said. "We passed through there not—what—a year back?"

"It wasn't a pleasant walk, even with more people to help. We were all in a different place, too. There was more to the crew than this small party," Cordial said. "And guides. Beautiful, lovely guides."

"Yeah, no guides this time," Sorella said. "I miss them."

"Do Maynard and I get a say?" Runt huffed.

Duncan turned to Runt, taller and leaner after a hard winter. He knew his way around a camp and could hold a blade without cutting himself. Even Maynard looked winter-thinned, as a hard road takes clay and molds it.

"Sure, Runt. We are going to this city for you and because we hope to see Doc—whatever he calls himself now," Duncan said.

"I say stay on the Queens Road. It's been safe so far. Even with the wanted posters, there hasn't been much foot traffic. If we see trouble, we go off the road and circle around. I say, stay the course. Maynard, your thoughts?"

Maynard, sitting on a branch in the dead pine tree, looked at Sorella, the actual leader of the band. She stood there, and Maynard looked at her, then down and away from her gaze, filled with guilt. "Sorry, Sorella, I'm with Runt. There's no need to head to Affectus. If anything, the Holy Imperium will soon drop the hammer on their pacifists, and the city will roll over for them." He fiddled with the burned wood from the pine tree, shoved it in his satchel, and shimmied down.

They were five days past Mount Nittany University and a month's journey to Olde Ridgewatch.

"I think there should be a tavern at the foot of the next major pass as we stay on the Queens Road. If we pick up the pace a bit, we should get there before nightfall," Gray Jim said.

"Fine," Sorella said with a huff. "I'm overruled, but it gives me bad vibes. Keep weapons at the ready, and piss in groups of two—unless we can make it to a keep or tavern. I want Duncan in front with Cordial by his side; Stitch, you and Gray Jim in the back; dwarve, you lead the wagon with Runt next to you; and Maynard, in the wagon."

They took their places. Sorella whispered to Maynard quietly, "Can you whip up a distraction if we need to make a fast exit?"

"Think so." He hopped down from the tree.

The packhorse pulling the cart shifted its head back and forth, and shit.

"Ask Cordial for help as needed."

They moved with a quiet unease, making solid progress toward the first pass east in the direction of Olde Ridgewatch.

"It should be up the way a bit. There's smoke on the horizon above the tree line. This inn makes these slow-cooked bore ribs. You could die for them. Angus, you should get the recipe from the cook. They're wonderful," Gray Jim said, sounding happier than anyone in the band since coming together.

"Ah, sounds tasty. How did you come about this place?" Angus asked.

"Oh, in my travels. Either a town treats a hangman like a king or a plague victim. Sometimes both, but I have to eat, so they feed me. Nobody wants to be on the bad side of a hangman." Gray Jim didn't talk much, but food got him going; he enjoyed talking about dinner when torturing people.

The road's width shrank, and the cart and horse progressed more slowly over the hilly portion of the road.

"Maybe we can trade the wagon and horse at the tavern. It's slowing us down," Maynard noted.

"Don't like it, but agree we're slowed down by it," Angus nodded.

The band had gotten along well enough since deciding to move east. Having never seen it, Runt looked forward to getting closer to the Atlantis Ocean.

"It's getting dark, but their cook fire is still burning. See there." Gray Jim pointed. "They had the prettiest serving wench there."

Duncan laughed. "I see now why you're excited."

Sorella slipped from the trees. She waved and ran toward them.

"What news, Silvercrow?" Duncan asked.

"The smoke ahead is the tavern, but it's not smoke from cooking. The place is burned down. The bodies look butchered and eaten while others were dragged off toward the woods in the north."

"Orcs and goblins," Duncan said loud enough for everyone to hear.

"Most likely a pretty large force, at least two dozen. They moved off toward the north, away from the road," Sorella said.

The band of travelers stood quieter now. Sorella, for her worth, didn't say anything about being right. Instead, she was calm and considered their options. Gray Jim scratched at his chin, angered by the news.

"No survivors at all? Shit. I'm so tired of the Commonwealth of Erie. It does nothing but shit on you. See, this is why I don't get my hopes up," Gray Jim growled.

"If any survived, they are food for orcs and goblins now. The tavern was large before it burned. It's why you could see the smoke from here," Sorella said.

"What's our best route now? Say we lose the cart," Duncan said.

"Stay on the road. Move swiftly past the tavern. There is a path with a fork in it. We take the one to the right and hope for the best," Sorella replied.

They went by the tavern at a quick pace. Sorella strung her bow; Duncan put on his armor and carried his shield on his back; both Cordial and Stitch became twitchy, jumping at the birds in the trees.

"When the birds fly away or you can't hear them, that's when there's trouble. Boys, don't forget," said Gray Jim to Maynard and Runt.

The burned inn brought memories of Wolf Hills back to Maynard, Angus, and Runt. Runt grabbed the pommel of his sword more tightly as the wind picked up. They moved away from the burned tavern, leaving the smoke behind them. They left the cart near the trail entrance, blocking the way. Maynard placed a vial he'd created under one of the wheels. He covered it with dried leaves and an old bird's nest and smiled. They moved on through the dwindling light. After a while, Maynard laughed a little.

"Whatcha do, Maynard?" Runt asked.

"I can't make them all of the time but figured a random blast of green and red flames might scare off whatever might want to follow us. Whoever moves the wheel on the cart enough so they can get around it will snap a glass vial, causing a reaction with the chemicals placed inside and the tinder below. It'll spook those shitheads, scaring the piss out of them," Maynard said with a smile.

"Let's move, boys, let's move. I don't care if it's dark," Sorella ordered.

They traveled the trail the best they could. Sorella called out for any odd footfalls or turns with Stitch's help. They made their way out of the trees of a large hill and into another open field. Both horse and human breathed wearily, walking on the broken trail. Laughter and other inhuman noises broke the hush of the walk. They sounded a little like what Runt had heard in the cave at the university. There was a snap, screams, and a speck of light behind them.

"Okay, everyone, let's go," Sorella said in a loud whisper.

They pushed on, past a clearing and onto another trail. Long, winding turns led into bushes and briars as they tried to lose their pursuers. By the morning, tired and the two horses hobbled, they trudged on, knowing they would need to stop soon.

Sorella pointed in the distance. She spotted a protective keep consisting of two large towers sunk deep into a valley surrounded by earthworks, stone, and wood fencing. A large hall and stable with a barn next to it lay between the two towers. Both structures had been built with stone, one in a circular fashion and the other with sharp, squared edges. The keep and barn were a mixture of stone, mortar, and log construction and looked fairly new. The towers looked as if they came from another age.

She breathed in deeply. "Never heard of this place but looks safer than our current situation. Let's get going."

As she finished speaking, a rider came out of the keep's gates and headed in their direction. He bore a flag with green and white colors. The rider circled at a distance as they walked into the open. His helmet's face was open. The rider looked at least fifteen years older than Gray Jim, well armed in plate and mail, spear in hand.

"Come, travelers, we don't get many guests as of late from the east, with the Queens Road near impassable around my keep. I'm sure you have stories to tell and news to give. We have ale, a warm fire, and food," the armored rider said. He pointed them toward the first gate and followed, an eye to the trail they had come from.

As the bastards moved toward the earthworks, they found a robust stream and a drawbridge braced by stone-held walls. The gates were iron with stones anchoring them down. Maynard looked at Runt with one eyebrow raised but said nothing. The inner gate and walls were stone and human-made, looking old but well maintained. The two towers stood as high as the older trees surrounding the valley. Both buildings provided a full circle of protection from the forest spread around the valley's hills, and the valley was open enough for farming.

"Sir, may I ask who this keep belongs to?" Duncan asked. "I have not seen such in my travels."

Sorella let Duncan take charge in matters like this, knowing certain men's attitudes became bruised around strong women.

"It belongs to Lord Washcreek of Liathland, known to his enemies as the Gray General."

"Liathland, you say? I thought we were in the Commonwealth of Erieland," remarked Duncan.

"Aye, you are, but this outpost, this keep was given to him after the Crimson Struggle, as a," the rider paused, "a gift by our esteemed great prince," he finished with a sour look.

"'Tis a beautiful gift, sir," said Duncan as he noted the knight's mocking tone.

"As you say. I am Sir Roland of the Eaglespire." He pointed toward one tower. "The other is the Owl Pillar." He pointed at the other tower. "My lads will take your mounts. Please meet me in the long hall once you're ready. I hope we'll have food and news to share," Sir Roland said. He steered his mount away, toward the Eaglespire tower.

They gave up their mounts to young handlers and walked to a large building in the center courtyard, pushing the kinks out of their legs from their journey. The building, a great hall, lay between the two towers, welcome and warming. The only structures other than the great hall and the stable behind it were modified field tents near the keep. Nobody operated the gates, and nobody walked the walls around the towers. Duncan thought this odd and nodded to Gray Jim, who signaled that he understood. The group opened the large doors to the great hall and entered. The room was sparse, with benches and long tables in the middle. There was a fire, and the walls were timber with plastered whitewash.

"You ever been this way before?" Runt asked Cordial.

"The Owl Pillar? I heard of it in passing. You know, in whispers and conversations. Servant's thick cock, my legs are tired. Give me cobbled streets, pockets to pick, and sweetmeats. Hate big, open spaces. Hey, Duncan, you think something's up?" Cordial rambled.

"We shall ask our kind knight why a hold with two grand stone towers and two sets of walls is nearly empty. Doesn't feel right. Keep sharp. Only draw your weapons when you see me do so," Duncan said. "Angus, please stay with the boys. Get our horses ready to leave if it all goes wrong. Stitch, stay by my side. Gray Jim, Sorella, and Cordial, make like grateful guests until we figure out what this place is all about."

Sir Roland walked toward them, still in his armor kit. His helmet was off, and he smoothed his finely combed mustache, long white hair wet with sweat. "My apologies for the sorry state of the keep, but time's been rough. The winter was long, and when the weather broke, our lovely neighbors—the goblins and orcs from the Blightbriar Mountain range—visited us, bringing death and despair."

They spread out in a half circle around the knight.

"Friends." He smiled, worried but not shaken. "I have taken off my helmet and welcomed you to this keep as guests. I wear my kit and sword because we could be attacked at any time by forces much darker than you could suppose. If you wish to take this place, you'll fight kids, a cook, and me. You may even win, but I promise several of you will die with feathers peppering your leather jerkins and chain mail."

Older adolescents with bows and arrows aimed at them sat above on ceiling beams, and two others stepped out behind the hall doors. More came through the kitchen door, all armed with bows, arrows, and knives at the ready. Both parties tensed.

"Hold now, everyone. We come in peace, and it's been a long road. You can rob us. We have not much to offer. We'd like to trade our news for food and a roof for the night. It would be much obliged," Duncan said calmly, hands out in front of him.

"Okay, that was our hope. Know we will defend our empty, modest home here," Roland said. His hand rested on the handle of his blade; his other hand was out and open, palm up, attempting to keep everyone calm.

"We mean no violence—just need rest," Sorella said.

"Fair enough. Everyone, relax and go about your business. Keep me updated on any movement outside of the walls."

A boy of fifteen came up to the knight and whispered in his ear.

"There's been movement in the woods you came through—goblin or cave spiders, most likely," Roland informed the Bastards. "We put sentries out to warn us if they come near the walls. Please come eat, quickly. We have venison, bread, and roots. Apologies, our hospitality has not been much. We're understaffed, as it were."

Duncan introduced everyone as the food came in. "We came from the likes of Steelsburg and wintered at Mount Nittany University," he said.

Duncan provided Sir Roland with basic information on what befell Steelsburg, leaving out his part in igniting the dwarven civil war. After finishing their food, the knight got up from his stool and paced.

"Your news confirms my worries, much so. Most of the folk from this hold followed Lord Washcreek, the Gray General, to the city of Affectus. There's a gathering to discuss what to do with Prince Damon and his treatment of the independent city-states. The delegation left before winter, and we lost others to the Smoldering Plague and stray attacks from goblins. The attacks on the stronghold have grown aggressive, which is unnatural. We received stragglers from villages and homesteads destroyed by further attacks as the winter rolled on. The survivors wandered in, and we welcomed them, mostly children. It's whispered the orcs have united under one leader, under one horn. They speak of a leader who regards herself as a queen or prophet of a mountain. Hearsay mostly, but stories seep from bitter truths. The wicked live outside these walls, and it's spreading," Sir Roland said.

"We can feel it as well," Duncan agreed gravely. "Go on."

"Refugees and children defend the two towers, Eaglespire and the Owl Pillar. My greeting to you was one of the first forays I've mounted in days. We lack enough strength to protect our outer walls in full force. A few kids are brave enough to slip out past the gates and wander the woods to provide intelligence as to what's happening," he finished and looked out the hall's window for a moment.

319

"You, Duncan, spoke of the Red Army. A detachment under the flag of the First Army commanded by General Flint passed through after Lord Washcreek's delegation left. Flint's men stripped this place bare and pressed our older ones into service. Their leader didn't think the place was defensible and told us to get out. Too many unfriendlies in the area. They left us for the birds, offering no coin or barter for what they took." He sipped a cup of wine as everyone rested. "I ask out of need: If you can stay on for a few weeks, give us a chance to get this place in better order. we would be obliged. We could use you older veterans to teach these kids self-defense and get our food stocks up," Sir Roland said.

Duncan looked around, considering. "We'll talk it over and get back to you in the morning. I think we could all use some rest under a roof."

"The hall is yours. If you need me, find a child nearby, and they'll likely find me in one of the towers." Roland stood, bowed, and walked away.

They looked on and waited until Sir Roland left the hall.

Cordial yawned, and Gray Jim got up, stretched his legs, and threw a log on the fire in the hearth at the back of the room. Maynard and Runt were asleep at the table.

"Stitch and I are going for a walk. You all rest up," Sorella said.

Maynard and Runt woke but didn't say anything. They moved over near the fire and lay down. Duncan nodded, and Angus stood, stretched his arms up, and walked toward the kitchen to speak to the cook.

Gray Jim put his feet up and drank from his cup of wine. "What do you think, Duncan?" he asked.

"Me, I think this place is a death trap waiting to close. He's right about the orcs. Those beasts and goblins don't attack walled strongholds like this. Even during late battles in the Crimson Struggle, it didn't happen. Not enough discipline to do so. If they joined as a war party, they were used in the vanguard. Sir Roland says they make attacks against this place. That goes against their nature," Duncan said.

"Hate those little goblins. They're a nuisance to this land. I got nothing against an orc—executed a few, tortured others, and counted one as a friend for a time," Gray Jim said. "But a goblin? They make no sense, man. They're wild and uncivilized and have no morals."

"Friend, you say?" Cordial asked. "You had an orc friend?"

"Yeah, but circumstances beyond my control ended it," Gray Jim replied. "Bloody Order of the Blue Rose—we call them Blue Templar. One ordered me to take my friend's horns. She was captured near a burned-down nunnery. Most orcs are killed on the spot, while some are thrust into slavery. My friend was knocked out and taken prisoner by this Templar and his monks. I was employed at a fort nearby and knew the orc from trading and drinking with her. They brought her back to the fort, stripped off all her clothes and armor. They left her chained like a dog. They wanted to set an example of her." He took a deep drink and wiped his mouth. "When you take an orc's horns, it's like ripping apart their honor, their souls. It's castration." He paused. "I couldn't look her in the eyes as I sawed down each horn to a fine nub. The screaming and grunting—I hear it still."

"What happened," Runt asked, "after?"

"I'm a hangman. After losing the horns, she went mad instead of being cowed into slavery. She tried to kill any that went near her. So, I did what my job required. I was ordered to nail her to a fiery cross," Gray Jim said. He downed his wine, angry tears welling up and slammed the cup down. "The Templar said a prayer to the Maker and lit the cross. I walked away after. The smell of burned orc flesh doesn't leave you, like the smell of a battlefield doesn't leave you. Sticks to you like honey."

"That'll do it. Remind me not to get too close to you," Duncan said.

"Oh, I won't, Duncan, but it doesn't matter. Death comes to all sooner or later, and I am death's hand." He stood and smiled. Duncan smiled back. "I'm trying to live with a small amount of honor, even in death."

"Well, I've escaped once, and I am grateful," Duncan said. He took a deep breath and closed his eyes, ready to sink into a nice nap.

The door swung open, and Stitch came through, breathing heavily. "Hey bastards, we got trouble!" he yelled.

The Bastards - Raining Arrows

Duncan rolled his neck, preparing for an inevitable fight. Gray Jim kicked at the boys, ordering them to gear up. Duncan moved his shield to his right arm and loosened his sword.

"Angus! Get the boys and get to the horses. Cordial, stay with 'em, and keep them safe. We'll meet you at the barn. If the battle goes bad, get out and head east. We'll try to meet in the next town east of here—wait three days at the most. If you don't hear from us, move on and think of us as dead. Stitch, you come with Gray Jim and me," Duncan said.

They all knew whatever had burned down the tavern would follow them. They were lucky enough to find a place to hole up and defend themselves against whatever followed them.

Exhausted yet relieved to know there would be a confrontation, Gray Jim walked over to his pack and grabbed his giant two-handed executioner's sword, unused since Runt had met him. The tall hangman typically carried a standard one-handed sword on his left side. He looked as though a bully had killed his favorite dog.

Maynard grabbed Runt's arm and dragged their travel bags with him.

Angus came out of the kitchen as the two boys half ran toward the door. "Sweet Vulcan's breath, what's happening now?" he said.

Cordial started, "Stitch said there's trouble and we should get the horses, get ready to travel if we can."

"Okay. There's a door in the kitchen. Let's head that way. Runt, you and Cordial grab food as we go—and a wineskin or a water skin if you can."

Angus jogged back to the kitchen as Cordial followed with Runt and

Maynard.

The others, Duncan, Stitch, and Gray Jim, moved toward the hall's front door to see if they could find Sorella and better understand the situation.

"What's that sound, Duncan?" Stitch asked. "Is it singing or a stampede of squirrels?"

The sound seeped near the front gate as a hole appeared in the ground. Duncan, Stitch, and Gray Jim looked on while the hole appeared. Giant spiders in multiple shades of gray, black and brown started crawling out and toward the towers, two and three at a time, each spider the size of a dog. A group of youths let arrows fly from the tops of the towers. The walls around the buildings stood unguarded as small goblins ran about, jumping up and down, hooting. They were bald, and others with full heads of hair had different numbers of small nubbed horns indicating how high in the social hierarchy they stood. They carried bows, spears, and other deadly-looking swords and clubs. They wore a shamble of clothes and armor pieces and used mail crudely forged and held together with bits of leather and string.

"Goblins, giant spiders, and orcs. I hate nature. This is why Cordial and I stay in cities—because of chaotic shit like this. Fucking giant spiders!" yelled Stitch. He looked at Duncan. "Lot of nastiness, boss."

"Yeah, I see. I dunno if those kids will survive this. We could run, but I don't think we should. Damn my father for leaving me. We can't leave these kids to die," Duncan said.

Gray Jim put his hand on Duncan's shoulder. "No, we should help those lads out. Besides, those wretches need to die."

"Where's Silvercrow?" Duncan asked with slight alarm.

"She was with the knight by the other tower." Stitch pointed.

Across the yard, Sorella Silvercrow created a line of archers as they attempted to take down the spiders that were pouring out of multiple holes in the ground near the wooden wall of the compound. Sir Roland lumbered toward the flank of an opening alone, carrying a broadsword and shield. He moved toward the giant spiders, nearly meeting him waist-high, and sliced through one, two, three of them. He stepped back, still swinging, trying to kill as many as possible and remain out of harm's way. If help didn't arrive soon, he'd be overwhelmed. They clawed at his sabatons and knees. A smaller spider managed to jump onto his back armor plate. They couldn't get through his armor and mail, but his sword swipes slowed down. The archers aimed but, in fear of hitting the knight, shot toward the hole where spiders and goblins crawled out.

Duncan and Gray Jim jogged toward the skirmish, no battle cry from either, just the silent breath of determination moving them forward. They proceeded methodically, as if killing giant brown spiders were an everyday occurrence.

The spiders continued to pour out from the ground, attempting to overrun the centuries old Eaglespire and Owl Pillar towers.

Duncan and Gray Jim waded into the fray, moving toward the knight. Duncan kept his distance as Gray Jim swung his greatsword in an orbit-like arch, sending death to anything moving in his direction. Duncan was more surgical, bashing at the beasts with his sizable circular shield and stabbing at an angle down toward the ones on his left, pushing them away again with the shield, creating a small opening with dead spiders on his left and right. Stitch moved around the chaos and toward Sorella. Her line of kids deteriorated as they headed for the safety of the nearest tower. When Stitch arrived, Sorella and one of the older sister girls were still pulling away at their bows, a pile of arrows at their feet.

"How are we doing, Stitch?" she asked, fatigued.

"Sorella, there's a lot. The outlook here is pretty poor," said Stitch. "Any chance we can get out of here?"

"They have several wounded inside this tower, and another group in the other is getting attacked as well. Where are the others?" Sorella asked.

"They were to go to the barn and get the horses ready. You hear the horrendous noise coming from the hole all the creatures are coming out of?" Stitch asked.

She stopped firing arrows. "It's coming from the largest hole. It may be what's causing all of this."

Duncan, Gray Jim, and Sir Roland continued to slay spiders and goblins as they pulled back toward Sorella and Stitch, who dropped arrows onto the spiders, trying to protect the three warriors.

Stitch put a shaft into a brown spider as its claw tore into the skin and bone of a boy near a palisade wall. The arrow slowed the spider for a moment before its poison-filled fangs sank into the screaming child's hip. The venom melted leather and cloth, and two other gray spiders devoured the child as he screamed.

Duncan wore a vest of jack plate, consisting of plates of armor sewn into a well-made leather vest and splint armor for his forearms and shins, while Gray Jim wore his trousers and winter gambeson, a padded defensive jacket. Both were more susceptible to wounds compared to Sir Roland of Eaglespire. The knight fought in full plate and mail with his cloth tabard clad in white and green of the House of Washcreek.

More spiders came out of the hole. One of the albino spiders spat toward Duncan and Gray Jim, splashing them with specks of a foul-looking liquid.

Gray Jim cursed. "Their spit, it's not fire, but it burns away anything it touches," he yelled toward Duncan, both covered in the gore of battle.

Duncan saw Sir Roland to their right, moving toward them after slashing a spider in its stomach, innards spewing out. He opened the clasp to his helmet mask.

"Get to the tower. We can figure out what to do there," Sir Roland said, breathing heavily.

Duncan and Gray Jim backed up toward Sorella as she, an older girl, and Stitch fired directly at the spiders scurrying toward them, no longer angling their shots due to the distance. Spiders, both dead and alive, enveloped the courtyard. They were close enough that Duncan could yell to Sorella. Gray Jim stepped forward and swung his greatsword, cutting through spiders and creating distance between the groups as their enemy reformed to rush them again. Duncan looked at the gate where the initial hole had appeared.

A goblin clad in torn pants and a long robe of dark chain mail arose, taller than the average goblin. His greenish bare chest showed various strings of beads, bones, and feather necklaces in different lengths under his robe. A mask of a giant bird beak covered the top half of the goblin's face, and terrible noise resonated from it. The beaked goblin's head bore a crown of sharp-pointed horns like a natural crown. They climbed on the walls and scampered on the ground, zipping around and aimlessly throwing javelins and arrows toward the tower where they stood. As the goblin leader emerged from the hole, four orcs appeared, taller than the goblin, two with swords and shields and two with long war spears, looking like the its bodyguards. They wore an assortment of ragged plate armor. All four were of the warrior class, featuring two bull-like horns each. These were not humbled slave orcs doing heavy labor in Holy Imperium cities with horns brutally chopped off. All four stood taller than Gray Jim and Duncan, who were burly men. The four orcs would give a mounted knight pause if it came to a fight.

Duncan and Gray Jim turned to Sorella, knowing the odds had just worsened.

"Get into the tower. Now!" ordered Sir Roland.

"This is a death trap. We'll never get out, and I'd rather take my chances in the woods," argued Sorella.

"No time, no time! We can't take these beasts on, not like this, and they'll run you down in the woods. Trust me, I've fought them in this valley all my cursed life," Sir Roland said.

The goblin leader screamed and sang a cursed song, commanding the spiders and goblins forward. He pointed to two of his orc guards and cackled a command. They moved off toward the other tower with spiders and a smaller batch of goblins following.

Roland pushed them all through the tower door, closing it behind them with a slam. Two chains were put over the door along with three separate metal beams. He inaudibly took a deep breath.

Stitch cursed, and Gray Jim heaved for air. Duncan checked his person for cuts and wounds.

"You placed a protective charm on this tower," Sorella noted to the old knight. "Is that why you feel so safe in this place?"

"We've been battling the orc and goblin tribes for years, and yes, I know how to protect myself and folks who listen," he replied.

Outside the tower, spiders spat acid, and other orcs and goblins threw javelins and shot arrows at the base walls and door but did not approach. Instead, they held back, as if getting too close would harm them. They howled, cursed, and angrily moved away from the tower.

Inside, Duncan, Sorella, Gray Jim, and Stitch were exhausted.

Sir Roland took a deep breath, leaning his back against the door. "Report!" he shouted.

"Sir!" a boy shouted from spiral steps above. "The Eaglespire holds and keeps the wild beasts at bay. We lost Becca, Travis, and his sister Splits to the spiders when they first attacked. As far as I know, the others are up in this tower. I don't have any reports about the Owl Pillar."

"So Eaglespire holds," Roland said, weary and worn from battle. "It's one of the few elvish- and dwarven-made structures I have ever known. There are old powers within these walls," he said to the Bastards. He looked up at the boy. "Do we have provisions? And are you sparing arrows for only kill shots?"

"Yes, sir," the boy yelled.

"Carry on. I'll be up shortly," he commanded. He looked at Sorella and the others. "Thank you for your feat of arms and help this afternoon. All is not lost. Where are the others you came with?"

"I told them to grab the horses and wait for us at the barn," Duncan answered flatly.

"I fear for your friends, but we'll not be opening the door until those vile creatures are gone from our sight. If they made it to the other tower, they would be as safe as us," Sir Roland said.

"And how safe is that," asked Gray Jim.

"This place is ancient. A mixture of elvish and dwarven runes protects it from the beasts still haunting these Blightbriar Wilds. Come now, let's see what we can see." He stood and went up the spiral staircase leading to the top of the Eaglespire.

They walked up the winding carved stairs as children, some as young as eight winters old, shot through arrow slits at spiders and goblins below. Sorella checked through the openings on the way up, only to see smoke and ruin at every glance. Finally, they reached the top and moved through a trapdoor in the tower's center. They stood hemmed in by stone barriers reaching the height of their hips, their heads covered by a wooden roof held up by four stone columns. The view impressed all as they peered out into the valley.

The mass of spiders disappeared, working their way back down the hole, leaving the dead bodies where they lay. A smaller pack of the dead lay near the other tower. The main hall burned along with the barn, tents, and everything else on the ground—all destroyed except the other tower and the stone and wooden fence surrounding the buildings.

Duncan, Sorella, Gray Jim, and Stitch looked on grimly, unsure of what had become of their compatriots.

The Bastards -The Other Side

A ngus went through the kitchen quickly, grabbing any food fit for travel. He ran his arm over the spice rack, dropping everything into a burlap sack. The dwarve had a thing for stealing spices. He tossed the sack to Runt. "If you see any fruit or butter, grab it—and sausages, too. Maynard, go to the closet and grab any wine and water skins. Hurry! Cordial, check the back door now!"

They moved deliberately, legs and arms tired and sore as the fear of the unknown spurred them onward.

Cordial carried his short bow, arrow notched. He cracked the door, poked his head out, and returned. "There're goblins in a pigsty. The pigs are running around and going crazy."

Cordial looked back at Maynard, Runt, and Angus. Everyone was eager to get out of the kitchen.

"Barn is to the right and back—move quickly," Cordial said. "Maynard and Runt, grab and saddle the horses. Angus, fill the saddlebags. I'll watch the doors and break for the back gate once we're ready. Hopefully, the others should be with us. If not, we go without them. They'll catch up."

Pigs and hogs screamed behind them as wooden boards smashed together and splintered.

"Move!" Cordial said.

Angus and Maynard ran, moving from the kitchen door to a well and toward the barn.

Cordial spoke like a hardened warrior commanding troops on a raid, realizing the situation before them was significantly dangerous. He pointed toward the pigsty to the left of the barn.

The few remaining pigs screamed in fright. Inside the fenced-in area, a handful of horned goblins grasped onto a pig or hog. They slipped and fell, hissing and laughing at one another. One grabbed a smaller hog, gnawing on its neck, blood, and foam spewing from its mouth. At the back of the sty stood a large, gray-skinned orc with two medium-sized bull-like horns. He was over six and a half feet tall, muscled, and bare-chested. The orc breathed strength and attitude. He carried a great saw-toothed sword, methodically swinging it, slaughtering pigs. His soiled and rotten britches were tied together with a rope. He looked like a giant, angry man-child with leathered skin. He smiled sharp yellow teeth and maniacally laughed as he butchered the pigs.

"What the shit?" Runt asked, looking back at Cordial as he took in the scene with wide eyes.

"Orc. Bad news. Move to the barn now—go," Cordial said, pushing the boy out the door.

Runt and Cordial ran toward the barn, where Maynard and Angus crouched, peering inside a small opening. The horses were all lay dead, ripped to shreds. One spider the size of a foal prepared a small casing of white web, wrapping a sliced-up horse for a meal later.

"More spiders like the one by the river," Maynard said. "This one is bigger."

"Horses are dead, and a quick escape isn't possible. Drop anything you can't carry at a run. Keep what you need. Let's find the others and figure out what to do," Angus said. "This is bullshit. I fought enough of these chumps for a lifetime already. I won't die by a damned goblin mount."

Gray, brown, and black spiders were a common nuisance and enemy of dwarves living underground.

"Let's get away from the barn and whatever is going on with the pigs," said Angus.

"Angus, do goblins ride spiders like humans ride horses?" Maynard asked. He was almost oblivious to the situation around him for a moment.

"Not the time, Maynard. Not the time," Angus said gruffly.

"No, you're right. Sorry," he whispered and pushed up his glasses. "Anyone else have an awful headache all of a sudden?"

Cordial and Runt ran up to the barn where Angus and Maynard waited, tossing useless gear to the ground.

"Keep those spices, Maynard. I'll go to the grave with those."

Maynard carried his satchel of books, sleeping gear, and a small bag with the spices and food like he was a mule.

"What's this?" Cordial said, coming up to Maynard and Angus. He had his dwarven one-handed crossbow out.

"Horses are dead, Cordial. We need to find the others, figure out another way," Angus said. "Didn't like riding them anyway."

"Not back there. Let's circle, see what's happening at the front," Cordial said.

"The pigs are being slaughtered and eaten by two orcs and ugly-looking goblins," Runt said.

They moved to the other side of the main hall where they first rested, then peered around the corner of the hall and toward the first tower, Eaglespire. Cordial peeked over Runt, with Maynard and Angus following. They both looked back, hoping whatever feasted on the dead horses and pigs didn't take an interest in them.

"Well, fabulous," Cordial said. "Angus, take a look. I don't think we can make it over to Duncan and Gray Jim."

Maynard covered his ears. "What is that noise?" he said, bent over in pain. "It's like the library all over again. Runt, I think that goblin is back."

"I hear it, like a weird humming," Angus said.

"My head, my head! It's like thousands of pins in my head!" cried Maynard.

Cordial and Angus looked on as a mass of dark matter moved around the feet of both Duncan and Gray Jim. They swatted and sliced at the ground around them. Sorella created a small line of archers and fired near the wall where a hole appeared in the ground. Near the pit, Sir Roland, clad in armor, swung his sword back and forth, stepping away from the gap. The noise Maynard complained about grew louder, and a large goblin and four orcs crawled out of the opening in the ground. Duncan and Gray Jim moved back, toward the Eaglespire.

Cordial stopped watching, looked at the wall nearest them, and realized the black things were spiders. The ones on the wall started to crawl toward them. The spiders moved in twos and threes. Others crawled from under the front gate near where they stood.

Angus pointed. "We can't make it to Duncan and Sorella. Best head for the other tower. It may withhold this onslaught. Best chance we have."

They jogged toward the Owl Pillar, hoping the bottom door was open and they could get in safely. Cordial led, attempting to cover with arrows. Angus followed, his cast-iron skillet now in hand, with Runt holding his sword and buckler and Maynard stumbling gracelessly behind, overburdened.

A goblin cackled and lunged toward Maynard. Cordial lifted his crossbow and pulled the trigger, catching the goblin in midair. The bolt sunk into its head, right between two of its small, rounded horns; it fell like a rag doll. Cordial reloaded the device, pointed, and aimed again—this time, behind Maynard, where another goblin slinked toward the group. Runt deflected a javelin and ran a goblin through to his left. As he pulled his sword out, Angus hacked another, and he heard Cordial release another bolt.

"Grab him with me. We need to get inside," demanded Angus.

Runt and Cordial snatched Maynard under his arms and dragged him to the tower, where Maynard banged on the door. Maynard doubled over, catching his breath. Cordial continued to put arrows into the spiders and goblins as they made their way toward the door. Angus swung his large cast-iron skillet like an axe, smashing a spider down like a fly. Green gore splashed at their feet. The situation turned urgent. The noise of battle continued, and Maynard pressed his palms into his eyes and tried to cover his ears in pain.

"Do you not hear the noise?" he yelled. "It's like in the library basement, only worse!"

"Open up in there! We're on your side! They'll eat us alive!" Angus screamed, hammering his fists against the door.

"Come on, please," mumbled Maynard, fingers in his ears, shaking his head in pain. He retched on the tower's side.

The spiders came in bunches over the wooden fences, moving into the courtyard between the two towers. Runt looked upon one of the beams holding the front gate, saw a goblin hissing, and pointed at them. The spiders crawled closer. Runt moved to the closest spider, the size of a feral cat, and started slashing, cutting off its legs and head.

"Come on, please," Maynard whimpered as he wiped vomit from his mouth, tears in his eyes.

Angus swore in ancient dwarven and spoke harshly at the door. Runt had only heard him talk like this late at night in his cups.

Suddenly, the door swung open. Angus looked inside, didn't see anyone, grabbed Maynard, and threw him inside. Goblins started throwing javelins in their direction from on top of the wooden wall surrounding the keep. Runt turned to his right and saw the main hall catch fire.

"Come now, Runt, we aren't heroes today!" Angus yelled, pulling him in.

Cordial followed, closing the ancient metal and wood door behind them. Angus looked at the door and moved a large metal beam into place, barring it closed. They glanced around at rough-looking small boys and girls armed with knives, clubs, and short swords staring back at them.

"Who are you, and how'd you get in?" asked the oldest boy, holding an exceedingly long dagger, his hair a mess with blood smeared on his arm and face.

"We're right surprised you're holding a pig sticker at our faces is what we are," Angus snorted. He swung his frying pan, knocking the dagger out of the child's hand, and pushed the other children back. The frying pan was made of dwarven iron, harder than any human metal, with a lip for draining liquid on each side. The lips of the spouts on either end were sharpened often and could cut through leather, skin, and bone if necessary. It was nearly a battle-axe but was also used to make dinner around a campfire. "Now put your weapons away before I pound the piss out of you. You ungrateful little stains," Angus roared.

The other boys and girls looked at the one boy with his dagger now at his feet. He held his hand up, glared at the dwarve angrily, and nodded his head; they lowered their weapons.

"You! Dagger boy with the blond hair, what's your name?"

"They call me Sunshine," said the boy.

"Okay, Sunshine, I'm Angus. This is my friend Runt, Cordial, and the right mess over there throwing up is Maynard. We were your guests minutes ago and meant you no harm. Now tell me again: who opened the door?"

"No one. We barricaded it and walked up to the windows above to shoot the spiders. Then it opened," Sunshine said. He sniffed a little as blood leaked from his nose.

"Angus, it opened when you spoke in dwarven," Runt said. "What did you say?"

"I cursed Vulcan's name and said 'open up' in our native language, as my mother taught me," Angus said.

"The door is magically sealed in dwarven runes, ancient runes, most of which I can't read yet," Maynard said, finally standing though still shaky. "You must have invoked the runes to open it in your blasphemy." He wiped his mouth of vomit and saliva. "The noise in my head is gone. It was worse than at Mount Nittany."

"Well, never mind, it's shut now. Kids, get to the windows and start taking any shots you can at those spiders and goblins, or this will go from bad to worse soon," Cordial said.

There was silence for a moment, and then everyone started moving. Cordial got those with bows up in the windows as best he could, throwing arrows through windows and arrow slits around the tower staircase. Angus and Runt made their way to the top of the tower along a spiral staircase and looked out to the other building.

"I see others over there. Look to be on our side. Can't tell who made it, though," Runt breathed.

"Me either. If they didn't make it, I think we won't know until those varmints leave," Angus spat. "Good grief. Right mess down there."

They saw smoke and flame as anything wooden burnt between the two towers.

Cordial came up through the trapdoor, stood, and pointed toward Eagle-spire, the other tower. "Nothing is attacking the tower. They stay far away from it," he said.

"Wonder if it has the same protections this one has." Angus looked down and saw no spider or goblin coming near the tower around the square-edged building. The other tower had been built with a circular construction; no spiders or goblins came within ten feet of it.

"Okay, you stay up here. Holler down or come get us. Let us know if you see anything important like fireballs or lightning coming from one of those wild creatures. I'll be back to let you know what's going on. I'll check on Maynard and see what we have to deal with here," Runt said.

He looked at the other tower through the smoke. Spiders and goblins moved around the grounds, devouring the dead. The fires burned themselves out, and the sky to the west clouded, ready for rain. The goblin leader, surrounded by four large orcs, blew a horn. At the sound of the horn, the spiders, goblins, and orcs left back through the pits in the ground. It could have been the coming dark clouds to the west or the fact that nothing more could be accomplished, Runt didn't know, but the attempted siege was over. The only remaining structures were the palisade walls surrounding the courtyard and the two towers.

The first reliable communication came from a boy, one of the knight's smallest and fastest runners from Eaglespire. Runt saw him running and yelled down the stairs to get the door ready. The boy jumped through the door, and it slammed shut behind him. No more than seven winters old, the boy reported who survived and their current stance on arrows and food. He then asked for the same, stating to remain in the tower until morning. Runt noted the boy acted more like an adult than a child in his speech and mannerisms. He felt relieved to hear their little party was still intact and felt sorrow as the children grieved for their lost friends.

Sunshine consoled the kids like a general after a tough battle. They heard spiders scurrying around at night but nothing else unfamiliar. It wasn't an easy night for those in the tower, and nerves were raw. Most everyone watched a window, and only two or three slept throughout the night. They took shifts and drank water, which remained clean, from the tower's deep well. Angus mentioned the tower's build and its artisanship, but Runt didn't grasp what the dwarve said and slipped into a fitful sleep. Late in the night, rain fell along with thunder and lightning, putting out the fires.

Cordial woke Runt in the morning, looking tired and weary but still wearing a smile.

"Escaped the arms of death yet again. It's been a Hades of a year," Cordial said. "They sent another runner—seems our attackers have pulled back. Oh, and Maynard found a trap door in the basement storage area of the tower. It's dwarven in make and lit by dwarven lights."

"Maynard's better?" Runt asked, relief flooding his mind. "Wait, you opened a random dwarven door nobody knew about? After this area was overrun with monsters crawling out of holes in the ground?"

"Yup, we've been discussing it using runners back and forth with the other tower. Sorella found one over there, too. The last runner walked over. I think we may be in the clear for now," Cordial explained. He threw off the beam behind the door and poked his head out.

"Looks like they pushed the dirt back through the hole over there by the gate. I bet they did the same for any other holes they made," Angus pointed.

Cordial, Maynard, Runt, and Angus walked out of Owl Pillar and toward Eaglespire as the sun came up on the wreck of the long hall. Duncan, Gray Jim, and Sorella met them in the middle of the two towers, taking stock of what had occurred outside. The Owl Pillar stood with its sharp features and Eaglespire, the perfectly circular tower, remained on the other side of the ruin of the rubble of the long hall. Sir Roland met up with the few boys and girls from Owl Pillar, talking closely among themselves.

"Thank you all for your help," he said as he walked over to them.

"It was nothing. We survived, but I don't know how. They should have overrun both towers but didn't," Angus said.

"Both towers are protected, one by elvish runes and the other by dwarven runes. They're both ancient and provide interesting benefits to those within. They've been around for hundreds of years before the Crimson Struggle; they're older than I know. This valley and its two towers are a beacon of light surrounded by these dark forests and the Blightbriar Mountains. This attack makes the intelligence we gathered more respectable. Feels like a clan of orcs has a leader and a mage. The goblin leader performed magic and commanded the others. Spiders don't normally follow goblin orders." Roland raked his hand through his hair and looked away from the group. "I sent birds to Lord

Washcreek and messengers requesting food, supplies, and soldiers, and yet received nothing in return." He sighed. "I guess you are all leaving. I can see it in your eyes. Let them know of our plight if you come across anyone from the House of Washcreek—or any of his bannermen. Let them know we need help. The towers will hold, but I don't know how long we can carry on inside them."

Duncan looked at Roland. "This is not the first time this has happened. How long have you been doing this?"

Roland didn't speak. Instead, he looked toward the hills where mountains grew and where the legendary hold the Gloomspire was rumored to exist.

Duncan grasped the man's arm. "We will help bury the dead and burn the remaining beasts. We hope to leave tomorrow morning. I'm sorry we can't do more, but we will send help if we can."

The rest of the day melted away through the toil of cleaning up after a battle, tallying up the dead, digging graves, and burning the corpses of the beasts. There were no sightings of spiders, goblins, or orcs, and birds and other animals returned throughout the woods surrounding the towers.

Sir Roland sent his two best scouts out, who returned by midday. They brought rabbits and two deer on their return, and dinner preparations began.

"Glad the wildlife returned so quickly. Those monsters tend to scare game away. It's how you know you're naturally safe—when the wilderness is alive. When the animals disappear is when trouble's come."

Sorella looked at him and measured his words.

"You speak like a wise man. How old are you, Sir Roland?" Angus asked, juices running out of his mouth.

The boys and Roland stopped eating and got quiet for a second.

"I am as old as I need to be, I guess. I'm near past thirty summers."

The children started eating and chatting again. Conversations went on, and friendly words remained. Sorella Silvercrow occasionally looked at Roland with a question in her eyes.

"Tonight, we'll sleep in the towers again. We'll start rebuilding the hall and barn after you leave," Sir Roland declared.

* * *

When Runt rose before the sun broke, he felt full of energy and stronger than the day before. Maynard was already up and reading by a candle.

"Man, I feel amazing. No aches, no pain—I haven't felt like this in weeks, if not months," Runt said.

"Me too. It's disturbing," Maynard said as he flipped a page in his book.

"What do you mean?" Runt asked.

"I mean, all my newest wounds, cuts, bruises, and other pain—it's all gone. My wounds healed from yesterday, but we only slept a few hours. We got a full night of rest. I'm fully healed and ready to take on the world. It's not normal," Maynard said.

"It's nothing," Cordial said as he met the lads. "First solid night of rest after nearly dying, you'll feel like you visited a harem." He paused and looked at the two younger boys. "By that, I mean relieved and grateful for the night before. Man, you boys need to get laid."

"What? How do you know we haven't already?" Maynard said, offended.

"Really, mate? Yeah, no doubt about it," Cordial said. He stuck his tongue out at them and walked away.

"Maynard, don't. I know you're a virgin, and so does he," Runt said.

"You are too, Runt," Maynard said in defense.

"Never said I wasn't. Can I ask you something?"

"Do I need to tell you how babies are made?"

"Seriously, Maynard," Runt sighed. "Why are all of you doing this for me? Helping me get to my father?"

"Doc told me to help, said you're more than the son of a soldier in the prince's Red Army. Said you could help start something," Maynard replied.

"Like what?"

"I dunno what he meant. He mumbled about a revolution."

Maynard looked at Runt for a long moment, closed his book, got up, and walked away. Runt nodded but didn't understand. He knew whatever was occurring was about more than getting him to his father, but he wasn't sure what to do.

Sorella Silvercrow led the way out of the shadow of the two towers onto a forest path with assistance from Sunshine. After about a half day, they walked out of the deep woods and moved toward the main road. Sunshine waved goodbye after pointing to a trail that would lead them toward civilization and Olde Ridgewatch.

"Without horses, we're about ten days out until we hit the city-state of Olde Ridgewatch, and Maker knows what. Let's try not to get into any further battles with singing goblins and giant spiders on the way," Sorella said.

"Sorella, love, any chance we can hit up an inn soon and take a day and really enjoy civilization?" asked Cordial.

"Civilization? Vineland hasn't been civilized since my elvish people governed the land," she said. "But yes, we could use an inn."

Gray Jim snorted and spat. Duncan looked at him, and Gray Jim turned away.

They trekked through a path of field grass, the sun warming them and the grass growing beneath their feet. They stopped at the side of a road, the first spot of civilization they had witnessed in days, a road hard packed with broken stone, well-worn and wide enough for two carts.

Sorella started forward, Duncan behind her, followed by Cordial, Stitch, Maynard, and Gray Jim. Angus pushed them on. Runt looked back on what had transpired and turned hopefully toward better days.

Alysha - Birth of a Maiden

Alysha polished the star metal weapon to a dusky shine, thinking of Jared Blackheart's shield, Midnight's Veil, and the violence behind it from last autumn. She wondered: if Midnight's Veil and this new weapon met, which would break? Exhausted, her arms and back ached for rest. Her challenging work had created a weapon of gravity and elegance. All three of the smiths had poured their time, sweat, and a small amount of blood into the work. Alysha drank from a clay pitcher and pushed her hair back from her face.

"What are you going to call it, Alysha?" Hob asked, excited.

"No idea," she said.

The weapon was a mixture of war-hammer and poleaxe. The closest Hob and Bob came to naming it was a short halberd or hammer glaive. Most halberds were five to eight feet in length, but the weapon they'd created was shorter than a long sword. It lay on the cloth; the shaft was star metal with a tightly wrapped handle of wire and leather at the bottom. The other end held a magnificent axe head nearly ten inches in length. A blunted head opposite with small metal divots looked like what Angus used to tenderize venison at the tavern. A short spike sat on top, between the axe head and the hammer end, where the cast star metal handle met. It was a blade, spike, and hammer able to bash armor, pierce flesh, and cut through sinew and muscle. It looked heavy as an iron brick, but the metal was light enough that Alysha could swing it one-handed, like an elvish tomahawk. The weapon was long enough to grip with both hands if necessary.

"It could maim a cow just sitting there. Not sure of a name yet, but it will come to me," she said. "I've been practicing with a two-handed sword and one-handed axe, but this is another deal. It's going to take time to get used to." She picked up the weapon and swung it around.

Bob walked into the room. "Cow Slayer it is!" He laughed. "It looks a bit like a bearded maul. There is a weight to it, but all three of us can swing it with one hand and be all right. Yeah, reminds me of a maul used for splitting logs, but the wedge portion with a thinner axe blade changes it up."

"No, it should get a proper name. Maybe it'll be earned soon," she said, thinking again of Jared Blackheart. "Maybe Stormkiss," she whispered. Alysha handed the bearded maul to Bob.

"When you were swinging it, it looked like it fit you well. Me, I like a nice, full-on, two-handed axe. This, this is perfect for you," he said. "We should get it blessed by the Holy Church."

Alysha looked at Stormkiss and thought for a moment. The name fit it in so many ways.

Both Bob and Hob worshiped at the Holy Church in Counselor City. They kept the Maker, the Child, and the Servant in their hearts and never missed making it to church on holy days. Alysha pantomimed the process as her mother taught her years ago, to keep up appearances and not let all know they worshiped the Profane. She took after her mother, like her younger brother, Runt. Benjamin, her oldest brother, was a true believer of the Maker, the Path of the Blessed, and had originally wanted to be a member of the Order of the Blue Rose or, like their father, a Knight of the Redcloak. She never prayed to the four Profane in earnest, not until she lost her mother and home and watched the servant of Judith struck by lightning at the altar. After struggling through a day at the anvil, she knelt and prayed to the Profane. Thinking of and thanking Jupitor, Guardian of Light; Sif, Matron of the Harvest; Stribog, Father of the Veil; and Judith, Maiden of Storms. Hob caught her once and raised his eyebrow but did not say anything. Bob was more devoted out of the two and would lecture her on the wrongness of her choices like the grizzled father figure he was, but Hob was more mother-like and took a softer approach.

She used to cry at night, thinking of her mother and brothers. Alysha used to think of Ryan Purenut, who taught her the basics of smith's work; she was appreciative of her earlier skills taught by him and missed his laughter and ability to treat her like an equal. All those memories used to create a feeling of sorrow, but sorrow faded to anger and resentment towards the Holy Imperium and the Holy Church if she lingered on them too long.

"I'd like to, and I know you won't approve, but I don't want to get this blessed by the Holy Church. I'd like to do something else with it, if you don't mind," Alysha said, lost in her thoughts.

"What are you thinking, young lady?" Bob said. "The other blade we worked on, the one from the Wolfe family, has already been blessed by the Holy Church. It's remade now, stronger than before, but has a slight star metal shine to it." He drew it out of its sheath. It was nearly twenty inches, straight bladed and double edged. The handle was the same, but the blade was shorter and carried the same shimmer as Alysha's halberd.

"I'd like to take this back to the place near where we found the star stone. There's an altar on the hill there where," she paused, "where my gods are prayed to and offer a blessing."

She took a deep breath and held it, awaiting Bob and Hob's decision. Bob's ears turned red and then faded. Hob walked over and patted Bob on the shoulder tenderly, as if they were married.

"The prince believes the Profane should be burned at the stake, Alysha. Don't forget. The Holy Imperium, including General Flint and Jared Blackheart, burn the Profane as heathens and sow their ashes into the crop fields. They think of the Profane as nothing better than manure." Bob turned his back.

The comment hurt, but this was Bob. He was an anvil and unbreakable. Hob kept his hand on Bob's shoulder.

"But we could stretch our legs and search for more firewood. Been a long winter, and the weather broke yesterday. If we hooked up the cart, we might find old pieces of tree fall to be dried and split in case we get a second winter storm. I dare say, if you came along and helped, we couldn't stop you from taking a short hike up a hill."

Bob scoffed and put his hand on Hob's for a moment. "She has you wrapped around her finger, Hob. Tomorrow, you hitch up the horse to the cart. Bundle up a bit. Winter isn't over yet. Not sure what the skies are bringing from the west. Best we hurry."

Alysha smiled. "Thank you! It's been a long winter, and I think we all could use some fresh air."

* * *

When Hob and Bob awoke the following day, they found Alysha outside, getting two horses ready.

"You're wide awake and ready to go," Bob said, smiling.

"Just want to make sure we're ready to get some wood, that's all," she said, bouncing with anticipation.

"Sure, sure. Well, Hob went to the tanner and requested a few pieces made. This used to be an axe harness. Your bearded maul can't be worn on the waist. You'd puncture an organ or cut yourself with the blade." Bob tossed the leather harness to Alysha. "Once you put it on, you can strap the bearded maul to your back with blade and spike down and at an angle. The leather cover snaps shut, but if you tug it right, the weapon breaks free as you pull it from behind and over your head. Loggers use it to carry their axes. I wouldn't wear it in the city. You'll get wild looks from arrogant folk. It's not unheard of for women to be mercenaries and all, but best not to draw attention. If you wear a cape over it, it'll be concealed. You'll have to take the cape off to get to it. Remember, anyone asks, it's for cutting wood." He winked.

"Wow, this fits perfectly. Thank you both," Alysha said, and she hugged Bob, who accepted the gesture unexpectedly.

"I have the short sword on my hip here. Not ladylike to carry a sword," Bob said and handed her the same dagger she'd carried the last time they'd gone out to get wood. "Can't be too careful, though."

They made their way out of Counselor City as the temperature rose and the last breaths of winter melted the snow and ice away. Hob nodded to the southern gate guard, Edwin Flatrock,

"Back before dark. New rules from the general," said Flatrock.

"Sure thing," Alysha said with a wink as they moved past him. "Just getting more wood for the fires, Flatrock. Back before you know it."

They moved south, back toward the hill and altar. Slush pushed away from the wheels on the cart, and Alysha was heartened to see the first flowers of the year peeking up where the sun broke through the clouds. Fresh tufts of grass peeked about in the morning. There was a slight fog below the pines, oaks, and maple trees to her left as the cart moved. The noise of the woods and the jostling of the cart relaxed Alysha. She felt gratitude toward Hob and Bob and all they had done for her this past winter. They made their way down the road, and the area started to look more familiar. They came to an open field with ankle-high grass, a hill, the stone altar above, and a forest along the edge of the field as the road pushed farther south toward Wolf Hills. Alysha felt the energy, and a smile crept up her face.

Hob looked back and noticed. "All right, so we can go check the woods over there for any easy dead fall wood. Alysha, why don't you go up the hill there and see if there are any old fallen trees around? Come on, Bob, let's go," he said. He grabbed an old jug of hard cider and two axes.

They moved away. Alysha tied up the two horses and cart to an overgrown bush so they wouldn't veer away.

"See you in a few, lass," Bob said.

"Thanks again, both of you," she said, walking up the hill. She noticed a small briar bush and rocks on the side, reminding her of a giant rabbit hole. The going felt easy, as her hard work over the winter had paid off. The winds shifted, and the earlier blue skies gave way to large rolls of gray and black clouds. The temperature started to drop.

"You there, stop where you are!" somebody yelled from behind her. "Where do you think you're going?"

Alysha turned back. Hob and Bob were about twenty feet from the wood line where armed soldiers came out of the morning fog. They wore tattered armor, mail, and leather bearing the colors of the Holy Imperium. Most likely, they were scouts looking for anyone from Grimwood. Their gear was worn, and they looked weary from days away from Counselor City.

"Looks like we found trouble," said one of the soldiers. "Hey, Blanchard, whatcha think?"

"Don't like this one bit, Arn, not one bit. Must be spies. Nobody else out in this type of weather," Blanchard said. "What say you, Ole?"

"I agree with my brother Arn—must be spies," griped another soldier.

"Now, see here, we were scrounging up wood. Been a rough winter," Bob said, trying to control the situation, his arms up and away from the short sword at his side.

Hob carried the axe used for clearing and cutting tree branches.

They were six soldiers around Hob and Bob while Alysha was halfway up the hill.

The leader of the soldiers, Richard, looked roughly built and walked with a swagger, even as his armor was caked in dirt and mud. "Nobody asked you. We were discussing whether you were spies or plain old traitors to the prince," he said. He removed his helmet and wiped a greasy hand through stringy straw-yellow hair. Two other soldiers stood, half helms on, not saying anything, and another stood near behind them.

"We work for the Holy Imperium and saw General Flint not three weeks ago in our shop," Hob said. He made an "oof" sound as the butt of a spear met his stomach, and he doubled over.

"Another word," said the soldier named Arn, "and the other end of the spear will be in your belly."

Bob moved slowly to pick up Hob, not saying anything.

"Lass, come down this hill. We want to know what you're doing up these ways," said Richard. "You boys, go get her and bring her to me."

Two half-helmed soldiers broke off and moved toward Alysha, up on the hill. She slowly inched down, hoping the situation wouldn't escalate.

"Come now, lass, let's have a look atcha," said one soldier. He approached her, carrying a spear, and sheathed a short sword. "Whatcha think of this, Purenut? She fixing to be a lovely lass," he said to the other soldier. "Now, whatcha thinking about giving us a kiss, and we won't hang those two as traitors to the prince?" The soldier had a wispy beard, as if growing it for the first time and trying to look older.

"Bring her down the hill, man," said the other soldier named Purenut, almost not caring. "Better bring her along. Richard don't want to spoil her. You know how Richard can get," he said. He shifted his shoulder a bit and pointed his spear toward Alysha. "Let's go. We'll stick you if you don't. Come on now."

"Ryan, is that you? Ryan Purenut from Wolf Hills? It's me, Alysha," she said, looking at him through months of beard growth. His eyes were sunken, and he looked thinner, tired, and a little in anguish.

"Get moving. You and those two fellows are in trouble. Keep quiet, or I'll put a piece of leather in your mouth and hogtie you," Ryan Purenut sneered. He pushed her forward, down the hill.

She looked back at him; anger flared in his eyes. They didn't disarm her, and her cloak hood was still up. The sky behind the hill darkened as clouds moved in. In the distance, thunder rolled against the trees.

"Hear that, Purenut? Says she knows you," Eric said. "How's a soldier like you know a lass like this?"

"She used to follow me around my father's blacksmith when we were younger," Ryan Purenut said. He jabbed at her with the butt of his spear. "Move on, girl, toward the two old farts down there."

"Why are you doing this, Ryan?" Alysha asked. "Do you know what happened to Wolf Hills? Do you know what soldiers like this did to your parents, your home?"

"Shut it, girl. Move along now," ordered Eric.

The other four soldiers stood in a half circle with Hob and Bob in the middle. They still didn't disarm anyone. Eric and Ryan pushed Alysha into Hob and Bob, so they were all together.

"Now, girl, tell us: what are you doing out in the middle of nowhere with these old-timers?" Richard commanded.

"You okay, Alysha?" Hob whispered as he helped her up.

"Yes, I'm fine. What do they want with us?" Alysha asked.

"I dunno—trouble. Looks like Bob may be able to get us out of this," Hob said.

"Sorry, fellows. We were pulling dead drop wood from the forest here," Bob said. "Not trying to make trouble."

"You're hauling logs out of the woods with this young thing?" Richard said. "Don't seem right. You're too old for her. Ain't he too old for you, lass?"

"She's our daughter now adopted. Her mother was killed this past autumn," Hob said. "We can get our cart and be on our way. We don't want no trouble."

Alysha's anger boiled over. "You pig, my mother's dead, just like your parents. People like you, Prince Damon's soldiers, slaughtered them like sheep this past fall!" she yelled and spat at Ryan.

"Ohhh, Ryan knows the lass," Richard said, laughing with mirth.

The other soldiers chuckled. "How do you know this girl, Ryan? Did you and this lass make it in the hay one fine summer night? Is this the one you talked about over and over like a cow in love?"

She looked at Ryan, his face red with anger, the ridicule from his fellow soldiers, and Alysha's spit raising his anger.

"Shut up, Richard. Just shut up," Ryan said, gripping his spear and aiming it toward Alysha. "I know her, yeah. We made it by a riverbank on a flat stone down from where we both lived last summer."

"You stain, you never made it with me!" Alysha screamed.

Hob and Bob gripped her shoulders.

"Quiet, Alysha," Bob whispered between his teeth. "You'll get us all killed."

"Shut up, girl," said Arn, reaching over and slapping her hard with the back of his hand.

She was stunned, her head dropping to her chest. She tasted blood on her tongue. Out of the corner of her eye she saw Bob's thumb push up the sword blade from the scabbard at his belt.

"How dare you!" Bob yelled, drawing his blade. Before he could finish pulling it out of its scabbard, Ryan Purenut stabbed him straight through the neck.

Hob raged with his axes as Bob fell, smashing Ryan's spear in two but missing Ryan by several feet. He stepped back.

"No!" yelled Alysha. She grabbed Bob as he fell to the ground.

"Kill the other; leave the girl," ordered Richard. "Good work, Ryan. Because you know her, you get her first. Then you can watch after."

Bob looked up at Alysha, struggling to speak. Blood gurgled out of his mouth.

The other soldiers—Eric, Arn, Blanchard, Ryan Purenut, and Ole—moved toward Alysha as she kneeled, and Hob stood, gripping his two-headed axe with both hands.

"I'll protect you, Alysha. If you see a break for it, run and stay low," Hob said. Tears creased the sides of his eyes, and his body swelled, muscles tensing. He raised his axe and screamed.

The soldiers hesitated, giving Hob a second to swing his axe at Blanchard, who was nearest to him. He missed but continued the swing and followed with a spin, catching Arn by surprise. He weakly defended the blow, and the axe caught his leg, cutting it deeply. Hob stepped back, and Eric stabbed him in the shoulder with his spear. Ryan stabbed as well, hitting Hob in his thigh with a sword. He screamed in pain. Alysha continued to kneel, holding Bob's slumped-over body.

"Run, Alysha, run!" Hob yelled as he swung wildly toward Arn and Blanchard, who closed in with sword and shield.

The words registered, but not as they should. Alysha unclasped her cloak and took out the bearded maul, Stormkiss, strapped to her back. She held it in front of her and grabbed her cloak with her other hand. She rushed toward the soldier named Eric and threw her cloak, blinding him. She swung under his spear shaft and connected between his legs on the left side, spilling blood onto the soft earth. Eric squealed and fell. Alysha moved as if she were in practice, stepped back, and circled to Arn and Blanchard. Hob, bleeding from his thigh and shoulder, fended off a blow from Ryan.

"When I finish your friend here, Alysha, I'll have you right there on the ground." Ryan laughed as he stabbed Hob, who fell to his knee and pushed the sword away from his head. Ryan pulled back and slammed the sword into Hob's shoulder.

Alysha didn't say anything. She gritted her teeth in anger and ran into Arn's shield. She didn't care if she lived. She wasn't going to die whimpering or whining. She would die biting, screaming, and chewing at their flesh. Arn fell back and slipped on his cut leg but managed to put up his shield for protection. Alysha swung with both hands on Stormkiss. The blade fell toward the shield and Arn behind it. The shield shattered as wood splinters and pieces of iron and copper broke away. The blade connected with Arn's forearm and continued down, into the ground.

"What the Hades? Can you lot not take care of an old man and a crazy bitch with an axe?" Richard yelled from a distance. He was checking the horse and cart for food and money.

Alysha drew the axe away as Arn gripped at his mutilated arm stub, not screaming, only in shock as blood spurted out and his face whitened. His arm and hand lay on the ground, separated from the rest of him.

Ole stabbed Hob in the back with a broad sword while Purenut pulled his weapon out of Hob's shoulder. The smith fell over, releasing his breakfast and guts onto the ground.

Blanchard swung his sword in a wide arch, and Alysha shifted to the side.

"Bitch, die," Blanchard said, wild, full of anger, and missing by a foot.

Alysha stayed low and hunched over, moving away as she pulled Stormkiss close to her. She punched up with the head of the axe toward Blanchard and hit his shield, shoving into it. He pushed back and knocked her off balance. Blanchard stabbed at her again, this time with more thought, and sliced into her right forearm. He tried again, defending himself with his shield and staying too close for Alysha to swing Stormkiss. She deflected the sword with the blunt end and trapped it against his shield. They wrestled their weapons together. Blanchard rammed the shield forward, catching Alysha in the face, dizzying her sight, and stinging her nose. She shoved back into the shield with her weapon set vertically between them. Blanchard's sword was stuck off to the side. They continued to press against each other, shield and Stormkiss together. He couldn't believe Alysha's strength as he tried to break away. He looked down and realized too late as she slid to the right of the shield and stabbed at his stomach with a dagger. He lowered his shield and dropped the sword.

"Oof," he managed to say as she stumbled a step.

She kicked him in his wound, and he fell to a knee, gripping the hole in his abdomen.

"Look what your lass has done," said Ole. "You go teach her a lesson,

Purenut." Ole shoved Ryan in front of him as a human shield. Ryan stumbled forward, sword in hand, half helm tilted off his head. "Richard, need you over here. This lass managed to screw up our unit. Best not take any chances. Looks like Blanchard could be done for."

"I'm fine, Ole, just fine," Blanchard said, off to Alysha's left. He was on his knee, holding the side of his stomach, no weapon in hand. He cried in pain, slobber coming out of his mouth—and blood as well. "Ole, I lied. I'm hurt, hurt real bad. Bitch got me. She got Arn, too. I don't think he's doing so good."

Alysha circled around and toward the hill. She had surprised herself during the fight; three against one was poor enough odds. If she were to die, she would do so near the altar. She wanted Judith to approve of her. Someone, something, should give a shit about her. It seemed fitting to depart on Judith's altar. She whispered a prayer while carrying the dagger, wet with blood and stomach juices, in her right hand. The blade was held toward her smaller finger to help make a cut and block blows. She spun Stormkiss in her left hand, looking confident while her hands trembled, and she held her breath as she took steps back up the hill.

She made it a quarter of the way up the hill before Ryan Purenut, her old boyfriend, charged at her with anger and fear in his eyes. He was tired by the time he made it a spear's length away; she nudged the sword out of the way with her weapon and let him fall onto the hill. She kicked him twice in the chest. The first stopped his momentum, and the other pushed him down the hill. She watched him roll, catching her breath, but only for a moment.

Ole and Richard came at her, leaving Ryan behind. Ole carried a tomahawk and a one-handed broadsword, while Richard carried a two-handed sword. Ole got to her first and swung a haymaker of a blow with his sword up high. Alysha tried to block with Stormkiss and used her other hand to help stiffen the impact. The weapons met, and she grunted from his strength. Ole swung his axe with his other hand, and Alysha dropped her dagger, moving to dodge the weapon. She stepped back and then forward again, thrusting the spike of Stormkiss toward Ole. The spiked head pushed into his right armpit. She felt the swing from Richard's two-handed sword and wasn't sure what to do other than fall to the ground quickly. Richard cut into Ole accidentally, missing Alysha. Richard's blade stuck in Ole with a sloppy, wet noise. He grunted and his life left through his throat.

"You are going to die, and I'll fuck your corpse, you nasty bitch," Richard growled. He removed the blade from what was Ole.

Alysha grabbed the dagger on the ground and lunged at Richard's boot from her stomach. She punched it as hard as possible, and it felt like she broke a finger, but the blade punctured Richard's ankle.

"Ahhh, fucking, ahhh," he said, dropping his sword and gripping his ankle right in front of her.

Alysha crawled, half on her knees, half on her stomach, and pulled the dagger out. She stabbed again, crying and stabbing, crying and stabbing up to Richard's thigh. They beat on each other. He punched her arm and face, broke her nose, smashed her eye, and screamed at her. Alysha stabbed him again, this time in the stomach, and his screams ceased. She could smell his insides when she pulled the blade out. Richard held his stomach and breathed as best he could.

Alysha's one eye was closed now, her nose wouldn't let her breathe through it, and blood filled her mouth from split lips and loose teeth. She sat up next to Richard as he leaned on his arm, holding his stomach, and she watched while he bled and coughed.

"Die—just die," she whispered in anguish.

She pushed him over, and he flopped for a moment. She tried to catch her breath. Everything hurt, and her eyes rolled up toward the sky. She smiled for a second. She looked down and saw Ryan slowly moving toward her up the hill. He picked up a sword from the ground. Alysha flicked the hair out of her one good eye so she could see him—this boy, this man, this thing—as he walked, sword in hand. She looked at the ground, grabbed Stormkiss, and pushed herself up, her other hand not working correctly, her fingers aching to the point where she could only make a fist out of them. She wiped her nose, clearing blood away, and stumbled up the hill, her hand slippery with snot, blood, and tears. The sky above beckoned with flashes of lightning from cloud to cloud and slow rumbles of thunder.

"This isn't over, Alysha. No, this isn't. Fuck you—get back here. It's not over with!" he howl, animal-like.

They trudged up the hill, ten feet from each other, as if it were an angry turtle race. As Alysha stumbled and walked up the slope, exhausted, she realized Ryan was catching up. She wasn't sure why, but she wanted to reach the summit, ready to die there. Alysha fell and looked back; instead of screaming, she laughed. She laughed at him and everything that had brought her to this hill again. There was nothing to lose, nothing left in her world now. It was all gone and done. No safe, warm place to live; no home; no parents; nothing. It was her and this weapon in her hand. So, she laughed at it all, at the atrocity of life. Finally, she got on her knees and pushed her ass in the air.

"Hey, Ryan, is this how you want me, you shit? You want me all broken-faced and bruised ass in the air after I butchered your friends?" She wiggled her behind and started crawling on all fours like a bear, trying to move faster, grabbing at the rough spring grass to move up the hill. She was close to the top now, to the altar of Judith. She could hear his breathing, and how she hated herself for thinking of him as special. She crawled forward. Snot and blood fell on the grass. Ryan grabbed her foot, paces away from the altar, and she kicked at him.

"No, no, not until we get to the top!" she screamed and pushed back.

He moved closer. "Shut up!" He punched her lower back, and she collapsed. She rolled over, holding Stormkiss like a cross against her chest. He looked down at her. "You used to be the most beautiful girl in Wolf Hills. Now, look at you. A fucking sow ready to be stuck and stuffed."

He held the sword over her, pointing down. She lay on her back, one hand at the top of her weapon, the other at the bottom. She could barely see out of her swollen eye. She looked at him with defiance. Breathing out of her mouth, she smiled.

"Isn't this how you wanted me, sweet Prince Ryan Purenut?" And she made a pouty face with her broken lips. "Like in the tales in my books, the blacksmith's boy here to save me from the evil soldiers. Too bad you're the one who needs saving."

"Fuck you! You said not until we get to the top—fuck you!" He switched his sword to his other hand, reached back, and smashed her head into the ground.

Alysha closed her eyes, and when they opened, she looked at the sky and the clouds as the lightning danced for her. Ryan dragged her another few feet to the hill's summit, all while Stormkiss dangled in her fingers.

"I don't know what I'm going to tell the captain. Bandits, I think. Yeah, bandits attacked us," he said to himself. He pushed her up against the altar, sitting her up, Stormkiss cradled in her arms like a baby. The blade cut into her arm, and she didn't care. "It wasn't supposed to be like this. We were supposed to get married next year. You messed it up, Alysha. I would have a nice bit of money saved up after serving. Why couldn't you wait for me? Fucking bitch."

"Didn't you hear me, you piece of shit? They're dead. Your mom, your dad, the entire town is gone—burned down," she mumbled, tired and sliding into shock. "Do you even know what's happening in Grimwood? In Vineland?" She spat blood and snot to the ground. It dribbled on her chin and face. "Where have you been? Do you even know where we are?"

"Shut up, Alysha. My parents aren't dead. I saw them at the beginning of autumn," he said, standing over her.

"Look at me, Ryan." She stared up at him, breathing deeply through her mouth. Bruised and beaten. He stood, straddled over her body as she limply sat against the stone altar, pushing herself up with the back of her head and the strength of her neck. "We're on top of a hill at the altar of Judith, Maiden of Storms. I'm still a maiden, Ryan. You never had me, and I won't let you. Your parents are dead by the army whose colors you wear." Tears and blood smeared her face for the storm to see. "The world is shit, and there is nothing left." Then, looking beyond Ryan at the storm, she breathed out as lightning sliced across the sky. "Storm's coming, so finish it, Ryan. Your world is gone, like mine."

"Shut up, just shut up!" he screamed, wavering as his battle rage weakened and lightning flashed through the clouds. He turned away from the storm and pointed his sword at her chest.

"Do you hear it, Ryan? Hear the rain and thunder," she said. "The lightning is mine."

He moved closer, pushing the blade of his sword close to her chest, unsure if he could kill her. She moved her head forward, spat a gob of blood onto his face, and grabbed at his shirt. He drew the blade back in fear while she pulled with all her weight and forced him down so he lost balance. His sword moved down and into her shoulder as she strained. Ryan fell onto her, and she guided his head, causing it to kiss the stone altar of Judith. The sword pushed deeper, lightning flashed, and she gasped. The rain fell, and she hugged his limp body. Her eyes watched the lightning dance across the sky.

The Bastards - Cobblestones and Stories

"What's the plan once we get into Olde Ridgewatch proper?" Runt asked, excited. He stood with his cloak hood up, covering his blackberry-dyed hair.

"The plan? A hot bath," said Sorella.

"Stiff drink," said Gray Jim

"A nice stew," noted Duncan.

"A card game and bar wench on my lap," finished Cordial. "Pardon me, Sorella, not sure where you sit on the thought of wenches at this point." He winked at her.

"Runt and I should figure out how to find his dad and talk with him," Angus said. "It might be a bit tough since there are wanted posters out for the boy. We also don't know if he's in Olde Ridgewatch proper or camped outside the city in Roxburrow, where part of the Holy Imperium's Second Army is located."

"We got a slight problem," said Stitch. His scarred face showed a frown. "Cordial and I could find room and board with a sleazy friend, but overall, we're broke. Bath, hard drink, and wenches ain't happening unless one of us is holding back on funds."

"Never thought you'd be the voice of sweet reason after all this time," said Angus.

"Do my best not to complain, but I'm dog tired," Gray Jim said. "We got Runt this far, and we all need rest. We should split up for a day or two and meet back together. Then finish our little task of getting young Runt to his dad."

"'It's okay, young man. We're all tired and road-weary," Angus said, looking at Gray Jim. They all laughed, as Angus had Gray Jim beat by over one hundred years.

They stopped and looked at their ragged, filthy clothes, beat-up leather, and rusty, road-worn armor. They were in abysmal shape.

"I'll look for the hangman of Olde Ridgewatch, see if they need help, and shack up with them until I can find a suitable job. This many people, I'm sure the city could use another hangman, corpsman, tanner, torturer," said Gray Jim. "Whatever I can do to make some coin."

"Anyone know a place to meet back up?" Duncan asked.

"It's been years since I've been to Olde Ridgewatch. I bet the city's changed," Angus said. "I think there's a tavern near the water called the Empty Gauntlet. We could meet there if we split up. If it makes it easier, Stitch, why not act as an indentured servant, so we don't get any odd looks as we get closer? This area doesn't take kindly to freed slaves. Let's head toward the barracks in Roxburrow and see if we can get information on Runt's dad without getting into trouble. Not sure how it'll go. I have enough money left for a room for Runt. I may be able to find an old friend or two in the dwarven ghetto near Mount Whoredom, the red-light district in the city."

Cordial, Stitch, and Sorella sold pelts from animals taken throughout the journey to the first tinker passing the road, giving them funds for the city.

The band represented an intimidating presence walking the main road toward Crimson Yard University, located outside Olde Ridgewatch. Six were armed with deep, sunken eyes full of mistrust and potential violence. Travelers coming and going gave them a wide berth as they walked the road. On the horizon stood Crimson Yard University, part of the Silver Ivy League, a series of institutions founded by the Goldthorn family. Growing from the university was the town of Roxburrow, and to the west was the port city known as Olde Ridgewatch, a peninsula surrounded on three sides by water and protected to the north by a large structure called Bawstone Keep.

"Aren't we supposed to find Doc?" Duncan asked. "He owes us payment for our duties."

They stepped off the busy road to let merchants, tinkers, scholars, and beggars move toward Olde Ridgewatch.

"Look, I've said it before. No one is obligated to come with me. I'm truly blessed to have you by my side. So, if I don't see you," Runt continued, "if we split and I don't. . ." He choked up a bit.

"Shut your hole, kid. We'll see this through. You deserve to be with your father and get answers as to why this all happened," Angus said gruffly.

"My fear after meeting up with your dad is you'll never want to again hang out with a failed squire, a degenerate apostate, a few thieves, a dwarve with no family, and a hangman with no job," Cordial said.

They laughed and looked on from the road, the smell of the ocean coming up from the east along with the sound of sea birds. Sorella and Stitch grew tenser the closer they got to Olde Ridgewatch.

"I'm going to head to the university, see if there's any word from Doc. I'll meet up with everyone at the Empty Gauntlet soon after," said Maynard. "If he's here, he'll be haunting a bar for sure."

"I'm coming along there with you, Maynard. Got a bone or two to pick with your mentor," Duncan said. "Runt," he looked the boy straight in the eye, "your choice here: head out with Angus to search for your father, or stay with me, talk to Doc, and see what he knows."

Runt looked to the west, past Olde Ridgewatch to the Atlantis Ocean, and thought for a moment. "Angus, why don't you and Stitch find out what you can about where my dad is staying? I'll head to Crimson Yard University with Maynard and Duncan and see if we can find Doc. He got us into this mess, and he'll have news on how to get to my dad. After, we'll make our way over to the Empty Gauntlet," he said. He felt a sense of accomplishment and relief, having finally made it to his destination.

"Boy, you have grown up so much. That's well thought out. More than just, Duncan wants to talk to that loon; see if he'll come to the Empty Gauntlet. If not, he'll get an angry dwarve hunting him down," Angus said.

Sorella sighed, looked at everyone, and then looked away. "Okay, that settles it. Cordial and I will find suitable accommodations for our original party of four, and we'll meet up with the rest at the Empty Gauntlet tomorrow to discuss what we know." It was on the cusp of dawn. "I'm not really welcome in this place. The people of Olde Ridgewatch are prejudiced against elves, and even if I look human, I'm still a half blood and don't want to draw attention. The same goes for you, Stitch. Keep your head down and out of trouble. You stick out more than I do. Acting as an indentured servant to Angus is a perfect idea." She placed her hand on his shoulders, like two old friends do when parting.

"I hear ya, Sorella. I'll behave," Stitch grumbled.

"Why do I have a feeling one of us will end up in jail before the sun sets?" Angus said. He hugged Runt, shook Duncan's hand, nodded, and waved. It was a short goodbye, but it was still a goodbye.

Stitch shrugged and walked off with Angus as if he were a servant. "You been holding out on us, old man," Stitch said.

"What? No. I feel responsible for the boy, so I tried to keep some coins tucked away in my boots. Makes me look taller, that's all. Besides, all those meals I cooked for this band, you all owe me money anyway," Angus said as they trekked toward Roxburrow.

"You lot—nothing ever changes. Always pinching a coin or gem away," Stitch said.

"At least we don't piss off tree branches like you all do, you tree fucker," Angus said. They both laughed and waved behind them.

From Roxburrow, Stitch and Angus walked toward the university before veering to the Neck, the only land route into Olde Ridgewatch. Sorella and Cordial split off to find their way, hoping to use a small boat and the cover of darkness to get inside the city. Gray Jim walked with Duncan, Maynard, and Runt on their way to Crimson University. After an hour, he parted, heading north to Bawstone Keep to inquire about potential jobs and to find out more about the Second Army of the Holy Imperium. He stated he'd follow up with them and leave word at the Empty Gauntlet.

"Duncan, you think Gray Jim is trustworthy. I mean, I have a bounty on my head and all," said Runt. "And he's constantly complaining about money."

"Runt, it's been a long time coming to get here. I saved myself and my friends, but it all came down to Gray Jim. He was the executioner and could have refuted my family claim during my death sentence, but he didn't. The man has integrity and fought to save us when he could have let us die. He's got his demons, but he wouldn't turn you in. He's one of us now," Duncan said. "There isn't much honor in this world, but he's got a bit left. Honor's harder to see with blood on your hands, but it's there just the same."

"Fair enough." Runt shrugged. "Can't shake the feeling he hates me, though."

"He was hard on you when you trained, sure, but he doesn't hate you, Runt. He hates the entire damned world. Angriest man I've ever met. Don't take it personally. What he's been through—it changes a man. Nothing meets his expectations. Ain't nothing we can do about it except be glad he calls us friends and that he's on our side," Duncan said. "You can't say you're the same person after what's happened to you. But I know there's still honor in your heart."

Runt sighed, and they walked on, worn boots kicking dust up into the air. The weather was mild, and it felt amiss. The wind would blow one way with a warm burst and gust in from another direction, cooler. Runt, Maynard, and Duncan began to feel out of place the closer they got to Crimson Yard University. The sun shined on their backs, providing a false sense of a warm spring day even as winter tried to hold on.

Maynard showed more life and energy than Duncan or Runt saw the entire journey. In a pitched battle, Duncan was in his element, and by a campfire, Runt felt at ease, but Maynard didn't take well to the wilderness, and the misery showed on him daily. Now he walked in the shadows of the educational capital of the Holy Imperium, the first institute created on this side of the Atlantis Ocean. He bounced about like a puppy.

"We're not actually going to find Doc at the university," Maynard said. "He's banned from it for numerous reasons. At least he's mentioned it in his ramblings. All the families ejected him from each of their libraries, leading to the threat of arrest if he were seen on campus again. We'll find him in one of Crimson Square's drinking holes or wine sinks." Maynard walked backward as he talked, as if he were a tour guide to Runt and Duncan.

They sold their horses and tack, gaining money before entering Twistbridge, Crimson Yard University's village.

"What did he do?" Runt asked.

"I can tell you later. The stories are best told by a fire, with warm wine in hand," Maynard said like an old angler not ready to tell how he almost caught a whale.

"Where the Hades have you been this entire trip, Maynard? I haven't seen you this excited since we were at Mount Nittany and the girls came back to campus," Duncan said.

"I've always wanted to come to Crimson Yard. This is the heart of Vineland, the educational epicenter this side of the Atlantis Ocean. Who wouldn't be excited?"

Maynard's enthusiasm creeped into Runt, and they picked up their pace. As they made their way on North Avenue, Duncan felt heavy and tired from the long journey. A brick road colored in red, brown, and dark-orange shades fell under their feet. There were open grass fields with sparse thickets of trees here and about. The fields looked almost ready for early crops. Runt and Duncan relaxed; the grass looked almost trimmed.

"I've never seen anything like this place," Runt said.

"It's special because it's the first and, thus, oldest in Vineland. They use goats, you know, to keep the grass the way it is, and the younger students. First-year students must pick up the goat shit, as a chore assigned from one of the houses of the university," Maynard commented. "The houses are old family estates where students live during their studies."

"Maynard, how do you know all of this about goat shit and house family fights?" Duncan asked. "You haven't been the most social person I met on the journey. Now, suddenly, you can't stop talking."

"You all know weapons, forestry, combat, cooking, and everything. I keep quiet, listen, and learn. I know books, and I know education. I try to learn of the mysteries of nature and break them down; this is where I feel at home, where the mind is the sword," Maynard said. "Everything we've done so far, I have written down or committed to memory. I now know unusual ways to cook from watching Angus. I know how to disarm a soldier carrying a sword by watching you and Gray Jim teach Runt, and I know the basics of picking a pocket from Cordial and Stitch. Not to mention the conversations with Sorella late into the night by the campfire, learning about elves and their ways," he said. "I'm not strong enough to forge through a pitched battle, Duncan, but I can hold my own in the right circumstances."

"Right," Duncan said. "Knowing and doing are two different matters."

"Sure thing." He let Duncan pass him on the road, accidentally bumping his shoulder. "Duncan, you must have dropped this back there. Seems to be short a few coins, though. Don't know what happened." He tossed Duncan a small purse he'd stolen from him moments ago.

"Son of a bitch," said Duncan. "Well, I'll remember you can handle yourself next time we get into a fight." He put his purse away.

They moved on from the conversation and carried on walking.

Both Duncan and Runt realized how unkempt they looked. Duncan's beard was wiry, and his mustache was floppy. His hair was longer, with leather straps tied to pieces to keep it away from his notched face. Duncan carried his round shield on his back, a bow and quiver tucked inside. His one-handed sword and knife sat at his waist. Runt wore similar gear, and they both carried the burden of exhaustion.

Maynard, who had struggled the entire trip while carrying books in his travel bag, seemed to be gliding on air.

The Crimson Yard University buildings lay hidden by a fence of old trees and hedges with occasional gaps where grassy meadows held lingering goats. They feasted on new tufts of grass an early spring had brought as the sun shined down upon them. The fields were budding shades of brown, green, and gray grass from the previous season.

"How do I know about goats and houses of Crimson Yard University? I read about this place. I spent a weekend studying it over the winter while you both worked guard duty. Never been here before, but I memorized the streets of the university, Olde Ridgewatch, Twistbridge, and Roxburrow. Did you know the Crimson Square is not a square in the traditional sense? It's more of a triangle and a neighborhood or borough if you will. Essentially, it's where the students go to get drunk, whore around, and find illicit drugs—and it's where we'll find my mentor. It's all a guess. The best bet may be to wait for him to make a fool of himself and try to stop it from getting worse when we find him. It's still early, so he may be sober. Or sobering up from last night."

Duncan and Runt walked as Maynard continued to talk.

Runt's neck nearly snapped when he saw the first female student. "There are girl students here," Runt said. "Her lips were red."

Maynard stopped and gawked for a moment as well. Duncan pushed them both down the cobblestone road. Runt rearranged his hair and pressed down his clothes.

"Yeah, during the Library Wars, they were allowed in," said Maynard.

"Library Wars?" Runt asked.

"Yes, the rival houses of Crimson Yard have a history of getting into friendly debates about which house has the best library. Generally, it ends in bloodshed. Thus, the university motto is 'We Bleed the Truth.' I guess the last one was before I was born," Maynard said as they walked in the Crimson Square.

"Right this way. It's time for breakfast anyway. I'll buy the food and the first round for the three of us," declared Maynard as he picked up his pace.

"Here we are—the Windmill Pub. You two head in there and order breakfast and drinks," Maynard said.

Duncan felt beat, and Runt looked even worse.

"Maynard, we're pretty much dead broke. We have the funds from selling the horses and tack, but it's supposed to be for room and board once we get into the city. How are you paying for this?" Runt asked.

Duncan looked around. It was jarring to see the buildings, the towers, and the city of Olde Ridgewatch before them after so much wilderness and wildness from their journey.

"I have two books I stole from Mount Nittany University. I've read them, and I'm bored of them. This town is hungry for knowledge and books. There's a place like a pawnshop across the street. I'll nick over there and check to see if Doc is in. If not, no matter. I should have enough money from the books for a month's rent and meals until I'm enrolled here. I can afford to buy my traveling compatriots a meal and drink," Maynard said.

"Okay, if you say so," Runt shrugged.

Duncan raised his eyebrow, said nothing, and lugged himself into the

Windmill Pub. The building was a reformed windmill now housing a pub and multiple loft rooms for students with facilities to rent out. It stood on a corner of a meadow near trees and hedges. Nearby buildings were one to two floors high, rectangular, and square in shape with pitched roofs. The base of the Windmill Pub was of large stone, while the rest of the building was deep-red brick with leaded glass windows. The building looked like an unfinished pyramid. Inside, stairs twisted their way up to the top of each floor. It was one of the tallest in the neighborhood, with only a clock tower and the steeple from the Holy Church reaching higher.

Runt and Duncan walked in and found a circular bar with tables surrounding it like tiny islands. A patron could sit at the bar in the center or make their way to one of the tables surrounding the bar. The walls around the inside held booths set up like school cubicles, with hard chairs, tables, and tall wooden walls separating the stalls. For privacy, there were doors attached. Patrons could study, drink, or meet in secret. Light came from a mixture of windows, candles, and dwarven-made fixtures throughout the establishment. The floor was stone as well.

The barkeep eyed them. "You two look rather rough. What can I get you?" the bartender asked before sipping ale from a tall tin cup. He was an older man with a freshly shaved, rounded face, large ears, a reddish nose, and lively cheeks.

"We'd like two beers and breakfast if possible. My boy should be by shortly to pay," Duncan said.

"Humph, okay, can do," said the man, smiling but serious as he poured beer from a copper nozzle below the bar. He pushed two tin mugs toward them.

Duncan looked at the beer and salivated.

"I'll serve breakfast shortly, but a long march on the road like you all had, I'm sure a drink would be much appreciated." He smiled. "Crimson Yard University has been weapon-free since . . ." He thought for a moment. "For some time. Can't remember for sure, but the Holy Imperium is strict about its rules. The same goes for Olde Ridgewatch. You need to check your weapons in, or you could be asking for trouble. Of course, it's not normally so strict, but the problems with Olde Ridgewatch made things a bit tighter with the

Red Army and those Bitterleak Black Eagles patrolling the streets."

Runt sighed, realizing his father and brother were so close, yet further obstacles lay before them. He just wanted to see them both and wasn't even sure they would know what he looked like now or if they would believe him about his mother's death or his sister's whereabouts. His journey felt like it would never end.

Runt - Beer for Breakfast

D uncan and Runt sipped their beer, drinking in the news about the Red Army and Bitterleak Black Eagles controlling the area. They knew they would be in and around Olde Ridgewatch but hadn't counted on strict martial law governing the city.

"What's happening in Olde Ridgewatch? We come from the west, and the news has been scant." Duncan took another sip of beer. "Servant's beard, this is amazing."

Runt took a drink and breathed out a deep sigh.

"Thank you. Out west, you said. Looks to be far out west. I'll do my best to fill you in shortly. Why don't you take a booth with a door in the corner?" The barkeep paused and smiled, then returned to a stoic face. "There's only one other patron this morning. The others are sleeping off a drunk upstairs or in school. Stay for breakfast and two drinks. Any longer, you'll have to check your weapons."

Runt nodded and walked toward a booth. Duncan was about to move with Runt when the bartender grabbed his arm.

"Say, comrade, a bit of an odd question, but how do you take care of a tree you want to grow?" the barkeep asked with a smile, but with a firm grip on Duncan's arm.

"What? What are you talking about?" asked Duncan.

"Oh, my mistake, friend, a bit of a gardening question. Having trouble with some hops I'm growing at home. Thought you may know," the barkeep said, now cheerful.

"I don't know much about gardening. The only way a plant gets watered by me is when I spill blood by it and hope no one steps on it. Let me know when a lad comes in wearing spectacles. He's the one paying." Duncan pulled his hand away and walked toward the booth.

"No problem, no problem. I'll get a few eggs and sausage ready for you."

Duncan slid into the booth, looking toward the door. He shoved his pack and shield in next to him.

"Beer's good," Runt nodded "What was that all about?"

"Hades if I know. He called me friend asked if I know about watering trees. This place gives me the creeps. Too many people on the streets, and we aren't even in Olde Ridgewatch," Duncan said. He smoothed out his mustache and pushed his beard down.

"We've been on the road for weeks, and moving from dark forests, open pastures, and broken roads, I'm just not used to civilization. Now we're a breath away from a sprawling metropolis," Runt said. "It's like reality crashing in on everything. I don't want to get too involved in anything—just need to see my dad and find out why I've a wanted poster out for me."

"You said that right. Here comes our food," Duncan said.

"Here you are, folks: two eggs each, sausages, and home fries. To help square up, give me news from out west. We haven't heard anything from any leaflets or newspapers," the barkeep said.

"Not much to say. We walked into trouble on the road by accident, but you'll have that. The Queens Road saw heavy use by an armed company of soldiers, leaving a mess nearly everywhere they touched. Not sure which army, but we think the Holy Imperium is attempting to secure holdings by the Erie Sea. My friends, including my son here, fought cave spiders, goblins, and a few orcs in the Blightbriar Wilds," Duncan noted. "We barely made it out of there—never thought those things left their caves."

Runt, noticing the lie, looked at his beer, tapping his thumb to the cup.

"Seems like a bit much. Just the two or three of you?" asked the barkeep, taking a sip from his cup.

"There was a bit more of us. We split up, though, once we got here," Duncan said. "And you, tell us: How's business? Anything a wandering band of travelers should know?"

"Okay, eat up. Business is all right, rooms are full of students. We get a nice bout of nightly singing from minstrels. As you can tell, they come for the atmosphere and beer."

Duncan drank deeply, as did Runt.

"This is excellent. You have the barrels behind the bar there?" Duncan asked.

"What? Oh, yes, it's a work of my own. A bit of a tinker myself, mostly self-taught. I did work with a dwarve for a bit, but we broke up our business deal. He tried to take credit for my beer-delivery system. So, I booted his ass right out of my bar. Little half shit."

Duncan raised his eyebrows but didn't say anything.

"Anyway, business is all right, aside from these new taxes. I barely keep my head above water when the university isn't in session, but I find ways to get by," the barkeep looking left and right as if anyone else was listening.

"Death and taxes," Duncan said, egging him on.

"Sure, sure, but I can't even stock *tea* because of the taxes, so I've been getting coffee from down south to supplement. It's cheaper. And had to fire a few local prostitutes—couldn't afford the taxes imposed on them. Not to mention, any pamphlets or posters I want to put up need to be stamped. I have to pay for the stamps. It's a nuisance." He sighed and brushed sweat off his head that didn't exist. "I'm getting taxed everywhere. I take a shit, and Prince Damon wants a piece of it. He wants to weigh it and tell me I owe him a ha'penny. All this for a party he's throwing in a few months." He paused, drank, and looked around, realizing he shouldn't have spoken as such. "Course I do my part. I'm loyal; it's just a struggle, 'tis all."

"Sounds like a hard way to run a business. Heard things are tightening up, thus all the troops. Should we be worried about anything in town, either from the Holy Imperium soldiers or other malcontents?" Duncan asked.

"Yes and no. It's a bit uneasy between the lads in Olde Ridgewatch and the Bitterleak mercs. The Red Army sends patrols out around here, but they mostly knock heads after dinner in the city. University tries to keep the students from taking too many beatings. The Crown pissed off the merchants, who upset a tax collector back in Olde Ridgewatch. City's been a mess before, but that's how it goes normally, you know? Ye Olde Ridgewatch, beans, tea, bricks, and bar fights. Well, the prince heard and dropped an army on the town like Vulcan's anvil, hoping to make everything calmer. Feels like it got worse. Trade's slowed, and it's difficult to get into town now. Soldiers walk the streets day and night, folk don't feel safe, and it feels a like a prison," said the bartender, "or a tea kettle, you know, over the fire. Eventually it's going to heat up too much." He motioned with his hand in a fist and released all his fingers. "Lid's gonna pop off one of these days. Bad vibes in ye Olde Ridgewatch."

"What do you mean you can't get in?" said Runt, taking another large sip of his beer, feeling the weight of the road fall off deep inside himself.

"City's tight like a virgin's shithole. There's only one gate inside the city to walk at the Neck. The rest is surrounded by water, so there's no way of getting in via land unless you have the right papers. Bawstone Keep monitors the ports around the town, so it's pretty tightly locked up."

"Bawstone Keep is one of the reasons we won against the Legion and the Nation, right? At any moment, they could rain fire, death, and steel down on anyone from the heights of the fortress," said Duncan.

"Sure, sure, like having your jealous wife watch your every move. Make no mistake, I love the Holy Imperium, but this could've been managed better. They should let the merchants have a say. Nobles are blocking this all up. Did you know there are two war galleys around the city and smaller boats patrolling the waters? We are at peace for the first time in decades, and it was better when we were at war."

"Like it's nearly a siege," said Duncan.

"Nearly so—you know much about sieges?" asked the barkeep.

"Ahh, fought in a few," said Duncan. He looked at the back of his hands for a moment and then up at the barkeep.

The door opened, and Maynard entered. He saw Duncan and Run and hurried to joining them. "There you guys are. Did well unloading the books. I'll be okay for now until I find a job and join the university. Oh, beer, thanks," he said without acknowledging the barkeep. He looked cleaner and more awake than Duncan and Runt. "Here you are, sir." He put money down for the beer and breakfast.

The barkeep took the payment. "I'll return with breakfast for you then." He turned and headed for the kitchen.

"What's the word?" Maynard asked. "What did the barkeep have to say?"

"Oh, we were discussing the beer, that's all," Duncan said.

"Glad Angus isn't here. The place doesn't allow any non-humans. I get the feeling there're a lot of places like this around here. For all the barkeep said about freedom from taxes, he doesn't feel keen on allowing other races to be involved," Runt said.

"In the store where I pawned the books, the owner tried to talk me down, saying anything written by an elve or dwarve wouldn't garner the same price as a human author. The place is a bit ass-backward. I tried not to be too much of an ass, but, well, I can't tolerate hatred," Maynard said.

He slid into the booth, sitting next to Runt. The doors stood open like a large confession booth for the Holy Church. Across the way, on the other side of the bar, a door opened from a similar booth, and purple smoke billowed out. A man stepped out wearing a tattered formal coat typically worn by Redcloaks for dinner parties and ceremonies at court; he looked oddly familiar to Runt. The coat was dirty and unkempt, with patches all over it and a melancholy dark-crimson hue.

Runt nodded to Duncan, a trait he'd picked up as they'd traveled with the party, communicating with his head and eyes. Duncan looked over. Maynard, who was mid-sentence, caught the gesture and followed their eyes.

The man stood straight, dusted off his coat, took his long-stemmed, dwarven-cut pipe from his mouth, and sauntered to the bar. He hopped over it with a daft and secure movement a man half his age would make, like a tumbler in a passing traveling band. He poured another beer for himself and secured a large knife along with a piece of fruit he found near a sink. He looked over and saw the three of them staring at him. The man glanced down, grabbed more pieces of fruit, juggled them, snatched another stein of beer, and walked around the bar to the trio.

"You mouth-breathing orcs, help an old doctor out and take this fruit," Doc said.

None of them did. They looked on in amazement.

"Well, speak. You act as if a goblin walked in wearing a dancing dress," Doc said.

"Mentor, what the—? How did you—?" Maynard asked.

"Hello, Doc. Glad you're here. You can start by paying for lunch," Duncan said, leaning back and putting his hand on his belt, inches from his knife. He fingered the amulet under his shirt with his other hand.

Doc looked at Duncan, his teeth gripping his pipe. He deftly put down the two beers, one near Duncan, and several pieces of fruit. He juggled the large knife to his left hand. One of the fruits, a melon Runt had never known existed, started to roll off the table. Doc slammed the blade through the fruit as if splitting a piece of wood, startling all three. He left a dent on the table. The knife stuck there.

"Not now, dammit. We have much bigger issues than my debts to you," Doc growled. He looked at Duncan. "I see you got my package."

"I should cut off your fuckin' tongue," Duncan stated.

"They have my staff, dammit. Do you understand? I am nearly fucking sober here. This is serious." Doc rubbed his eyes. "They have my staff."

"Your staff? But how did you lose it?" Maynard asked. "Wait, who has it?"

Runt was quiet. He respected yet disliked the man standing in front of him.

"I went toward Affectus to gather news, talk to a few friends, and learn more about Mr. Runt's family. And I got more than I planned." He paused. "I lost it. And I think I can get it back, but I need Runt's help," Doc said. "Forsaken Templar got involved."

"This must be pretty serious if you're sober," Runt said. "Let's get to my dad, and we can square away this staff thing."

"Mostly sober, sure, sure. But that's just it; your father has my staff," Doc said and paused, swatting away imaginary flies. "The beer here is exquisite. The owner's quite talented, if he is a bit of a racist piece of shit, but hey, we all have sins to carry." The barkeep, coming out of the kitchen, looked at Doc. "Speaking of this fine establishment. We're talking about you and your craft beer. I'll be joining my comrades here for the remainder. Please bring another round, and yes, I will be paying. We're celebrating a reunion."

Doc finished his beer, grabbed the one in front of Duncan, and started drinking. Duncan eyeballed him.

"You get used to it," Maynard said.

"I forgot about Doc's little quirks," Duncan said. "Raving loon, I tell you." He stopped again. "We came to get Runt to his father, Doc, not to get your staff back."

For all the time Runt had spent with Doc, he looked out of place without his staff. He'd only used it the one-time Runt could remember and had only performed magic once or twice during their travels.

"This could get interesting. I've got a feeling your staff is pretty important," Runt said excitedly, able to take his mind off his family for a moment.

"You're damned right it is. Do you know anything about so-called legendary weapons?" Doc said.

"You mean like the first sword and shield of the Maker, owned by the Blackheart family?" Runt asked. "I can't remember either name. One is called Midnight's Heart, I think?"

"Yes and no. There's a rumor the Blackheart family has a sword named Twilight and a shield called Midnight's Veil, each unquestionably unique," Doc said.

"I met one of the brothers up north. You may remember, Doc," Duncan said. "Right before we lost someone important to us."

"Oh, yes, Joseph Blackheart, known as The Brokenhearted One, the hero of the Battle of the Reaping." Doc put his fingers up in the air to mime quotation marks when he said "hero." "What a piece of shit, taking credit for what I did, for my win," he said. "I haven't evaluated the sword and shield the Blackhearts possess. The family keeps them close, and they're one of the most powerful families this side of the Atlantis, but I can tell you my staff is special and should not be in anyone's hands but mine."

"We both performed atrocities we'd rather not remember on the Plains of Ursula. The weight from the Battle of the Reaping just gets heavier." Duncan looked down into his beer, thumbing the stein with his finger.

"You're right, you're right." Doc stopped drinking and looked at Duncan. Usually, Doc acted like a half-mad hermit drunk on his moonshine, half a smile and a glazed-over look like a fresh cinnamon roll in a bakery, but the look he gave Duncan now, and the look Duncan gave back, told an entire story in a moment. "Best not dwell, best not ever." Doc took a deep pull from his stein. "The Brokenhearted One, the little fraud, has one of the Paragons. It's named Twilight, and his knuckle-dragging, mouth-breathing brother, Jared, has the shield known as Midnight's Veil. Knights and even mercenaries name their weapons, and kings, despots, emperors, and other power-grabbers have named weapons and armor, but very few feel like they break natural laws. Weapons so special and so old they give the owner power or energy, an edge in battle few can meet."

"So, the book I searched for explains these, Paragons?" Maynard said, eager to join in the conversation. He'd been full of confidence and self-esteem, but Runt could tell he'd reverted to his old self. Maynard had become the student again. "I can only read a little of it. *Gaston's Chronicle of Weapons,*" Maynard said. He took it out of his satchel and placed it on the table.

"Excellent work. Maynard, I'm proud of you. This little journey you took with Runt and Duncan made you grow so much." Doc grabbed the book and examined it, giving it a short sniff.

Maynard felt warm inside. Compliments from Doc were as common as a cardinal in the winter.

Doc said quietly. "There's no better high in life than that of knowledge and the power and pleasure it gives you." He flipped through the book and continued to speak. "Maynard will follow along better but let me try to explain. There are different origin stories, right? Yes, different religions give ideas about how it all started. Forget all of it for a moment. What I'm trying to get to is my theory, my idea. Look, there are families, *old families*, here and across the ocean. I believe if you look back long ago, we all grew out of them. Each family coveted power, secrets, and knowledge, just like Prince Damon and the noble families do today. They didn't want this knowledge to get out. It was too much, too corrupting, too powerful, and too deadly—not only for the victims of this knowledge but also for the users. Anyway," he waved his hands as if to ward off thoughts on creation and religion, "what I'm saying is these grand old families—most of this is forgotten. Those weapons fell into antiquity. History is littered with the rust of empires. Maynard and others like me seek the truth about the nature of Midgard. It's the difference between a mage and a professor. Do you see? I'm saying there are weapons capable of amazing feats, and these weapons shouldn't be in the wrong hands. Like Gaston's staff in the hands of the Red Army."

"Are you saying your stick is one of them? Are you telling me the sword Brokenheart has is one of them? Is that why he beat me and killed—" Duncan started in on Doc.

Runt watched as the two started to speak at the same time.

Duncan thumbed his amulet.

Doc held up a hand, silencing the former squire. "Yes, you weren't outmatched. He had an advantage not many, if any, could defeat. The little shit is on par with an average sword in battle, but when he holds Twilight, he's nearly unstoppable."

Duncan sat back and twirled his mustache. "Shit, I need to get one of those."

"Yes, but first, I need my staff, Gaston's Beard, back." He paused and looked around. "We need—no, we *must*—get it back."

Maynard looked at Doc, as did Duncan and Runt. There was silence. Even Runt knew about the staff of Gaston, one of the first users of magic in the known world. It was a children's story spoken over the hearth fire before they slept.

"Gaston, like the wizard from fairy tales? Like from the knights of the circular table?" asked Runt.

"Sort of, Mr. Runt, sort of. There was a man who owned the staff before me, and his name was Gaston. As Maynard is now my student, I was one of his," Doc said.

"Oh, I had no idea," Runt said. "Is the staff the reason you can do—what did Maynard call it—high art?"

"The Paragons are only as useful as the person wielding them. They take your abilities and push them beyond what anyone else is capable of. I can perform the high art, but instead of, say, lighting a candle, I can light a castle on fire with Gaston's Beard. Either way, to create the art, you need to take from nature, an animal, yourself, or" he said more quietly, "from someone else."

"How? What do you mean? Can I just take a life and make sparks fly out of my hands?" Runt said.

"No, it's more than that, or everyone would be slinging fireballs all over the place and shooting sparks out of sticks like foolish children in school. But if a person gives up their life, it's different," Doc said before looking away.

The apprentice stared at his mentor as he took a deep, slightly shaky sip from his cup.

They talked, ate an early lunch, and drank a mixture of elvish pale ales and dwarven lagers. Customers came and went as they continued to catch up; they made plans, but none seemed to pan out. They couldn't crack how to get into Olde Ridgewatch or how to get Runt to his dad.

"I could walk up to a guard, say I'm the general's son?"

"The general's son? Your father would barely know what you look like. It's been over ten years since you've seen your father or brother," Duncan said.

"Don't be so hard on the boy, squire, but he's right," said Doc.

"Call me squire again, and I'll cut you, Young, from groin to neck," Duncan growled.

"Fuck you! Don't call me—" Doc began.

"Wait, what? Doc, what's your name?" Runt said.

"My name is my name, and . . ." Doc looked away, puffing on his pipe as he lit it. A sweet tobacco smoke filled the booth. He kicked the door open to let out the smoke. "Names have power. Call me mentor or Doc."

"Whatever. You have so many aliases it's not even funny," Duncan said, chuckling. "His name is Hunter Young, Sir Hunter Young to those who remember when a long-dead king knighted him, but he is also known as Doc, Doctor Young, or as Maynard says, mentor. He is technically a Redcloak, but Prince Damon does not recognize him anymore. And he owns no land."

"Why haven't you knighted, Duncan?" Runt asked. "I thought all knights could ask a person to kneel and make them a knight."

"They can, but after the battle up north, I spoke the truth to powerful people, General Thomas Casting and his Council of Crows and Prince fucking Damon." Doc rapped his fist against the table. "They took everything away from me except my staff, and now it's gone, too."

"What did they take away?" Runt asked.

"General Casting called me a looney-cracked miser and got Prince Damon and the council to agree. So, they exiled me, took my knighthood, family estates, and my favorite dog," Doc said. "They tried to take away my power by putting a binding ring on my fingers, three to be exact, but failed. I was the first to break a binding, and I broke all three, so they can eat Prince Damon's dick and die."

"I want to know what you said. What truth did you speak to this council. This Council of Crows," Maynard said softly. "You never told me what it was."

"No, Maynard, not the time or place," Doc replied sharply.

"Mr. Hunter Young was poking the prince's muse at the time and caused an incident." Duncan said cooly. "She was one of the three Ladies of Wightland. Which one was she? Lady Grapeseed, or was it Lady Rowan, or was it, Lady Blacklace? I can't remember."

"You swine, how dare you!" Doc's eyes were starting to glow.

"It was Lady Rowan, I believe. You made her garden grow." Duncan chuckled. "I remember now. You did her from behind at court in a broom closet."

Doc stood and took his pipe out of his mouth but said nothing.

"They were going at it like beasts. It was Lady Rowan, the quietest of the three sisters—not Lady Grapeseed, the poisoner, or the other sister, Blacklace, who was exiled from the court for witchery. Lady Rowan, in the closet, moaning and screaming like a drunk cat in heat during a full moon. Everyone could hear it," Duncan said venomously. "And here I am trying to be his bodyguard because who wants a squire who failed three knights before him? And they're making this ruckus in a closet while the prince is holding court."

"We weren't making it like dogs. Lady Rowan had a revelation—she can see things others can't—and I took her into the closet so only I could hear what she had to say."

"You had time to go into a closet with a courtesan but couldn't knight me, you drunken fool," Duncan interrupted.

Why doesn't anyone believe me? She can tell the future, you ingrates!" Doc huffed. "I've only loved one person. My daughter and she's dead and gone because of me. Hades, you all are awful people. I lost everything after the Crimson Struggle, and you mock me. Bastards, all of you!" He chewed on his pipe like a sad puppy, blustering. "You're worse than the bleating voices in my head."

"We lost a lot of loved ones during the Battle of the Reaping, Doc," Duncan said. His irritation abating. "I'll never forget your daughter Doc. You know that."

Doc stared at Duncan for a moment, a deep understanding passing through the men. The tension cleared.

The conversation shifted and their tone adjusted moving from past war stories to the trek across Vineland from Steelsburg to Windmill Pub where they now sat. Runt and Maynard laughed, and even though Doc's eyes were partially glowing, he soon laughed bitterly with them. Then, there was a knock at the booth door and the barkeep from earlier asked if they wanted another round, which they did. Duncan bought Doc a glass of whiskey and calmed him down. The door opened, and Runt could see the place had filled up; two barmaids walked around, making sure customers were dealt with, and two more barkeeps worked behind the bar.

They drank through the morning into the afternoon.

The barkeep's name ended up being Mitt, the establishment's owner. "Lunch is served," and he handed them bowls of stew, dark bread, and more beer. "Say, earlier I heard you lot were interested in getting into the city. I know it can be hard to do unless you have business. It's starting to snow outside. A bit late for this kind of weather. I mean, it was a good week of warmer weather and we saw grass for the first time, but I guess one can suppose it could snow in March. I'm trying to say: I need assistance in getting merchandise into the city, and you four could help. Lost a few boys who couldn't make it in from the outskirts of town and could use some help."

Doc didn't say anything. He lit his pipe for what felt like the tenth time today and leaned back, away from the table, the color of his face draining.

Duncan was the first to speak. "What're you looking for us to do?"

"Got a cart of beer and wine that needs to get to my cousin's beer hall. See, I produce it, and he uses it. I have the papers to get into the city and distribute the stock. Your jobs would be to guard it and get it unloaded. What you do after is none of my concern."

"I'd say we're interested," Doc said. "We've been trying to get this young lad into Olde Ridgewatch to meet up with friends he hasn't seen in years."

"The odd thing is, with the Holy Imperium soldiers and other reprobates all over the city, you would be kind of guarding it against them. You can't bring a blade, shield, or anything dangerous in, so guarding it would involve only your presence. A few staves could be used from the cart in case you need to knock some fools about, but the goal is to drive the cart through the gate, let the guards check your papers, head to my cousin's beer hall, and unload the wine and beer barrels," Mitt said.

"All this is on the up and up. Taxes paid for and papers legit?" Doc said.

"Aye, sure is. I have this bar to take care of, and I prop up my cousin's beer hall as well. I got too much in it to not be," Mitt said. "Stamps are legit and paid for."

Duncan eyed the barkeep, who returned his look square. He nodded and shook on it.

Runt was going to see his father.

The Bastards - Chest Pains

Winter lay in the shadows, not ready to fade. Benjamin Ashburn looked south toward the Atlantis Ocean, saw the darkness in the clouds, and felt a chill as the wind picked up. From the long winter, he knew a storm could spin in from below and drop massive amounts of rain and snow. Lightning flashed in the distance.

"Don't expect rain tonight, even with the strange lightning in the east. It's going to snow on us again," Ben sighed.

"Can we just get this patrol over with?" Stu whined.

They both put on proper clothes before they went out. Along with half kits of armor, they each carried a dwarven crossbow and short swords. They felt the weight of soldiering in Prince Damon's army upon their shoulders. The winds from the sea mixed with the weather front from the west, creating looming dampness, making it harder to grip the handle of a sword or club.

"Don't expect much tonight. Too cold, too windy, and this fucking snow," Stu said.

The snow fell in large flakes; its weight was visible in the dark clouds above the ocean.

"Let's get on with it," Ben replied, wariness creeping up his spine. "Still feels off today out there. I went outside past the barracks for a minute. Weather's shifting."

"What's up now?" Stu asked.

"Price went up again for a warm cup of wine down the way. Feels like the prince taxes the air we breathe. The newest ones—these taxes on alcohol, tobacco, and brothels—are awful. This is starting to get to folk. Warm weather came in, and townsfolk grumbled. They put up with it during the winter, but things are thawing now, and tempers are rising." Ben said. "It's our job, and all to keep the city under control by Prince Damon's justice and authority. I thought soldiering would be different, I guess." Ben thought about the money he'd spent recently. Since he'd joined the army, he hadn't enticed himself too often, but he had seen prostitutes before and had spent money on a drink or two.

"Whatever. Let's get through tonight," Stu said, blowing on his hands.

"Sorry, just complaining. But I swear, all they do is give us night duty," Ben said.

"We got to put in our work, man, and keep affairs straight, even if we disagree with it. We've no say in the laws and politics made above us. Shit, nobody does."

"Maybe we should have a voice in what the laws and punishments are," Ben said under his breath.

"Whatcha say there?" asked Stu.

"Nothing, nothing." Ben shook his head. "Let's just get going."

Both Stu and Ben wanted to become knights and make their fathers proud. Knighthood was bestowed by a lord or another knight to those showing prowess in a pitched battle, a duel, hunting a foul monster, or other dutiful measures.

Ben continued to prep for the evening, wearing plain leather gloves to keep warm as the temperature dropped. He was tired of serving and unsure of his life as a soldier. He thought of home often and considered quitting after his initial two years of service. Ben checked his crossbow and ensured the mechanism's action clicked, and Stu picked at the spear of his blade. Ben was a crack shot in practice, one of the best in the command, and actively improved his longbow skills. He tucked his sizable wooden club opposite his short sword. The general, his father, had advised all on patrol of the city to limit using edged weapons to keep the populace in line and to not agitate the locals of Olde Ridgewatch. Regrettably, it hadn't had the desired effect on the local population. Stabbings had slowed, but beatings had become more common.

* * *

A mutual distrust grew between citizens of Olde Ridgewatch and the standing army, but it was not all-out warfare. General Benedict Ashburn, Benjamin's father, imposed martial law, pulling back enough to show restraint, but it wasn't enough. A growing portion of the population felt the soldiers assigned to the area were more oppressors and invaders who caused terror instead of keeping law and order.

First, the barracks were too small, so soldiers quartered in people's homes. At certain times, this would be an honor. But ye Olde Ridgewatch was hard-nosed and didn't like to change its self-sustaining ways.

The new taxes, labeled the "Party Tax," caused resentment among the lower classes. The initial tax collectors met opposition, even when they hired bodyguards. The first few tax collectors were found strung up by hempen rope from trees across Olde Ridgewatch. The hangings occurred at night. So, the Holy Imperium and Bitterleak soldiers retaliated, found suspects, and put them to death with no trial, only a quick beheading in the streets.

A week later, the housekeeper for the mayor of Olde Ridgewatch, loyal to Prince Damon, found a barrel at the gate of the mayor's house filled with tea, piss, and another tax collector's body. The body was soaked and swollen, his face smashed in.

Days later, a city council member and newly appointed tax collector was found strapped naked to his prized horse, lipstick all over his body, his genitals sewn into his mouth. His wife's screaming had brought all the attention needed for the Holy Imperium Army's reprisal.

A group calling themselves the Bastards of Liberty sent a young man named Emanuel Shapespin to supply terms to General Ashburn. The Bastards of Liberty were composed of smugglers, thieves, and lawyers who were angry at the new taxes levied by Prince Damon and his court. Ben had heard rumors about the Bastards of Liberty infiltrating city-states like Olde Ridgewatch, Grimwood, Affectus, Bison City, and Hudson City. Sir Ashburn listened to Emanuel Shapespin in his study over tea. The case presented to General Ashburn was compassionate and thoughtful.

General Ashburn asked to see Sir Fredrick Burrow, commander of the Bitterleak mercenaries supporting General Ashburn's army. Sir Burrow walked in wearing scaled gauntlets and slapped Emanuel Shapespin until he lay unconscious. Sir Burrow tied him up to his warhorse and dragged the boy down the street. Emanuel woke and screamed, sliding down the cobbled road until Sir Burrow stopped at Emanuel's ancestral home, cut off his head, and staked it on the home's gate. Emanuel Shapespin's mother screamed from her window during the beheading. Burrow kicked down the house's front door and dragged Ms. Shapespin out of her home and placed her head next to her son's. He burned down the house, which had previously survived the family for generations.

With the Party Tax in place, the murders of well-known family members of the city, the gossip about the dwarven civil war from Steelsburg, and an army marching west toward Grimwood, anxiety was created in those living in Olde Ridgewatch. General Ashburn's strict adherence to law and Fredrick Burrow's mercenary retinue caused nothing but dissidence among the locals. Those nobles loyal to Prince Damon and Burrow's mercenaries heard rumors of hired elves performing hangings, burnings, and drownings of tax collectors. The distrust now went both ways.

* * *

"You were complaining about the wine. I'll grab a wineskin to take with us tonight, but we better have a cup or two before we start," Stu said.

"Yeah, sounds like a plan. You buy the first round, I'll get the second," said Ben.

They headed out toward the Empty Gauntlet, a local haunt where soldiers of the Red Army mixed with locals.

* * *

Maynard and Runt started loading barrels onto a cart behind the Windmill Pub. Two barrels already stood in the cart when they began.

"Didn't think it was cold earlier; can't believe it's snowing now," Runt said as he and Maynard hefted a barrel.

The weather had changed quickly. The past two weeks of early spring had fought and lost to the last grips of winter as it moved into the early evening.

"Yeah, but we drank a bit today already. Probably didn't feel the weather change," Maynard said.

"You're right." Runt nodded. "Well, this gets us into the city. Once in, do I just walk up to where my dad is staying and say, 'Hey, remember me, your son? Mom's dead, no idea where my sister is, is Ben around, and, oh, I missed you? Did I mention it was a bunch of damned Red Army soldiers who did it?' I'm excited and kinda pissed. I haven't heard from him in a long time, you know?" Runt said. His tone mocked the tragedies he had endured in the past months.

Maynard looked at Runt. "Don't lead with how they died. Tell him your mom passed, your sister is missing, and you need help. My concern is, how the Hades do you get to him? He's the general of an army and, well, kinda in charge of Olde Ridgewatch. It would be like trying to get a hand on the prince just to say you touched him."

The door to the pub slammed shut as Duncan helped Maynard and Runt finish loading the cart. Doc and Mitt followed out shortly after sharing one last drink together. They shook hands with the barkeep and got on their way, situating themselves on the short-walled cart drawn by two draft horses. They hoped to make it into the city before the snow fell any harder. The trek to the gate took over an hour. They hit the queue to get into Olde Ridgewatch through what everyone called the Neck, their nerves shivered in the wind.

* * *

The Neck was a thin strip of land with the ocean on one side and a bay on the other, protected by a human-built and dwarven-engineered stone wall. The wall kept those inside the Neck sheltered from each side's ocean and bay waters. It also forced all foot and horse traffic in and out of Olde Ridgewatch into one lane. The only other way into the city was via boat. Each stone wall was as wide as two and a half carts and higher than any man could stand. One or two guards walked up and down the walls, watching peasants and merchants coming into the city from the farm town of Roxburrow or Crimson University. Runt looked over his shoulder and saw lightning flash across the clouds from the east. Everyone waiting in the queue felt the walls brace against the snow and waves. Nor'easter storms like this limited access to the city during the winter months.

"Most folk favor staying inside when a storm rolls into Olde Ridgewatch. They fear the Atlantis Ocean will swallow them up. At least, those new in town," said an old farmer, looking at the cart Runt, Maynard, Duncan, and Doc rolled on behind him. "Keep moving on, Taug, keep moving," the farmer groaned.

He poked the female orc slave named Taug with a short spear, grazing the skin. She shuffled forward, shackled at the neck, with a pair of chains leading to her arms. Her white and red hair fell in wisps over two nubs where her horns used to grow. She wore a binding ring on each finger. The orc looked comatose. She stood a near foot taller than the old farmer.

Duncan and Doc looked on and mumbled to each other. Runt sat in the back of the cart; his view obstructed by the beer barrels.

The people in the queue at the first gate of the Neck waited eagerly to get in before the weather worsened. Mitt, the barkeep, had provided the band with a wine barrel tapped at the front of the cart so they could drink to stay warm. Doc and Duncan started in on it as soon as they were rolling.

"I didn't think it was going to get worse. This is bullshit!" Runt spat as he braced against the wind.

"Not bullshit, Runt, just ye Olde Ridgewatch doing its best to welcome us," Maynard shouted over the sound of waves crashing against the Neck's walls. He wore his robe hood up to keep the wind and snow away from his face and pulled up his coat collar so just his spectacles showed.

The cart moved forward through the Neck as water on both sides of the cart splashed over the walls. The road between the walls of the Neck was made of flat, well-placed bricks aged by the ocean. Runt listened to the roar of the water against the stone. The horses pulling the cart didn't enjoy the closed-in space and noise. They shuffled on and stopped as another queue formed near the entrance to the city and the end of the Neck.

"This is a bit of a mess, ain't it?" Duncan said to Doc as he took a swig of wine.

"You said it, Duncan. We need to get out of this weather soon. I don't think this storm will let up until tomorrow afternoon," Doc sighed into the wind and snow.

They were next in line. To the front of them stood the Neck's gate, guarded by two soldiers in dark-gray, seal-skin cloaks with fur on the top to protect them from the elements. They quickly got people in or recommended that they turn around and walk back. A guard waved them forward.

"Walk up to the front of the Neck and close this son of a bitch down. This storm is going to get worse. I don't want to deal with anyone getting drowned or frozen to death!" yelled the head guard to another over the falling snow. "If the water pushes over the top of the Neck, this turns into a death trap. Get the soldiers off the walls here, or we'll lose one."

Orders given, and orders taken.

"Ahoy! Here to deliver stock to a beer hall," Duncan hailed, handing the paperwork to the guard in charge.

The guard looked at the papers and checked the names of the barrels. "Oy, all you carrying is beer and wine?" he asked. "Stamps look legit."

"Yes, sir, we cracked one open for the ride in. Here's a taste," Doc said, handing the main guard a wooden cup.

"Hold up a moment. Hey, John, bring over the boys!" yelled the guard. He looked at the papers further.

Duncan smirked at Doc, feeling there would be no trouble with the guards. The snow blew up in their faces. Duncan looked back at Maynard and Runt, who stood on the back of the cart, bracing against the wind. It was too cold to say more. Four more soldiers walked up and spoke to the main guard, but Duncan and Doc couldn't hear over the wind as Runt and Maynard shivered near the back, waiting.

The main guard came up to Duncan again. "My boys need a sample each, and you can move on. Welcome to Olde Ridgewatch. You're the last group to pass through. We're closing and locking the gate, and the port won't see any other ships until the storm passes."

Duncan relaxed. "Bring them over. Make sure they have a big cup, and we'll fill them up and be on our way," he said into the blowing wind. "And thank you."

After the drinks, the cart moved through the gates and into the city. Initially, it had been a farming community, but the first inhabitants stole the art of brick making taught to them by local dwarves and built the area to become one of the main ports of Great Brightland's colonies. Now, hundreds of years later, the newly formed Holy Imperium wanted to manage it not as a town but as a significant part of its new country.

Olde Ridgewatch held several high-fortified towers overlooking portions of the city and bay. Originally built as light towers, General Benedict Ashburn commandeered them and affixed them to be more dangerous. Each building protected a bit of the city and ocean with mounted scorpions, a type of large crossbow capable of damaging ships or large crowds of people. The city's roads twisted around buildings, making circles and squares for public meeting gatherings, leaving large trees as the city became more "civilized." Neighborhoods coveted the few remaining trees in the city, treating them like pets, with their own names and customs. Those in town held dances and weddings, using the trees as centerpieces for their celebrations. Local justice was served at the trees. The older families said the blood from executions strengthened the trees and the city with every drop.

The cart moved forward, leaving tracks and horseshit. They moved through the city as chimneys spewed smoke from coal fires and Doc began to sing a song, the cart's wheels crunching in the snow. Duncan joined, and at first, it was sad and slow like a funeral hymn. Then it reached up high, and the tempo moved faster. Two terrible singers inebriated and trying with a fuzzy head and full heart to give the song its proper respect.

Maynard and Runt sat on the back of the wagon as it twisted its way through the city. As they shuffled down a side street, a group of the Holy Imperium's Red Army soldiers walked toward them. They wore cloaks, gambeson shirts over vested chain mail, gloves, and woolen crimson-and-white striped pants.

Two guards carried spears, while the others carried crossbows illegal to anyone but Holy Imperium soldiers or those of dwarven heritage. Under the cloaks, smaller one-handed swords used in shield work and guard duty were concealed.

"Oy, past curfew. You better have an excuse, or it's the stocks for the lot of you," one guard hollered as the cart approached toward them.

Duncan slowed the two draft horses and yelled against the wind, "Sorry—just making a late delivery. We have all our paperwork here."

Doc bundled up his jacket, no longer wearing his shaded glasses, and looked away. The guards blocked their way as the wind blew snowflakes, whipping them around the cart and into their faces. Two guards stomped their feet and muttered to themselves, their breath blocking their faces. Another lit a cigar off his lantern while the lead soldier inspected the papers.

"Where you headed?" the soldier with the cigar asked before spitting out pieces of tobacco. A foot soldier's boredom showed on his gray mustache and portly face.

"We were told to deliver this cart to Dick Holmes of the Empty Gauntlet beer hall up the way," Doc said, coming to life. He took a sip out of his cup to keep him warm and give him strength. "You fellows need a quick top-off to keep you warm on this frosty night? We have a small barrel of red wine we were given."

"Papers look acceptable. We could fine you for being outside after dark, but the beer and wine's good at the Empty Gauntlet, even if old Dick overcharges and under pours. Let's have a fill-up. You two keep walking. We'll be right with you."

The two guards nodded and started walking on.

"No need to start the young men too early on the sauce," said the mustached guard.

"Certainly not. Don't want to make them delinquents and drunks," said Doc. "Wine is evil. It's why I stick to beer, which doesn't dull the mind." He handed the two men two wooden cups.

Both guards drank two rounds, nearly finishing the small barrel off.

"Ahh, that's the ticket. Now, you be on your way," the main guard said.

"You lot remember you see anything suspicious—any looters, scoundrels, or rebels—report them to the nearest official right away. Been talk of an insurgence, people upset about taxes and other fake news, from anonymous pamphlets and newspapers."

Duncan snapped the reins and moved into the wind as it blew across the stones on the road. The snow fell but pushed horizontally as the wind commanded it. The cart wobbled down the street another fifteen minutes until it came to the front of a brazier near a beer hall. A few drunks warmed themselves outside the swinging sign of the Empty Gauntlet. They moved on past the sign and down an alley. The horses let out a huff as they were pulled to a stop. Duncan knocked at the side entrance of the beer house, laughter and songs echoing through the wall.

"Coming, coming! What now? I'm trying to run a business," a short fat man said, his voice like a frog had swallowed gravel. "Oh, you must be my delivery. A bit late, don't you think? You got the manifest with you? Busy night tonight. They're really cutting it loose in there."

Duncan handed over the papers.

"Let's get this unloaded. Start rolling the barrels to the back of the building to the cellar. Afraid the cart won't fit anymore. Once done, we'll warm you up and get some dinner in you."

Doc hopped off and walked back to the boys to monitor the unloading. "Maynard, you know I can't lift shit. I'll take a few of the smaller wine barrels. You two, start on the bigger beer barrels, and we'll get this finished up. Maker's tits, it's cold." Doc coughed and spat blood. "Then we'll eat and find a place to sleep. Tomorrow morning, we'll meet up with the rest of your friends."

"Right, let's get this done. I'm over this weather already," said Maynard.

"You and me both," said Runt. He gripped the barrel Maynard was pushing off the cart.

They rolled the barrel past the cart to the back of the alley, where a cellar door stood open. Runt and Maynard maneuvered the barrel into the cellar with the help of two dwarves. Once the barrel was in the basement, the dwarves rolled it out of sight.

After Maynard's first barrel, Runt returned to the cart to find Duncan laughing with a man shorter than him, skinny, with longish hair.

"Well, mates, we meet again! Thought you lot wouldn't make it into the city. The place is in a real lock down now," the rogue-looking man with a curved-up smile said.

"Stitch, how did you get in here?" Runt asked.

"I've got my ways. Angus and I got in with ease, no papers needed. Met an old friend on guard duty who let Angus and me in. Old favor paid off. Angus headed to his friend's house for personal business but should be along. I stopped in here to get me a job working for old Dick. Right, let's get back to it. My blood ain't made for this weather," the elve said.

"It's good to see you again. I was worried," Duncan said, clapping Stitch on the shoulder. "With the heavy military presence and all these new laws, we thought some of you may not make it in." They lifted more barrels off the cart to roll to the back. "Any word from Cordial, Gray Jim, or Sorella?"

"Nothing yet. I checked on old friends, but no word from either of the two. The town's in a state. During the day, the Holy Imperium soldiers walk around like they own the place. Most of the officers are quartered in houses here in the city, but they can't really control all of it, the slums, back alleys, sewer systems, and dark places are riled up. Accordingly, they travel in twos and threes day and night to stop drunken crowds from causing trouble."

"Trouble from what?" Runt asked. He stood, pushing on his lower back, having moved four barrels so far.

"Prince's taxes on brothels, beer, and wine are pissing off not just the poor but the merchants, too, plus the Red Army is now in charge of collecting, and they're not too kind on being stiffed. There's animosity between the Holy Imperium and the locals. Something is brewing, and I don't mean the beer in these barrels. Two Holy Imperium soldiers fought with the locals in a tavern a few weeks back. One soldier went missing. The other lost his foot to a hand axe used for splitting wood."

"Shit, wow," Maynard breathed.

"Guess there was a trial, and two locals were hanged in the town square, but it wasn't a normal hanging. After the trial, the bodies were brought down at night, buried properly like heroes, and given tombstones." Stitch took a drink from the nearly empty wine barrel.

Doc and Duncan stood by the front of the cart. Doc smoked his pipe, taking the story in as the snow drifted down from the sky.

"Captain Burrow of the Bitterleak Black Eagles said the burial was illegal, dug up the bodies, and tossed them into the ocean."

"Bad vibes here. I need to get my staff, and we need to get out of here. They'll drop an anvil on this city soon—blood in the snow. I can feel it. Did you see the towers in the city? This place is under siege from within," Doc said, pipe gripped between his teeth.

"Don't like this either," Duncan said. "Let's finish up, get inside,"

The wind picked up, blowing the brazier at the front of the alley. It remained lit, but the path darkened.

Runt climbed into the cart, rolling a barrel over to the edge. "This one seems lighter and not evenly weighted. Weird." He tapped it, and the sound was off. He stood it up, nudged it toward the edge, let it stand, walked back to the end of the cart, and checked on the other one. "This one, too. Echo is weird, and it's lighter." He rolled it over to the first one.

"It's okay, Runt. Nudge it toward me. I'll grab it, get it off the cart," Stitch said. "Hate the snow. I'm over winter. The slush and bitter cold."

Runt pushed the barrel off the edge. Stitch caught it and let it down easy.

The rolling of the barrels and people walking had cleared snow in the alley. Small drifts appeared, covering the edges of the two buildings on either side, leaving the center clear. Shadows danced around them from the lit brazier at the top of the alley, near the tavern's front door, while one lone torch hung near the back, by the cellar. The wind continued to play with the direction of the snowfall.

"Who goes there?" yelled a voice at the top of the alley. The wind quieted, and the yell made the horses rear up and shake the cart. One horse shit, leaving its steaming mark on the ground.

Runt lost his footing and fell forward, tipping the second barrel and himself over the edge. He flipped as he fell and landed on his back, the wind knocked out of him. The barrel fell, cracked open, and spun away from Stitch. Maynard walked up to see what was happening. The broken barrel turned and wobbled away from Runt, toward the front of the alley and the voice.

"Red guard coming through. State your name and business being out this late past curfew," the soldier said.

Four Holy Imperium soldiers stomped past the edge of the brazier at the front of the alley and looked down at Stitch, Runt, and the others. Stitch stood with a barrel at their feet. Maynard came behind Stitch, and Runt lay dazed on his back, a half-broken barrel several feet in front of him.

"Sorry. Delivering wine and beer to this beer hall, trying to keep your fine selves quenched after a hard night of work," Stitch said, trying to use what little manners he could summon.

The four guards walked forward. Each carried a crossbow or spear.

Maynard moved closer to Stitch to get a better look at the guards.

"Wasn't talking to you, ya fuckin' slant-eared tree-humper. You better have your papers, elve, or your dark, sharp ears will be hanging on my necklace before the sun shines in the morning," the head guard spat at Stitch. "Now, spectacles, what's your business?"

The soldiers seemed bent on trouble, judging from their tone and mannerisms. The guard with the loudmouth was bearded, his face well suited for the weather. He wore red soldier leathers, a breastplate covered by a furred cloak. The other three were not as adorned but were menacing in their gear and status all the same. The snowfall was still large, thick flakes.

Stitch took a step back and lowered his shoulders with a decisive understanding of the situation, feigning weakness even as he fumed with rage. Maynard knew Stitch carried a small arsenal inside his coat pockets, even in a town where no swords or bows were allowed.

"We're hired outside of town to make a delivery of beer and wine to the Empty Gauntlet. The barkeep has our papers inside," Maynard said.

"Does he now? Best go get them," the guard with the beard said. He looked over to the youngest guard and nodded; the younger of the two disappeared back to the front of the alley.

"What can I do to help you hard-working folk?" Duncan said, stepping between the guards and Maynard.

"Hi, Duncan. I was telling the guards about our delivery and that we've got the proper paperwork," Maynard said calmly.

Runt rolled onto his knees and looked up at the guards as he caught his breath and held his side, which felt like a rib had popped when he fell.

The red guards, three now, walked closer to the group, now about twenty feet away.

"Aren't you a big pile of shit stacked up high? Bring me your papers now, before I have the lot of you arrested," the leader with the big mouth said.

"Sure thing. Heard the commotion, so my old friend went to grab the paperwork from the owner. Should only be a moment," Duncan said. He put his hands up in a gesture that said, "take it easy, we don't want any trouble."

"You there, get on your feet and move toward your friends. We don't want any funny business. Been reports of hoodlums knocking on doors to wake sleeping soldiers. When the door is answered, they run away. Except one was not. One was tarred and feathered a few nights back, nearly died," said the loudmouth guard.

"We are new here, sir. We—" Runt said. He stood and pushed on his lower back with his hand.

"Didn't ask you, did I? If your man doesn't get here in the next moment, I will impound the lot and throw you all in the stocks, where you can die from this weather," the guard said.

Lightning streaked across the sky, almost feeling as if it had traveled a distance to reach the group.

Maynard stood by the wall. Duncan was next to him, and Runt moved gingerly to stand at Duncan's shoulder. The guards inched closer, their crossbows pointed lazily but still in their direction.

"Where's the ale from, and how many were you carrying?" one of the other guards demanded.

"Near Crimson Yard University. Don't know how many, don't count too well," Stitch said, playing dumb. He moved behind Duncan and now stood with Runt on his left, creating a half circle.

The fallen barrel lay on the other side of the cart near the dark-red alley wall. The wind stopped blowing as the snow fell from the darkness above. Runt squinted a bit to see.

"Atticus Stitch, what in the blazen Hades is going on? Get my beer and wine in the cellar before it gets frozen solid," the one-legged beer hall owner said as he hobbled toward the commotion from the bar's back door. Dick Holmes hobbled over and stood, blocking the broken barrel where oddly no liquid seeped out even though there was a large gash in the side. "God save the prince, what have you done now, you lousy elve?"

He looked at Stitch and winked. "Sorry, I can't find acceptable help these days. Bought this one as he was driven in from the forests. He's an alright lad, mostly, but shit for brains at times. Taught him a lesson last year for having a big mouth, as you can see," Dick lied. "I brought your paperwork." He looked up at the guards.

Behind Dick, two more people showed, a cook and barmaid.

"What's the issue? You boys need a drink before you finish your rounds? I got a jug right here," the barmaid said. She wore a cloak, but the inside of her shirt showed off her assets.

The fourth guard returned with two more, one with a crossbow and a spear. They were the two younger men they'd glanced at earlier, on their way in.

Dick walked up and handed the papers to the leader.

He squinted at the paperwork, angling it toward the best light as the snow fell.

"This paperwork is two weeks old—unless you're trying to pull a fast one on me. I suggest you find me the right paperwork. Do it now, or you'll hang," the guard barked.

"Shit, sorry. My brother couldn't get the shipment in until today. There may be an updated one inside," Holmes said.

"You grabbed the wrong papers? It's freezing out here, and you lot are all making us wait," the guard who stood next to the leader said. "Something's up here. Gotta bunch of misfits and bastards unloading booze in the night with the wrong paperwork."

"My lords, really, I grabbed the wrong paperwork. Please, give me a moment," Holmes begged.

"You men, impound all this. The bar will be fined, and anyone protesting will be arrested and thrown in the stocks," said the lead guard, taking control of the argument.

Duncan whispered, "Not our fight. Let's get out of here; back away," to Maynard, Runt, and Stitch, but Stitch edged toward the barmaid and cook.

"Sides, your ale is shit anyway, especially if you employ sharp-eared forest savages," the lead guard spat as he picked up Dick Holmes. He tossed him toward Duncan and the rest, where he fell on his ass with a thump.

"Hey, he fought a war for you—lost a leg, too, you fuckwits," the cook said, fist waving.

The barmaid held a large bread pin behind her back. In her other hand, she held a jug of ale. Dick sat on his ass, struggling to stand, his fake leg askew. A snowball flew from behind, landing between the guards and Dick, and silence followed for a moment.

"Go back to Hudson City, you fuckin' lobsters!" a voice yelled.

More snowballs fell, a few hitting the guards in the back. They instinctively ducked like children at play, grown men dodging snowballs.

Runt couldn't see the people throwing the snowballs, but they appeared to be in front of the alley. Laughter lingered in the distance. The snowfall, red bricks of the buildings, and brazier in the distance deluded visibility, which created a weird grayness to the entire scene.

Maynard and Runt laughed. Duncan smiled, and the barmaid giggled. Further snowballs hit the soldiers, stunning and confusing them.

"Stop this in the name of Prince Damon, damn you!" bellowed one guard who carried a spear.

The tavern's patrons funneled out from the back door and gathered toward the cart, while a few others exited the front of the Empty Gauntlet, moving down the alley, grabbing more snow from the small drifts. They starting to peg the guards from both sides. Doc stood with a group by Maynard. An odd smoky light came from the brazier at the front of the alley, casting more shadows than light. Doc was mumbling under his breath.

"Fuck the prince and the horse he rode in on!" a bar patron yelled.

"Imperium scum!" Someone yelled from the front of the alley. The Holy Imperium guards looked toward the front of the alley. Another snowball hit a guard in the arm.

"Liberty from the red guards!"

The crowd was drunk and enraged. Another person yelled. The six guards looked around, crowded together, and moved toward the wall, realizing they were outnumbered even with weapons in hand.

"Stand down, you miscreants! Stand down," the lead guard yelled. "Men, do not fire. They will torch us all if we fire," he said in a lower tone. Snowballs hit the two younger guards several times, and a bottle shattered on the ground on the other side of the guards. "You lot, stand down and return to your homes!"

"Sod off, you holy pricks! Go back home!"

"This is our town!"

"Liberty from the prince!"

A rock hit the side of the lead guard's face. Additional bottles flew and hit the walls. The second guard, a blond man of about thirty summers, grabbed at the bearded guard's jacket arm. "Sir, we need to get out of here, come back with reinforcements. They mean to hurt us."

"I know, you dolt. I told you to get more guards. You brought me two greenhorns," shouted the lead guard wiping his cheek.

The crowd continued to jeer and yell profanities.

"Now, see here, disburse, and no one will be arrested," the lead guard said. He stood up tall and tried to yell with authority. "Comply!"

"Fuck off!" Someone yelled.

The crowd at the front of the alley grew as tavern patrons and neighbors joined to see the revelry in the alley.

The guards moved along the wall toward the back of the alley, away from the crowd of intoxicated locals.

Runt and Maynard joined in, sending snowballs toward the guards as they walked toward the cart. Stitch stood on Duncan's right side. Duncan reached toward him as he laughed at the guards, his hand inside his jacket.

"Don't fuckin' do it, Stitch. You'll turn this into a riot. Don't do it," Duncan said through his teeth.

Stitch yelled at the guards, calling them every foul word he could think of. His face showed anger and frustration at years of slights toward his heritage.

Runt came up past Duncan, pushing him out of his way, and threw a bottle toward the soldiers not more than ten feet away. It shattered above their heads.

"Nicely done, Runt," Stitch laughed.

"Thanks," Runt said as he scooped up more snow from the ground.

The two younger red guards, Ben and Stu flinched from the glass bottle as it broke over their heads, each gaining cuts on their faces. Ben carried his crossbow and recoiled as another bottle hit nearby. "Sir, what do we do?" he yelled to the commanding officer. The bottle cut below his eye and started to bleed.

The crowd was manic; men screamed, and women yelled. "Go back to Thamesbridge and wank off!" Large drunken sailors spat at the red guards, grabbing their crotches and yelling, "Piss off! This is our land!"

Stu pushed back at the crowd using his long spear to keep sailors and patrons at bay. The crowd grabbed at the spear and tried to take it from him.

Ben aimed his crossbow at them. "Step back, or I shoot!" he yelled, but either they didn't hear or they didn't care.

Finally, the lead guard realized the situation was desperate.

"We're going to make you a bloodstain!" a grandmother yelled and threw another bottle.

A snowball filled with rocks hit Ben in the face, and he stumbled forward. The lead guard with the big mouth and beard grabbed him and dragged him up.

"Steady, help will come soon enough. They can't scream like this for more than a few minutes before more guards come," said the lead guard, trying to gain composure. Another bottle slammed to the ground in front of them. "Span the crossbow, boy. We'll put fear into them. But don't fire; there are only three dwarven bows and a lot more of them," commanded the lead guard.

The crowd screamed and cursed, some carried broken chair legs and a few torches. The commander looked at the elve slave who had started this all. A snowball hit the commander in the back of the head, and he stumbled forward onto his knee. He looked down and saw a broken barrel with sharp metal sticking out.

The commanding guard fell toward the wagon. Runt saw Stitch lunge and grab at him, feigning aid with his right hand. He stopped the guard from falling and helped him up to a standing position. Stitch's left hand struck under the man's other arm with one of his favorite stilettos, leading to an exit wound that would be nearly impossible to repair. Stitch had spent many an evening sharpening it so it would sail through cloth and chain mail, if necessary, to find skin, muscle, and organ, ready to bring death to its recipient. The blade sank deep between the arm and ceremonial breastplate. Stitch moved his hand back and put the blade in the inside pocket of his jacket so nobody could see as he pushed the commander to stand.

The commander felt a sharp pain under his arm as he got back up from stumbling. "That's odd," he said to himself. He caught his breath for a moment, but the pain continued. His chest warmed; he looked down to see hands release his coat and move away. He breathed in deeply again, and nothing came. He looked down at the barrel. *Why was there metal inside the barrel?* he thought. *Why was there shiny metal inside the barrel?* He tried again to breathe in deeply, but only a little air came into his chest. Screams and jeers continued around the commander. His ears started to ring. Faces blurred in his vision, spittle came out of his mouth, and he fell to his knees.

Runt had thought this was fun moments ago, but the playfulness of the crowd had changed to anger, and now it bordered on violence. He felt hatred for the guards and what they represented, even with minimal knowledge of taxes, laws without representation, religious scrutiny, and illegal trading. He wanted justice for his family. Runt pulled Stitch away and they staggered into the front of the crowd of bar patrons.

The lead guard stumbled, and the crowd surged. A young guard's long spear kept the group from tearing them apart.

Another bottle flew. Ben scratched at his face. He yelled, "Back off, you ingrates!" He saw a man with a bottle and rag pushed inside its neck, the rag aflame. Ben yelled, "Fire!" He slipped, dropping his crossbow, and it fell toward the cart and fired.

Stitch smiled and watched as another rock hit a guard in the head. Another guard stumbled as well, dropping his crossbow. The crossbow went off. The bolt nearly hit Stitch, passing by his side. There was a grunt behind him.

Stitch tensed his neck and shoulders, leaving the red guards to the crowd and hoping Duncan was not hurt, considering how big a target he presented. As he looked at Duncan, he relaxed, glad to see his old friend safe. No blood showed on Duncan's chest.

* * *

Runt tried to grab Stitch's shoulder to pull him back deeper into the crowd. Duncan yelled to get Stitch back, away from the guards. One soldier turned toward Runt crossbow in hand. The face seemed familiar. It reminded Runt of climbing pine trees around his house in the valley, looking across from him as he cleaned sap off his hands. It looked like his older brother, Ben, a soldier in the Red Army, on his way to becoming a knight like their father, like they'd spoken about summers ago. The soldier angled the crossbow toward Stitch and Runt, which didn't seem right.

* * *

Ben didn't register that it was his brother, Runt, across from him, as the years had changed them both. He wore a beard now and looked fatigued and slightly skittish. The snow twisted and turned, bottles, and seashells smashed on the ground in front of him and against the wall, and his hand flinched, and he bumped into Stu's arm.

* * *

"Ben! It's me, Runt!" Runt yelled and waved his hand, holding a snowball full of stones and leaves. He looked at his hand. *What was he doing?* Runt had toiled and fought from Grimwood to Olde Ridgewatch, walking and riding from his ravished home to see his father and brother, and here was one of them. He dropped the snowball. Duncan pulled Runt away from the crowd, and a bolt from his brother's crossbow entered the left side of Runt's chest. He gasped, tasting the frigid air, gurgled blood, and thought of the pine trees near his home.

* * *

Ben stumbled dropping his crossbow on the ground. The lead guard fell back onto his knees in front of him, blood soaked the bricks in the alley.

"Murder!" Someone in the crowd yelled.

A bottle hit Ben in the head, bounced, and broke on the ground. A sharp pain seared the side of his skull. He blinked for a long moment, seeing bright lights. Ben looked back at his comrades and witnessed two red guards fire their crossbows toward the cart with beer barrels. Both guards dropped their crossbows as if they were red hot and tugged at their swords. The only reason to drop a crossbow was the immediate need for a short sword. His head was muzzy; he mimicked his comrades and pulled out his sword. Ben's movements felt slow and stupid. He looked at his fellow soldiers, registering their movements in his head, and saw guardsmen with swords scream and lunge toward the crowd as blood dripped into his eyes, burning through his tears and down into his mouth. He turned, wiping his face, and saw Stu lunge at the mob with his spear tip forward and plunge it into an older woman. A bottle with a flaming rag arched in the air, falling toward his friend. Ben barged into Stu, knocking them both over. The bottle hit the cobbled stones, lighting Ben's cloak on fire.

* * *

Stitch saw Duncan holding Runt as he lay propped up, slightly off the ground, his eyes flickering and rolling to the back of his head, his body not moving as it should. "What, no!" Stitch cried, and he turned and grabbed to drag Runt inside.

"Get him inside now!" Duncan commanded.

Two sharp pricks jabbed Stitch in his back, penetrating his shirt, jacket, and cloak. Stitch touched the bolt tips sticking out from his chest. The crowd roared and screamed, but he didn't care anymore. He wanted to make sure

Runt was alive, but his eyes grew heavy, and he fell onto the bricks in the alley as the snow continued to drift down.

* * *

To be continued in Maiden of Storms
Book Two of The Conspiracy of Crows Trilogy

Dramatis Personae

Five Known Races of Vineland
Humans, Elves, Dwarves, Orcs, & Goblins

In Antiquity
King Christopher Goldthorn and Erica the Red: deceased
Ruinthorn Family: near-deceased bloodline
Hawthorn Family: near-deceased bloodline
Perri Stonegazer: dwarven mage, deceased
Bearfric the Righteous Hand: a member of the Broken Flowers, deceased
Umar and Jezebel Everfall: deceased
Gaston: mage, deceased

Wolf Hills
Maria Ashburn: wife to Benedict Ashburn, mother of three
Rhett "Runt" Ashburn: son of Benedict Ashburn, youngest of the Ashburn family
Bella "Alysha" Ashburn: middle child of the Ashburn family
Pete: Wayward Tavern owner
Angus: dwarven cook of the Wayward Tavern
Ryan Purenut: oldest son of the Purenut family, apprenticed blacksmith
Helena Catseye: Alysha Ashburn's best friend

The Wolfe family
James Wolfe: Wolf Hills's war hero, deceased
Junior Wolfe: oldest son of James Wolfe
Felix Wolfe: brother to Junior Wolfe

Counselor City
Hob and Bob: local blacksmiths
Edwin Flatrock: town guard
Thomas Huber: merchant
Douglas Huber: son of Thomas Huber
Robert Flint: Redcloak general of the Holy Imperium's First Army

Ian Shortstride: scout, close friend to Robert Flint
Richard: leader of a group of Holy Imperium soldiers on patrol
Blanchard: Holy Imperium soldier on patrol
Arn: Holy Imperium soldier on patrol
Eric: Holy Imperium soldier on patrol
Ole: Holy Imperium soldier on patrol

The Genteel Monks
Jared Blackheart: second in command of the First Army, leader of the
Genteel Monks
Bernard Caldwell: Jared Blackheart's lieutenant
Mother Softfellow: priestess/nun of the Genteel Monks
Professor Nester: accountant for the Genteel Monks
Claudette Leigh: scout

Hagarville Valley
Dean Slither: dean of Mount Nittany University
Hattie: student librarian
Olde Ridgewatch
Benedict Ashburn: Redcloak general of the Second Army
Alfie Von Dyke: squire to Benedict Ashburn
Fredrick Burrow: leader of the Black Eagles
Sir Donald Williamson: semiretired knight
Stewart "Stu" Slickback: archer in Sir Donald Williamson's lance
Benjamin Ashburn: son of Benedict Ashburn
Dick Holmes: runs the Empty Gauntlet beer hall
Mitt: cousin to Dick Holmes, runs the Windmill Pub
Emanuel Shapespin: a member of the Bastards of Liberty
Taug: orc slave

Hudson City
Prince Damon: House of Farover, royal leader of the Holy Imperium

The Council of Crows

Minister of the Treasury: Madam Diana Thompson

Minister of the Navy: Admiral Howl

Minister of the Army: Thomas Casting of the Longview family

Minister of Education: Victoria Parish, secretary to the Council of Crows

Minister of Laws: High Judge Sternball

Minister of Letters: Stephanie Shannon of House of Breechrun

Bishop Devon: Leader of the Hudson City Holy Church

Lord Protectors of the Holy Imperium

East: Thomas Casting, also Minister of the Lords and Minister of the Army

West: General Jacob Blackheart, Fourth Army

North: General Robert Flint, First Army

South: General Hammer Clinton, Third Army

Members of Court

Brock Rustblade: captain of the Copperheads (city guards of Hudson City)

Murrow Edward: editor and owner of *The Post Enquirer Newspaper*

Conway and Winston: writers for *The Post Enquirer Newspaper*

Victor Parish: footman and fixer for Thomas Casting

Joseph Blackheart: youngest son of Jacob Blackheart

Sir Leadwall: second in command to General Hammer Clinton's army

Jessie Stainfurd: wife of Murrow Edward

Nicholas Firemane: fourth son of the mayor of Hudson City

Ladies of Wightland

Lady Grapeseed Wightland: a disgraced lady of Prince Damon's court

Lady Rowan Wightland: assumed deceased

Lady Blacklace Wightland: exiled from court

The Wildcats

Jasper Pinehard: captain in the Wildcats, the prince's closest friend

Austin Casting: guard in the Wildcats, cousin of Thomas Casting

Pap: oldest of the Wildcats's guards

The Bent Plow Company
Gunther "Gunny" Wilmot: captain of the Bent Plow Company
Bo: Gunny's second in command
Hilda: daughter of Bo
Ralph: member of the Bent Plow Company

The Squire and his Crew
Wyatt Duncan: failed squire and thief
Sorella Silvercrow: member of the Society of Shadows
Cordial: handsome thief, member of the Society of Shadows
Atticus Stitch: member of the Society of Shadows

Steelsburg
Dufin: owner of the Cracked Brick Tavern
Betsy: wife of Dufin, runs the Cracked Brick Tavern
Gray Jim: personal executioner for the Clearstone family

The Dwarves of Steelsburg
Cormac Clearstone: head of the Cormac family
Morrin Clearstone: daughter of Cormac Clearstone
Heddwyn Clearstone: son of Cormac Clearstone
Rodric Blitzsteel: head of the Blitzsteel family
Gruff Blitzsteel: son of the Blitzsteel family
Ella Blitzsteel: heir of the Blitzsteel family
Gwawl Blitzsteel: honor guard to Cormac Clearstone
Griff Grudden: city guard
Gruff Blitzsteel: city gatekeeper
Toplin Bitterspear: guard of Steelsburg's northern gates
Fredrick and Lawrence Bitterspear: felons

Other Players

King Geordie of Great Brightland of House Troulbuss
Queen Layla of House Troulbuss
Lord Washcreek: semiretired soldier known as the Gray General
Bradley Railhead: dwarve who provides supplies to Hudson City
Roland of Eaglespire: knight of Owl Pillar and Eaglespire Towers
Hunter "Doc" Young: the last battlemage of Vineland
Maynard: apprentice to Doc, student at Grimwood University
Olivia Franklin: editor of *Hudson City Journal*
Samuel Hawthorn: mercenary/witch hunter

Acknowledgments

Thank you for joining me on this adventure. I have more stories to tell. I hope you all stay to read more. To my friend Ty Tracey, thank you for the late-night talks and texts about all things writing. Katrina Robinson, thank you for your professional guidance and work fixing my grammar. David Gardias thank you for your fantastic artistry on my book cover. To my alpha and beta readers, your comments and feedback helped me reach the finish line. Finally, to my wife, son, and daughter, thank you for putting up with me talking about a fictional world as if it were real and letting me pursue this obsession.

About the Author

Matthew Zorich is based in Ohio and has always been an avid reader, becoming obsessed after nearly losing his eyesight in his twenties. He graduated college with a degree in journalism from The University of Akron. Comics, novels, and periodicals lay all over his house while several cats, his two children, and his incredible wife put up with his book hoarding. Along with reading, he appreciates long walks with loud music and enjoys a fine bourbon while gaming with his friends.

You can connect with me on:
- 🌐 https://www.raccooncountypress.com
- 🐦 https://twitter.com/MatthewZorich
- 📘 https://www.facebook.com/MatthewZorichauthor
- 🔗 https://www.instagram.com/matthew_zorich_author
- 🔗 https://bsky.app/profile/matthewzorich.bsky.social

www.ingramcontent.com/pod-product-compliance
Lightning Source LLC
Chambersburg PA
CBHW021844010726
47493CB00005B/1552